SHE STOOD THERE IN THE NIGHT, IN THE WIND, A FIERY, NEAR-NAKED TEMPTRESS . . .

Afraid to move, afraid to breathe, West stood concealed in deep shadow, an unashamed voyeur. She was so alluring, the sight of her sent an involuntary shudder of pleasure through his body. . . . West felt the slithery black satin of his robe rising with his untimely arousal. . . . He wanted her so badly, it frightened him. Frightened him because it was Elizabeth—not just a beautiful woman. He wanted *her*. Only *her*. And because he was terrified, he grew angry. Angry with himself for being so weak. Angry with her for making him weak.

Slowly Elizabeth, clad only in clinging aqua satin and lace, turned about, threw her head back, and leaned languorously against the railing.

Hot silver eyes blazed, then turned icy cold in the darkness. Under his breath West uttered the oath, "Damn you, Mrs. Curtin."

The
Legend of Love

Nan Ryan

A DELL BOOK

Published by
Dell Publishing
a division of
Bantam Doubleday Dell Publishing Group, Inc.
666 Fifth Avenue
New York, New York 10103

"Victorio Gold Hunt" article in the Afterword reprinted with the permission of Peter Copeland and *The Albuquerque Tribune/* Scripps Howard News Service.

"Lost Treasure of Victorio Peak" map in the Afterword reprinted with the permission of Carol Cooperrider and *The Albuquerque Journal.*

ISBN: 0-440-20604-9

Printed in the United States of America

Published simultaneously in Canada

September 1991

10 9 8 7 6 5 4 3 2 1

RAD

ACKNOWLEDGMENTS

With sincere thanks to my caring editor, Damaris Rowland, for keeping a close continuing watch over my books through each stage of production and for considerately updating me every step of the way. With a sure hand and a beautiful telephone voice.

Thanks as well to my knowledgeable and enthusiastic agent, Aaron Priest, for always affording me the best advice and representation available.

To the library staff of *The Albuquerque Journal* for invaluable research assistance for *The Legend of Love*.

And as always, to my valued readers. I appreciate you all and I'm truly grateful to those of you who have written me such kind and encouraging letters.

The treasure which you think not worth taking trouble and pains to find, this one alone is the real treasure you are longing for all your life. The glittering treasure you are hunting for day and night lies buried on the other side of that hill yonder.

B. Traven
The Treasure of the Sierra Madre

The
Legend of Love

Part One

❧❧❧❧

1

Shreveport, Louisiana
The last capital of
the Confederacy

April 1865

"And it is the decision of this special Military Tribunal that you, Elizabeth Montbleau, having been judged guilty of the willful murder of the gallant Colonel Frederick C. Dobbs, Confederate States of America, will be taken at once to a place of execution where at sunrise tomorrow, April 18th, 1865, you will meet your death by a firing squad. May God have mercy on your soul."

Elizabeth Montbleau looked directly at Colonel Davis M. Clark, highest ranking officer of the five-man Confederate Military Tribunal, as he spoke those dooming words.

Her hand tightened reflexively on the drawstrings of her small reticule and her heart almost pounded its way out of her chest. A flush of icy heat swept through her slender frame and her stomach contracted painfully. But she did not make a sound. Did not beg the tribunal for mercy. Expressed no remorse for what she had done.

Dusk was descending over the northern Louisiana fortress and Elizabeth stood, as she had throughout the long, warm afternoon, with her feet together, her hands at her sides, her back as militarily rigid as the condemning officer she faced. Her chin was tilted minutely upward and her blue eyes did not glisten with unshed tears. Her lips quivered not at all, nor did her body tremble.

No sooner had the sentence been handed down than the temporary court's double doors burst open. A gust of cool April air rushed into the stuffy room. Flames flickered and wavered in globed glass lamps. Shadows danced on the stark gray walls and on the rigid faces of the seated tribunal.

Four young, uniformed soldiers marched forward and Elizabeth knew they had come for her. She gave one last slow, deliberate look at each of the five stern men seated behind the long table, turned on her heel, and left with the escort.

Outside on the flat stone porch she paused, drew a deep breath of the fresh night air, and mentally girded herself for the humiliating trek to the fort's stockade.

It was the longest walk of her life.

Holding her head high, she looked neither to the left nor the right. But shouts and catcalls and whistles from loitering troops followed her as she was ushered across the silent parade ground, past the row of officers' quarters, between the barnlike infirmary and whitewashed bakery, until finally they came to the fort's small brick military stockade set apart at the far east perimeter of the quadrangle.

Glad it was too dark to see their faces clearly—and they hers—Elizabeth Montbleau sighed with relief when she reached the rectangle of light that was the stockade's open front door. Inside, a burly, barrel-chested guard was seated behind a small, scarred desk, head down.

He looked up. His light eyes immediately widened and he swiftly pushed back his chair and rose. Lank blond hair stuck out in unruly tufts all over his large head. His wide nose appeared to have been many times broken. A snaggle-toothed grin spread across his broad face and made him appear not quite bright.

"Delivering the prisoner, Miss Elizabeth Montbleau, for immediate incarceration," said Lieutenant Clayton Bailey, chief of the escort. "You're to see to it, Private Stark, that the prisoner is kept behind bars at all times until the hour of her execution."

The foolish grin never leaving his ugly face, the beefy night guard, looking only at Elizabeth, nodded and saluted the lieutenant with a hurried, jerky movement. Left alone with the prisoner, he eagerly circled his desk, wiped his hamlike right hand on his trouser leg, and offered it to her.

"I'm Davy Stark," he said in a gravelly voice. "Might as well get acquainted before I lock you up."

Elizabeth ignored the outstretched hand. She said nothing. She clung tightly to her reticule and glared at him, her eyes icy. Davy Stark shrugged massive shoulders, hooked his thumbs into his low-riding gray trousers, and slowly circled her as though examining a bit of merchandise.

Gap-toothed grin still firmly in place, he eyed her up and down and soon decided she was not really to his liking. He preferred big, bosomy, wide-bottomed blondes. This red-haired girl had barely any meat on her bones, her eyes were blue, and her skin was so white, he had a notion that if a man so much as grabbed her arm, he'd leave his fingerprints.

Furthermore, she had that haughty, don't-you-dare-touch-me look in her chilly blue eyes, as if she thought she was a mite better than him.

Continuing to circle her slowly, he decided it wouldn't hurt to give it one more try. This pretty little redhead might not act so distant and uppity if she thought she could trade a favor for a favor. She might get downright friendly with old Davy Stark if she thought there was any chance of escaping. 'Course he had no intention of letting her get away, but she didn't have to know that.

Stopping directly before her, Stark crossed his huge arms over his chest, grinned suggestively, and said, "I guess I ought to get you on back there to the cell." He paused, winked his left eye, and added, "Then again maybe you'd like to try to convince me not to do it for a while yet."

"On the contrary," said Elizabeth in a calm, even voice, "I *demand* that you lock me up at once." Her eyes narrowed. "A darkened death cell is far preferable to spending any more time with you, Private Stark."

It took a second for her reply to register. When it did, the private's wide gap-toothed grin disappeared and his light eyes filled with disappointment, then anger.

"Suits me just fine, you snooty red-haired skinny bitch." He picked up the lamp from the corner of his desk, grabbed Elizabeth's arm, and roughly propelled her toward a narrow hallway. "Damned cold-blooded murderess and still you think you're better than me," he muttered. "Well, missy, I'll lock you up all right. Be happy to. And when you start begging me to let you out—and you will—don't count on me paying you no attention whatever."

At the end of the short, shadowy hallway, Elizabeth, remaining silent, paused before shiny steel bars. Private Davy Stark pushed a long, nickel-plated key into the lock and the barred door swung open. Grinning again, he motioned her inside, saying, "Get on in there, where you belong."

Elizabeth swept inside, slowly turned about, and said in conversational tones, "Good night to you, Private Stark." She yawned dramatically to show she was relaxed and perfectly calm. "I think I'll get a little sleep."

Davy Stark laughed aloud. "Do that, missy. Yes, sir, you just try and do that." He turned and went back down the hall, taking the laughter and light with him. Elizabeth's breath came out in a rush and she automatically reached out to clasp the bars with both hands.

The steel cylinders were cold and solid. All at once she was overcome with a frightening feeling of suffocation. It stole the very air from her lungs. She felt faint, dizzy, as though she might black out.

But she did not.

She released the bars, turned slowly and squinted, attempting to adjust her vision to the darkness cloaking the cell. A small wedge of moonlight, spilling through the one high window, revealed a wooden crate, just inside the bars, pushed up against the west wall. On its top were a pitcher, a basin, and a small linen towel.

Not moving, Elizabeth continued to look about. She saw no cots or bunks. Only loose straw scattered about on the hard stone floor. She squinted, peering into the cell's back corners, untouched by the moonlight. Total darkness. She could see nothing. She considered feeling her way further into the thick blackness in search of a bed.

Promptly, she dismissed the idea. No telling what kind of disagreeable night creatures lurked back there in the darkness. The prospect of disturbing a black widow spider or a hungry rat unnerved her. Elizabeth shivered involuntarily.

The chill passed and she was warm again. Too warm. It was close and stuffy in the stockade cell and just looking at the strewn straw made Elizabeth's skin prickle and itch. Tossing her small reticule down, she opened the top two buttons of her bodice and fanned herself with an open hand.

She looked again at the pitcher and basin. Could it be possible there was actually water in the pitcher? She ventured forward, picked up the pitcher, and was relieved to find it full. She eagerly poured water into the empty basin, set the pitcher aside, and bent to scoop up handfuls of water to splash over her hot, flushed face.

The cool water on heated flesh felt so good, Elizabeth pulled aside the collar of her dress, dipped her cupped right hand into the basin and brought a palmful of water up to bathe her perspiring throat. Lost in the luxury of the moment, she sighed gratefully and stood there in the moonlight, leisurely bathing her face and arms and throat. Eyes closed, face tilted up to the moonlight, she picked up the linen towel and patted her clean skin. Face covered with the towel, Elizabeth caught the scent of . . . what? She wasn't sure. She sniffed curiously and detected the faint but unmistakable aroma of tobacco.

She frowned, lowered the towel, and shuddered with revulsion. Obviously it had not been laundered since the last prisoner had occupied the cell. She shook her head, threw the soiled towel down, and turned away, allowing her throat and arms to remain wet.

She shrugged. Dirty towel aside, the cleansing of her hot skin had been enjoyable. The thought occurred to her that this simple act of bathing her face was to be her last joy on this earth.

That sobering reality immediately sapped all the strength from her legs. They turned to water beneath her. She picked out a spot on the straw—a place where the moonlight was likely to remain longest—and sank down to the floor. She curled her long, slender legs beneath her, spread her skirts out over her feet, and leaned her back against the wall's cool, hard surface.

Slowly tipping her head back against the wall, Elizabeth could no longer put off thinking about what awaited her. Dread and fear rushed in to overpower her. When dawn broke, she would be taken out of this small cell, marched to the fort's high stone wall, and . . . and . . .

A sulfur match flared in the darkness.

All thought of tomorrow was immediately forgotten as Elizabeth's heart lurched, then stopped beating entirely. Her mouth fell open. Awestruck, she watched in mute fascination as the tiny flame was placed to the tip of a long, thin cigar. The cigar was slowly puffed to life.

The match was extinguished.

But a circular pinpoint of light remained, glowing red hot in the invisible lips of a mysterious specter.

2

Elizabeth's hand went to her throat. She tried to speak, to move, and found she could do neither. Frozen in place she could only stare, transfixed by that circle of bright orange light in the darkness.

Heart thundering, she swallowed, then swallowed again as the orange circle grew larger. Moved closer. And closer.

All at once a dark head emerged from the stygian blackness, slowly rose, and there before her was a man's face, awash in the moonlight.

Darkly tanned with hooded, drowsy eyes, a high-bridged nose, prominent cheekbones, and a full, firm mouth yawning broadly in a thick black curly beard that covered his jaws and chin.

Those sleepy eyes widened, flashed, and boldly assessed her. The yawning mouth stretched into a wide, threatening smile that split the darkly whiskered face, revealing a double row of white, gleaming teeth.

Then a deep, sleep-heavy voice said, "Sweet Mother of God. Have I already been shot and gone to heaven?"

His voice shattering the tense silence snapped Elizabeth out of her temporary paralysis. She sprang to her feet with the quickness of a cat and began shouting at the top of her lungs.

"Private Stark! Private Stark, come here at once! Hurry, please hurry!"

She clung to the cool steel bars and screamed for the night guard while from behind her that low, masculine voice murmured, "Forgive me, miss. I didn't mean to startle you."

Elizabeth whirled around and her fear accelerated. The bearded man had come to his feet and now stood not six feet from her. He was tall and slim and dangerous-looking.

"Don't come any closer!" she ordered, her back pressing against the ungiving bars. Then again, without turning away, "Private Stark, come quickly!"

The stocky night guard, carrying the lamp, came sauntering down the corridor, taking his own sweet time. At last he stood before the locked cell.

"What's all the shouting about, missy?"

"You must let me out of here," Elizabeth shrieked, spinning to face him. "There's a man in this cell!"

"Oh!" said Stark, grinning his gap-toothed grin. His eyes lifted briefly to the tall, bearded countenance, then returned to her. "Where? I don't see no man, missy."

"Are you deaf and blind!" She whipped her head around, her red hair blazing in the glow of the lamp Stark held. "There! Him! He'd been hiding in the darkness and—"

"What, that there?" Stark cut in. "That what that is?" He made a face then and said, "I ain't so sure. Don't smell like no man I ever knowed. Smells like a Yankee to me."

Elizabeth's eyes widened more than ever. "Stark, get me out of this cell or—"

"No, sirree, that ain't no man," Stark broke in

again. "That there's an animal. A dirty, stinking Yankee spy!" He spat on the floor.

"Well, now my feelings *are* hurt," said the bearded man, a definite edge of sarcasm in his low voice.

Elizabeth looked from one to the other. "Dear Lord, you're both crazy! Stark, I demand that you take me out of this cell immediately."

"Do you now, missy?" The beefy night guard moved closer, reached out and wrapped his short, stubby fingers around the slender white ones clinging tightly to the steel bars. "I told you a while ago you'd be begging me to let you out. 'Member that?"

Struggling to free her hand from his, Elizabeth said, "Let go of me!"

He didn't. Stark stood there chuckling, enjoying her anger and impotence.

"Drop her hand," came the bearded man's low, commanding voice.

Stark's gap-toothed grin broadened with defiance. "You stay out of this, Yankee."

Before the sentence had completely passed his lips, Elizabeth felt a hard chest slam up against her back and saw a gray-sleeved arm flash through the steel bars. Tanned fingers gripped Private Stark's fleshy throat and the low masculine voice took on a deadly, mean edge when the Yankee said, "The lady asked you to let her go."

Sputtering and nodding, his fearful eyes beginning to water, Private Stark's sausage fingers immediately released Elizabeth's. At once the Yankee spy's hand left Stark's throat and retreated to settle on the bars alongside hers. The burly private swiftly backed away, coughing and gasping.

The Yankee remained where he was. His other hand came up to curl around the steel bars and Elizabeth was trapped inside his long enclosing arms.

She felt the faint vibration of his chest against her

back when he said to Stark, "Apologize, Stark. Come here and tell this young lady you are sorry you were rude."

Stark, rubbing his red throat, looked warily at the tall, bearded Yankee. He moved a bit farther back from the bars, far enough to be sure he was out of the Yankee's reach.

Then his gap-toothed grin returned and he said, "I ain't gonna do it. And she ain't no lady. You two deserve each other. A dirty Yankee spy and an uppity southern bitch! Sweet dreams to the both of you."

Stark turned and started back down the corridor. Watching him walk away, Elizabeth was torn. She was left with the Yankee. She considered calling Stark back. He looked far less threatening than the tall, bearded man who stood uncomfortably close.

When Stark lumbered out of sight, taking the lamplight with him, Elizabeth immediately began to squirm and hotly order the bearded man to back away from her. She was more than a little relieved when his hands fell away from the bars and he stepped back.

She whirled about to face him and held a hand out protectively before her. "Don't come any closer. Not one step, do you hear me?"

"Well, I like that," he said, feigning injured feelings. "Fight for a lady's honor and this is the thanks you get."

She glared at him. "Not one step closer!"

"Whatever you say. But, please, at least allow me to introduce myself, I am—"

"I don't care what your name is," she cut in quickly. "I *know* who you are. You're a filthy Yankee spy."

He simply smiled at her. "Found guilty as charged. On most counts at least. I am most definitely a Yankee and I was convicted of being a Union spy. But I do take exception to being called filthy. Cleanliness has always been important to me. Why, before supper, I washed up and . . ."

The tobacco-scented towel flashed through Elizabeth's mind. Dear Lord in heaven, she had washed her face in water used by a dirty Yankee spy!

". . . and before the war," he went on, "I always—"

"I am not the least bit interested in your life's history, Mr. . . . Spy."

"Ah, well, a pity. Perhaps you'd like to tell me a little about yours. Or why you've had the misfortune to be thrown into a military stockade with the enemy."

Elizabeth crossed her arms over her chest. "I am not telling a Yankee spy anything."

"And who could blame you?" He stuck two lean fingers inside his half-open gray tunic, drew out a fresh cigar, and placed it between his gleaming white teeth. "Tell you what, though"—he struck a match with his thumbnail, lifted it, cupped his brown hands, and puffed the smoke to life—"if it's any consolation, you won't have to put up with this offensive Yankee spy for long." He took the lighted cigar from his mouth, blew a perfectly formed smoke ring, and stated dispassionately, "I'm to be shot at sunrise tomorrow."

"So am I," Elizabeth said automatically.

His flashing eyes widened. He jammed the cigar forcefully back into his mouth and said from between clenched teeth, "Holy God! They're going to shoot a helpless young woman? Jesus!"

"Stop your swearing, Spy. Whatever I may have become, I was raised a lady. Perhaps up North it is acceptable for Yankees to swear before a lady, but down here no gentleman does so."

His sudden deep laughter surprised her. He took the cigar from his lips, and said, "Let me get this straight, miss. Here in the old South it's permissible to shoot a young lady, so long as you don't swear while you're pulling the trigger?" His eyes twinkled with mischief as he studied Elizabeth's rigid face.

The moonlight was flattering, so he was not certain if she was really as lovely as he perceived her to be. Couldn't be positive if those large, luminous eyes flashing so indignantly at him were green or blue. Wasn't sure if the long, tousled hair spilling down her back was brown or red. Didn't know if the pale skin was as flawless as it appeared.

"Did you hear me?" her voice, lifted in frustrated annoyance, cut into his appraisal.

"No. No, I didn't." He took a step closer. "What did you say?"

Elizabeth was struck by his leanness. He was tall— at least six two—and broad of shoulder, but slender, the lanky frame bordering on thinness. The gray trousers hung loosely on his slim hips and the matching tunic fit across his shoulders but was slack around his trim waist. Half open down his torso, the tunic's brass buttons winked in the moonlight and the parted opening revealed a dark, hard chest covered with thick black hair.

Instinctively Elizabeth backed away from him. "I . . . I won't allow you to poke fun at our customs and beliefs. You have no idea why they are to execute me so—"

"Then tell me," he smoothly cut in, "what have you done that's so terrible? You don't appear to be all that dangerous to me."

Thinking to herself that the spy *did* look dangerous, Elizabeth was determined she'd not let him suspect she feared him. "You're no priest that I should confess my sins to. I've no intention of baring my soul—much less to a Yankee spy. In fact, I've no intention of continuing this conversation."

"Fine, but please," he said, his gaze traveling down her slender form, "tell me just one thing."

"I'll tell you nothing, Mr. Spy. Keep your questions to—"

"The color of your dress, miss?"

"My . . . my . . . what difference does it make?"

"Blue, I'll bet."

"What if it is?"

"And it matches your eyes?"

"How did you know?"

"I didn't. You've just told me." He smiled at her, his white teeth gleaming from out of that forest of black facial hair. "I like blue eyes."

"I don't care what you like, Spy." Elizabeth commandingly pointed toward the darkness from which he had materialized. "Kindly get back over there on your side of the cell. For these final hours, I may have to share this space with you, but I refuse to associate with the enemy."

He nodded his assent. "A loyal Rebel to the end." He leisurely backed away until he was completely swallowed up in the darkness. A pause. A rustling of the straw. Finally, silence. Then, from out of the blackness came that deep, bodiless voice. "Admirable, though, and quite touching, miss."

Elizabeth gave no reply. She knew he was making fun, but she didn't care. All she wanted was for the devilish bearded Yankee to leave her alone. She wouldn't press her luck by arguing.

She strained to locate him in the darkness, but could not. The wispy hair at the nape of her neck lifted. She sensed that behind that teasing smile and calming voice was a dangerous man. The way his arm had flashed through the bars and grabbed Stark's throat had been frightening and impressive for its sudden violence. If he chose, he could seize her just that swiftly and she'd be totally helpless.

Elizabeth stood in the moonlight, blinking, wishing he would light another cigar so that she could establish his exact position. As if he had read her mind, a match flared and he puffed a fresh cigar to life. He was in the darkened corner and the glowing cigar told her that he was lounging on the hay, his back against the wall.

Relieved, Elizabeth turned away, went to the moonlit corner opposite him, sank down onto the scattered hay there and waited. She listened intently and watched alertly for any sign of movement that might signal danger.

Finally she sighed and relaxed a little.

Long minutes passed.

Silence.

Then, from out of the darkness: "Should you need me, I'm right here for you, miss."

Elizabeth jumped, startled. She hurriedly laughed to show her poise and contempt. "I need no one. Least of all you, Mr. Spy."

3

Soon a deep nighttime silence settled over the stockade, the stillness broken only by the gentle sigh of the south wind pressing against the small, high window. Outside, the air was cool and sweet, but little of it found its way down into the close, stuffy cell.

Where Elizabeth waited with the bearded spy for their dual dawn execution, it was warm and uncomfortable. The scattered straw did little to cushion the hard stone floor. Her full skirts, bunched around her legs, were cumbersome and hot. The satin of her chemise clung damply to her tired back, her long red hair stuck to her neck and throat.

Her face was shiny with moisture and she could feel beads of perspiration pooling between her breasts. She twisted and fidgeted and exhaled loudly. She put her hands under her heavy hair, impatiently swept the flaming tresses up atop her head, and twisted the long locks into a plump rope. But her arm soon tired, so she sighed and released the wild mane. It spilled back down around her shoulders. She bowed her head.

In seconds she raised it, made a face, and wondered how she could be worrying about something as trivial as heat and discomfort when in just a few short hours she would face a firing squad.

It was foolish, she knew, and yet she yearned for a bath and a soft bed. She envisioned a big marble tub with lots of soapy bubbles and gallons of cool, soothing water. She pictured a high feather bed with silky sheets of fresh snowy white and downy pillows in lace-edged pillow slips. And herself, squeaky clean and pleasingly cool, lying atop that inviting bed.

Physically exhausted from her long afternoon before the tribunal and lulled by the silence and the heat, Elizabeth allowed her thoughts to become focused only on pleasant things. On much-missed luxuries and half-forgotten gaiety. Refusing to dwell on the horror that lay before her, she daydreamed of the past in the stillness of her last night.

She relived some of her favorite occasions, pulling up from memory happy times and beloved faces that filled her with joy. It became a welcome diversion, a mind exercise requiring total concentration. The intriguing game transported her out of the too-warm Louisiana stockade and into a carefree world.

When the bell in Shreveport's riverfront Presbyterian church tower chimed midnight, Elizabeth, abruptly brought back to the present, was amazed at how rapidly the time had passed. Only a few hours left. Dawn would break and then they would . . .

Elizabeth realized she had all but forgotten about the Yankee spy sharing her death cell.

She raised her head and looked across the small chamber, saw the orange tip of his cigar glowing in the darkness, and wondered what he had been thinking as he sat there silently smoking. Was he reliving his past? Was he recalling happy times with a wife or sweetheart somewhere?

Was he afraid to die?

Hers had always been a curious nature. She wanted

to know what was on the Yankee spy's mind. More importantly, she longed to hear the soothing sound of a firm male voice, even if it belonged to the enemy.

Her life was rapidly ticking away and there was nothing she could do to stop it. As the hour of execution neared, her fear of death escalated. There was only one person to whom she could turn in her need.

Elizabeth cleared her throat. "Ah . . . Spy, are you . . . are you afraid to die?"

For a few seconds there was no reply. Then, "No, miss. Not particularly. My only concern is that the firing squad we're to face are a bunch of peach-fuzz-faced kids and likely the worst shots in either army."

Elizabeth was immediately defensive. "Young boys are all that the beleaguered Confederacy has left, Spy! It is not their fault they aren't expert marksmen!"

"Your loyalty is laudable, miss. Nonetheless, the results are the same."

Elizabeth opened her mouth to make a cutting reply, then changed her mind. Like it or not, what the spy said made sense. On her walk to the jail this evening she had seen nothing but untrained boy soldiers. The Yankee was right. Those young, green recruits were likely less than expert shots.

Elizabeth's apprehension grew. She mulled the situation over in her mind and came up with a solution to the problem.

"Spy, can you see me?"

"Why?"

"Just answer the question!"

"No." His eyes, at that particular moment, were shut. So it was not a lie when he said, "I can't see you."

He immediately opened his eyes and smiled. She was perfectly framed in the moonlight and he had been leisurely observing her off and on all evening. He had seen her squirm about on the hard stone floor. Had seen her impatiently sweep her long, thick hair up atop her head. Had seen her smile dreamily and sigh wearily. Had seen her frown and shake her head. Had hardly taken his eyes off her.

"Good," Elizabeth said, then jerked up her blue skirts, reached for the bottom of her lace-trimmed white petticoat, and pulled it up past her knees.

His dark head came away from the wall. He sat up straighter and his teeth practically cut his cigar in two. He had no idea what she was up to, but whatever it was, he didn't mean to miss it. While he stared intently, she held the hem of her petticoat in both hands and yanked on it with all her might.

Obviously, she was trying to tear it. He was tempted to offer a hand, but didn't dare. He swallowed with difficulty when finally she lifted the stubborn petticoat all the way up to her face. His narrowed gaze swept appreciatively over shapely thighs and womanly hips covered only by silky pantalets and stockings.

He grinned when she put the petticoat's hem into her mouth. With her small, perfect teeth she ripped the fabric, then tore a long, narrow strip from the petticoat.

Puzzled but fascinated, he watched while she tore three more strips from the undergarment, and was so entranced he didn't realize that the cigar in his mouth had burned down.

"Ouch! Damn to hell!"

Elizabeth, her blue skirts and white petticoat pulled up around her waist, jerked her head around. "What is it?"

"I burned my lower lip."

"Oh? Did you doze off?"

He smiled. "Yes. Fell asleep with the damn thing stuck in my mouth."

"Since you're awake, will you come here, please?" She tossed her skirts back down over her feet.

"On my way," said he, grinding out the smoked-down cigar beneath his boot heel. He rose and crossed to her. She looked up at him and wondered if she could trust him. He looked tall and menacing standing there. She motioned him down to the stone floor. Leisurely, he eased down into a crouching position directly in front of her.

"What is it, miss?"

"You got me to thinking."

"Did I?"

"Yes. You see, you're absolutely correct. The men on the firing squad are unproven and that could mean pain and suffering for us. Like you, I don't mind dying, but the prospect of suffering frightens me terribly."

"Ah, now, miss, I should never have said anything." He tried to sound reassuring. "It will be swift; we won't suffer."

"No use taking a chance. I've come up with a fool-proof plan." Proudly, she lifted the white strips of material. "I tore these from my petticoat."

"Really?" He could hardly keep from grinning.

"Yes, and if you sit down here on the floor, I will sew a white cross directly over your heart." She almost smiled at him. "That way, the worst firing squad can't miss their target."

He smiled fully at her. Permission no sooner granted, he quickly turned about and sat down beside her. He leaned back against the wall, put a dark hand to a shiny brass button in the center of his gray tunic, and asked, "Shall I take this off?"

Her swift reply was, "No. I'll have to do my sewing with you wearing the tunic. Otherwise, how would I know I had the cross in exactly the right place? Directly over your heart." She looked away, drew from her reticule a needle and thread, and turned back to him. "Ready, Mister Spy?"

"Ready, miss."

Elizabeth first laid a hand over his heart, atop the gray tunic. She felt a slow, steady beating. "That's the spot," she said, placed a strip of the fabric vertically over his heart, and came at him with her needle.

He reached out, caught her wrist. "You aren't going to stick me, are you, miss?"

"No, Spy. While I sew, I'll keep my other hand inside your tunic so that if anyone gets pricked, it will be me."

He immediately released her wrist and Elizabeth went to work. From low-lidded eyes, he watched as she painstakingly stitched, her lovely face one of total concentration. Her left hand was inside his half-open tunic, its soft back against his bare chest. The delicate knuckles brushing his flesh caused his heart to skip a beat, and he wished she would turn her hand over and touch him.

Really touch him.

Elizabeth kept her eyes on her work, anxious to be done. She didn't like being this close to the Yankee spy, didn't like having her hand inside his tunic. Of necessity, the back of her hand was pressed against his chest. The texture of crisp dark hair and the fierce heat of his smooth flesh was such a curiosity, Elizabeth found she was half tempted to turn her hand over and touch him.

Really touch him.

None too soon she completed her task. The sewing was finished, nothing left to do but snap the thread. Elizabeth never gave it a minute's thought. She leaned her face down to his chest, and bit the thread in two. A snowy white cross was now neatly stitched on the left side of his gray tunic. It would give the firing squad a target which could not be missed.

"Thank you. I appreciate this, miss," he said, and meant it.

"I'm glad." She proudly examined her handiwork, then guilelessly asked, "Now, will you kindly return the favor?"

"You mean—"

"Yes, Spy. Will you please sew a cross over my heart so I won't have to suffer?"

Charmed by her mettle, the bearded man nodded, took the needle and thread from her. Unceremoniously, he laid his right hand over her heart, atop her blue bodice, his long dark fingers gently pressing the soft undercurve of her full, high breast.

Elizabeth's heart immediately speeded; he felt its rapid beating against his palm.

"That's it. That's the spot," he said softly.

"Spy, wait!" she said, pushing his hand away. "I'll take off my—"

"No," he interrupted, "I'll have to sew the cross on while you're wearing your dress." Smiling in the shadow, he added, "Otherwise, how will I know if I have the cross in exactly the right place? Directly over your heart."

Skeptical, Elizabeth reluctantly said, "Well, all right. But make it snappy, Spy."

"Unbutton your bodice, miss."

"Unbutton my . . . now, really, this whole thing is—"

"Then I'll do it," he said, and with one dexterous hand he flipped open the buttons halfway down to her waist while she wordlessly stared at him.

His hand slipped inside her opened bodice. Her face flushed hotly when the back of his hand touched her breast through the thin covering of her chemise. But he seemed not to notice. He was, she told herself, solely intent on sewing the cross over her heart. Likely he didn't even realize that his hand was touching her. After all, it was only the back of his hand brushing her lightly.

Still, Elizabeth was acutely aware of that strong male hand inside her bodice. A little involuntary shiver raced through her as she guiltily considered what it might feel like if that dark, long-fingered hand suddenly turned over and he touched her.

Really touched her.

"I didn't stick you, did I?" His low, even voice startled her.

"No. No, it's just . . . will you kindly hurry?"

"Sure thing," he said. And didn't hurry at all. While he worked deliberately slowly, his thoughts were no longer on the white strip of cloth he was stitching to the bodice of her blue cotton dress. Nor were they on the dawn date with a Confederate firing squad.

Her lovely face was only inches from his own, her soft lips slightly parted. The intoxicating scent of her clean hair filled his senses. The back of his hand was resting against her rounded breast with only the seductive satin of her chemise between. He wondered what she would do if he turned his hand over and touched her.

Really touched her.

As he languidly stitched a white cross to the blue bodice of the ivory-skinned southern beauty, his thoughts turned from death to life. More specifically, to one of life's greatest joys.

Lovemaking.

4

Sweet desire began its slow, sure burn through his
body. The blood flowing through his veins started to
heat pleasantly. His heart expanded, kicked forcefully against his chest. The hard muscles in his flat
abdomen tightened. His breathing deepened, became
more rapid.

She was young and pretty and he had been too long
without a woman. He wanted her. It was as elemental
as that.

So little time. He would have to work fast. But not
too fast, or she'd never consent.

"There. Just about done," he said, and looked up.
When her eyes met his, he held her gaze for a lingering second, then purposely directed her attention to
the needle in his hand. A needle still connected by
thread to the bodice of her dress. He gave the thread a
mild jerk. He wanted her to recall that when she had
finished sewing the cross on his tunic, she had leaned
down and bitten the thread in two.

His silent statement was quite clear. Elizabeth did
remember and became immediately edgy. Her gaze
flew back up to his eyes and she murmured, "No . . .
I . . ."

He just smiled at her. Slowly he lowered his dark head. Her heart galloping, Elizabeth watched, wide-eyed, as his bearded face moved down to her left breast. When his face was no more than a fraction of an inch from her, she saw his wide mouth slowly open and she trembled.

His sharp white teeth gleamed in the moonlight. He bit the thread swiftly in two and she was free. But for another heartbeat, his bearded face remained where it was and gently nuzzled. Elizabeth's breath left her body in an astonished rush.

He raised his dark head, held out the needle, and smiled at her. She started to speak; he stopped her before she could issue the command that he return at once to his side of the cell.

"Miss," he asked gently, "will you allow me to sit here beside you for a few minutes?"

"Whatever for?" was her shaky reply.

"Even Yankees," he said, easing himself over to sit flat down on her right side, "are human beings. I have a name and I—"

"I told you once, Spy,"—she sensed sure danger—"I don't care to know who you are."

"But I care who you are." His voice was velvet in the still, warm night. "Won't you please tell me your name so I—"

"No. I will not. And . . . and must you sit so close?" She scooted over several inches.

Undaunted, he stretched his long legs out before him, placed his flattened palms on his thighs, and said, "Show a little compassion, miss. I've been away from home for years. Been locked up in this stockade for a week. I'm a lonely man."

His dark head swung around and he looked directly at her, his eyes flashing in the moonlight. While his riveting gaze held hers, his hand slowly lifted from his thigh. He turned it over and offered it to her.

Elizabeth, snared by those hypnotic eyes whose color she could not determine, shook her head no. But at the same time she placed tentative fingertips atop his warm, open palm. And then tingled from head to toe when his long, lean fingers closed firmly around her own.

He said, barely above a whisper, "My God, you've got the smallest, softest hand I've ever held."

"You really shouldn't be holding my hand," she told him, feeling strangely warm and short of breath. He smiled engagingly, laced his fingers through hers, and drew her hand up to his chest. She gave a couple of halfhearted tugs to free herself, but wasn't certain that's what she actually wanted. He read the indecision. He didn't let her go.

Instead he sighed as though contented and began to speak of inconsequential things. His voice, low and gentle, was seductively soothing. The rich timbre of that deep male voice had a definite calming effect on Elizabeth's raw nerves. Slowly, cautiously, Elizabeth began to relax ever so slightly.

She exhaled deeply, slowly, and leaned her head back against the wall. She rolled her aching shoulders a couple of times. She allowed her tense body to go slack, her limbs to fall limp. The subtle change was duly noted by the bearded man seated beside her.

He was tempted to speed up the process, to get on with it, to take her in his arms and kiss her half senseless. But he continued to speak in low, soft tones, patiently drawing her along the pleasing path that led to lovemaking. Almost absently, and talking all the while, he changed her small white hand from his left to his right, leaving the left arm free.

Elizabeth noticed the switch, but didn't see that it made any difference. She no longer tried to pull away. Surely there could be no harm in just holding

hands, and the sound of his deep voice in the night
was a comfort.

He pressed her hand to his chest and casually
slipped his arm around her slender shoulders. He felt
her stiffen and she turned her face away. He patted
her tense shoulder reassuringly, then rubbed her
slender arm slowly up and down until he felt the
tenseness leave and she slouched back against his
solid shoulder.

Drawing her steadily closer, he said, "Look at me."

Slowly, Elizabeth turned her head, looked into his
eyes, and said unconvincingly, "You really should
move back over there where you belong, Spy."

His long dark fingers tightened possessively on her
shoulder. "I know," he said. "But I don't want to go."
He lifted her hand to his lips, kissed its back, and
Elizabeth felt the pleasant tickle of his beard against
her skin. She couldn't keep from smiling.

But then he turned her hand over and pressed his
lips to her palm, and her smile disappeared. He
opened his mouth and let her feel his tongue teasingly trace her lifeline. She involuntarily shivered
and felt her throat and ears flush red with heat. His
bearded face still buried in the softness of her palm,
he said, "Let me stay. For just a while. Just a little
while longer."

He slowly lifted his head to look at her and in his
flashing eyes was the unmistakable plea to let him
stay. She knew she should say no. Knew to say anything else was courting trouble. This dark, bearded
man was a Yankee, a spy, the enemy. Possibly very
dangerous. How could she consider even speaking to
him, much less allowing him to sit this close, to hold
her hand, to kiss it.

His mesmerizing gaze shifted to her parted lips and
he spoke the plea aloud. "Let me."

Flustered, half frightened, half attracted, Elizabeth

nervously cleared her throat. He was waiting for an answer, but his close masculine presence was so strong, his deep voice so seductive, she couldn't remember the question. And just what exactly was he asking her to let him do?

"Let you . . . ?"

"Stay," he said, and drew her so close she could feel his heartbeat against her right breast.

"This . . . this is crazy," she murmured breathlessly. "You are crazy." He released her hand, tipped her chin up, and urged her head back to rest on his supporting arm. "We are crazy," she added, the fabric of his gray tunic mildly abrasive to her cheek. She felt dizzy, weak. "*I* am crazy . . ." she whispered helplessly.

"It's the world gone crazy, not us." All at once his eyes darkened with emotion. He stared at her mouth until Elizabeth felt her lips begin to tremble from his unnerving scrutiny. She tried to make them stop, couldn't. She heard him murmur, "Will you kiss me? It's been such a long, lonely time since last I kissed a beautiful young woman." He paused, drew a deep, ragged breath, and lowered his dark face to hers until only an inch of space remained between their lips. "Kiss me, miss. Kiss me."

Her answer, of course, was an emphatic no, but Elizabeth found to her horror that her voice wouldn't work. She couldn't speak, couldn't make a sound. Violently she shook her head no.

She was still shaking her head when his mouth possessively closed over hers. She continued to move her head from side to side, clearly protesting the intrusion, determined to free her lips from his.

To her surprise, after only a few seconds, he released her. The strong arm around her abruptly drew her back up to a sitting position, then fell from her shoulders. The tanned fingers playing so tantalizingly on her face and throat departed. He leaned back against the wall, draped a forearm over his bent knee, and looked off into space.

Elizabeth was both pleased and puzzled.

Pleased that the enigmatic Yankee spy apparently did not intend to force himself on her. Puzzled—and a little offended—that her kiss stirred him so little, he hadn't bothered to try a bit harder.

He shifted slightly beside her and Elizabeth's heart lurched, her breath caught. He *was* going to try again! Instinctively, she leaned closer, tilted her face up for his kiss.

But he didn't kiss her. He slumped more fully back against the wall, lolled lazily on his spine, tipped his dark head back. Watching him closely, Elizabeth's parted lips dropped open in disbelief when, turning his head to glance indifferently at her, he yawned sleepily.

And closed his eyes.

Elizabeth frowned. She was thoroughly confused and more than a little insulted. She stared at him. His long, lean body was in an attitude of complete relaxation. Any second, he would fall asleep, if he hadn't already.

Good!

That's exactly what she wanted him to do. To go to sleep and leave her alone. He had no business thinking he could hold her hand and kiss her. He was a dirty Yankee spy who could not be trusted.

Elizabeth continued to stare at him.

In the dim light it was impossible to tell what he really looked like. She knew only that he had a bushy black beard, and a too-lean frame, and bold, bothersome eyes. In the harsh light of day, when he was cleanly shaven, he was probably ugly as sin.

"Spy," she said softly.

"Hmmmm?"

"Look at me."

His thick black lashes stirred restlessly, rose, and his smoldering eyes were fixed on her. She felt a jolt of electricity. She smiled at him and said, "I . . . I suppose if you want to kiss me one time it would be all right."

He didn't move a muscle, just stayed there as he was, lounging back against the wall. He said, "I don't want to kiss you, miss."

"You don't?" Her voice was shrill and her finely arched eyebrows shot up.

"Not really." he said. "I want"—and his low voice became a gentle caress—"you to kiss me. Kiss me. Come kiss me."

Elizabeth pretended exasperation, but she turned fully to him, leaned close, placed her hands on either side of his bearded face, and gently cupped his jaws. She expected him to reach for her at any second. He didn't do it. He remained as he was, in a posture of repose, waiting for her soft mouth to settle on his.

Her heart beating loudly in her ears, Elizabeth cautiously placed her lips on his. She kissed him. It was a sweet, soft kiss and she was amazed by the warm smoothness of his lips.

But she was tickled by his beard. Her hands still clinging to his face, she raised her head, wrinkled her nose, and laughed helplessly.

"The beard tickles?" he asked, his hands slowly lifting to span her small waist.

"A little," she said, and rubbed at her itching nose.

"I'd shave for you if I could," he said, drawing her to him and kissing her. Those dense, tickling whiskers caused Elizabeth to continue laughing, even as his lips were on hers. He didn't mind. He purposely tormented her, kissing her eyes, her nose, her cheeks, while she collapsed in peals of laughter. His lips came back to hers and against her mouth he said, "I love to hear a beautiful woman's laughter."

Weak, her stomach jerking, she said, "It's a good thing, because when you kiss me, I can't keep from laughing." She wiped at the tears of laughter rolling down her flushed cheeks.

He looked at her lying in the crook of his arm, laughing. Her lovely eyes were shut. Her wild, gleaming hair was spilling over his arm and down to the straw-covered floor. Her slender body was shaking against his. She was incredibly desirable. His pulse began to beat rapidly and violently. The stirring of desire became a fierce hunger.

"I . . . I'll quit laughing now, I promise," said Elizabeth, and continued to laugh. "I will, I will," she gasped, pressing her face to his half-open gray tunic. The crisp, thick hair of his chest now tickled her nose and she went into fresh fits of laughter. Like a child that begs a parent to quit tickling him, then immediately begs for more when the parent stops, Elizabeth purposely rubbed her face against the abrasive, tickling chest hair and sputtered giddily, "I . . . I . . . can't . . . can't stop. . . . I'll never stop laughing. . . ."

He said, "Would you like me to make you stop laughing?"

"Y-yes, but you . . . you can't do it, Spy. Nobody could . . ."

The smile left his dark face. He slid long fingers into her cascading hair, tightened them on the gleaming tresses, urged her head up and back until his face was just above hers. He looked into her eyes. A vein throbbed on his forehead. His open mouth descended slowly to hers.

"*I* can."

5

His mouth covered her parted lips. Spasms of laughter still surging through her, Elizabeth began to cough and struggle. His invasive lips lifted, but his burning eyes bore directly into hers with a hot intensity that was sobering. Never had a man looked at her the way the Yankee was looking at her.

Elizabeth's laughter began to ebb away and soon it died completely. She swallowed anxiously and kept her eyes open as his lips slowly, surely descended to hers again.

It was a kiss unlike any she had ever known or dreamed of. His lips were blazing hot. Hot and smooth and incredibly persuasive as they molded hers to his. His marvelous mouth took her breath away, made her forget entirely that a black, ticklish beard covered his lower face.

For a dazzling moment in time he kissed her in the most deliciously dangerous way. It thrilled and frightened her. He literally took her breath away. His magnetic mouth drew all the breath from her body and made it his own. Forcefully, he sucked the very life and will from her. And the strangest thing about it was, she didn't mind. She wanted him to have it.

She gave it to him freely. Eagerly breathed and blew against his fiery lips.

Just when she began to feel light-headed and weak and feared she would black out and sag lifeless in his arms, he gallantly offered the gift back. Gave her his hot, reviving breath. Sweetly, his lips sealed tightly to hers, he rhythmically pressed air into her mouth and down into her starving lungs.

Elizabeth sucked anxiously at his heated lips, inhaling deeply, drawing life-sustaining oxygen from him.

And when she was filled to overflowing, she sighed and tore her mouth from his. Dazed, she laid her head back on his hard, muscled arm and waited for her breathing to become slow and regular, for her heart to stop its frantic racing.

He waited too. He held her as gently as if she were a child. He placed his dark hand directly atop her rapidly beating heart and waited for its fierce rhythm to slow.

Too weak to protest his boldness, Elizabeth lay there and mentally swore that she would put an end to this risky foolishness as soon as she was herself again. She'd scramble hurriedly out of his arms, shoot to her feet, and send him back across the cell.

It never happened.

When her heartbeat had slowed to near normal and she made an attempt to rise, that commanding male mouth was immediately back on hers, his strong arms crushing her to his hard chest.

If the last kiss had been dangerously stirring, this kiss was explosive. His silky tongue slid between her lips and teeth, thrust deeply into her mouth and touched hers. Elizabeth felt her stomach flutter crazily and the muscles in her inner thighs jump involuntarily. A new kind of heat swept through her and traveled with amazing speed to every part of her body. Her toes and fingertips actually tingled.

Alarmed and astounded, Elizabeth tried to escape that dazzling mouth, those tightly embracing arms.

The Yankee wouldn't let her go. He deepened the kiss. She struggled, valiantly fighting what she felt happening to her. It was no use. His burning lips, his nipping teeth, his thrusting tongue, soon conquered completely.

Never in her nineteen years had she been kissed the way this Yankee spy kissed her, and she was as powerfully drawn to the sexual danger this dark stranger exuded as an infant is drawn to a red-hot stove. She felt the blood scalding through her veins, felt every bone in her body begin to melt in the incredible heat.

Her breasts swelled against the tight bodice of her blue dress. Her stomach, beneath the full gathers of her skirts, contracted sharply and became almost concave.

It was a one-sided contest. Elizabeth never stood a chance. She was naive and passionate. The Yankee was experienced and overwhelming. She was all but powerless against such a skilled, determined lover. Dazed by his blazing kiss, engulfed in rising passion, she clung helplessly to him, marveling at the things his mouth was doing to hers.

When at last that fiercely potent kiss ended, when his lips lifted from hers and his strong arms loosened and she was free, Elizabeth no longer wanted to go. She didn't move an inch. She didn't want to leave him. Didn't want him to leave her. She wanted— needed—to feel warm and wonderful for just a while longer. Wanted to taste more of those magical kisses. Wanted to feel his dark hands caressing her back and shoulders.

The message radiated from her shining eyes.

Armed with that knowledge, the Yankee again stretched his long, lean legs straight out before him. Half turning, he kissed her, and put both hands to her narrow waist. His mouth never leaving hers, he quickly lifted her onto his lap.

When the kiss ended, Elizabeth opened her eyes, gasped for breath, and threw back her head when she felt his lips seek out the hollow of her throat.

"No," she murmured, but her hands clutched at the dark shaggy hair at the back of his head, "you mustn't . . ."

He said nothing, just kept kissing her throat and reached for the tiny buttons of her bodice, buttons with which he was already familiar. Effortlessly he slid several from their buttonholes and his lips moved down the slender column of her throat.

"You . . . must . . . stop," Elizabeth whispered, her eyes closed, her head thrown back. "You must . . . Spy . . . please . . ."

He didn't stop. His deft fingers continued unbuttoning her dress. His tormenting tongue kept stroking her sensitive throat. When his bearded face moved brazenly down inside the parted blue bodice, Elizabeth whispered harshly, "No, I said no." But at the same time she instinctively arched her back and pressed closer to his face.

The dress was half open to her waist. His lips had reached the lacy edge of her satin chemise. Her fingers nervously clasping the thick hair at the sides of his head, Elizabeth held her breath, teetering on the brink of total surrender.

With his hot face he pushed the lace trimmed chemise down dangerously close to a throbbing nipple. Stopping less than an inch from the taut, aching crest, he kissed the pale, burning flesh of her soft breast. It was a sweet, warm, gently plucking kind of kiss that made Elizabeth instantly wonder how it would feel if he kissed her nipple that same way.

He lifted his dark head and sat her back. She swallowed and looked at him, her eyes aglow with the

beginning of full-blown, all-consuming desire. Her in-
nate sensuality thoroughly awakened, Elizabeth was
unconsciously bent on tempting and teasing this
dark, exciting man upon whose lap she sat.

She put out the tip of her tongue and moistened her
parted lips. She seductively tossed her hair about,
then raised a hand and swept the flaming tresses
down over her left shoulder. She inhaled deeply, allowing her swelling breasts to rise and press against
the lace border of her chemise. She restlessly
squirmed, her bottom moving provocatively against
his groin and thighs.

For a time he let her play. Let her sigh and writhe
and drive him half crazy with growing lust. From
low-lidded eyes he watched her closely, fully enjoying
the game she played. It was highly effective and he
had no doubt she knew exactly what she was doing.
She was an irresistibly alluring little tease if ever
there was one, and he was becoming achingly
aroused.

Hers was an inborn eroticism made all the more
potent by her fresh, innocent beauty. Enhanced by
the moonlight, her unbound hair spilling down over
her shoulder, she appeared to be a sweet, chaste angel
descended from out of the heavens.

But if she looked angelic, what she was doing to
him was downright earthy and he was confident this
devilishly desirable woman could take him straight to
carnal paradise.

He reached for her, buried his face in her hair, feeling as if he couldn't wait one more second to make
love to her. Against the silky tresses filling his senses
with their sweet fragrance, he said raggedly, "Ah,
sweetheart, sweetheart, send this weary soldier to his
grave a happy man. Let me love you before we go."
He lifted his face and looked into her eyes. "Give me
one last moment of bliss."

Before Elizabeth could give him an answer, his lips captured hers. It was a different kiss this time. He kissed her with such devastating tenderness, Elizabeth sighed and laid her hand on his chest. The tender kiss began to change, to graduate in intensity until they were kissing each other wildly, hotly.

Elizabeth's hand roamed restlessly over the Yankee's chest. Her fingers closed around a shiny brass button and in her excitement she jerked it loose. It fell from her hand and rolled across the stone floor.

The Yankee captured Elizabeth's wandering hand and guided it inside his half-open tunic while her hot, wet mouth remained fully on his. Her fingers burrowed into the hair covering his hard chest, eagerly learning its crisp, pleasing texture. She found it heavily dotted with diamonds of perspiration and found that tremendously exciting. This man was uncommonly warm, the smooth dark flesh beneath the crisp, damp hair feverish with heat.

She was warm as well. Intoxicated by his savage kisses, his powerfully persuasive voice, she began to feel that what he was suggesting was not such an outlandish proposal. At dawn she would die without having really lived. She would go to her death without ever experiencing the sweet mystery of physical intimacy.

Unless she allowed this Yankee spy to make love to her.

His lips moved to that sensitive spot just below her right ear and his breath scorched her when he murmured thickly, "Sweetheart, I'm not a wild animal. I'm a man. I want you so badly."

"Spy . . . Spy . . . Spy," she whispered, the last of her defenses toppling.

His face lowered into her open bodice. His fingers tugged at the tiny bow of her chemise. It came undone, and after that, the tiny hooks holding it to-

gether. He swept the flimsy garment aside and Elizabeth trembled, then gasped in shocked pleasure when
his burning lips found and closed around her right
nipple.

The flames licking at her body became a raging inferno. She clasped his dark head and pressed him to
her, lost in a sweet new sensation and wondering why
his blazing lips sucking on her nipple could cause
such a gentle throbbing between her legs.

The Yankee knew her total surrender was imminent, and it couldn't come soon enough for him.
While his tongue and teeth toyed with the rigid little
bud enclosed in his mouth, he became more and
more conscious of the blood pounding hard through
his veins. His breath was growing short. He sensed
the same thing happening to her and that added to his
excitement.

His hand moved to her skirt. His long fingers
closed into a fist, bunching the blue fabric and tugging it upward. Elizabeth made no move to stop him.
She did not protest when his tanned fingers first
rested briefly on her knees, then gently nudged them
apart. Her breasts were wet and tingling from his
kisses when his bearded face finally lifted.

Her breath coming in shallow little pants, she made
one last effort to preserve her modesty, but he shook
his dark head and her hand fell away, leaving the
bodice open, her naked breast exposed to his heated
gaze.

His fingers moved up her right leg, gently stroking,
caressing her thigh through the silky fabric of her
pantalets. She swallowed and looked at his face. His
eyes were so darkened with passion, it was as if he
had just come out into bright sunshine from the darkness.

Elizabeth tried to look away, but found it impossible. Held by his hypnotic gaze, she continued to look

directly into his eyes even as his warm hand moved slowly up her leg until it was directly between her thighs. His hand was gentle as he possessively cupped her, but she knew he was in a highly sensual state of urgency, could feel the hardness of him rising against her bottom.

His long fingers gently pressed the soft material of her pantalets against her soft, hot flesh and the heel of his hand pushed tightly against her contracting belly. Those fingers began to move in a slow, erotic circle and the deep timbre of his voice sent tingles of joy up her spine when he said, "Yield to me, sweetheart. Give it to me. Let me love you, miss."

"Yes," she whispered, afraid but aroused. "Yes, Spy, yes."

6

Her inhibitions gone, Elizabeth Montbleau gave herself to the Yankee spy. She did so with such appealingly sweet trust, the Yankee was resolved to provide her with a degree of ecstasy surpassing any she'd known with past lovers.

Amidst burning kisses and murmured endearments he lovingly undressed her, caressing each inch of ivory flesh he bared. Elizabeth never considered helping with the task. Although unschooled in the ways of passion, she possessed an inborn sensuality. She found it gloriously erotic and highly pleasurable to have a man undress her. Especially, since he skillfully managed it with her sitting atop his lap.

To her passion-clouded mind, it was an amazing feat. Even more amazing was the fact that he handled it so deftly she suffered no embarrassment or shame. Somehow it seemed very natural and right for this dark, bearded Yankee to be undressing her in their moonlit cell. And it was thrilling in a way she'd never been thrilled before.

In minutes all her clothes had been magically swept away and she sat on his lap wearing nothing but the dewy perspiration of growing sexual excitement. His tanned hands dropped away, he laid his head against the wall, and openly admired her. She felt the heat of his eyes on her bare body but experienced no compulsion to turn away, to try to cover her nakedness. Truth to tell, she liked his hot eyes touching her flushed flesh.

Maybe under different circumstances she would have behaved very differently. She'd never be sure. She knew only that this night was to be her last and there was no time to waste on maidenly modesty. This dark, bearded Yankee was no nervous bridegroom, nor she his frightened bride.

"You're very beautiful," he said hoarsely, his hands lifting to stroke her delicate back, her flat belly, "but tell me, what color is your hair?"

"Red. Dark red," she murmured a little breathlessly.

"Red," he repeated approvingly, his eyes sweeping over the tousled locks falling around her bare shoulders. "I like red hair, I like—"

"What color are your eyes?" she softly interrupted. "Are they green?"

He drew a curling lock of red hair over her shoulder and toyed with it. "What color do you want them to be?"

"I've always been partial to green."

"Then green they are," said he, knowing it made no difference. If she preferred green to silver gray, why not let her suppose his were her favorite hue.

He released her hair and his fiery lips paid homage to a bare ivory arm as he leaned away from the wall, shrugged the gray tunic from his wide shoulders, and murmured against her flesh, "Help me, miss."

Elizabeth was more than willing. Stirring to the touch of his hot, bearded face nuzzling a bare, tingling breast, Elizabeth pushed the tunic off his shoulders and down his long arms. His thanks was a quick, searing kiss to a diamond-hard nipple. He raised his dark head, reached behind him, and withdrew the discarded tunic.

With an arm clamped around her narrow waist, he began spreading his gray tunic out on the scattered hay. Realizing that he was concerned with her comfort, Elizabeth was touched. She leaned over, reached for her blue dress, and drew it toward them. He smiled at her and together they carefully spread her dress so that it touched his tunic.

Their bed was now ready, the last one they would ever lie on.

As they looked at the makeshift bed, the Yankee said regretfully, "Sorry it's not sheets of silk, sweetheart."

Elizabeth's brazen reply was, "Make me forget that it isn't, Spy."

His head swung around and he looked at her, swallowing hard. He lifted her up in his powerful arms like a child, and rose agilely to his feet. For a moment he stood in the moonlight, holding her to his chest, his tall, spare body tensed, his need for her growing by the second. Elizabeth clung to his neck, her unbound hair spilling over his arm, her fingertips nervously tracing his collarbone.

The sound of Private Stark's loud snoring suddenly shattered the nighttime quiet and Elizabeth flinched, horrified.

"I had forgotten about the night guard! We can't . . . Oh, Spy, what if Private Stark . . ."

"He won't," the Yankee quickly assured her, pressing her closer. "He'll sleep soundly until morning. I know. I've been in the stockade for a week."

"Yes, but if he should . . ."

His lips stopped her worried questioning. Kissing her into silence, he went down on one knee and placed her on the spread clothing, following her down. His tanned hands gently stroked the length of her back, her rounded buttocks. Relaxing a little, Elizabeth turned more fully to him, laid the back of her hand on his chest and trailed her knuckles down across the hard muscles to his belt buckle.

He drew her slender leg up to curl over his hip, laid his head down on a bent arm, and faced her, leaving enough space between so they could look into each other's eyes. His hand continued to tenderly stroke her flared hip and smooth thigh. Hers continued to explore his hair-covered chest, his corded ribs, his drum-tight stomach.

After a while he drew her closer, so close she could feel the hair on his chest tickling her bare breasts, his heart beating against hers, the throbbing hardness restrained by his gray trousers. Urging her leg to curl up higher around his back, he kissed her, and his splayed hand moved across her belly and down, to touch and stroke.

He lifted his head and looked at her as his tanned fingers slipped fully into place and cautiously caressed her. Elizabeth stared straight into his eyes, her own widened with shock and with wonder.

"Spy, Spy . . ." she murmured breathlessly, feeling as if a liquid fire was raging through her veins and spilling onto his bold, coaxing fingers.

"Yes, sweetheart, I know, I know," he whispered, brushing kisses to her ears, her throat, her breasts. Elizabeth writhed and breathed through her mouth and her hips lifted and surged against his caressing hand.

She was hot, she was cold. She was restless, she was relaxed. She was anxious, she was eager. She wanted nothing more. She wanted something more.

The Yankee rose to his feet and took off his tall black boots and stockings. He unbuckled his belt, unbuttoned his gray trousers, and sent them swiftly to the floor. Elizabeth caught only a glimpse of the hard muscle and bone of his dark, spare body, and of the awesome erection thrusting skyward, before he was back with her.

He stretched out close beside her, his hand again sweeping over her silken skin, his achingly aroused flesh pulsing against her thigh. He kissed her a long time, then savoring the pleasure until he could stand it no longer, he moved between her parted thighs and thrust himself very gently into her.

Elizabeth felt an immediate flash of fiery pain and automatically stiffened beneath him. She pushed on his chest and turned her face away to evade his kiss.

He encountered a slight barrier and felt the sudden tenseness of her body. For one split second he wondered; could it be? Overpowering desire immediately drove the foolish notion from his head. He sank more deeply into her. Her tight, hot flesh sweetly closed around him and quickly he realized she was only playing the tease, behaving the coquette.

Elizabeth reinforced that belief when she again became pliant and moved with him in slow, erotic rhythm. Her hands clung to his hard biceps, the nails cutting into his flesh. Her feverish lips sprinkled kisses along his gleaming shoulder, her teeth nervously nipping. Her soft receptive flesh was so accomplished at taking him, squeezing him, setting his blood afire, he knew it would be impossible to hold back until she was ready.

It had been too long since he had last made love and this beautiful woman was too desirable, too practiced at pleasing a man. Wishing he could stop himself, knowing he couldn't, the Yankee continued to thrust into her, moving more rapidly now.

Feeling as though she would surely be torn apart, Elizabeth felt him grow within her until at last great throbs rolled through his spare frame. His eyes

closed, the tendons in his neck stood out in bold relief, the veins in his arms bulged below the dark,
smooth skin. He gave a great groan and lay still atop
her, his heart hammering wildly against hers, beads
of sweat rolling down his face, his chest.

Elizabeth lay quiet and still beneath him, aware
that something powerful had happened to him, and
knowing that she was responsible. She was relieved.
She had been concerned that he would be put off by
her sexual ignorance. She was afraid she wouldn't
please him, that she wouldn't know how to give him
pleasure.

She softly sighed, pleased with herself. It was obvious that she had given him a great deal of pleasure.
Much more, it seemed, than she had derived from the
intimate act, but then she supposed that was normal.
She'd heard the gossip of young wives who were
deeply in love with their husbands. Most admitted
they obtained far less bliss from making love than
their spouses. Some didn't even like it, found the act
of love revolting.

Elizabeth didn't feel that way. She had enjoyed tremendously the touching and kissing, and after the
first few seconds of terrible pain, it had felt almost
good. She liked it. In a way.

The spent man lying atop her *was* pleased with her.
She had brought him splendid, glorious ecstasy. Now
she was lying calmly beneath him, stroking his back,
his shoulders, sweet and uncomplaining. She was a
good sport, he gratefully decided, a very good sport.
His lovemaking had been that of an inexperienced
young boy, climaxing almost as soon as he was inside
her. Yet, no murmur of disgust or criticism.

Well, he would make it up to her. Any woman as
unselfish as this lovely red-haired beauty deserved
better than he had given her. Next time he'd see to it
she got the joy she had earned.

Elizabeth smiled shyly at him when he raised his dark head, brushed a kiss to her cheek, and slid from her. He rolled over to lie flat on his back, reached for her, and pulled her atop him. She lay with her arms folded over his chest, her chin propped up in her hands, her toes digging into his shins.

It was, she thought, strange that although they had just made love, she still felt all tingly and flushed and excited. When his tanned hands began to sweep enticingly over her shoulders, her back, her buttocks, Elizabeth couldn't lie still. Her breasts, flattening against his chest, still ached, the nipples were still taut. She stared at his full, sensual lips and realized she still wanted to kiss him, wanted to more than ever.

Elizabeth raised her head, shoved her tumbled hair back over her shoulder, and put the tip of her forefinger to the cupid's bow of his lip. She traced the curving line of the top lip, then traced the full bottom lip. His lips parted. She traced them again, touching gently, her fingertip gliding over his smooth wide mouth.

His hands came up to cup her rib cage, his thumbs stroking the sides of her breasts. "Use your tongue."

"Wh . . . what?"

"Trace my lips with your tongue."

It sounded like a wonderful idea to Elizabeth. Sliding up a little on his long body, she braced a hand on either side of his head, leaned close, and put out the tip of her tongue. She touched it to the left corner of his closed mouth and began to slowly move her tongue along his top lip until she reached the other corner. She repeated the teasing exercise on his lower lip. When she started on the top lip again, his mouth opened slightly. She licked at his lips until they were shiny wet and her hair was falling over her head and around his bearded face.

When his hands came up to sweep the hair back

from her eyes and his mouth closed over hers in a sweet, hot kiss, Elizabeth sighed with pleasure. He kissed her long and ardently and she became aware of the stirring readiness of his body against hers.

Was he going to make love to her again?

"I'm going to make love to you again, sweetheart," he said softly, "and this time I won't let you down."

Let me down? What's he talking about? Baffled, she started to ask what he meant, but never got the opportunity. His lips got in the way.

The pair spent the rest of the night making love. Elizabeth learned what the Yankee had meant when he'd said he wouldn't let her down. He kissed her and touched her for a long, lovely time before he again came into her. There was no pain this time, none at all. Inside her he moved slowly, slowly, gentle to the last, until she felt that great explosion of heat and joy.

Eyes widening with wonder and shock, she clung to his wide, slick shoulders and cried out in ecstasy, "Spy! Spy! Oh, my darling Spy!"

"Sweet miss," he murmured, and let himself go at last. "Baby, ah, baby!"

Both were so fully satisfied, they lay silently in each other's arms, sighing, relaxing. They dozed. Sometime later Elizabeth awakened to the sound of Private Stark's loud snoring. Harsh reality immediately washed over her. She was in a Confederate stockade. She was going to be shot at sunrise. She trembled violently.

And felt a strong arm tighten reassuringly around her. She lifted her face. He kissed her warmly, and made her forget what lay ahead. There was only the here and the now. Only the two of them. They made wild, exciting love this time and afterward, when the Yankee collapsed on his back, Elizabeth smiled, kissed his damp chest, and whispered, "I think it's time you learned my name, Spy."

"Tell me, miss."

"I'm—"

"Rise and shine, you two prisoners." Private Stark's booming voice came from the jail's front room.

An expression of horror froze Elizabeth's face. She quickly scrambled up, realizing now that she'd not heard Stark's loud snores for the past few minutes.

"Give us five minutes, damn you!" the Yankee called out. "Some coffee from the mess!" He was on his feet in a flash, helping her dress, standing in front of her to shield her should Stark lumber down the hall too soon.

"I ain't giving you nothing. They'll be coming for you any minute and . . ." his words trailed away. Then Elizabeth heard him say, "Mornin', sir. Mornin', Padre."

She heard other voices. It was time. They had come for her and the Yankee. While she hurriedly buttoned her bodice she looked up at the high window and saw the first hint of the last gray dawn of her life. She glanced at the Yankee. His back was to her as he buttoned his gray trousers.

She reached down for her shoes and saw, gleaming in the shadow, the shiny brass button she had pulled from his tunic in her excitement. Wistfully, she picked it up, closed her fist around it, and decided she would keep it. To the end.

The Yankee was buttoning his tunic when Private Stark came swaggering back, a smile on his ugly face. "You got company," he said. He pushed the key in the lock, swung the cell door open, and invited them to follow him.

There was no time to say good-bye. Elizabeth and the Yankee looked at each other. He smiled at her, briefly touched her shoulder, and followed her down the hall.

The early morning air was cool and moist as the

provost marshal and the black-robed padre escorted them outdoors, around the brick jail, and toward the execution ground. Elizabeth's thoughts were of her father and how it would break his heart when he learned of her shame. The Yankee's only thought was that he would meet his death aboveground in the bright sunshine. That was enough for him.

There in the rising sun, forming a neat line, was a firing squad of nervous, callow youths. Again Elizabeth exchanged glances with the Yankee. He touched the white cross sewn over his heart and gave her a bracing look. She bravely smiled at him.

They were marched directly to the high brick back wall. Their hands were tied behind them, and in Elizabeth's closed fist was the shiny brass button. She held it so tightly, it cut into the flesh of her palm, but the minor pain was a solace.

The Yankee shook his dark head no to the offer of a black felt blindfold, so Elizabeth did too. Nodding, the provost marshal walked away, and for a few seconds there was total silence. Elizabeth could hear the beating of her heart.

The soft, even voice of the padre offered up a prayer for their immortal souls and the provost marshal, hands behind his back, stepped alongside the firing squad and issued the command.

"Port-arms." Eight rifles were raised in neat precision. "Ready." The raised rifles were slapped up against eight young cheeks.

"Aim—"

"Halt!" shouted an arriving courier, bringing his horse to a plunging stop only feet from the firing squad. Dismounting quickly, he tossed the reins to the ground, saluted the provost marshal, and said excitedly, "Lee has surrendered! The war is over! The Confederacy has fallen!"

While the stunned firing squad lowered their guns

and the provost marshal read the dispatch the young soldier handed him, the courier strode forward, looked at the tall trussed man, and asked, "You the Union spy going under the name of Colonel Jim Underwood?"

"The very one," the Yankee replied, smiling, knowing he was now the senior Union officer present.

And in total command of the camp.

As the defeated Southern officer untied the Yankee victor, he said respectfully, "Sir, the female prisoner? What shall we do with her? Does her execution stand?"

His hands free, the Yankee asked, "What's the charge?"

"Murder, sir."

His expression changing none at all, the bearded Yankee could hardly keep from smiling. So that was it. The beautiful little murderess had somehow learned about the war's end. Had known all along that before the night ended, word would come. Word that *he* was now the officer in charge. The man with her fate in his hands.

That's why she had so eagerly come into his arms. Had allowed him to make love to her through the warm spring night. To save her lovely, evil little neck. She was a seductive, wily female who knew her ultimate fate and salvation rested in his hands. Willingly, wisely, she traded a favor for a favor. And there for a moment or two he had even thought her to be a virgin!

"I'll handle this, Major." He dismissed the provost marshal and turned to Elizabeth.

She was glaring at him. Angry. He had no idea why.

Elizabeth *was* angry. Angry with him. Her jaw set, teeth clenched, she glared at him, quickly putting two and two together.

He knew! The unprincipled Northern spy had

known all along that the war had ended. Acting so brave! That's why he hadn't been afraid to die. He knew he wasn't going to die. Knew he would never face the firing squad.

He knew all along that before the night ended word of Lee's surrender would reach the camp and he would be safe. He had only let her think it was to be their last night so that he could coldly seduce her.

The Yankee stepped up directly before her. Elizabeth looked up at the tall, bearded man with whom she had just been intimate. He began to smile sardonically. He shook his dark head.

"You knew, didn't you, sweetheart?" he asked in a low, soft voice.

"No," she replied angrily, "but you did, you deceitful Yankee bastard!"

Part Two

7

New York City

Autumn 1868

A child's merry laughter carried on the chill September air. Elizabeth Montbleau looked up from her book and smiled. Benjamin Curtin's golden curls danced in the sharp south wind as he energetically skipped rope.

His fair face was flushed with good health and good humor, and even at a distance Elizabeth could tell that his enormous green eyes were flashing with joy.

"Watch this, Miss Montbleau," the lively seven-year-old called, and Elizabeth waved to him and closed her book.

When he had her undivided attention, Benjamin Curtin unsuccessfully tried to cross hands with the jump rope, imitating his older brother, Daniel. Benjamin's spindly legs immediately became tangled in the badly thrown rope and he took a tumble. Elizabeth came to her feet.

"I'm fine," called the adorable Benjamin, jumping

quickly up and brushing at the dusty knees of his gray corduroy knickers. "I'll master it yet!"

"You'll never be able to do it," needled his brother Daniel, leaning against the school's high stone fence, his own jump rope slung around his neck, a smug expression on his face. "Give it up, Benny. You aren't coordinated."

"Of course, he will master it," Elizabeth called, tempted as she had been so many times before to give Daniel's ear a painful twist.

Drawing her woolen shawl more tightly about her shoulders, she sat back down on the stone steps, her gaze on the pair of young blond boys.

The Curtin brothers were without doubt two of the handsomest children enrolled at the Boltwood School for Young Gentlemen, New York City's most exclusive private school for boys aged five to fifteen. Benjamin was also one of the sweetest.

Elizabeth smiled, recalling that sunny morning in September of 1866 when she had nervously climbed Boltwood's stone steps for her first day of teaching. The aging three-story red brick building had looked intimidating with its many wide windows and the gabled and turreted white roof rising to meet the blue Manhattan sky.

Taking a deep breath, she had resolutely climbed the steps and walked into the stately Madison Avenue institute with its slate blackboards and kneehole desks and learned professors. It was not by chance that she would be the first female ever to teach at Boltwood. While she was grateful for the opportunity, she was apprehensive as well. Would her fellow instructors accept her? Would the students? The boys' parents?

Cautiously she entered a wide center corridor to find dozens of loud, boisterous boys pushing and shoving as they swarmed into appointed classrooms.

Pressing her back up against a wall, she waited for the storm to pass. When it did, she saw a small blond boy pressed up against the wall directly opposite her.

He looked as frightened as she felt.

She smiled, crossed to him, put out her hand, and said, "I'm Elizabeth Montbleau and this is my first day at Boltwood."

His small hand stole shyly into hers. He lifted his blond head, and a pair of huge green eyes, swimming with unshed tears, began to sparkle as she smiled down at him.

"I'm Benjamin Curtin. It's my first day too," he told her, his rosy cheeks dimpling appealingly. "My mother is away, so my father told Daniel to take care of me today. Daniel's my big brother." His narrow shoulders lifted and lowered in a sigh. "Daniel ran off and left me as soon as we got inside and I don't know where to go."

Elizabeth laid a gentle hand on his shoulder. "It appears we're both lost. Why don't we find our way together, Benjamin."

He smiled at her, his two front baby teeth missing. He was, she decided, the cutest child she had ever seen. Together they went in search of their classrooms and found they were one and the same. The first period of the morning, she taught the five-, six-, and seven-year-olds. Benjamin Curtin was five years old.

Before that first day had ended, she had met the other Curtin brother. Nine at the time, Daniel was an older version of the appealing Benjamin. But it was in looks only. She quickly learned that Daniel was argumentative, a complainer, and a troublemaker.

Looking now at the two blond boys, Elizabeth regarded the pair much as she had on that day more than two years ago. At seven Benjamin was still

sweet, agreeable, and loving. The rapidly growing
eleven-year-old Daniel was quarrelsome, hard to handle, and untrustworthy.

More than once Elizabeth had wondered if Daniel's
disagreeable temperament had come from his
mother. She had met the boys' father on more than
one occasion when he visited the school. Edmund
Curtin was a soft-spoken likable gentleman, unfailingly gracious and friendly. His wife had never set
foot inside Boltwood.

"He's here, Miss Montbleau," Benjamin called excitedly, and Elizabeth looked up. She had agreed to
have dinner with the Curtins. They were worried
about Benjamin's continuing low marks in school.
But Benjamin was unaware of the visit's true purpose, and he was delighted that his teacher was finally coming to his home.

Rounding the corner was the Curtins' fine coach,
pulled by a matched pair of elaborate traces. A blond,
smiling Edmund Curtin stepped down from the carriage and strolled quickly forward, a spring in his
step. Benjamin hurried to him, smiling up at his father when Edmund Curtin ruffled his hair. Daniel
stayed where he was.

Extending a hand as he approached Elizabeth, Edmund Curtin apologized. "Miss Montbleau, I do hope
you'll forgive me for being late. I was unavoidably
detained on Wall Street." He shook his head wearily.
"Mining stocks have been erratic of late."

Elizabeth smiled understandingly. She was aware
that Edmund Curtin and his younger brother, Dane,
whom she had never met, were wealthy native New
Yorkers whose family fortune was tied to mining
shares in the volatile stock market. The brothers controlled mines—gold, silver, and copper—in Arizona
and the northern states of Mexico.

"No apologies necessary, Mr. Curtin," she assured him, warmly shaking his outstretched gloved hand.

He drew a gleaming gold-cased watch from his trouser pocket, looked at it, and said, "You're a tolerant young lady, Miss Montbleau. I meant to be here by four. It's a quarter of five. Louisa will have my scalp. Shall we go?" He offered her his arm.

Elizabeth placed her hand inside his bent elbow. At the waiting carriage he handed her up into the burgundy upholstered interior. The boys scrambled up after her, young Benjamin taking the seat beside her. Their father got in last, settled himself across from her, tapped on the coach's top, and they moved out onto the avenue.

They had only a few blocks to travel, but an early dusk was settling over the city when the carriage reached the Curtins' Fifth Avenue mansion. They were met at the door of the three-story brownstone by a British butler. They stood beneath a lighted brass overhead lantern in the vestibule while the liveried butler took Elizabeth's shawl and Edmund Curtin's gloves and cane.

They moved into a wide hallway, where Elizabeth had only a moment to appreciate the magnificent wooden staircase with its intricately carved balusters. At their father's urging the boys hurried up the stairs to change for dinner. Elizabeth, smiling after them, looked up through the opening in the oval-shaped staircase and saw a huge skylight framing a large portion of the rapidly darkening sky.

She was shown into a vast sitting room off the hall, where a cheerful fire blazed brightly in a marble fireplace. The big, handsome room had archways decorated with molding and sculptured ornamentations. The ceilings were exceptionally high. The large windows were covered by interior shutters with movable slats.

A gleaming teardrop chandelier cast prisms of light on the cream-covered walls, French gilt furniture, and fine oil paintings. A large gilt-framed oval mirror hung over the fireplace, reflecting the taste and beauty of the room.

Standing in that warm, luxurious home, Elizabeth realized she had all but forgotten that people actually lived in homes like this. That *she* had once lived in a home much like this one. Only hers had not been a three-story brownstone on Fifth Avenue in New York City, but an eight-columned white two-story mansion on the bluffs of the Mississippi River in Natchez.

"We're delighted you could join us, Miss Montbleau," said a fashionably gowned, slightly overweight woman with glossy black hair who swept into the room just as Elizabeth was about to sit down. "I'm Louisa Curtin. Welcome to our home."

"Thank you so much for inviting me here, Mrs. Curtin," Elizabeth said, trying not to stare openly at the huge blue-white diamond glittering atop her hostess's bare décolletage. Louisa Curtin was known to have one of the largest and finest jewel collections on all of Fifth Avenue. Transfixed by the large, flawless diamond, Elizabeth could hardly take her eyes off the valuable gem.

"It is stunning, isn't it?" said Louisa Curtin, catching Elizabeth looking at the famous twenty-carat Star of the West diamond, the most prized of all her jewels.

"Yes," Elizabeth said, "it certainly is."

"Sit down, sit down," said Louisa, waving a small bejeweled hand. Walking straight to her husband and lifting a pale cheek for him to kiss, Louisa Curtin scolded, "You haven't offered Miss Montbleau an aperitif, Edmund." Not giving him time to answer, she came to sit beside Elizabeth. "Edmund's brother,

Dane, will be joining us for dinner. I hope you don't mind."

"Certainly not," said Elizabeth.

"Dane lives just around the corner on Fourth, though he's rarely home." She laughed girlishly and added, "Edmund says the same thing about me. Don't you, dear?"

"My lovely wife is a very busy woman," was Edmund's gracious comment. "Several of our city's more worthwhile charitable and eleemosynary organizations depend almost exclusively on my tireless Louisa."

Again Louisa laughed. "Edmund's so stuffy," she added, as though he were not present. "I just can't drag him away from the precious metals markets, so what choice do I have? Either I venture out alone or draft one of Edmund's friends to escort me." She sighed, looking as though she felt a little sorry for herself.

Then Louisa brightened and began chattering gaily about her many civic obligations and her frequent trips abroad. She explained, as if she had been asked, that the travel was tiring but necessary to her role as one of the guardians of New York City's culture.

For more than ten minutes Louisa Curtin spoke of her duties, stopping only when her young blond sons came bounding into the sitting room. At the intrusion, Elizabeth caught just a hint of a frown cross Louisa Curtin's round face.

What happened next caused Elizabeth to frown.

Daniel nodded almost imperceptibly to his mother, then crossed to a square table where a chess set was laid out. But the warm, affectionate Benjamin ran straight to his mother and threw his short arms around her bare neck. Louisa Curtin turned her dark head away and forcefully shoved her son from her.

"Benjamin!" she snapped irritably. "You'll ruin

Mommy's gown." She pushed on his narrow chest with a diamond-bedecked hand and wrinkled her small nose.

"Yes, ma'am," said Benjamin, the expression of hurt in his big green eyes missed by his mother, but not by Elizabeth.

While the dejected little boy moved toward his father, Louisa Curtin, patting her sleek, upswept dark hair, quickly regained her composure, turned to Elizabeth, and said, "I'm sure you want to freshen up before dinner, Miss Montbleau."

"That would be nice," Elizabeth replied, stealing a glance at Benjamin and giving him a secret smile.

The small, voluptuous woman rose and Elizabeth followed her up the grand staircase. Louisa paused before a closed door of gleaming mahogany. "Take as long as you like, Miss Montbleau." She smiled and was gone.

The soft bouquet of lilac soap scented the white airy bath, a room as large as most bedrooms. Beveled mirrors multiplied her image, dozens of clean white towels hung on gilt racks, and rich wool carpet, as luxurious as the beige Aubusson downstairs, covered the floor.

Elizabeth washed her hands, patted her face with water, and saw reflected in the mirror a big long white tub on claw feet against the wall behind her.

For a second she had an almost uncontrollable urge to strip off her worn woolen dress and underwear and climb naked into that shiny tub. How wonderful it would be if she could skip the meal with the Curtins and spend the entire dinner hour luxuriating in their bathtub, experimenting with the varied stoppered bottles of oils and trying all the different bars of scented soaps.

A little wistfully, Elizabeth blotted her damp face with one of the fluffy towels, dried her hands, and left the big inviting bath. Lost in guilty thought, she descended the carved wooden staircase and at its base came face to face with a tall blond man.

He stood squarely in her way, his arms crossed over his chest. He looked dashing in a finely tailored suit of dark brown wool. An impeccably dressed man, his shirt was snowy white linen, his perfectly tied foulard a rich tan silk. His blond hair gleamed brilliantly in the light cast by a crystal wall sconce and his lips were stretched into a wide grin over even white teeth.

"You must be the boys' teacher," he said, thrusting both hands out to grip the polished banisters, trapping her where she stood. "I'm Dane Curtin. My nephews have told me all about you." Against his brown waistcoat a gold Phi Beta Kappa key caught the gaslight as he said, "Think you can teach me anything?"

"A great deal, Mr. Curtin."

Taken aback, but intrigued by her quick confident reply, Dane Curtin glanced about, leaned close, and said, "Oh, yes?" His smile broadened as his gaze dropped to her lips. "Tell me, what can you teach me?"

"First, some manners, Mr. Curtin."

8
♪♪♪

"I'm retiring," said West Quarternight, the reflection of the campfire's flames flickering in the depths of his silver-gray eyes. "Giving it up." He yawned and ran tanned fingers through his shaggy jet-black hair.

Grady Downs hooted at West Quarternight's ridiculous statement. Grady laughed and elbowed the gigantic Navajo Indian sitting cross-legged on the hard ground beside him.

"Sonny," he addressed West, "you ain't about to quit." Grady shook his white head from side to side and his sky-blue eyes twinkled.

"I am, Grady." The tone of West's voice was flat. He rose to his feet with an easy, uncoiling motion and stretched his hands to the fire's warmth. It was a cold night in the New Mexico high country. Chill mountain winds ruffled West's dark hair and pressed his fringed buckskin shirt and trousers against his back and legs. "The way I figure it," he said, "I've got enough to make it from now on, if I don't do any high living."

Grady Downs wouldn't have it.

"You ain't quittin'. He ain't quittin', is he, Taos?" He looked for support to the big Indian, hoping to read affirmation in the blinking of his flat black eyes, the extent of the Navajo's reaction. Addressing West again, the wiry white-haired man said indignantly, "Is this the thanks me and Taos get for taking you in and teaching you everything we know? You up and quit on us just like that?" He snapped his fingers. "Why, without us, you'd still be back there in them Kentucky hills starving, not having enough sense to . . ."

Unruffled, West grinned, turned, and went to his stashed bedroll. He crouched down on his heels, unbuckled the fat bundle, spread his blanket on the ground, stretched out, and laid his head on his saddle, rolling his eyes heavenward.

Grady Downs's tirade continued. He was picking up steam, working himself up into an angered frenzy. He went on and on to the silent Navajo about the youth of today having no respect for their elders.

". . . and guess he's plumb forgot, Taos, that if it wasn't for me and you, he'd be nothing but a not-too-bright womanizing broke Kentuckian who couldn't guide his own self out of these here mountains back down to Santa Fe. No sirree! Mr. Weston Dale Quarternight's one ungrateful, selfish youngster if ever there was one. Never would have made one penny on his own. And you can mark my words, without the two of us around to tell him what to do, and when to do it, he'll . . ."

Smiling, West Quarternight folded a long arm beneath his head and looked up at the cold, starry sky. He couldn't totally disagree with the feisty white-haired mountain man's unkind assessment. If he hadn't walked into that Kansas saloon one summer afternoon over three years ago, where *would* he be today?

He thought back on that unhappy stage in his life. After the war he had left Shreveport, Louisiana, immediately and headed for his home in the Kentucky hills, only to find that everything that had made it his home was gone.

He didn't stay.

He drifted over to St. Louis, got a job dealing faro in a saloon, and heard a player say the westward moving railroad was paying decent wages. He turned in his green eyeshade for a spade and worked twelve to fourteen hours a day in the Kansas sun, laying track. And hated every minute of it.

On a day when the temperature on the scorching plains soared past the century mark and not one breath of air was stirring, he wiped his sweating brow on a forearm, looked out across the flat prairie, and decided he'd had enough.

He handed the heavy spade to a smiling Chinese workman, picked up his shirt, drew his pay, and left. In Junction City he headed for the nearest saloon. He walked through the slatted doors of the Plainsman Saloon in the middle of the quiet afternoon. The Plainsman was near deserted, save for a table of so-ber-faced poker players in the corner and a small white-haired man standing alone at the long, polished bar. West stepped up to the bar and ordered an Old Crow whiskey.

He felt the customer's eyes and turned his head. Smiling at him was a trim little man with snowy white hair down to his shoulders, a full white beard and drooping white mustache, dancing blue eyes, and ruddy cheeks. His back ramrod straight, the immaculate stranger wore a western-type pullover shirt as white as his hair, trousers of dark twill, and high, shiny black boots. A holstered gun was buckled low on his hips and a large turquoise stone, framed in hammered silver, dangled from a leather thong around his neck.

"Something on your mind, friend?" West asked, threw back his head, and downed his shot of whiskey.

Without an invitation, the smiling man moved down the bar toward him. Stroking his flowing white beard, he said, "Sonny, you're gonna look back on this day as one of your luckiest."

West motioned the barkeep for another whiskey. "I assume you're about to tell me why."

The white-haired man nodded happily. "I'm pretty good at sizing folks up and I'd say you ain't got no family, no money, and no job. Am I right?"

West shrugged. "And that makes me lucky?"

"No, that makes *me* lucky." The white-haired man put out his hand. "I'm Grady Downs, son. At dawn tomorrow, I'm guiding a small party of wealthy Easterners from here to the New Mexico Territory. Know how much I'll charge 'em?" Without waiting for a reply he went on, "Two hundred fifty dollars apiece! Seven of 'em comes to seventeen hundred fifty dollars. Not bad for a couple of months' work, is it?"

Interested, West said, "Let's get to the part where I'm lucky."

Grady Downs chuckled. "I'm coming to that. I'm gonna pay you two hundred dollars for coming along, riding shotgun for me."

West looked him squarely in the eye. He'd never been west of Kansas and he was restless, eager to get away, to try something different. He had heard about the Apache and Navajo and Comanche and Ute Indians that roamed the mountains and deserts of the West, terrorizing travelers along the Santa Fe Trail.

"You'll pay me five hundred dollars," he said, and Grady Downs laughed and slapped him on the back.

Together, they escorted the Easterners westward without incident. The trip was pleasant enough, despite the fact that Grady Downs was the world's greatest talker. He started talking the minute he opened his eyes in the morning, was still talking at night when West fell asleep.

His squinted eyes constantly sweeping the changing terrain for signs of trouble, West only half listened to the tales of Grady's many hair-raising adventures. But slowly, and almost without realizing it, West revealed a great deal about himself to the little white-haired mountain man.

They had hardly reached the New Mexico Territory before a gigantic Indian appeared from out of nowhere. He came riding a big paint pony directly toward them. West's hand automatically slapped the butt of his holstered Colt, but Grady Downs laughed and said, "Sonny, don't shoot old Taos. He's my best friend and you'll be calling on him to save your life more than once if you stay in the Territory."

Grady had been right about that.

Taos stood six foot six in his moccasins, weighed an even three hundred pounds and every ounce of it was bone and sinew. His chest was awesomely massive. Muscles of steel bulged and bunched in his long arms and powerful thighs. He was keenly intelligent, but silent. He never spoke a word.

Grady had found the young Taos twenty years before, badly wounded and left for dead with his father, mother, brothers, and sisters all lying dead around him in the foothills above Taos, New Mexico. He judged the boy to be twelve or fourteen at the time. He had nursed the Navajo back to health and given him the name Taos.

The boy grew into a giant of a man who was as protective of Grady as if Grady had been his own father. In no time, Taos became just as protective of West. When West proposed that the three of them set up a land-and-mineral exploration company and start contracting to guide prospective purchasers, geologists, and expeditions throughout the New Mexico

Territory, the silent Taos persuaded Grady the idea was a good one.

With people pouring into the West, business had flourished. Their reputation as the most knowledgeable guides west of the Rockies quickly spread to the big cities in the East and they were booked for months in advance.

In those rare periods when they were idle, Taos and Grady disappeared into the mountains, where they lived out in the open, the New Mexico sky their only roof, the alpine meadows their bed. West had gone up with them a time or two, but much preferred to engage a room in Santa Fe's La Fonda Hotel, or the old Exchange in Las Vegas, New Mexico.

Or to ride down to the vast Baca Rancho in the southern part of the Territory. Senora Baca, the blond, beautiful widow of the late Don Javier Narcisco Baca, was always glad to see him and had her own special way of making him feel welcome.

West sighed now as he studied the star-studded black sky. Grady, Taos, the Baca widow, hell, the whole Territory had been good to him. Yet that old restlessness was plaguing him again. That feeling that he wanted to be somewhere else, doing something else. He was tired of his life and its sameness. He felt the terrible hand of his great pursuer, boredom.

Well, it was September. He would stay on through the winter, honor the contracts already signed, then quit. Leave the business with Grady and Taos. Ride on down south and visit the friendly Doña Hope for a few days and from there . . . who knew. Maybe he'd go to old Mexico or out to California to see if any gold was left.

". . . and if Sonny actually thinks he can just up and quit us, he's got another think a-coming. We got contracts to honor, Taos. We gave our word. Hell, he knows that . . ." Grady Downs's voice became a low, lulling hum, and West's eyelids grew heavy. He drew a long, slow breath, closed his eyes, and fell asleep.

Benjamin and Daniel Curtin were sent upstairs as soon as the early dinner had ended. The adults remained at the dining table, enjoying their strong English coffee and fluffy French pastries.

Dane Curtin, seated directly across from Elizabeth, swirled brandy around in a crystal snifter and openly stared at her, the hint of a smile on his full lips. She paid him no attention. He was quite handsome, but she detected in him some of the characteristics she disliked in his nephew, Daniel.

Dane corrected his brother Edmund on several inconsequential professional points, complained that the roast beef was not tender, and with scarcely concealed malice teased his sister-in-law about setting a record by spending an evening at home. Louisa Curtin shot him an angry look. Pleased, he grinned and winked at Elizabeth.

Elizabeth assumed that any minute he would be the one excusing himself to go out for the evening, and as far as she was concerned, the sooner the better.

Shortly, Louisa Curtin set her fragile china coffee cup in its matching saucer, patted her red lips with a white linen napkin, and said, "Miss Montbleau, Edmund and I need to discuss Benjamin's learning problems with you."

Elizabeth nodded, giving the woman her undivided attention. "Yes, of course. I'm so pleased that you've—"

"Ah . . . I'm afraid you will have to excuse me though." Louisa pushed back her chair and rose. "I'm late for the opera already." She smiled sweetly at Elizabeth, nodded to the two men who had risen as soon as she stood up. "Edmund will be happy to handle everything, Miss Montbleau. He's always so good with the boys." She rushed from the dining room, her long gunmetal taffeta skirts rustling with her steps, the magnificent Star of the West diamond flashing on her bare bosom.

Elizabeth barely managed to hide her dismay. When the two men sat back down, she smiled at Edmund and continued speaking as though Louisa Curtin were still at the table.

Edmund revealed his deep parental concern as he talked of his son's learning problems. They spoke at length of Benjamin, and in the end Elizabeth agreed to tutor Benjamin twice a week at the Curtin mansion. When the schedule had been decided and Elizabeth's fee agreed on, she told the Curtin brothers that she had enjoyed the evening, and that she needed to get home to her father.

To her surprise and displeasure, Dane Curtin insisted on driving her home. An open one-horse gig was brought around to the mansion's front gate and Dane took her arm and led her out into the chill night. When he climbed up beside her and unwrapped the reins from around the brake, he smiled and said, "Better scoot closer, it's mighty cold this evening."

Staying where she was, Elizabeth replied, "I'm quite comfortable, thank you."

"Then since you are, would you like to take a ride down the river or along—"

"No, Mr. Curtin. I must get home. My father is not well."

"Then home it is." The well-sprung gig rolled along the grooved Belgian blocks of the busy street. "Which is where?"

"Four blocks off Broadway on Twenty-fourth Street."

"Twenty-fourth Street?" His classic features took on a frown as he turned to her. "But, Miss Montbleau,

Twenty-fourth Street is where our . . . the . . . ah
. . . that's—"

"Yes. Where the stables are," she said, without the
slightest trace of embarrassment. "Father and I live in
a small apartment behind the stables." She looked
squarely at him, daring him to say more.

He didn't. The urbane, sophisticated man found it
rather charming that the beautiful young teacher was
not ashamed to admit she lived and cared for a sickly
father in a shanty behind the city's smelly stables.

Never in his life had he known a woman who
worked. It was a bit of a novelty, like her flaming red
hair. It might be a lark to escort her around town,
take her to the theater, to some of his crowd's many
parties. He could imagine the mouths of his hostesses
dropping open when he presented his red-haired
teacher to the snobby guests.

They turned onto Twenty-fourth Street. The high-
stepping horse pranced down the dark street fronted
by nothing but stables. In the middle of the fourth
block a narrow lane on the left leading between the
stables was barely visible in the dim light.

"You may stop here, Mr. Curtin," Elizabeth told
him. Nodding, he pulled up on the horse and Elizabeth turned, smiled, and said, "Thank you for driving
me home. Good night."

She made a move to get out of the gig. He caught
her arm, pulled her back. "Do you really suppose I'd
let you walk alone through the darkness?"

"I've done so many times, Mr. Curtin."

"Well, you won't this night," he said, bounded
down, and hurried around to help her from the gig.

The pair went into and down the darkened lane.
Dane Curtin held Elizabeth's arm while she led the
way. At a corner they turned into a narrow alleyway
—more of a cobblestone path—and moved quickly toward a lighted window several yards away.

Pausing before the wooden front door of her modest apartments, Elizabeth offered him her hand. "Thank you, Mr. Curtin, I appreciate your—"

"Dane," he corrected, and took her hand in both of his.

"Thank you, Dane."

"You're welcome, Elizabeth." He moved a little closer. "Come to a wine supper with me tomorrow evening."

"No, I'm sorry. I can't."

"Can't? Or don't want to?"

"Good night, Mr. Curtin."

9
៹៹៹

In her narrow bed that night, sleep eluded Elizabeth.
She found herself comparing the way she and her father lived to that of the Curtins. For the first time in
ages she felt a measure of the old hatred and resent-
ment that had once threatened to consume her.

Fighting those destructive feelings, wanting to
leave the past buried and forgotten, she tried to fall
asleep. But the thin mattress on which she lay was
lumpy and worn and beneath her cheek the un-
bleached muslin pillowcase was rough and scratchy.
Tossing restlessly, unable to get comfortable, Elizabeth sighed with frustration.

She missed—would always miss—the feel of the
fine silky linens that had graced all the tall four-post-
ers in the big white mansion high on the bluffs of the
Mississippi.

That stately mansion built by her long-dead grand-
father, Edgar Montbleau. The spacious mansion now
owned and occupied by a rich Northern carpetbag-
ger.

Yankees living in her home! Sleeping in her bed!

Elizabeth shut her eyes tightly, and her hands
curled into fists, the nails cutting into her palms. She

felt a heaviness in her chest, an overwhelming longing for the happy, tranquil days of her youth. Before
the war. Before the Yankees.

There had been no Yankees in the white-columned
mansion on that glorious early spring day in 1861
when she had returned home after completing her
schooling in New York City.

Warm and sunny, the humid air sweetened with the
scent of early-blooming roses, it had been a perfect
day. She'd had no way of knowing that instead of it
being the first of many such perfect days, it would be
the last.

Elizabeth began to smile as she recalled with vivid
clarity everything about that wonderful April day.
The entire family and half the servants had been
down on the private jetty when the sternwheeler,
Eastern Princess, had rounded the last bend in the
river. From the tall texas deck she had waved madly,
her heart pounding with happiness and excitement.

It was like a holiday with old friends coming to call
and lots of presents and hugs and kisses and a big
midday meal with all her favorite foods. And then,
that evening, had come the best part of all.

The guests had all gone and she had sat on the veranda steps in cool spring twilight while her distinguished gray-haired father dozed peacefully in his favorite white wicker chair and her beautiful red-
haired mother rocked contentedly beside him, smiling serenely.

Her brothers, Dave and Tommy, grown up and
handsome in their finest clothes, had burst out onto
the veranda, scuffling and laughing. They quickly
kissed their mother's pale cheek and ruffled Elizabeth's hair, then bounded down the steps and out to
the waiting carriage, and were off to the latest gala
party.

Elizabeth watched them drive away and smiled,

knowing that in only one more year, when she turned sixteen, she, too, would be off to the gay parties.

But there were to be no more parties.

The very next day, Pierre Beauregard commanded the attack on Fort Sumter, South Carolina, and the war started. The three Montbleau men immediately formed and armed a troop for the Confederate Army and rode away from home. Forever.

After six lonely months in the empty mansion on the bluffs, Elizabeth and her mother, Helene, went to Atlanta to wait out the war with her mother's sister, Aunt Julie. It was there they got news of the boys' deaths.

Tommy and Dave were killed within days of each other. Tommy, the youngest, was the first to die. He lost his life in a charge at the bloody battle of Gettysburg on July 1st, his twenty-first birthday. Tommy was luckier than Dave, he was killed instantly with a bullet through the heart.

Dave, down in Vicksburg, less than a hundred miles from his home, starved to death in the long, terrible siege. A big-framed man, he survived for several hard, hungry weeks, taking his place in the trenches, too weak to stand.

His commanding officer said when it was finally all over on that July 4th, 1863, Captain David Edgar Montbleau never saw the victors come marching into the city, never heard the Union band play "The Star-Spangled Banner."

He had died at dawn that day.

Elizabeth consoled her mother when the boys were killed, one terrible blow coming right after the other. But there was only Aunt Julie to console Elizabeth when her beautiful mother, Helene, died. The regal, patient, loving Helene Montbleau literally worked herself to death in a sweltering Georgia field hospital outside Atlanta in the hot summer of '64.

Fleeing Sherman's invading troops, Elizabeth and Aunt Julie went south to a cousin in New Orleans. Aunt Julie stayed there, but Elizabeth was never happy in that Yankee-occupied city where life went on just as if there were not a bloody war taking place in the rest of the country.

When a band of war widows and sweethearts enlisted the help of anyone they could find to go upriver to northern Louisiana to work in an overcrowded Confederate field hospital, Elizabeth overruled her Aunt Julie and went with the valiant ladies. She wanted to help. To do her part.

So she went to Shreveport, Louisiana . . . and . . . and . . .

Elizabeth gritted her teeth in the darkness. She had tried, in vain, to blot out all that had happened in Shreveport. She would *not* think about it now. She willed herself to skip ahead, to dwell on the relief and happiness she'd felt when she was reunited with her father.

She had finally found him in an eastern hospital, badly wounded and permanently crippled. His dulled eyes lighted with hope when he saw her, and she knew as she gripped his frail hand that she would find a way to take care of him, just as he had always taken care of her.

Miss DuGuire, the headmistress of the girls' school she had attended, immediately came to mind. Perhaps Miss DuGuire needed an instructress at the school.

The stocky, gray-haired spinster was glad to see Elizabeth. She was understanding, but apologetic. Enrollment at the Academy for Young Ladies had drastically fallen off since the days before the war. It had been necessary to let two of her teachers go—instructors who had been with her for more than a decade.

Seeing Elizabeth's disappointment, the sympathetic

headmistress said, "But don't you worry, my dear. I'll call in a favor. The headmaster over at Boltwood owes me one." She smiled mischievously.

"Boltwood? Isn't that a boys' school, Miss DuGuire?"

"It is." Miss DuGuire pursed her thin lips, then smiled and said, "But I happen to know that they need an instructor badly."

"That may well be, but—"

"Elizabeth Montbleau, you are going to be the first female teacher at Boltwood! Leave everything to me." The portly woman giggled like a young girl.

Elizabeth would never know what kind of favor Miss DuGuire called in, but that same afternoon a tall, painfully skinny man with a beaklike nose, small brown eyes, and a few wispy gray hairs forming a horseshoe around his gleaming pate, arrived at Miss DuGuire's Academy off Madison Square.

Professor Charles F. Durwood III, Harvard graduate and confirmed bachelor, had been the headmaster of Boltwood for twenty-five years. Elizabeth found him to be shy, stuffy, and humorless when he interviewed her, so she couldn't believe it when he formally offered her a position at the all-male Boltwood Academy.

Her salary, she felt certain, was much lower than that of the male professors, but she was grateful to Charles F. Durwood III. And to Miss DuGuire. The money she made teaching at Boltwood afforded her the small two-room apartment for her sickly father and herself.

Normally Elizabeth felt very grateful for what little they had. At least they were together and there was always food on the table and enough clothes to keep them warm and money to buy her father's medicines.

She should be ashamed of herself. There was no excuse for feeling this anger and self-pity all because she had visited the luxurious home of the wealthy Curtin family.

Elizabeth sighed loudly and turned on her stomach. She punched her lumpy pillow, laid her head down, and closed her eyes.

And immediately came to the decision that with the extra money she would earn tutoring young Benjamin Curtin, she'd go right out to buy a pair of fine silk pillowcases edged in delicate Belgian lace.

For weeks, Elizabeth said no.

Every time Dane Curtin invited her to join him for dinner or the theater, she politely but firmly turned him down. Naturally her puzzling reluctance to go out with him made her all the more attractive. Dane made it a point to be at his brother's Fifth Avenue mansion each time she came to tutor young Benjamin.

He teased and flirted and remained undaunted when she repeatedly turned down his invitations. He couldn't believe it when finally she said yes.

It was on a splendid sunny afternoon. From an outdoor balcony Dane secretly spied on Elizabeth and Benjamin. Inside his nephew's upstairs bedroom, teacher and pupil sat cross-legged on the floor and studied, as though they were best friends, as if Elizabeth was the same age as Benjamin.

Enchanted, Dane watched with envy as the flame-haired teacher encouraged and praised and showed her student an abundance of affection. Young Benjamin glowed from all the attention. His school marks had improved dramatically.

When the session ended, Dane came to his feet and made his presence known. He joined the pair in young Benjamin's room, bent and gave his nephew a big hug, and complimented him on his work. He did it because he knew it pleased Elizabeth as much as it pleased Benjamin.

Elizabeth was smiling her approval when Dane straightened. He smiled, too, and said casually, "Have dinner with me tonight at Delmonico's."

Continuing to smile, she said, "All right."

Dane's green eyes widened with surprise. "Did I hear correctly?"

"Is eight agreeable?" Elizabeth said, gathering up her books. "I'd like to be home no later than ten o'clock."

Elizabeth enjoyed the evening. Dinner at the fashionable restaurant was such a treat she couldn't believe that the time had passed so quickly when Dane Curtin said, "We'd better be going if you're to be home by ten."

At her door behind the stables on Twenty-fourth Street, Dane said, "Tell me, Miss Montbleau, that we'll be doing this again." He kissed her cheek.

"We will, Mr. Curtin," she replied. "I'd like that. I'd like that very much."

He smiled, kissed her cheek again, and as she stood watching, he turned and walked slowly away. When he'd rounded the corner at the alley, he ran as fast as he could back to the waiting carriage.

"You know where to go, Darcey," he said to the liveried driver atop the box.

Moments later Dane rang the bell of the most imposing dwelling on Fifth Avenue. A butler let him in and silently pointed a white-gloved finger toward the marble staircase. Dane bolted up the steps two at a time.

She was waiting in her upstairs bedroom, still dressed to go out for the evening. An expensive Paris gown of yellow silk was molded so tightly to her thick waist, the seams were pulling. The shiny yellow bodice strained across her enormous breasts and dipped low in the shadowed valley where beads of sweat were pooling.

Her naturally curly black hair had been fashioned atop her head but had begun to droop and straggle down her short neck and to frizz about her plump, pouting face.

Dane Curtin fought down his distaste and hurried forth to greet the twenty-three-year-old Marjorie Ann Bishop.

"Darling, I'm so sorry. I'm dreadfully late and I know how disappointed my angel must be."

The woman's small, plump hands went to her wide hips. "I am angry with you, Dane Curtin," she whined. "I shall never speak to you again."

Knowing exactly what he had to do to appease the overweight, spoiled, decidedly unattractive young woman, Dane Curtin fixed a picture of the beautiful flame-haired Elizabeth Montbleau solidly in his mind and rushed forward to take in his arms the sole heir to one of the largest banking fortunes in America.

Marjorie Ann Bishop's mood began to soften the minute his arms came around her. Her breathing grew raspy and loud in his ear when she felt his hands on her bare back and shoulders. She whispered excitedly, as if she hadn't told him a dozen times before, that her parents were still in Europe.

"Undress me, Dainee," she murmured anxiously. "Rip my clothes off."

A muscle in Dane Curtin's jaw throbbed. God, if only he could turn his back and she'd quietly undress, get into bed, and turn out the lamp. But he knew better. Knew there wasn't a chance of getting off that easily.

For just a second longer he pressed her dark head

to his pleated shirtfront, drew a deep, spine-stiffening breath, and prepared himself to begin the charade that would keep her happy.

But first he asked if she had done her part. Had she been a good girl? Was she playing the game fairly? Was she wearing beneath the billowing yellow ball gown the adornments he had requested?

She was, she was, she breathlessly assured him. She had on even more than the last time. Some really fine ones she'd found in her mother's bedroom wall safe!

That last statement helped a great deal. He was curious and that curiosity, along with the fresh vision of a red-haired charmer, would see him through.

Dane's fingers slid up into Marjorie Ann's dark frizzy tresses and closed around a handful of the coarse, curly hair. Immediately he tightened his grip and jerked her head back forcefully.

Quickly he closed his eyes so he wouldn't have to look at the rouged face and large red mouth. He bent to her, brutally kissed her, and felt her plump body sag against his.

Now they were ready.

He lifted his head, shoved her away, and ordered, "Get undressed! Take everything off!"

Almost swooning with excitement, Marjorie Ann Bishop said the same thing she always said, "No! I will not, sir! I am a lady and you can't—"

"Then I shall tear them off," he thundered, right on cue.

Marjorie Ann couldn't keep from giggling happily when he reached out, grabbed the low, tight bodice of her yellow silk dress, and yanked it down to her waist.

When her heavy, naked breasts spilled out, Dane Curtin was not totally repelled because Marjorie Ann had well prepared herself for the evening's exercise.

Sparkling blue-white diamonds and blood-red rubies and glittering green emeralds—more than she'd ever worn before—adorned the stretched white flesh of her big-nippled breasts.

In minutes the pair were lying on the huge cano-pied satin-sheeted bed that sat atop a large pedestal. Directly across the spacious room was a white marble fireplace, blazing cheerfully, over which a ceiling-high mirror reflected every movement made on the white bed.

Both were naked. Both were excited. Both were ready to play.

The very pale, very plump Marjorie Ann Bishop lay on her back, propped up on the many satin-cased pillows. Her fleshy bare arms were folded beneath her dark head, her short pudgy legs were parted, dimpled knees bent, toes curling into the satin bedsheets.

All over her bare milky body were precious gems; gems it had taken her personal maid, Pearl, using theatrical spirit gum hours to glue on, one by one. They had started in the early afternoon. Marjorie Ann had taken a nice long bath in lilac-scented suds, then Pearl had dried her off, made her sit on a velvet vanity stool before the mirrored walls of her rose-hued dressing room, and set about her task.

It was slow, tedious work because Marjorie Ann fastidiously searched through the many fine gems laid out on their beds of black velvet. When she found one that suited her fancy, she lifted it between her short fingers, studied it, and decided at exactly which spot on her body she wanted to wear that particular diamond or ruby or emerald.

It had been after six that evening before all the carefully picked and counted jewels were in place.

Now lying sprawled out on her bed, shamelessly watching in the mirror across the room, Marjorie

Ann smiled with pleasure as the delicious game she so enjoyed began.

The object was to have this naked blond Adonis search for—and find—every precious gem glued to her bare body. And she was ingenious at finding new spots on her generous anatomy to hide the glittering precious stones.

Once he located a diamond or an emerald or ruby, he was to patiently, carefully remove the sparkling bauble.

With his mouth.

When all the glittering diamonds and rubies and emeralds had been cautiously bitten or sucked from her tingling flesh and deposited back on their bed of black velvet, the game was near completion.

Some evenings her lover became so aroused in his search for treasure, he made fierce, driving love to her, bringing her to ecstasy again and again. Other nights Marjorie Ann had to content herself with the rapture she experienced during the jewel hunt and seizure.

Dane Curtin was feverishly aroused on this warm spring night. His burning desire, however, had nothing to do with the sighing, moaning woman squirming on the white satin bed.

While his lips and tongue toyed with a flawless blue diamond hidden behind Marjorie Ann's left knee, he envisioned the beautiful, sedate red-haired teacher who had smiled so dazzlingly at him across the candlelighted table at Delmonico's.

In his fantasy, Elizabeth Montbleau was lying naked on that linen-draped table at Delmonico's with diamonds scattered over her flawless flesh, all sparkling in the candlelight.

The large blue-white diamond came loose. While it rolled down the underside of her flabby thigh, Dane Curtin anxiously mounted the panting Marjorie Ann, drove deeply into her, thrust fast and furiously a half dozen times before exploding in release.

His eyes closed, his neck bowed, he rasped hoarsely, "Teacher, teacher . . . oh, God, teacher."

10

After that first pleasant evening at Delmonico's, Elizabeth began seeing Dane Curtin regularly. She was flattered by his attention and she found that it was great fun to explore the big, exciting city on his arm.

He showed her a side of New York she had only wondered about. He took her to the glittering theaters lining Broadway. At the Reesbeck she sat entranced as a European company brilliantly performed *Hamlet,* an incredibly talented dark young man in the lead as Shakespeare's Danish prince.

Not a week later Dane took her to the famous Wallack's Theater, right next door to the Reesbeck. Flower girls circulated outside the theater among the well-heeled crowd and Elizabeth laughed with delight when Dane generously bought her fragrant bunches of carnations and roses and tulips.

One chilly Saturday afternoon they visited the Eden Musée, a museum filled with wax figures of sensational crimes and horrors. Childlike, Elizabeth stared wide-eyed at the frightening wax statues reigning eerily over the dim, windowless chamber. Frightened by the amazingly lifelike murderers and ugly gargoyles and chilling vampires, she clung tightly to

Dane's arm. He hugged her close and teased her, saying perhaps he should bring her here every day.

He took her into New York's finest shops, some below Canal Street, the rest along Broadway to Fourteenth and over to Union Square. They went to A. T. Stewart's gleaming marble palace, where the mannerly clerks welcomed him by name. To Lord & Taylor, where Elizabeth blushed at seeing filmy underwear displayed, her eyes clinging to a wispy, daring white negligee shot with threads of gold. To Arnold Constable, where, Dane informed her, he purchased all his fine linen shirts and silk foulards. And finally to Tiffany's with its sparkling glassware and glittering diamonds and shiny gold baubles.

Urging her toward one of the glass cases, Dane insisted on buying her a little trinket. A gift. He chose a delicate butterfly brooch of gold filigree and told the clerk to put it on his bill. The clerk, a well-groomed, nervous little man, wrung his hands worriedly. He dared not remind Dane Curtin, in front of the lady, that he was overextended and was no longer able to charge at Tiffany's until he paid his bill.

Dane had counted on the man's impeccable manners and knew he was safe. He proudly pinned the filigree butterfly to the high lace collar of Elizabeth's white blouse. His fingers toying with the miniature butterfly's golden wing, he said, "This is only the beginning, Elizabeth."

"Dane," she replied, "you are too generous."

He smiled. "One day I'll cover you with fine jewels," he said, and felt himself become half aroused at the thought of playing the treasure hunt game with Elizabeth instead of Marjorie Ann Bishop.

One quiet, cloudy Sunday they strolled along Fifth Avenue, stopping to peer in the windows of the hotel shops that fronted the thoroughfare. When they reached the scarlet carpet outside the canopied front entrance of the Fifth Avenue Hotel, Dane paused and said, "Have you ever stayed at this hotel?"

"No. No, never."

"Shall we, then?"

A small twinge of alarm shot through Elizabeth's breast. Had Dane Curtin somehow found her out? Is that why he had kept after her all those weeks, why he had continued to ask her out? Because he knew she was not the lady she pretended to be? Did he somehow know about her shame in Shreveport, Louisiana?

"Dane," she tried to sound indignant, "how could you suggest—"

"Oh, my dear, no, no." He smiled and shook his golden head. "You've misunderstood, and it's my fault." He laid a gentle hand to her waist. "I meant only that I'd like to show you the downstairs lobby. It's quite grand and I thought you'd enjoy seeing it."

Relieved, Elizabeth laughed and her face flushed with color. "Please. I'd love to have a look around."

Inside Elizabeth saw what they meant when people described the Fifth Avenue as deluxe. The painted paneling. The waxed mahogany. The emerald-green ferns. The thick, rich carpets. Uniformed young boys stood at attention or rushed about the lobby and up and down the stairs. The hotel director stood near the ebony registration desk, where handsomely attired guests signed the hotel book.

"Ever ride in an elevator?" Dane asked.

Elizabeth's blue eyes lit up. "Could we, Dane?"

"Right this way," said he.

Inside the magic box, Elizabeth clung tightly to Dane's hand and felt her stomach rise to her throat as they slowly ascended the six floors to the hotel's top story. Staying inside the elevator, they rode back down. When they reached the ground, Elizabeth was

reluctant to get off. With her eyes she silently pleaded and Dane laughed and indulged her.

He confided, "I'm told that when the Prince of Wales was here some years ago, he would ride in the elevator whenever he had a few spare moments. Simply for the thrill of it."

They rode up and down several more times before Dane finally said, "The hotel restaurant serves the best peach melba in New York. How does that sound?"

"Wonderful."

And so it went.

Life was suddenly fun again and Elizabeth was grateful to Dane Curtin for making it so. She realized that perhaps she had misjudged him on their first meeting. He was nothing at all like his disagreeable nephew, Daniel. Dane was respectful, easygoing, always a gentleman.

Then came the day her frail father died and Elizabeth, heartbroken, was extremely grateful she had Dane's strong shoulder to lean on. He was her rock of strength at a time when she needed him most. She greatly appreciated the caring and understanding he showed her.

Dane offered to help her sort out her father's few belongings, and it made the gloomy task more bearable. While Elizabeth carefully placed clean, worn nightshirts in a large wicker basket, Dane crossed the room to a scarred chiffonier and began removing the items from its top.

Finished, he went into Elizabeth's small bedroom, walked to the chest, and saw nothing there but a small bottle of perfume, a lace handkerchief, the gold filigree butterly he'd bought her at Tiffany's, and a pair of tan gloves.

He was about to turn away when a small object caught his eye. From underneath Elizabeth's tan gloves, he plucked a brass button from the white doily draped atop the chest.

He lifted the button and studied it closely. At its center was the letter A. Although he had not fought in the war, he recognized the button as being like one worn by his brother Edmund, an officer in the artillery. A slight frown creased his high forehead.

"Elizabeth," he called, "I thought you told me that your father was with the cavalry during the war."

"That's right," she replied, placing a pair of darned stockings in the wicker basket.

Button in hand, Dane came to her. "Darling, this brass button was lying atop your chest."

Elizabeth felt her knees go watery. "Yes, it's . . . it's from Father's uniform," she lied, reaching for it.

Dane withheld it. "Elizabeth, the cavalry's buttons carried the letter C. This one has an A." His eyes lifted to hers. "A for artillery."

"Does it? I never noticed." She reached for it, took it from him, and shook her head as though puzzled. "Father must have borrowed a tunic from someone in the artillery."

"I suppose," he said. "What next? Shall I begin carrying some of the baskets out to the carriage?"

Her hand closing around the brass button, she said, "Yes, why don't you. We're almost finished." She slipped the button into the deep pocket of her woolen skirt.

"What's this?" Dane asked, lifting a long, rolled-up leather scroll from atop one of the packed baskets.

"Oh, that," Elizabeth said, and a smile came to her lips. "I'll show you."

Taking the scroll from him, she untied the grosgrain ribbon wrapped around it and spread the worn oxblood leather map and several sheets of brittle yellowing paper out on the small eating table.

"This," she said, "was something my father kept

with him at all times." She laughed softly and admitted, "He even took it with him when he went away to war."

"Sentimental value," Dane reasoned.

"More than that. This is a map and deed that was given to my father a long time ago by an old sourdough whose life he saved." She pointed to a gaping hexagonal hole, the size of a man's hand, directly in the center of the ancient map. "Somewhere in that missing section, a vast fortune in gold was supposedly hidden." She laughed, unable to recall anything more about the absurd legend surrounding the map.

More interested than he let on, and not nearly as wealthy as Elizabeth supposed, Dane laughed with her, but he moved closer, studied the map intently, and said casually, "I guess the sourdough never mentioned what part of the country this map is supposed—"

"He did. He told Father it was in the New Mexico Territory. The southern part, I believe. Something about vast caverns miles underground." Shaking her head, she added, "Needless to say, Father never did make it back out West to hunt for his hidden treasure."

Dane hardly heard her last remark. He was too busy reading the yellowing papers, which appeared to be a valid mining claim and deed. The deed was in the name of Thomas S. Montbleau, Sr.

Slowly refolding the yellowing deed, Dane's thoughts raced. He knew Elizabeth had lost the rest of her family during the war. Now, with her father's death, she was the only Montbleau left.

Dane felt excitement stir within him. Elizabeth was the sole heir to anything and everything the old man had owned.

"Couldn't be worth anything, could it?" Elizabeth broke into his thoughts.

He gave her an apologetic smile. "No, darling, I wouldn't think so."

Nonchalantly, Dane folded the deed, placed it atop the worn oxblood map, and began to roll the map back up. He tied the grosgrain ribbon around it and tossed the oxblood map back atop the bundle where he had found it. All the while he was very carefully committing the map to memory.

"Should I throw it away then?" asked Elizabeth.

Too loudly, he shouted, "No!" Immediately his tone softened, and he said, "You might want to give it to your children one day."

She liked his answer. "Yes," she said, "I'll save it for my children."

He reached for her, drew her into his embrace. Against her blazing red hair, he murmured, "I want at least a half-dozen children, don't you?"

Her arms locked around his trim waist, cheek pressed to his shirtfront, she replied happily, "At least."

Elizabeth tipped her head back to smile up at Dane. He lowered his lips to hers and kissed her. Needing him, wanting more than anything in the world to love him, Elizabeth put everything she had into her kiss.

When at last their lips parted, Dane Curtin was trembling, his breathing rapid and heavy. It was all he could do to keep from throwing Elizabeth down on the bed and making hot, quick love to her.

Wishing at this moment she were not an innocent refined young lady, the kind who had to be slowly wooed and always treated with the utmost respect, he fought the surging passion she so easily evoked in him.

Elizabeth fought as well. It was not surging passion Dane's prolonged kiss inspired. It was the lack of it. Her face against his shoulder, she kept her eyes tightly closed and pressed her slender body to his tall frame, hoping, wishing, praying to feel just a spark of the raging fire she'd known in the arms of a bearded Yankee spy one April night nearly four years ago. A man whose caresses she had found so stirring, she'd plucked a button off his tunic in her excitement. The button she had kept all these years that was now cutting into the flesh of her left thigh as Dane's hard leg pressed against hers.

Her hands anxiously roaming Dane's back, Elizabeth inhaled deeply. He smelled good, so clean and nice. He was a well-built man, leanly muscled and slender. With his classic facial features and his golden hair and emerald-green eyes, he was strikingly handsome.

Not only was he physically attractive, he was also highly intelligent and extremely rich. He was all any woman could long for or dream of. And he was obviously very fond of her. There was little doubt that one day he would ask her to marry him. She'd be the worst kind of fool not to accept should he propose.

Elizabeth pulled back a little and looked up at Dane. While passion flashed in his expressive green eyes, he made no attempt to overpower her, to make love to her. They were alone in her apartment. A lesser man might try to take advantage of her grief, her vulnerability, but not Dane. He was a gentleman. He respected her.

At dusk they were finished with their chore. They went out for supper at a small, quiet cafe off Union Square and were back to her small room by nine. Dane told her he had an early morning appointment, would she forgive him if he went on home.

It was then Elizabeth smiled, took the worn oxblood map from its basket, handed it to him, and asked if he would keep it in a safe place for her.

"Count on me, my darling," he told her.

She felt certain she could count on him and that

was a warm, comforting thought. Knowing it was
only a matter of time before he asked her to be his
wife, Elizabeth pushed aside both her doubts about
loving him and her guilt over past transgressions, and
said softly, "Dane Curtin, may I tell you that I think
you are one of the finest men I have ever known."

"Dane Curtin, you are one of the biggest cads I have
ever known."

"A fine way to speak to your intended."

Dane opened his arms wide and the angry Marjorie
Ann Bishop sighed and came to him. Scolding him
soundly for showing up at half past nine when he had
promised to be there no later than eight sharp, the
woman to whom he was secretly engaged wrapped
her short, fleshy arms tightly around his neck.

"You are so mean to me, Dainee, and I don't like it."

"Mean to you, dearest? How can you say such a
foolish thing?"

"Because it's true. You won't let me tell anyone
about our engagement. Why not?" She tilted her head
back and looked up at him.

He favored her with one of his most dazzling
smiles. "Because secrets are such fun. You know that,
sweet. Like our treasure hunts. Our own special
secrets."

"I suppose you're right." She made an unhappy
face. "But we can't have one of our secret treasure
hunts tonight."

"No?"

"Mother and Father came home unexpectedly this
afternoon." Her double chin sagged to her huge chest.

Relieved instead of disappointed, Dane Curtin put a
finger beneath her chin, lifted it, and whispered,
"Damn them! All day I've been looking forward to my
evening alone with you."

"You have, Dainee?" Her eyes lighted. "I know

what, we'll go for a carriage ride through the park and I'll undress and—"

"Out of the question, my love. You think I'd risk compromising you like that? Suppose someone saw us?"

Her face fell. "You're right. It's too dangerous. Oh, well, come into the drawing room and say hello to my parents."

"Dane Curtin, you're one of the biggest scoundrels I have ever known."

"Why, Edmund, such a thing to say to your only brother."

Edmund, standing with his back to the fireplace in the drawing room of his Fifth Avenue mansion, glared at Dane, lolling on a long beige brocade sofa.

After staying at Marjorie Ann Bishop's for only a very few minutes, Dane had come by to show Edmund the worn oxblood map Elizabeth had given him.

"She wants me to keep it in a safe place," said Dane, pouring himself a splash of brandy into a sparkling crystal snifter. Smiling, he added, "The map might prove useful when Tom Lancaster and I go out to the New Mexico Territory next month to survey and evaluate those mineral holdings we have there."

Edmund's calm eyes shone with disapproval. "Dane, I don't like this . . . this relationship you're having with Elizabeth Montbleau. It's not right. Has it occurred to you that she might be falling in love with you?"

Dane took a sip of his brandy. "It has."

"I don't want to see her get hurt. She's a fine young woman and she's just lost the last member of her family. How do you suppose she'd feel if she knew that you were all but engaged to the Bishop heiress?"

Dane's pleased smile never slipped. "She wouldn't

like it, that's why she won't find out until she's so
much in love with me it won't matter." He downed
the last drink of brandy. "You must understand that I
care deeply for Elizabeth, but I can't marry a woman
with no money. My God, man, she thinks we're all
rich. She has no idea that an unstable stock market
could make paupers of us any day."

"For God's sake, Dane. Keep your voice down. Do
you want Louisa to hear you?" Edmund said nervously.

"Edmund, we both know that if Jim Fisk and Jay
Gould's attempt to corner the gold market proves successful, the market will crash and we'll be ruined."
His blue eyes snapped with anger. "Damn the greedy,
thieving bastards. There's nothing they won't do to
gain even more wealth for themselves."

Edmund nodded worriedly. "I know, I know. But,
you mustn't be like them. Those men are unprincipled and—"

"Edmund, just how do you suppose your free-
spending wife would react if we suddenly lost all our
wealth?" Seeing the fear leap into his older brother's
eyes, Dane hurried on. "Even if Louisa agreed to stay
with you, she'd be miserable without the luxury
you've always provided. Face it, we can't live as beg-
gars, and that's what we'll be if the market crashes.
For your sake as well as for mine, I'll have to marry
Marjorie Ann Bishop. There's no other choice."

Edmund's shoulders slumped wearily. "Then leave
Elizabeth alone."

Dane came to his feet, crossed to the drink trolley,
and poured himself another brandy. "I can't do that. I
want her. Besides, it's not necessary. After I'm married, I'll set Elizabeth up as my mistress, buy her a
fine house, make it my home away from home."

Edmund shook his head. "Money is everything to you, isn't it? The only thing that really matters."

Dane's green eyes gleamed. "Where's the crime in that?"

11

On the eve of the brand-new year, Elizabeth was alone in her cheerless rooms on Twenty-fourth Street behind the stables. She was achingly lonely.

Dane and a business associate, Tom Lancaster, had left New York the day after Christmas. He hated leaving her, Dane had told her, but the trip was necessary. It could be postponed no longer. He and Lancaster were obligated to travel to the faraway New Mexico Territory for the purpose of surveying and evaluating land and mineral holdings.

Now, with Dane gone for less than a week, Elizabeth was beginning to realize just how empty her life would be without him. Boltwood was closed for the holidays and time hung heavy on her hands. Edmund, Louisa, and the boys had left the same day as Dane. They were spending the remainder of the long holiday with the wealthy Belmonts at their country estate far from the city.

At the stroke of midnight on that solitary New Year's Eve, Elizabeth took down a near-empty bottle, poured the last of her father's amontillado sherry into a glass, and raised it in a toast.

"To 1869, a brand-new year filled with hope. May it

be the best one of my life," she said aloud. She looked at her dreary surroundings and added, "And the last New Year's Eve I spend in poverty!"

On a blustery day in March of 1869 the already nervous New York Stock Market hit a new low. The Curtin brothers were financially ruined.

Badly shaken, reluctant to mention it to his wife, Louisa, Edmund Curtin arrived at the Fifth Avenue mansion as a cool dusk was settling over New York City. In the wide downstairs corridor, a couple of steamer trunks stood open. Puzzled, a frowning Edmund was about to ascend the stairs when the front doorbell jangled.

At the foot of the stairs he paused and waited while the butler answered the door. Out in the cold stood a uniformed messenger, who handed the butler a small yellow envelope.

The curious butler held out to Edmund a small silver salver atop which lay the yellow missive. Wondering if somehow the entire world already knew he was destitute, if some forgotten creditor was immediately calling in a debt, Edmund picked up the telegram with shaking fingers.

Irrationally annoyed when the butler did not immediately move away, Edmund snapped, "That's all, Johnson. Don't you have work to do?"

Apprehensive, Edmund Curtin hurried into the empty downstairs drawing room and tore open the small yellow envelope.

Edmund,
Have found missing hexagon. Coordinates seem right. Know I am near underground cavern where gold is buried. Only matter of time before I locate it. You must see to it that Elizabeth Mont-

bleau becomes my wife. As her husband, I can
best protect her interests.

                                            Dane

Edmund read and reread the telegram. Could it be
possible? Was Dane actually near to finding a fortune
in gold? Enough gold to save them all from disaster?
Would it be so terribly wrong to persuade Elizabeth
Montbleau to marry Dane at once? The gold was their
only hope. His only hope. Besides, Dane was genuinely fond of Elizabeth and she of him.

Struggling with his conscience, Edmund was still
staring at the telegram when his dark-haired wife,
Louisa, swept into the room.

"So you're finally home," she said, coming to him,
lifting her cheek for a kiss. She saw the message.
"What is that?"

"Nothing, really." He slipped the yellow telegram
into a pocket.

Not particularly curious about its contents, Louisa
nodded and announced, "Edmund, I cannot stand
one more day of being shut up in this house. The winter has dragged on forever and I feel I shall go mad."
She flounced away, crossed the room to close the
shutters against the approaching night. "I've decided
to take the boys out of school and sail to Europe tomorrow."

Another man might have been dumbstruck to hear
his wife had made a sudden decision of such magni-
tude. Edmund Curtin was not. Louisa was a spoiled,
willful woman who always did as she pleased. Long
ago he had given up on keeping her in line. This
would not be the first time she had become bored
with New York and gone to Europe without him.

All he said was, "Do you think it's wise to take the
boys out of school, my dear?"

"You've said yourself that travel broadens horizons

and serves as a good education. It's high time the boys spent a few months in London."

So that was the end of it. Her mind was made up, passage had been booked on the Cunard line, and she would expect him personally to be available to drive them to the docks at three the very next afternoon.

"Now I must fly," said Louisa, lifting her skirts and hurrying away. "I'm going to dinner and the theater with the Morgans. See to it the boys are fed. And don't wait up. There's an after-theater party at the Seligmans'."

"Have a pleasant evening, my dear," said Edmund, and knew, as he watched her leave, that spoiled though she might be, and selfish, and yes, even foolish and irresponsible, he could not live without her. He loved her. Had loved his beautiful Louisa since the first night he had seen her at a summertime ball when she had just turned sixteen. In his eyes she was still the flirtatious young beauty of that long-ago May evening.

Suddenly terrified by the prospect of losing Louisa, he hurried from the room, climbed the stairs, and rushed into his paneled library. Not stopping to light a lamp, he went to the wall safe behind his mahogany desk. He carefully turned the small wheel-lock to the correct combination and the door swung open.

He reached inside and withdrew a forest-green jeweler's bag. He turned and poured the contents of the heavy bag out on his desk. Glittering diamonds and rubies and emeralds sparkled, reflecting the suffused light coming from the gaslights lining the street outside.

Louisa's jewels.

Her jewels were all that was left of the Curtin fortune. Valuable though they were—particularly the sparkling twenty-karat Star of the West—their worth was not nearly enough to save a way of life.

Edmund dropped down into his chair behind the desk, put out his hand, touched the twinkling stones spread out before him. A fear as cold as the stones gripped his heart. He felt dizzy and light-headed. His mouth was dry and his heart pounded.

Everything he had was rapidly slipping from his grasp and he was helpless to stop it.

Or was he?

Edmund had rehearsed what he would say at least a hundred times. But now as he climbed the stone steps of Boltwood, he could remember nothing of the carefully written speech he had intended to make to Elizabeth Montbleau.

He had just come from Pier Fifty-three, where he had waved to his departing family as the big ocean-going vessel was tugged out of the harbor toward the open sea. He had waited only until he was sure Louisa had retired from the deck and could no longer see him, then he had hurried to the carriage and ordered the driver to take him to Boltwood straightaway.

Now, pulling the lapels of his cashmere greatcoat up around his freezing ears, Edmund drew a deep breath of frigid air, opened the front door and ducked into the wide hallway of Boltwood. Noisy, laughing boys swirled past him, anxious to be outside, happy the school day was at an end.

Hat in hand, Edmund waited. When all the shouts and squeals had died and the old building was silent, he saw Elizabeth coming down the corridor. She smiled upon seeing him, and put out her hand. He took it in his gloved one.

"I miss the boys already," Elizabeth said. "I do wish Louisa could have waited until the end of the school term."

"Yes, so do I. But you know Louisa." He smiled sheepishly.

Fond of the gentle man, Elizabeth responded, "Well, travel is an education in itself."

Edmund took Elizabeth to a small coffeehouse nearby and over hot chocolate topped with marshmallows, told her he had heard from Dane. She herself had received no letters, so Elizabeth was relieved.

"Thank God, I was afraid something had happened to him. Is he well? Will he be coming home soon?"

"He's well and he's very lonely." Edmund coughed nervously, then proceeded, feeling like a conspirator in some evil plot. "He said he misses you terribly and his only regret is that he didn't make you his wife before he left New York."

Elizabeth glowed. "Such a sweet thing to say."

Edmund swallowed hard. "He . . . ah . . . Dane says it was a dreadful mistake and one he wishes to rectify at once."

Elizabeth nodded. "So he'll be back soon and—"

"He wants you to marry him immediately. Right now."

Elizabeth's eyes widened, and she tilted her head to one side. "I'm very flattered but we both know that's out of the question." She laughed and added, "A wedding with no bridegroom? Impossible."

"But it isn't," Edmund quickly corrected. "You can be married by telegraphic proxy. It's done all the time. It's what Dane wants."

Puzzled by the strange turn of events, Elizabeth was dubious. Why would a man who'd not bothered to write her in all the weeks he had been away suddenly feel he couldn't wait to marry her?

Edmund's hand covered hers atop the table. "For all his seeming confidence, Dane is unsure of your feelings for him. That's why he wrote to me, instead of you. He said that if you really love him, you'll marry him immediately."

Elizabeth pondered those words. "If you really love

him, you'll marry him immediately." Suddenly she felt like the worst kind of hypocrite. She was fond of Dane Curtin, but she was not in love with him, was not sure she ever would be. Worse, Dane thought her a lady above reproach. Suppose he found out that nothing could be further from the truth.

What if, years after she had become his wife, Dane learned she was responsible for a man's death? She had never told him—had never told anyone—about Colonel Frederick Dobbs at Shreveport landing. She had never even told her dear father, much less Dane. Now it was too late. Her path was chosen.

It was too late to tell him about the night she had spent with a Yankee spy. Dane had always behaved the gentleman because he assumed that she was pure, an innocent. Would he be shocked and disgusted to learn she was not a virgin? Would he be able to tell? The Yankee hadn't realized that she *was*. Maybe Dane wouldn't know that she wasn't.

Tired of being lonely, tired of being poor, Elizabeth felt she couldn't let the opportunity pass her by. She would take a chance on her past staying dead and buried. She would be a good and faithful wife to Dane Curtin. So good, so faithful, he would never know that she was not deeply in love with him.

Elizabeth looked up. Edmund Curtin was waiting for her answer. Almost holding his breath as though her decision meant as much to him as it did to his brother.

Looking straight into Edmund Curtin's eyes, she smiled and said, "I will marry Dane immediately."

The shocking news came not two weeks after Elizabeth Montbleau became the bride of Dane Curtin by telegraphic proxy. The Curtin-Lancaster expedition was missing, possibly all dead, in the southern wilds of the New Mexico Territory.

Elizabeth and Edmund were horrified. What should they do? What *could* they do?

As soon as the initial shock had passed, Edmund Curtin became his calm, decisive self. Insisting that Elizabeth try to get some rest in one of the many guest rooms upstairs, he left the Fifth Avenue mansion.

He was back before the sun went down. Silently he climbed the stairs to his library, closed the door behind him, and withdrew the green jeweler's bag from the wall safe. Thankful that Louisa had not chosen to take her most valuable jewels abroad, he slipped the bag into the inside breast pocket of his well-tailored gray frockcoat.

When he came back downstairs, he found Elizabeth waiting in the drawing room. She rose and looked at him expectantly.

He announced, "Elizabeth, I am going to the New Mexico Territory to search for Dane. Martin Exley, the Santa Fe agent for the Curtin company, is handling all the arrangements on that end."

"I am going with you."

"Elizabeth, that isn't prudent. The New Mexico Territory is still quite untamed and dangerous. Besides, you have obligations . . . the school and—"

"None of that matters." Impatiently, she shook her head. "My husband is missing and we must find him." She paused, then said, "But, Edmund, what about the stock market crash? Surely that has affected your precious metals holdings?"

"Somewhat," was all he said.

"It's a long journey to the New Mexico Territory and we may have to stay for several weeks, perhaps even months. The expense? Can we afford it?"

Edmund couldn't tell her the truth. That in fact he couldn't afford *not* to go. That finding Dane and the hidden gold was his only hope. That he was gambling all he had left in the world.

Edmund patted his breast coat pocket, where the heavy green jeweler's bag felt solid and comforting. His palm rested directly atop the hard, large twenty-karat Star of the West diamond.

"Leave that to me," he said calmly. "We Curtins always go in style."

12

An old Navajo woman, her hands adorned with silver and turquoise rings, sat unmoving on the broad, flat *portal*, the porch of Santa Fe's El Palacio Real, the Palace of the Governors. Her ancient face was as burnished brown and deeply carved as the rugged Sangre de Cristo Mountains. She leaned back against the wall of the one-story adobe building, her watery black eyes blank, the wrinkled, tissue-thin lids drooping and closing.

Dozing and dreaming of days gone by, the old Indian woman was neglected by most, tolerated by others in the Queen City of the New Mexico Territory. A fixture there on the *portal*, where the seat of government was located, she had long ago forgotten where her home was. She recalled only that once she had lived high in the Jemez Mountains, the wife of a powerful Navajo chieftain to whom she had borne three strong sons.

The old woman wondered where her boys were. She asked anyone who would listen if they had seen her sons. They were only young children, her boys. Babies, really. Or were they? Had they grown into men already?

She had long since blotted out the painful truth. Had managed totally to abolish the horror of an early-morning attack on her husband's high meadow village. No longer recalled standing naked in the stream, washing herself, and looking up to see a detail of mounted blue-coat soldiers bearing down on her. Had eradicated the pain and degradation she'd suffered as they used her to satisfy their lust. Had incised from the far reaches of her memory the recollection of crawling back to camp on her hands and knees, bloodied and suffering, to find her husband and her three sons lying dead, their bodies riddled with bullet holes.

She remembered none of it.

So she supposed that her husband had grown old and died in his sleep, as she soon would. But in her mind the boys were still little and she looked for them as she sat there on the government building's broad porch in the warm March sunshine. Studied the face of each dark-haired male child and every strong young man that happened past.

The old woman suddenly sensed someone's presence.

Her sagging lids lifted to see a tall, lanky man crossing the plaza, coming straight toward her from out of the glare of the sun. The woman blinked and squinted, straining to see him better.

His long, loose-limbed stride was familiar, as was the set of his wide shoulders. He was hatless. The west wind was tossing locks of his raven-black hair about his head and pressing one end of his white silk bandanna against his tanned, cleanly shaven jaw. His shirt was of dark navy gabardine and his trousers of tan hard-finished twill. A pair of silver inlaid spurs dangled from his belt and on his feet were boots of shiny black leather.

The old woman's mouth gaped open as the tall

young man steadily advanced on her. Hopefully she wondered if he might be one of her sons. Time got away. Maybe the oldest was grown now.

The tall man stepped onto the flat porch, crossed to the old Navajo woman, and crouched down directly before her.

"Is it . . . ?" Her questioning eyes grew almost round.

"No," he said gently, reaching for her gnarled right hand and holding it in his own. "No, Micoma, I'm not your son." He smiled at her. "It's West. West Quarternight."

A smile immediately came to her thin cracked lips and her eyes disappeared into the laugh-line creases of her wrinkled skin. Her hand gripped his with incredible strength as she nodded happily and repeated, "It's West. West Quarternight."

"Any messages for me this morning, Micoma?"

It was not an idle question. He meant it. West, as did all Santa Fe, knew the Palace of the Governors' porch was Micoma's main headquarters. In a hurry one day, he had left a message with her for Grady Downs. Micoma was flattered that he had trusted her and she had delivered the message word for word to Grady. A day or two later, Grady left a message for West with the old woman.

In no time, Micoma became West's personal message bureau. Everyone in the Territory knew that if they couldn't find Quarternight, they could leave word for him with the old Navajo woman. Amazingly, she never once forgot to relay the word. That, despite the fact that more than once she had thought —hoped really—that the dark-complexioned, black-haired West might be one of her own boys, grown.

"Anybody looking for me, Micoma?" West asked, and she silently began to nod. He knew she was carefully going over, in her head, the exact words she was to pass on. "Take your time now, there's no hurry," he said softly.

Normally an impatient man, West was extremely patient with the old Navajo woman. He knew if he waited, if he didn't rush her, Micoma would quote verbatim what she had been told to pass along.

So West crouched there on his heels, smiling at her, holding her hand, waiting, tolerant of her as he was of no one else.

At last, forming her words very slowly and precisely, Micoma said, "White Hair has been contacted by Mr. X." West grinned, knowing she meant that Grady had been contacted by Martin Exley, a Santa Fe based agent for several large Eastern Companies. "White Hair say that Mr. X have contract for you."

West's grin broadened. "Did you remind White Hair I will not take any more contracts?"

Micoma smiled her toothless smile and nodded. "I did. But White Hair say you will take this one. Say he will talk some sense into you." She paused. Then, black eyes twinkling, she added, "White Hair say you have rock-hard head." She chuckled and West laughed with her.

"Is White Hair in Santa Fe this afternoon?" he asked.

"Waiting at End of Trail Saloon," she said.

"Well, I guess I better go over there and talk to the old buzzard; tell him again, no more contracts."

Micoma liked that. Smiling, she said, "Tell old buzzard, no more contracts!"

"That's right," West said, and dropping one knee to the stone porch, he shoved a hand deep into his pants pocket and withdrew a silver coin. He pressed it into Micoma's palm and closed her brittle fingers tightly around it. "Promise me you'll buy yourself a hot meal."

"Too old to promise anything, West Quarternight."

West touched her wrinkled **brown** cheek, rose to his feet, turned and walked back **across** the dusty plaza, thinking that if anybody had a hard head, it was Micoma.

And Grady Downs.

How many times did he have to tell Grady that he was through as a guide, quitting?

"Damn it, Grady, how many times do I have to tell you I'm quitting?"

"Now, Sonny, just you wait till you hear what I've got lined up for us."

The two men stood at the long polished bar in the End of the Trail Saloon. The small saloon just off the east side of the plaza, marking the end of the Turquoise Trail, was Grady's favorite watering hole. It was shadowy and quiet and served, Grady claimed, the best Kentucky bourbon in all of Santa Fe. And the barkeep was an impressionable Alabamian who would listen attentively to Grady's tall tales by the hour.

Tossing down a straight shot of that fine Kentucky bourbon, West wiped his mouth on the back of his hand and said irritably, "I warned you not to go lining up more contracts. You and Taos want the work, fine. But count me out. I'm not interested."

"Will you just wait until you hear what I've got to say?"

"No," West told him. "I won't. You're wasting your breath. The way I figure it, we'll finish with our final contract around the last of April or the first part of May. Then I'm long gone. Riding out of New Mexico for good."

As though West hadn't spoken, Grady said, "You know that Curtin-Lancaster expedition that came through here a month or so ago? Them rich boys

from out of New York City that was a-heading down
to the south part of the Territory? 'Member them?"

"What about them?"

"They're missing! Them and all the Mexicans they
hired to go down the trail with 'em. Vanished right off
the face of the earth!"

West skeptically raised a dark eyebrow. "And now
we're supposed to find them? We're booked the next
four or five weeks."

Grady was sure he sensed a trace of interest on
West's part. Hastily he said, "Sonny, the Curtin fellow
that's lost, he's got an older brother back there in New
York City. The brother's fixing to come out here and
search for the missing expedition. He wired Martin
Exley to contract for qualified guides to lead him. The
timing's might near perfect. Curtin should reach
Santa Fe around the time we'll be coming down from
the Four Corners."

"The answer is still no." West downed his second
whiskey and said, "Nice talking to you, Grady. Now,
if you'll excuse me, I think I'll hunt a poker game."

"Speakin' of poker, guess it's time I show you my
hole card," said Grady, grinning from ear to ear and
stroking his flowing white beard. Abruptly, he
reached up and slapped the taller man on the back
and named an incredibly generous sum of money
which he claimed on his mother's grave Edmund Curtin was prepared to pay. Spot cash.

Frowning now, West remained silent. He motioned
the bartender to pour him another whiskey. He
reached into the breast pocket of his tailored navy
shirt and withdrew a long brown cigar. For a long
moment he idly rolled the cigar between his thumb
and forefinger.

Grady waited, as silent as West. Afraid to speak,
afraid to move, holding his breath.

West stuck the cigar between his lips, bit down on it

with even white teeth, and languidly leaned across the bar to the lighted match the barkeep held out. He lifted his head, slowly drew smoke deep down into his expanding diaphragm, then released it. He took the cigar from his mouth, stared at the hot orange tip.

Finally his head swung around, he grinned boyishly and said, "Grady, tell Mr. X to inform Curtin he's just hired himself the best damned guides in the Territory."

"Praise the Lord!"

Elizabeth Montbleau Curtin got her first look at Santa Fe, New Mexico, late one clear May afternoon. She stood alone on the jutting precipice of a hill overlooking the ancient city. The sun was low on the western horizon, its fanlike rays tinting the billowing clouds varying shades of red and staining the rugged mountain peaks a deep purple.

Below, in the darkening valley, at the base of the soaring Sangre de Cristo mountains, lights began to twinkle on, one by one, enchanting her, inviting her to come down. Elizabeth felt her weariness melt away and a tingling excitement stir the blood in her veins.

"Ready, Elizabeth," called Edmund.

"Coming, Edmund," she said, and took one last lingering look below, inhaled deeply of the fresh ponderosa-scented air, and hurried to climb back into the coach for the last leg of their journey.

The entire valley was cloaked in darkness when the stage drove up San Francisco Street, Santa Fe's main thoroughfare. But gaslights lined the avenue and a mix of people, as diverse as those living in New York City, milled about on the streets, talking, laughing.

The coach came to a stop before the La Fonda Hotel, on the plaza. Elizabeth preceded Edmund inside the two-story adobe structure. The beamed ceiling

was high, the floor was of polished tile, the walls of
dark wood adorned with colorful Navajo blankets.

Edmund engaged a suite on the second floor; two
bedrooms joined by a common sitting room. Once
upstairs, Edmund directed a pair of mannerly brown-
skinned Mexican youths to take Elizabeth's many
bags into the room to the right of the parlor, the
larger, grander of the suite's two bedrooms.

Elizabeth followed the boys into a spacious, cheerful room dominated by a huge pine bed, its headboard soaring halfway to the high ceiling. A matching
pine highboy on the west wall was as tall as she. A
long Spanish baroque settee upholstered in pressed
red leather faced a pair of sturdy armchairs before a
fireplace of natural stone. A fire, newly laid and burning brightly, took off the nighttime chill.

As soon as the boys left, Elizabeth crossed to a pair
of carved wooden doors, pushed one open, and tentatively peered out. She was delighted to find that her
room, fronting the city's *placita,* opened onto a wide
wraparound balcony bordered by a solid, waist-high
adobe railing.

Smiling, she held the heavy door partially open
with a knee and a shoulder while she swept a heavy
wool shawl up over her head and around her shoulders. Then she eagerly rushed outdoors to get another
look at the lights of the sprawling high-desert city,
glittering like diamonds in the darkness.

But just as she gripped the rough railing and leaned
out, a match flared in her side vision, startling her.
Elizabeth's shawled head snapped around and her
heartbeat immediately quickened.

A tall man, his back to her, stood a few feet away
on the balcony, coatless in the night. His dark head
was bent forward, his arms lifted. The fabric of his
black shirt pulled tautly across his back and shoul-

ders as he cupped his hands soldier-style around the red glowing tip of a cigar he was lighting in the wind.

Before he could see her, Elizabeth dashed back inside, slamming the heavy carved doors shut. For a long moment she stood there, her back pressed against them, her breath coming fast.

Then she laughed at herself, and blamed her irrational fear on exhaustion. She was being silly. A dangerous journey was finally behind her. She had reached Santa Fe and was now safe.

Totally safe.

13

♪ ♪ ♪

The next morning dawned bright and clear in Santa Fe, New Mexico. The sky was a deep shade of azure, the air dry and crisp in the seven-thousand-foot-high capital city.

By early afternoon, when Elizabeth and Edmund left the La Fonda for an appointment with Edmund's agent, Martin Exley, the day was sun-kissed and balmy.

Dressed in a smart traveling suit of rust cotton, a high-necked blouse of pale peach batiste, her abundant red hair swept up under a becoming hat with the brim pulled low, Elizabeth took Edmund's arm as they crossed busy San Francisco Street.

After dodging carts and carriages and mounted cowboys, the pair reached the safety of the sidewalk and paused to look in shop windows lining Washington Street.

Wishing they had time to go inside and browse, Elizabeth gazed in the window of a small store filled with beautiful silver Indian jewelry and colorful clay pottery. Next door was a saddle shop, the strong scent of leather carrying out onto the sidewalk.

Just beyond the saddlery a small open-air restaurant was crowded with men, white and brown, consuming huge portions of spicy native dishes made of corn, chili peppers, pinto beans, squash, and beef. Past the café, a saloon called The Nugget was filling with afternoon drinkers and card players.

One player, a man with jet-black hair and silver-gray eyes, sat at a green baize table with his back to The Nugget's slatted swinging doors. A brown cigar clamped firmly between his teeth, the silent man unemotionally studied his cards. The other players, anxiously studying him, caught the slightest narrowing of his unreadable gray eyes.

The player's opponents never knew that his almost imperceptible movement was not a reaction to the last card he had drawn, but rather to the faint scent of perfume—vaguely familiar—drifting into the smoke-filled saloon from a woman passing the saloon within six feet of where he sat.

Directly past The Nugget saloon, at the corner of Washington and Palace Avenue, a furniture store displayed heavy, intricately carved pieces fashioned from native woods.

On busy Palace Avenue, Edmund and Elizabeth turned west and soon were strolling past the low-slung one-story adobe Palace of the Governors on the plaza's north side. Large gatherings of men stood talking under the roofed portal of the old government building.

But it was a woman who caught Elizabeth's eye.

Seated cross-legged on the stone porch in the shade, her back resting against the building's adobe exterior, an ancient-looking Indian woman seemed oblivious to all the activity going on around her. Her wrinkled lids drooped low over flat black eyes. Eyes that looked neither to the left nor right, as if she were certain this life no longer had anything of interest to show her.

Abruptly releasing Edmund's arm, Elizabeth ventured closer. When she stood a few feet away, the old woman's gray head slowly lifted. Elizabeth smiled with uncertainty at the somber woman, and was genuinely surprised to see a wide, toothless grin quickly spread over the wrinkled brown face and the black eyes suddenly sparkle with life.

An arthritic hand covered with silver and turquoise rings lifted and motioned Elizabeth closer. Elizabeth didn't hesitate. She hurried forward and quickly sat down on her heels facing the woman, the rust cotton skirts of her suit mushrooming out around her.

"I'm Elizabeth Curtin," she said warmly, reaching for the dry, withered hand adorned with glittering silver.

"I am Micoma," said the Indian. Then immediately asked, "Have you seen my sons?"

"Your sons?" Elizabeth was puzzled. "No, no I haven't."

"Your hair is strange hue." The Indian woman had already forgotten her sons, for the moment. "Never see hair like that. Take off bonnet."

Elizabeth immediately reached up, withdrew the long hat-pin from the straw crown, and plucked the hat from her head. The slanting rays of the early afternoon sun fell full on her, bathing her with bright, unfiltered light.

"There. How's that?"

"Look like head on fire," said the Indian woman, fascinated.

Elizabeth laughed, then glanced up at Edmund, waiting patiently. "I must go, Micoma. Will your sons be coming for you soon?"

"Yes, they come soon."

"Good." Elizabeth impulsively took the small copper brooch from her suit's high collar, leaned forward, and pinned it to the old woman's chamois poncho. "I want you to have this, Micoma. You can tell your sons it came all the way from New York City."

Micoma beamed happily. As Elizabeth started to rise, she reached out and stopped her. "Wait," she said, and took a shiny silver ring set with a turquoise stone from her finger. "For you."

"Oh, Micoma, no . . . I can't—"

"You take." Micoma's black eyes shone like polished quartz. "Keep. You tell your sons come all the way from Nacimiento Peak."

Uncertain what she should do, Elizabeth looked up at Edmund. "She wants you to have it," he said gently. "To refuse might hurt her feelings."

Her hearing as keen as ever, Micoma nodded. "Might hurt old Micoma's feelings, Fire Hair."

Elizabeth laughed. "Thank you, Micoma. I will treasure this ring always."

"Go now," said the old Indian. "Be late for appointment."

Elizabeth's finely arched eyebrows lifted. "And how do you know we have an appointment?"

Micoma gave her a sly smile. "Hear everything, know everything,"—her smile fled—"but sometimes forget."

Leaving the old woman looking after them, Elizabeth said softly to Edmund, "I hope her sons come for her soon. She's surely tired of waiting and should be taken home."

"She'll be fine. Now, we really must hurry. We're still a couple of blocks from Exley's office."

The pair hurried on down Palace Avenue, turning right when they reached Grant Street. Halfway down the block they paused before a two-story stucco building. A dentist occupied the ground floor. Directly above, gold lettering on the frosted glass window proclaimed "The Curtin Company, Martin S. Exley, Agent."

"Legends abound here in the Southwest," said Martin Exley, standing before a mounted wall map of the New Mexico Territory. "So, of course, there's a legend surrounding your father's leather map and the hidden gold, Elizabeth.

"As you know, the map revealing the location of the gold was given to Thomas Montbleau by an old sourdough called Sid Grayson. Now, Grayson was a drinker and a gambler. One night in Silver City, Sid got lucky. He broke up a big poker game—this is well documented—won over ten thousand dollars. One of his opponents was young Jamie Pena, Spanish land grant family and all that goes with it. Pena felt sure his luck had to change, so he wanted to cut high card with Sid for the ten thousand dollars. Only one problem, he was out of money. *No mas dinero.*

"Pena offered Sid a map that had been made from a chart left by the first conquistadors. A treasure map revealing a cache of gold. Gold had been mined and smelted by Indian slave labor, then hoarded and hidden in an underground cave. The gold was cursed by the spirits of the Indians who had died while mining it. And so, it was constantly guarded by evil, winged ghost-creatures of the night.

"Well, Sid agreed to cut high card for the map against his ten thousand dollars. They shuffled, cut, and Pena turned up the queen of diamonds. Sid the king of clubs. Pena promised to take Sid to the stashed gold the next day, but a jealous husband buried ten inches of fine Toledo steel in Pena's heart later that same night. Sid Grayson searched for that gold until the day he gave the map to your father, Elizabeth." Exley smiled and said, "That's the legend of the lost Grayson gold."

Martin Exley went on to tell them that years ago he had heard about the *conocimiento de Grayson*, or chart of identification for Grayson. Further, he himself had visited the archives in the Palace of Governors and found, to his surprise, that Elizabeth's father had put enough faith in Sid Grayson's story to have the claim registered in his own name, Thomas S. Montbleau, Natchez, Mississippi. Which meant, if any gold was found, it would legally belong to Elizabeth, since Colonel Montbleau was deceased.

"Then, in your opinion, Dane and his partner are actually onto something, Mr. Exley?" asked Elizabeth. "I mean, with part of the map missing, how—"

Exley said, "The missing hexagonal section left us buffaloed for a time, but Dane was finally able to match up some known coordinates and felt sure they knew the approximate region to look for the claim, and hopefully, the gold. Only trouble is, this is wild country and it stubbornly refuses to give up some of its longest kept secrets. The boys could be walking right over the gold and never know it."

"But you are convinced there's gold out there," said Edmund.

Exley answered, "Through the years more than one wild-eyed old sourdough or grizzled mountain man or frightened Mexican peasant has stumbled back to civilization, half dead, babbling about 'rooms of gold guarded by creatures of the night.' Is there anything to it? Is it a dream based on fact? Or imagination? Hallucination? Lies? I don't know. I do know that Fisk and Gould threatening to corner the gold market made us believers. We thought we had nothing to lose."

"Exactly when was the last time you heard from my husband?" asked Elizabeth.

"The last communication was on March twenty-first. Lancaster sent word from the little town of Las

Palomas. Las Palomas is about two hundred fifty miles south of Santa Fe. They were camped there on the Rio Grande and were to head due east when they got back on the trail." He shrugged. "I've heard nothing further."

"Is there any chance that Dane and Lancaster are simply in an area too remote to communicate with you?" Elizabeth asked hopefully.

"Absolutely. When the boys turned east, they rode straight into some of the roughest country in the Territory. To reach their destination, they'd have to cross several mountain ranges, not to mention the badlands and the white sands. It's the section of the Territory that the early Spaniards called *Jornada del Muerto,* the Journey of the Dead."

"Sounds perilous," said Edmund.

"It is, Ed. Some strange, unexplained things have been happening of late down in that part of the country. Last week the body of a young woman turned up in Malaga." He glanced at Elizabeth, then added, "The woman's body, which was left on the plaza during the night, was unclothed. The New Mexico Rangers report there were strange markings on her throat. While I'm sure the incident has nothing to do with the missing expedition, I do wish I could persuade you to remain here in Santa Fe, Elizabeth, while—"

"I am going." Elizabeth's voice was firm.

"In that case, you're fortunate. I've contracted with the best guides in the Territory. West Quarternight was to arrive in Santa Fe either yesterday or today."

"Good," said Edmund. "I'll invite Mr. Quarternight to have dinner with us tomorrow evening. We'd love to have you come as well, Martin."

"Sorry, Edmund, but we've a houseful of guests in town for the Governor's Spring Baile tomorrow night. Oh, Good Lord . . . that reminds me, I took the liberty of telling Governor Mitchell he could expect the two of you." He suddenly frowned. "I hope I haven't spoken out of turn. The governor is now insisting on making you his guests of honor."

"We're flattered and pleased, aren't we, Elizabeth?"

Elizabeth smiled warmly. "We're more than anxious to meet the governor's friends."

"Wonderful," said Martin Exley, relieved. "So we can expect you to join us tomorrow evening at the Palace of the Governors for the baile?"

"Certainly." Rising, Elizabeth added, "And Friday night Mr. Quarternight can join us for dinner. Will we see him at the Governor's Spring Baile?"

"My dear lady," Martin Exley said flatly, "I'm afraid West Quarternight was not invited."

Wishing *she* hadn't been invited to the Governor's Spring Baile, Elizabeth could no longer put off dressing for the grand affair. The sun had been down for more than an hour and soon Edmund would be knocking on her door.

Elizabeth sighed and rose from the red leather settee where she'd been lying since finishing her bath. She yawned and stretched before the fire, thinking she must surely be the laziest of women. She had not been out of the suite all day and oh, how she had enjoyed it.

Edmund had gone out briefly, returning at lunchtime to say he had bumped into West Quarternight, who had agreed to have dinner with them Friday evening. He added that he thought it a good idea for them both to rest through the afternoon so they'd be fresh for the baile.

Now the afternoon was gone and it was time for her to dress. Elizabeth chose a beautiful ball gown of pale gray silk. After she'd slipped it on and stood examining herself in the free-standing mirror by the highboy, she wondered at the gown's plunging neck-line.

Frowning, she jerked at the bodice, attempting to pull it higher on her bare bosom. It was impossible. The shimmering fabric outlined her full breasts, pressing their contours tightly and dipping so low between, she felt exposed.

Finally, she shook her head and shrugged. Her fine clothes had been hand-picked by a trusted Lord & Taylor clerk, as was the Curtins' custom, and paid for by Edmund Curtin before leaving New York. In the hurried week prior to their departure, he had purchased for her a complete wardrobe of fine traveling suits, elegant high-necked blouses and well-tailored skirts and jackets in an array of spring colors.

Planning ahead, he had insisted she have several expensive riding habits and elegant ball gowns. He had even bought her some fine lingerie, those selections made sight unseen, trusting the reliable female Lord & Taylor clerk to choose the appropriate undergarments for a bride's trousseau.

Apparently the clerk had been a true romantic at heart. Elizabeth had never seen such wispy bits of sheer white gossamer meant to serve as a lady's underthings. The first time she slipped into a new chemise and a pair of daring thigh-high underpants, she felt and looked more naked than when she wore nothing at all.

Edmund's knock startled Elizabeth. It was time for the governor's baile.

14

Smoothing the skirts of her gray silk gown with nervous fingers, Elizabeth hurried to open the door. Edmund stood in the portal, debonair in dark evening clothes, a snowy white shirt, and spotless white kid gloves.

Downstairs a crested carriage—sent by the governor—waited to collect the visiting couple. It whisked them around the plaza to the Palace of the Governors, site of the glittering baile. A cortege of carriages lined the avenue in front of the palace and laughter and excitement filled the warm spring night. The city's gentry—wealthy ranchers, aristocratic grandees, and the politically influential—dressed to the teeth, arrived en masse for the governor's annual gala.

Dreading the long, wearing evening that lay ahead, Elizabeth nevertheless smiled, took Edmund's hand, and stepped down from the carriage. Her gloved hand resting on his arm, she swept into a long, large room where copper-and-crystal chandeliers cast honey-eyed light on a large, polished floor of gleaming oak. Huge clay pots filled with colorful blooming cactus bordered the dance floor. Slim Mexican waiters in black charro pants and white bolero jackets passed

among the well-turned-out crowd bearing silver trays
of French champagne. At the far end of the long
room, an orchestra tuned atop a bunting-draped dais.

On seeing the visiting pair enter, the smiling, well-
tailored governor of the New Mexico Territory hurried forth to greet Elizabeth and Edmund. Governor
Robert P. Mitchell gallantly kissed Elizabeth's hand,
then turned to shake Edmund's.

Welcoming them both profusely, the governor said,
"Mrs. Curtin, I do appreciate your coming here this
evening when I'm sure you would much prefer solitude." Feeling as if he had read her mind, Elizabeth
smiled warmly at him. He said, "Your selflessness,
gracious demeanor, and beauty is a credit to your
husband, my dear."

"You're very kind, Governor," Elizabeth replied.

"Come now, both of you. Let me introduce you to
my friends."

The governor, deftly stepping between them,
ushered them forward into the crowded room. He
made sure they met his lieutenant governor; the territorial commissioner; His Eminence, the respected
Bishop Lamy; a host of dignitaries and their wives; as
well as the Territory's wealthy Old Guard.

Elizabeth, radiant with her flaming hair swept atop
her head and her gray silk gown accentuating her
slender figure, drew nods, smiles, curious stares, and
whispered comments as she moved through the cele-
brated crowd at the governor's side, shaking hands
and finding something to say to everyone she met.

"Elizabeth, may I present Doña Hope," the governor said, stopping before a striking blonde wearing a
champagne-hued gown of shiny satin. "Doña, this is
Mrs. Dane Curtin."

"Mrs. Curtin," the doña acknowledged, "welcome
to Santa Fe."

"So nice to meet you, Doña Hope," Elizabeth replied.

Smiling, the women automatically sized each other up. They were the same height exactly and approximately the same weight. While Elizabeth's hair was fiery red, Doña Hope's was silver-white. Her large almond-shaped eyes were a deep brown, Elizabeth's a sparkling blue. Elizabeth's berry-red lips were full and had a pouty, bee-stung appearance; Doña Hope's mouth was wide and lush and sensual. Both women had skin of fair, flawless softness. Both wore gowns of daring but tasteful elegance.

Doña Hope's distinguished-looking escort was introduced as S. Dwayne Haggard, owner of Santa Fe's First Territorial Bank. A man of medium height whose light-brown hair was beginning to gray at the temples, S. Dwayne Haggard's smile was genuine, his manner friendly. As he spoke, his possessive hand never left Doña Hope's waist.

The orchestra began playing. The twittering and laughter increased as every eye came to rest on Governor Mitchell and his honored guests.

The governor bowed grandly to Elizabeth, took her hand, and led her onto the empty dance floor. She stepped into his arms and they began the waltz. The Governor's Spring Baile was officially under way.

Other couples poured out onto the floor to turn and spin and enjoy the dancing. While Elizabeth waltzed with Governor Mitchell, she casually questioned him about the attractive blonde, Doña Hope. He told her the señora was one of his city's most sought-after women. Not only was she breathtakingly lovely, Doña Hope was the wealthy widow of the late Don Javier Narciso Baca. Upon his death, she had inherited the don's six-hundred-thousand-acre rancho in the southern part of the Territory.

"Six hundred thousand acres?"

"One of the larger of the old Spanish-American land grants, although not near the largest. Don Javier was grandson of the rancho's original owner."

Elizabeth said, "Doña Hope is quite young to be widowed. Was her husband, Don Javier Baca, killed in an accident?"

The governor laughed, then shook his head. "Mrs. Curtin, when the don died of a heart attack three years ago, he had just passed his seventy-first birthday."

Elizabeth's eyes widened. The governor went on to explain that Don Javier was a vigorous man until his death. A full-blooded Spaniard, he had been a confirmed bachelor until he had met the lovely Hope Hayward on a trip to San Francisco. While in the city he visited the theater, saw the white-haired Hope onstage, and fell instantly in love.

As smitten as a schoolboy, the fifty-nine-year-old don stayed on in San Francisco until he could persuade the young actress to marry him. A month later, the don and his beautiful blond bride returned to New Mexico in time for her twentieth birthday.

The governor glanced across the room at Doña Hope. "That was fifteen years ago, though it doesn't seem possible. Doña Hope is the same dazzling beauty at thirty-five that she was at twenty."

"She is very beautiful," Elizabeth agreed, wondering if the governor himself was half in love with the blond widow. From the soulful looks the blond widow drew from a number of the gentlemen present, it was evident she could have any man she wanted.

While Elizabeth danced with the governor, Edmund sipped chilled champagne from a stemmed glass and made conversation with the other guests. Laughter and music and the scent of expensive per-

fume filled the big hall, while outdoors a million stars
came out to twinkle in the black New Mexico sky.

The party had been in progress for little more than
an hour when Elizabeth, again dancing with the governor, felt her bare back lightly bump another lady's
bare back. Both couples paused.

Elizabeth turned at the exact moment Doña Hope
turned. The two women smiled and apologized, the
men nodded, and they changed partners for the remainder of the dance.

While Elizabeth made polite small talk with the
brown-haired banker, S. Dwayne Haggard, Doña
Hope put her wide red lips close to the governor's ear
and whispered that with all the champagne she'd con-
sumed, she would have to be excused for a moment.
Would he kindly allow it?

"But, of course," said Governor Mitchell, charmed,
as always, by the beautiful blond widow's straightfor-
ward manner. "Promise we'll finish our dance later in
the evening."

"I promise," said she, lifted the skirts of her champagne-satin ball gown, and walked out of the
crowded hall.

Over Elizabeth's head, J. Dwayne Haggard had seen
the exchange and he frowned as the blond widow
hurried through the arched doorway and disappeared.

While the room continued to swell with the town's
elite ladies and gentlemen, one not-so-elite gentleman
—who was not invited to the governor's elegant party
—waited alone at the La Fonda Hotel for one of the
so-called ladies to slip up to his room and out of her
fancy ball-gown.

West Quarternight didn't bother to rise from his
bed when the lovely Doña Hope swept breathlessly
into his room without knocking. Naked, stretched
comfortably out atop the bed covers, his long arms

folded beneath his pillow, West leisurely turned his dark head and smiled at the woman who had begun anxiously undressing the moment the door closed behind her.

Caring not at all that the jealous, possessive banker who had escorted her to the baile might be wondering where she was, the blond widow—four years West's senior—dropped her expensive champagne-satin ball gown to the carpeted floor.

Impatiently she struggled with her tight waist-cinching corset, then swept her satin chemise up over her head and her satin underdrawers down over her shapely hips. She kicked off her satin dancing slippers and, looking straight at the dark, naked man on the bed, slowly, seductively, peeled her silk stockings down her long, slender legs.

Wearing only a pearl-and-diamond choker and matching earrings that dangled almost to her bare ivory shoulders, Doña Hope swayed provocatively to the bed, her brown, flashing eyes going to West's bare groin.

Pleased that the male flesh which had been totally flaccid when she had come through the door was now hard and pulsing and ready to give her exquisite pleasure, Doña Hope leaned down and gave West's mouth a hot, wet kiss, allowing her soft breasts to fall onto his broad, bare chest.

West kissed her back, his tongue sweeping the insides of her mouth, but his arms remained folded beneath his pillow. He didn't reach for her, didn't attempt to pull her down to him.

But then, he didn't have to.

When the passionate doña tore her burning lips from his, she climbed astride his hard thighs, licked her fingers wetly, then caressed his straining masculinity until it glistened in the light of the bedside lamp.

Her brown eyes darkening with desire, she raised herself up to her knees. And taking him gently with both hands, placing only the tips of her fingers just below the throbbing, mushroom-shaped head, she guided him a mere half inch up into the hot wetness of her pliant, yielding body.

For a long second they stayed like that, she kneeling above, her hands tenderly pressing him to her in an erotic initiation to invade and conquer, her heated gaze holding his. He lying below, arms still folded, long, lean body seemingly relaxed, his sexual force still leashed.

Giving him one last smoldering look, Doña Hope arched her body and threw her head back. Her hands fell away from him. The spread fingers settled atop her own creamy thighs. Doña Hope, knowing exactly how to please a man as well as herself, sighed with bliss as she slowly inched her way down on him, gloriously impaling herself on that expanding male power.

All the while, West watched the pleasurable flesh-melding ceremony with heated silver eyes.

When she began the movements of loving, West's hands finally came out from under the pillow to settle on her flared, grinding hips. It was not the first time the pair had made love. There had been many such occasions in any number of locations. They knew they could draw out the ecstasy or bring it about in a heartbeat.

Both were aware that Doña Hope would be missed if she stayed away too long from the baile. They didn't have much time. So West guided Doña Hope's hips with his hands, urging her creamy bottom to slap down against his hard pelvis as he rose to meet her with deep, penetrating thrusts.

In minutes Doña Hope was shuddering atop him, her eyes tightly shut, her breath coming fast, her long red nails scraping down his chest. At the same time, West pumped the hot liquid of lust high up into her.

Afterward, while she stood naked before the tall pine bureau and washed him from her flesh, the doña told West about the illustrious Eastern guests of honor at the Governor's baile.

"A Mrs. Elizabeth Curtin and her brother-in-law, Edmund Curtin of New York City, are there," she said, reaching for her discarded chemise.

Shoving a pillow up against the tall headboard, West reached for a cigar, lit it, inhaled, and blew the smoke out slowly as he watched the beautiful blonde step into her lacy underdrawers.

"I know all about them," he said evenly. "The Curtins are the reason I'm back in Santa Fe."

Ignoring the quick look of displeasure that flared in the blonde's brown eyes, West told her that he had been hired to escort the pair on a foolhardy trek deep into El Malpais and beyond in search of the missing Curtin-Lancaster Expedition.

"The man you met, Edmund Curtin, is brother to one of the missing men." West drew on his cigar. "The woman is Dane Curtin's wife."

Doña Hope's delicate jaw hardened. "And the wife actually means to go out on the trail with you?"

West shrugged bare brown shoulders. "Apparently that's their intention. I met Curtin only this morning."

"I see," said Doña Hope. "And you've not yet met the wife?"

"No, I haven't. Curtin has invited me to join them for dinner tomorrow night to further discuss plans for the trip. I suppose I'll meet her then."

Dressed again, Doña Hope came to the bed, sat down on its edge and laid a hand on West's flat belly. Petulantly, she said, "Darling, I hope you don't like red hair. The missing man's wife is quite beautiful and she has flaming red tresses."

West Quarternight dropped his cigar in a crystal tray on the night table. He grinned, reached out, and curled a forefinger down into the plunging V of Doña Hope's champagne-satin gown. Slowly, he pulled her to him. When her parted red lips were inches from his own, he shifted his gaze to the white-blond glory framing her lovely face.

He said, "Never could stand red hair."

15

Across the plaza, inside the crowded El Palacio Real ballroom, Elizabeth Curtin wished she could slip away from the spring baile as the beautiful Doña Hope had obviously done. After meeting everyone present and joining in endless conversations and dancing with countless gentlemen and sipping two stemmed glasses of French champagne, Elizabeth felt flushed and weak and extraordinarily tired.

The orchestra completed a number, and the latest in a long line of dancing partners released her. Elizabeth looked up to see Governor Mitchell reaching for her hand. He did not lead her into another waltz. The perceptive governor led her right off the floor.

At the edge of the crowd he leaned down and said, "Mrs. Curtin, you aren't feeling well." It was a statement, so Elizabeth didn't bother to deny it. Governor Mitchell smiled kindly and continued, "It's the altitude, my dear. It takes some getting used to. It's harder on women than it is on men, so until you're acclimated, you must not overdo."

"Perhaps that's it, Governor," Elizabeth replied. "I do feel a bit faint."

"I knew it. May I suggest that you return immediately to your hotel suite." When Elizabeth graciously protested, Governor Mitchell insisted. "You've stayed long enough. You've charmed everyone, done your duty beautifully. Now go; get some rest."

The governor quietly informed Edmund of Elizabeth's intended departure. Worried, Edmund immediately offered to go back to the hotel with her. Elizabeth told him she wouldn't hear of it. The governor called for his carriage and personally rode with her around the plaza, ushered her safely into the lobby of the La Fonda, and bade her goodnight.

Sighing with relief, Elizabeth climbed the stairs, eager to get out of her dress and into her bed. In the broad corridor outside her door, she lifted her small silk reticule, pulled the drawstrings loose, and reached in to feel for her brass door-key. Not immediately locating it, she withdrew her hand, lifted the small evening bag closer, and looked inside.

She didn't see the key.

Frowning, Elizabeth moved nearer to a lighted wall sconce suspended overhead directly between her door and the door to the room next to hers. Standing beneath the sconce, she moved over a little further, toward the other door, positioning herself so that the light would spill down into the reticule.

Sure enough, there was the brass key, in the very bottom of the silk bag. She was reaching for it when the door before her abruptly opened. Startled, Elizabeth looked up and found herself standing face-to-face with Doña Hope.

Equally startled, the doña gasped and swiftly jerked the door shut behind her. But not before Elizabeth caught a fleeting glimpse of a dark man lying stretched out on the rumpled white bed. Naked, he lay on his stomach, his head turned away, his jet-black hair ruffled against the pillow.

For a long, awkward moment, both women were speechless.

Finally Doña Hope forced a smile and said, "This is not what you think it is, Mrs. Curtin."

"Whatever it is, is no concern of mine, Doña Hope." Elizabeth smiled back.

"I wholeheartedly agree, so I'd like to know what you think you are doing here?" The doña's chin lifted a little defiantly.

Elizabeth didn't like the blonde's attitude. "Now that," she smiled confidently, "is no concern of yours."

She turned away, moved to the door of her own room, patiently unlocked it, and stepped inside.

"Wait," said Doña Hope, hurrying forward, putting out her hand to keep Elizabeth from shutting the door. "You're staying here? This is your apartment?"

"Have you any objection?"

"Yes! I mean no! That is, I . . . no . . . certainly not, but . . ." Doña Hope stammered.

" 'Night, Doña," said Elizabeth, and continuing to smile, she slowly closed the door in the blonde's face.

Inside, Elizabeth leaned back against the heavy door and shook her head. Poor S. Dwayne Haggard. While he had been looking everywhere for her, the beautiful Doña Hope had been here in the hotel with another man.

A dark, naked man with jet-black hair.

All at once Elizabeth felt a chill skip up her spine. Sure it was effects of the thin mountain air, just as Governor Mitchell had suggested, she pushed away from the door, eager to get undressed and into bed.

But once in bed she couldn't sleep. She tossed and turned, restless, despite her exhaustion. Exhaling disgustedly, she punched at her pillow, turned onto her stomach, and shut her eyes.

And saw again, behind closed eyelids, a dark naked man lying atop a big white bed.

Suddenly feeling uncomfortably warm, Elizabeth kicked off the bedcovers. It did no good. She was still too warm. She raised herself up on her elbows and looked across the room. The windows were closed.

That was it. The room was close and stuffy. She rolled over, sat up, bounded from the bed, crossed the darkened room, briefly considered opening the heavy double doors onto the front balcony. Then quickly remembered the tall, dark stranger from the night before, standing on the balcony lighting a cigar in the wind.

She made sure the balcony's double doors were securely locked, then turned to raise a window beside them. The night air was fresh and cool and Elizabeth inhaled deeply and allowed the breeze to press her gown against her heated body.

Returning to bed, she wondered: Was the dark stranger she'd seen lighting a cigar and the naked man next door one and the same?

Ashamed of her preoccupation with the dark man, Elizabeth willed herself to think of something else. Of someone else. She chose her husband, Dane. She concentrated and called up from memory his blond good looks, his cultured voice, his ready charm. He was alive out there in the desert, she knew it. And they would find him. When they did, Dane would have a perfectly logical explanation for his mysterious disappearance. And maybe . . . the buried gold.

Yes, she would soon be with her husband. Her blond, handsome, rich, loving husband.

The night breeze cooling her, Elizabeth soon fell asleep.

But she dreamed. And it was not her blond, handsome husband, but the dark, mysterious stranger who followed her into those dreams:

The dark man lay stretched out on his stomach on an enormous white bed, his head turned away. He was naked and his body—dark all over—was nothing short of divine.

His shoulders were broad and powerful, his arms long and muscular. His smooth back was deeply clefted and beautiful, narrowing symmetrically to his ribcage and trim waist. His bare buttocks were taut and gently curving, his long legs leanly muscled. Even his bare brown feet were pretty.

Elizabeth eagerly stripped off her nightgown. Naked, she climbed onto the massive bed and crawled across it on her hands and knees. It took forever to reach him. When finally she did, she laid a hand on his bare shoulder. Immediately he turned onto his back, his eyes opened, and he smiled at her.

She had only a second to admire his handsome face, his broad chest with hard, flat muscles and thick growth of raven hair, his corded ribs, his tight belly. He drew her down to him, and kissed her.

It was a sweet, wonderful, dreamy kiss that went on and on, his lips warm and gentle, moving coaxingly on hers. At some point in that exquisite kiss, their positions changed. When his lips lifted from hers, Elizabeth was lying on her back, he was above, looking down at her with love and passion shining in his beautiful eyes.

They were no longer on the big white bed. They lay atop a fluffy white cloud floating through the heavens. At first Elizabeth was afraid she might fall off, or even through, the cloud.

But his loving gaze told her that she wouldn't. He had her. He wouldn't let her fall. So she relaxed and dangled a foot over the cloud's side and drifted happily along, high above the towering mountains and tall green trees and scattered villages far below.

Happy as she'd never been before, she looped her

arms around his neck and drew him back down to her, wanting more of his incredibly splendid kisses. With his sensual mouth covering her lips and his hard, lean body pressed to hers, Elizabeth was not surprised, nor was she frightened, by the fierce heat that radiated from him, burning her flesh, setting her blood afire.

Soon she, too, was hot, devastatingly hot. She gloried in the heat because he was the source, this dark, naked god of love, this unselfish provider of ecstasy. Trusting him totally, Elizabeth closed her eyes and sighed and writhed as his burning lips pressed kisses on her parted lips, her bare shoulders, her sensitive throat.

And the heat continued to soar.

A brightness began to shine blindingly through her closed eyelids. Elizabeth's eyes fluttered open and she could see nothing but a glaring white sun. Close, dangerously close. Its fierce gravity was pulling them directly toward the fiery ball.

Then her lover's face came between her and the sun, and she tried to warn him, to tell him they were in imminent danger. But she couldn't make her voice work and he seemed unconcerned. He smiled at her and it was then she suddenly realized he had a thick black beard.

He lowered his bearded face to her breasts. The hair of his head ruffled against her chin and that on his face tickled her sensitive skin. His lips were scorching hot as he kissed her burning flesh.

She tried in vain to caution him. Tried to make him stop before it was too late, before they were both incinerated in the fiery inferno drawing them steadily closer. But he wouldn't. He kept on kissing her, and kissing her, his lips and tongue driving her wild. His bearded face moved lower and lower as they were pulled closer and closer to the sun.

Frantic to be free, to save herself, she struggled, fighting the perilous pleasure. Attempting to rise, she managed to roll into a sitting position, putting her stiffened arms out beside her. At that same instant his dark, bearded face moved down over her belly and went between her legs.

"No," she murmured as his strong hands urged her legs wider apart and his dazzling mouth sank into the fiery red curls between. "No, no," she pleaded as his heated lips opened over her wet, burning flesh. "No, no, no," she screamed as together they were sucked into the sun.

"No, no!" Elizabeth moaned, and bolted upright in her bed. "No, no, no," she gasped loudly, trembling, looking about in confusion. Soaked with perspiration, her heart hammering in her chest, she tried to recall the dream that had awakened her.

And could not.

"No, no." Her anguished cries awakened the man in the room next to hers and he bolted up. "No, no, no," it came again, and West Quarternight shot up from his bed, reflexively reached for his heavy Colt .44 and hurriedly crossed to an open window, the gun leveled, the hammer cocked.

His lean body tensed, he stood naked in the darkness, waiting, listening. In seconds he began to smile and lowered his weapon, feeling foolish. He went back to the bed and laid the Colt on the night table.

What he had heard was a woman's cries of ecstasy. He was sure of it. There had been that unique, breathless sound to her *no*'s with which he was more than familiar. Those sweetly pleading *no*'s mixed with startled gasps of delight. That's all he had heard. The occupants next door had been making love.

Grinning, West got back into bed, stretched out, yawned, and closed his eyes. In minutes he was sound asleep and soon he dreamed.

But he did not dream of women and of making love. He dreamed of being in a dark tunnel deep down under the surface of the earth. He was belly flat in the small, airless tunnel, squirming and pulling himself slowly forward, inch by agonizing inch. Captain Brooks was right behind him, their freedom less than twenty yards ahead when the tunnel started caving in on them.

Cut off, trapped, West clawed at the smothering dirt, calling to Captain Brooks. Blinded and coughing, he dug frantically with his bare hands, searching, begging Brooks to answer, knowing they would both suffocate if he didn't get them out!

"No, no," West moaned, thrashing wildly about, trapped in the smothering tunnel. "No, no, no," he gasped, feeling the last of his air supply being sucked from his starving lungs at the moment he touched the stilled fingers of Captain Brooks.

Coughing and choking, West awakened with a start. His breath coming fast, his heart thundering, he sat in the darkness, trembling, his chest and face wet with sweat. But oddly, as it sometimes did, the recurring nightmare faded as soon as he woke and in seconds had totally left him. Try as he might, West could not recall the frightening dream.

Running his fingers through his damp hair, he sighed and lay back down. Chilly now, he pulled the sheet up to his chest and closed his eyes. And fell back once again into a deep, dreamless sleep.

At midmorning on Friday, West Quarternight left his room. Walking directly through the hotel lobby, he never noticed a well-dressed lady seated on a long leather sofa, head bent, reading the *New Mexican*.

Nor did the woman notice him.

West walked out of the hotel, looked up San Francisco, then down. He stepped into the street, crossed it, then crossed the plaza to the Palace of the Governors. A smile spread over his face when he saw Micoma in her usual place on the palace *portal.*

"How are you this morning, Micoma?" he said, crouching down on his heels to smile at her and to wait for her inevitable question about her sons.

But it didn't come.

She said nothing. Just smiled toothlessly, her old black eyes sparkling, as if she knew some pleasant secret. West narrowed his own eyes and cocked his head.

"What's on your mind? There's something you're dying to tell me."

The old Navajo chuckled, but still said nothing. West noticed the copper brooch pinned to her poncho. Tapping a forefinger to it, he said, "Where did you get this pretty brooch?"

"From woman with hair on fire. You know her?"

He shook his head. "No, but if I meet a woman with her hair on fire, I'll see if I can't put it out."

"You can't," said the old woman, who crossed her arms over her chest and added, "Be very careful her fire not burn you, West Quarternight." And then she laughed.

"I'll watch my step," he said, rose to his feet, and left her there. Still laughing.

Restless, West sat in for a few hands of poker in a saloon, got bored, and cashed in. He returned to the hotel. He thought about taking a nap. Back in his room, he reached up behind his head, jerked his pullover shirt off, and dropped it to a chair, but left on his boots. He lay down on the bed, immediately got back up. He paced, poured himself a drink, and wandered out the open double doors onto the hotel balcony.

He lifted a booted foot up to rest atop the adobe railing, draped a bare forearm atop his bent knee, and looked indifferently out over the town. His sleepy-lidded, bored eyes took in all the activity below. It did not interest him.

Draining his glass of bourbon, West was ready to go back inside when in the distance, across the plaza, a flash of fiery red caught his eye. A woman was coming in his direction. A well-dressed woman who was young and slender. She moved with an easy, fluid motion, the skirts of her pale blue suit swaying gently with her steps.

Her hair was red, ablaze in the sunlight.

His gray eyes never leaving her, West watched the young woman move closer until she stood directly across San Francisco Street. She paused to wait for a couple of wagons to roll past. She was beautiful. Very beautiful. Something about her was familiar. As if he had met her before.

It hit him like a bolt of summer lightning.

The passionate little Southern belle from the Shreveport stockade! It was her. No doubt about it. Hers was a face and body no man could forget.

Grinning now, West lifted his hand and waved to her, but she wasn't looking up. He didn't know her name. Had never called her anything but "miss."

"Miss!" he shouted, "Red, up here. Up here, miss."

She hadn't heard, didn't look up. Her attention was on someone coming toward her. West wondered who. A moment later, he found out.

Edmund Curtin stepped out of the La Fonda, crossed San Francisco, smiled at the red-haired beauty, and took her arm. Together they stepped into the street and walked toward the hotel while West, unseen by either of them, gaped in disbelief.

The truth dawned.

That hot-blooded, flame-haired murderess from the Confederate death cell was now the respected Mrs. Dane Curtin of New York City.

And his boss.

16

As the appointed hour drew near, West Quarternight caught himself feeling mildly excited about having dinner with the Curtins. A man who approached most everything with a weary indifference, he was surprised to find he was looking forward to the evening with a degree of anticipation.

West hummed as he shaved meticulously. When he had completed the task, when his tanned face was smooth and totally devoid of dark whiskers, he leaned forward and carefully studied his reflection in the mirror.

Blotting at his chin with a corner of the white towel draped around his neck, he gazed intently at his face, frowned, picked up the shaving mug and brush and again lathered up. Handling the sharp straight-edged razor as deftly as a skilled surgeon, the man who often didn't bother to shave at all, shaved a second time.

Satisfied at last that all traces of his dark, heavy beard had been scraped away and that his face would remain shiny smooth for the entire evening, West reached up and turned out the twin gaslights mounted on either side of the tall mirror. He struck a sulfur match and held it to the wick of a lone white candle resting in a terra cotta dish. He turned, bent from the waist, and set the candle on the floor.

He discarded the towel draped around his bare shoulders and the one wrapped around his slim hips. Naked, he stepped into a high-backed porcelain bathtub filled with steaming hot water. He stayed there for the next twenty minutes, shampooing his dark hair, scrubbing his back with a long-handled brush, soaping up every part of his long, lean body. Scouring himself as if it had been weeks since last he bathed instead of only that morning.

While the flickering candle cast dancing shadows on the Mexican tiled walls of the big bathroom, West splashed about in the tub, singing a mellow song, wondering if the beautiful Mrs. Dane Curtin would remember him.

He looked different now than he had that night in Shreveport. Not only had a bushy, black beard and mustache concealed his face then, he had been undernourished and thin, at least twenty-five pounds lighter than he was now. And too, they had spent the majority of their time together in a darkened jail cell, where it was impossible to ascertain even the color of each other's eyes. West grinned, recalling that she had told him of being partial to green eyes, so he had let her think he had green eyes.

Smoothly shaven and scrubbed clean, West walked into the adjoining room, where his clothes were laid out. He shoved his long arms down into the sleeves of a fine white cotton shirt, buttoned it, then stepped into a pair of well-tailored gray linen trousers. He dropped down onto a chair and drew on his mirror-polished handmade black boots.

He spent the next ten minutes brushing his clean dark hair, finally dropped the brush atop the pine highboy, and reached for his suit jacket. The last thing he did was turn up the collar of his freshly laundered shirt, drape a braided black-and-gray bolo tie over his head, and settle it beneath the turned-up collar. He drew the tie secure with the turquoise and silver bolo ring Micoma had given him, turned down the collar, shot his long arms out to effect just the right amount of shirt cuff showing . . . and West Quarternight was ready to renew old acquaintances.

Edmund Curtin had failed to tell him the number of the Curtins' suite, so West hurried downstairs to inquire. He was directed right back up the stairs to the apartment next to his own.

His room was number twelve. The Curtins were in suite eleven. When he stood before number eleven's main door, an alarming warmth suddenly crept up the length of his body. He shook his head, waited until it had passed, then raised his hand and knocked.

Inside, Elizabeth, busily checking to make sure everything was ready and waiting, called to her brother-in-law through the closed door of his bedroom.

"I'll get it, Edmund. Take your time."

Crossing the suite's burgundy-carpeted sitting room, she gave the low-dipping bodice of her pale peach silk gown one last tug, patted at her upswept red hair, and paused directly before the heavy carved door. She summoned up an engaging smile for the waiting desert guide whom she envisioned as a rough-hewn buckskin-clad bear of a man, ill-at-ease in civilization and woefully shy and uncomfortable around women.

Smiling warmly, Elizabeth opened the door.

And found her vision filled with a tall, strikingly handsome man who appeared totally relaxed as he stood with one long arm raised and propped against the doorframe.

Elizabeth stood paralyzed, the foolish patronizing smile frozen on her face. Her first impression blurred into one mesmerizing essence, then separated into each individual aspect of his compelling good looks.

Thick, well trimmed hair of midnight black. A smooth, tanned complexion, clear of any blemish. Heavily lashed, low-lidded eyes of smoky gray. High, prominent cheekbones. A straight, princely nose. A finely sculpted jaw. Wide, sensual lips that were turned up into a hint of a grin.

The suit he wore was the exact color of his eyes. The gray linen fabric stretched across broad, powerful shoulders, and with his long arm raised, the jacket hung open to reveal that he wore no waistcoat. Beneath a shirt of pristine white, the thick black hair of his chest was a shadowy testimony to his rugged maleness.

Forcing her gaze up to the silver and turquoise adornment at his brown throat, Elizabeth finally found her tongue.

"Ah . . . Mr. . . . Mr. Quarternight?"

"You can call me West," he said, lowering his arm and thrusting out his right hand, his gray eyes glinting with an amusement she did not understand or share.

"I'm Mrs. Dane Curtin, Mr. Quarternight." She frowned and withheld her hand. "You may call me Mrs. Curtin." She stepped back. "Won't you come in?"

Still grinning, West stepped leisurely past her, so close she caught the faint scent of shaving soap. Unhurriedly, he walked across the large sitting room. Expecting him to turn any minute and catch her watching him, Elizabeth, a hand at her throat, stared at his back and watched the muscles of his wide shoulders pulling beneath the well-fitted gray linen suit coat.

Wondering why this dark man made her feel uncomfortable, and praying that Edmund would soon join them, Elizabeth drew a shallow, nervous breath and moved forward to make their guest feel welcome.

Pretending to fuss with a perfectly arranged bouquet of wildflowers atop the damask-draped table at the room's center, she glanced hurriedly at West Quarternight and said, "Please, Mr. Quarternight, have a seat."

"Why, miss," said West, continuing to stand, "I wouldn't think of sitting down until you're free to join me."

"You called me miss, Mr. Quarternight."

"Did I? Forgive me, Mrs. Curtin." He smiled, and added, "Won't you come over here?"

Trapped, Elizabeth told herself she was acting impolite and foolish and there was no excuse for either. This man had been invited here and had done nothing to warrant her bad manners. Should Mr. Quarternight have to pay for the fact that he was not the wild, woolly-looking creature she had expected?

From the table's colorful centerpiece, Elizabeth plucked a purple columbine and, turning, smiled graciously at the tall man standing with his back to the brightly burning fireplace.

"I'll be happy to join you, Mr. Quarternight," she said, and walked toward him. When she was no more than three feet away, she held out the purple flower. "This would make the perfect boutonniere for your lapel."

"Yes," he said, "it would." But his eyes were on her face, and he made no effort to take the flower from her.

Puzzled, Elizabeth moved one step closer and lifted the purple columbine up toward his face. "Well, then . . . here . . . don't you want it?"

"More than you know," he said. Still his arms remained at his sides.

Elizabeth exhaled in exasperation. "Then take it."

"No," he said, his voice suddenly low and soft. "You give it to me." Elizabeth's lips fell open; anger flashed in her eyes. She lowered the flower and started to back away. With a swiftness that startled her, West Quarternight reached out, wrapped dark fingers around her fragile wrist, and held her fast. "I'm only asking you to place the blossom in my lapel," he said, his gaze holding hers. "Since I'm all thumbs, won't you do it for me?"

Knowing instinctively that this tall, dark man was *not* "all thumbs," Elizabeth said commandingly, "Let go of me, Mr. Quarternight."

West released her immediately and for a long moment they stood there, not moving, not speaking, silently sizing each other up. Never a woman to allow anyone to get the better of her, Elizabeth consciously willed her tensed body to relax. There was, she reminded herself, absolutely no logical reason to be ill-at-ease and jittery.

Lifting her chin and throwing back her bare shoulders, Elizabeth said, "I'll be happy to help you with the boutonniere." She smiled and added, "Come a bit closer, won't you, Mr. Quarternight?"

West stepped closer. Stood so close she would have to tip her head back to look up at his tanned face. But Elizabeth didn't look at his face, didn't want to be snared again by that compelling gray gaze. She kept her head bent, her attention on the stubborn buttonhole of his gray linen lapel. She painstakingly attempted to tuck the small purple flower with fingers that had become unfamiliarly clumsy.

"Thanks, Mrs. Curtin," West said, when at last the vivid blossom was secure in his lapel.

Elizabeth's head turned and came up just as his turned and bent forward. Their noses bumped slightly and their lips were less than an inch apart. Elizabeth felt his warm, fresh breath on her face.

"I'm sorry," he said, and automatically clasped her bare shoulders with strong brown hands. His lips moving against her cheek, he asked, "Have I hurt you?"

Elizabeth went hot from head to foot, then icy cold. She pushed on his solid chest as if he had violently attacked her. "No, no, of course not," she said, backing away, quickly putting space between them. "And you won't!" she added inanely.

"He won't what?" said Edmund, smiling as he entered from his connecting bedroom.

"I won't disappoint her," said West smoothly. "Your sister-in-law was gracious enough to say she's heard I'm the best guide in the New Mexico Territory. I said I hope she won't be disappointed." He looked at Elizabeth, smiled, and waited for her to stammer or deny it.

Calmly, she said, "And I told Mr. Quarternight he is surely too modest. I'm certain we won't be disappointed in his services, will we, Edmund?" She turned and smiled at West. He alone saw the fiery snapping of her sparkling blue eyes.

"From all I've heard," said Edmund, crossing to properly greet West, "we're in the best of hands."

"I'll try to live up to my reputation," replied West.

Suggesting they relax and get better acquainted, Edmund went to the well-stocked drink trolley. While Elizabeth took a seat on the leather sofa, Edmund poured ruby-red Madeira into stemmed wineglasses from a cut-crystal decanter. West Quarternight remained standing.

After handing a glass of wine to Elizabeth, Edmund held out a glass to West and said, "Sit down, sit down. We've a good hour before dinner."

Elizabeth suddenly wanted to kick herself. She had thoughtlessly sat down right in the middle of the sofa and now it was too late to move. West Quarternight would sit down beside her, there was no doubt in her mind. West moved and Elizabeth braced herself. Her fingers tightened on the delicate stem of her wineglass.

West took one of the matching wingback chairs directly opposite the sofa, folding his lanky frame into it, stretching his long legs out before him and leaning back. Surprised, Elizabeth glanced at him. For a moment his silver gray eyes penetrated hers, sending a shiver of excitement and alarm racing through her.

Edmund joined them. He sat down on the sofa beside Elizabeth. Balancing the wineglass on a knee, he said, "West, we're both glad you could have dinner with us this evening. There's so much to discuss, so many plans to be made."

Elizabeth was silent while the two men spoke of the upcoming mission, of her husband's missing expedition, of what might have happened. She caught herself leaning forward as West Quarternight spoke dispassionately of her husband's fate.

"I wouldn't worry about the various legends surrounding the Grayson Gold. You'll soon learn that the Mexicans and the Indians are highly superstitious people. They believe in ghosts and evil spirits and they spread tales about 'winged creatures of the night.'"

He took a drink of Madeira. His lips gleamed as he continued, "I'm familiar with every rock, every tree, every butte, every stream of the route the Curtin-Lancaster expedition was to take." He paused, then said, "The Spaniards didn't call it *jornada del muerto* for no good reason. Very inhospitable country." His eyes came to rest on Elizabeth. "You might want to consider staying here in Santa Fe, Mrs. Curtin."

"We've been through that already, West," Edmund answered for her. "Both Martin Exley and I have tried to persuade her to stay here, but she is determined." He turned to Elizabeth. "Aren't you, my dear?"

"I am," she said, with far less fervor than before, half wishing she could back out.

"Well, it's up to you," said West. "But let me make it clear to you both, if you back out once we're on the trail and don't go all the way, we still get paid. The full amount."

"Why, certainly," said Edmund.

A uniformed hotel steward arrived with dinner. While the three of them sat down at the table draped with beige damask and set with orange-toned pottery and heavy silver, the white-jacketed steward pushed a serving table on wheels into the suite.

First came the cold consommé, followed with roast rib of beef, sautéed potatoes, string beans, and hot bread.

The meal was superb, but Elizabeth couldn't enjoy it for stealing glances at the man who seemed so strangely familiar. His presence was unsettling. Something about the man made her feel both excited and guilty.

And nervous, terribly nervous. The nervousness showed. She accidentally dropped her fork. It clattered loudly onto her stoneware plate, then landed on the burgundy carpet.

West Quarternight's dark head swung around, and he fixed her with those silver-gray eyes and smiled. Not five minutes later she spilled a drop of the ruby-red wine on the bodice of her pale peach silk dress and those bothersome silver eyes were on her again. They quickly came to rest on the telltale spot directly atop her left breast.

She wanted to die.

Coffee and dessert were served. But Elizabeth was afraid to touch the delicious-looking apple suet pudding with hot syrup cream sauce. Her hands folded in her lap, she waited for the long, miserable meal to end. Long after both men had finished and had lingered over their brandy and coffee, West Quarternight finally suggested it was time he leave. Elizabeth was relieved.

She dropped her napkin on the table and rose so rapidly, her full cup of now-cold coffee overturned and spilled. But not on her. The coffee spread directly toward West Quarternight. He saw it coming, but not in time to get out of the way. He was half out of his chair when the dark brown liquid splashed the lower part of his white shirt front and dribbled down his gray linen trousers.

Crimson with embarrassment, Elizabeth, apologizing for her clumsiness, grabbed up her napkin and started blotting at the stains, moving the napkin hastily down his body, until she realized with horror that she was frantically patting at his crotch.

She jerked her hand away and, refusing to meet his eyes, said, "I'm sorry . . . I . . . never meant to . . . I . . ."

"Think nothing of it, Mrs. Curtin," he said evenly and rose fully from his chair.

Her face and ears were burning. She was vaguely aware that the two men stood and talked for a few minutes longer, Edmund totally taken with West Quarternight, while she felt that if he didn't hurry up and leave she would explode.

Finally they all moved toward the door. West opened it, then turned to face them. His manner was maddeningly calm. He seemed totally unperturbed and in charge. Elizabeth wondered how any man could stand with coffee dripping down his belly and onto his crotch and appear to be so annoyingly cocksure!

At last he said goodnight, turned and walked out, and Elizabeth felt like shouting for joy.

But before Edmund could close the door, Quarternight paused, turned, and came back.

Turning teasing gray eyes directly on her, he said, "Tell me, Mrs. Curtin, have you ever spent any time in Shreveport, Louisiana?"

Elizabeth's heart stopped beating. Her face drained of color as she watched his sensual lips turn up into a devilish smile.

"Never!" she said, her voice rising dangerously close to a shout. Then, more softly, her face mirroring her shock, "No, Mr. Quarternight," she lied, "I've never been to Louisiana."

17

"Impressive, isn't he?"

"Who?"

"Why, West Quarternight, of course," said Edmund, closing the heavy carved door behind the departing West. "Elizabeth, aren't you feeling well?"

"I feel just fine," she said irritably and swept across the sitting room to stand before the fireplace. Staring into the flames, she added, "Why do you ask?"

Edmund came to her. "My dear, I asked because you obviously haven't been yourself this evening."

Elizabeth whirled to face him. "Edmund, let's retain another guide. Someone older, more experienced."

Taken aback, he stared at her, baffled. "But why, Elizabeth? Quarternight may be just thirty-one, but he comes highly recommended and he seems to—"

"Yes, yes, but there's something about him that's . . . I don't know . . . I've the strongest feeling he's not entirely trustworthy."

His brow furrowing, Edmund said, "I can't for the life of me imagine why you would feel that way." A worried expression came into his green eyes. "Did something occur before I joined the two of you that—"

"No, no, nothing happened," she said impatiently. "It's his manner. He's impolite and arrogant and . . . and . . . unfeeling. You heard the way he talks about Dane and the others as if finding them means nothing more to him than . . . than—"

"Than just another assignment?" Edmund finished her thought. "Elizabeth, we can't expect West Quarternight to feel the way we do about Dane's plight. West is a cool professional. He doesn't know and love Dane the way we do."

Elizabeth had trouble meeting Edmund's eyes. "You're right, of course, but I do wish Mr. Quarternight were a more gentle, sensitive man. I wish he were more like you, Edmund. Like you and Dane."

Edmund smiled at his sister-in-law. "Granted Quarternight may not be the kind of man that sheltered, well-bred young ladies admire, but he is perfect for our needs. He strikes me as being totally fearless and imperturbable."

"Cocky and uncaring fits him better."

Edmund laughed. "Would it shock you to learn that I'd give anything to be a bit more like West Quarternight?"

"Edmund Curtin!"

"It's true. There are times when every man wishes he was a bit more daring and dauntless." Edmund suddenly turned wistful. Thinking aloud, he murmured, "My darling Louisa might have behaved differently if I . . . I . . ." He caught himself, and fell silent.

Elizabeth gently patted his shoulder. "You're twice the man West Quarternight is, Edmund."

"And you are a sensitive and remarkable young woman. How lucky Dane is to have you." His melancholy abruptly disappeared and he smiled warmly. "I wouldn't worry about Quarternight. You won't have to be around him much. Now, if you'll excuse me, it's been a long day and I'm rather tired. I think I'll retire."

"An excellent idea," said Elizabeth. "Good night, Edmund."

"Good night, my dear. Shall I turn out the lights here in the sitting room?"

"I'll do it. You go on."

He said goodnight again and went to his room, closing the door behind him. Elizabeth stood watching intently for several long minutes, waiting until she saw the spill of light beneath his door turn to darkness. Releasing an anxious breath, she flew about the spacious sitting room, putting out the lamps.

She rushed into her own bedroom, locked the door, and spent the next half hour pacing the floor and worrying. A million disjointed thoughts raced through her tortured brain as she restlessly paced.

How could this be happening? How could it possibly be true? *Was* it true? Was the bearded Yankee spy she had so urgently made love to four years ago in a Confederate death cell here in Santa Fe? Was the dark, thin man the Confederates had called Colonel Jim Underwood one and the same as the superbly built guide, West Quarternight?

Was West Quarternight the dark stranger she had seen on the hotel balcony her first night in Santa Fe? Was he, as well, the dark man she had caught Doña Hope leaving naked on the bed? During this evening's dinner, he had casually mentioned that he was staying in the room just next to the Curtins' suite. He was either in the room next to Edmund's bedroom or the one next to hers.

Elizabeth stopped her pacing. She turned and stared at the wall, the one farthest from the shared sitting room of the suite. All at once she knew hers was the room next to his. Could feel it. Sense it. On the other side of that wall was West Quarternight's room. Was he there? If so, was he alone?

She desperately needed to speak to him. To know for certain that West Quarternight was her . . . her Yankee lover. And if he was, could she trust him to keep quiet? Would he tell all he knew about her? If he did, what then? What would become of her?

The prospect chilled her.

Of one thing she was certain. If West Quarternight informed on her, a man as fine as Dane Curtin would want nothing more to do with her. She would find her marriage annulled before she was ever really his wife!

Her head pounding, her heart in her throat, a very worried Elizabeth Curtin thought . . . if she were to slip quietly out the door that led directly from her bedroom into the wide corridor . . . if she knocked softly on his . . .

Elizabeth quickly put out all the lamps. In the darkness, she tiptoed to the door. Holding her breath, she opened it and peered out. The broad, gaslit corridor was empty. Thanking her lucky stars for small favors, she darted outside, hurried over and knocked lightly on West Quarternight's door.

"It's open," came a low, masculine voice.

Elizabeth rolled her eyes heavenward, turned the brass knob, took one last nervous look around, opened the door, and whirled quickly through it. Once inside, she stood like a frightened child, facing the heavy carved door, trying to calm her nerves before she turned to meet his gaze.

Wondering just how long he would allow her to stand there in awkward misery before he spoke, Elizabeth took a deep breath and slowly turned around. And almost swallowed her tongue.

"What kept you, Mrs. Curtin?" West asked, a mischievous grin on his handsome face, his heavy-lidded silver-gray eyes boldly sliding down her body. "I've been waiting for you."

Elizabeth was unable to put the brash man in his place with a wilting retort. She was far too shocked, and too rattled, by the fact that he was addressing her from his bed. He lay there looking totally relaxed, his torso bare, the white sheet resting well below his waist. At the sight of him, so apparently naked beneath only a silky sheet, a tremor swept through Elizabeth's body, making her feel both electrified and immobilized.

Whatever else the shameless, ill-bred man was, his dark good looks were nothing short of a study in male perfection. It was more than she could do to tear her gaze from those bronzed, muscular shoulders and that appealing mat of jet-black hair covering his broad bare chest.

"I usually rise when a lady enters the room. You *will* excuse me if I don't get up." His low, teasing voice brought her back to her senses.

"Don't you dare get out of that bed, Quarternight or Colonel Underwood or whoever the devil you really are!" Elizabeth said forcefully and stormed to the bed.

"Ah, now I see. You want to get in here with me," he said. Smiling at her, he added, "Still a woman after my own heart." He lifted a long arm, held out a hand to her.

"You're out of your mind to think we're anything alike, Quarternight," she snapped. She stood directly beside the bed, glaring down at him. "So stop talking nonsense. I've come here to—"

"Sweetheart," he interrupted, "I know exactly what you came here for."

"I doubt that very much, Quarternight! You just think you know everything, but let me assure you,

you are wrong. You probably suppose that I . . .
I . . ." He was looking up at her and Elizabeth suddenly detected a hint of honest understanding in his
expressive gray eyes. Hopefully, she asked, "You do?"

"Yes," he assured her. He reached out very, very
slowly, and wrapped his fingers around her forearm.
"To take up right where we left off."

He snatched her down so swiftly Elizabeth had no
chance of stopping him. Too stunned to scream, she
found herself draped across his torso and a strong
arm wrapped tightly around her back, pressing her
close. She felt her breasts flattening against his hard,
bare chest, his heart beating against her own.

"My God!" she gasped. "Oh, God."

"Now, darlin', you can just call me West," he murmured, just as his lips captured hers. Right from the
start it was an intrusive, erotic kiss that instantly fired
Elizabeth's blood and anger. While his silky tongue
slid quickly past the barrier of her parted teeth, Elizabeth struggled and squirmed and made loud sounds
of protests in the back of her throat.

Still West held her.

Elizabeth doubled up her fists and beat wildly on
his chest and shoulders and ears, not caring how
badly she hurt him. Hoping to high heaven she did
hurt him.

After what seemed an eternity, his burning lips left
hers and his steel-hard arm loosened its imprisoning
hold. Snarling furiously at him, Elizabeth was up off
the bed in a shot, her blue eyes flashing fire, her teeth
grinding.

"Well, perhaps I made a mistake," he said, rubbing
at a reddened ear that was ringing. "Exactly where
did we leave off when last we were together?"

Her cheeks blood-red with rage, Elizabeth made a
bitter face of disgust, snatched up a streamer of the
silk sash going around her waist, and roughly wiped

her mouth on it, determined she would rub away all traces of his kiss. She harshly continued to rub long after any lingering taste of him—and all her pale red lip rouge—had been removed. He watched her the whole time, amused by her fervor.

"Now, is that polite?" he said, pretending to be hurt.

"You just shut up!" she snapped, dropping the sash. Her hands went to her hips and she said, "Why on earth did you do that? Why did you kiss me?"

"Didn't you come over here to get kissed?" Crossing long arms over his bare chest, he leaned his dark head back against the pillowed headboard and grinned. "Maybe you want me to help you get undressed first."

"Help me get un . . . you actually think that I . . ." Elizabeth glared at him. "Your conceit is colossal."

He shook his head and gave her a self-deprecating smile. "You mean, I've made an embarrassing blunder, Mrs. Curtin?" He wrinkled his brow as if trying to understand what was going on. "Forgive me, I'm a bit confused. I expected you. Looked forward to your coming. And you did come, didn't you?" He sighed loudly. "Now you tell me you don't want me to make love to you. Is that what you're saying?"

"That's exactly what I'm saying! Where did you get the ludicrous idea that I would ever—"

"If that's not the purpose of your late-night visit, Mrs. Curtin," he interrupted her, "what is? Why are you here?" He rubbed his firm chin and did his best to look earnestly puzzled.

Elizabeth was not fooled. She was overwhelmed by the desire to slap that false expression off his handsome face! She knew damned well that he knew *exactly* what she had come here for.

To talk straight. To find out what he was up to, this aggravating man who held her very future in his hands. Did he plan to pull her newfound world out from under her? She had to know. She was smart enough to realize that appearing upset and frightened would only please him. So, she calmed herself.

Softening her voice, Elizabeth said truthfully, "Actually, I imagine you know the reason, Mr. Quarternight." She waited, foolishly hoping that he would make it easy on her. He did not. He just kept looking up at her with his head cocked to one side, a dark eyebrow raised quizzically.

"I . . . we . . ." She cleared her throat. "Although you look quite different, I take it you are the same man who . . . who . . ." She lowered her eyes in shame, fumbled for the words, finally said, "Must I go on?"

"Suppose I say it for you. It's true, sweetheart. I'm the Yankee spy you gave yourself to in order to save your precious hide."

Elizabeth's head snapped up. "That's a lie!"

"It's a fact, Mrs. Curtin. Granted, I look a bit different now, but I'm—"

"That's not what I'm talking about!"

"Then what? I seem to—"

"I did not make love to you to save my neck!" she hissed. "Just the opposite! You took advantage of me with your spying foreknowledge—"

"Mrs. Curtin, I've a feeling the man hasn't been born who could take advantage of you." He smiled broadly. "But I won't hold that against you. Not at all."

"You don't know what you're talking about. I'm not like you think. Why, that night in Louisiana when I . . . that you . . . it was . . . it was—"

"Good," he interrupted. "It was damned good. Good the way only lovemaking between two people not emotionally involved can be good. It was so good I haven't forgotten it and neither have you. So let's stop all this foolish talk and see if we can't recapture the past. I'll bet it will be just as good."

Horrified, Elizabeth said foolishly, "It was not good! It was awful . . . awful—"

"Awful good. Admit it." He leaned forward, drew one knee up, and draped a bare forearm atop it. "I'm naked, sweetheart. Get naked with me. Let me undress you like I did that night in the stockade. Sit here on my lap in the bed and—"

"I will not listen to another vulgar word!" she said, clamping her hands over her ears. "Will you kindly shut up!"

He grinned. "All right. So you didn't come here for old times' sake. Why did you come?"

Cautiously, Elizabeth lowered her hands. She said, "Well, I just needed to . . . I mean, I thought perhaps I could—"

"Persuade me to keep quiet about your past?"

"No," she quickly responded. "Persuade you to give up this assignment."

"Now, why would I want to do that?" West again leaned back against the pillows. He stretched out his long legs under the sheet and the folds of the thin silk outlined more than his legs. Elizabeth's mouth went dry.

"Why?" she said, and her voice sounded strained even to her own ears. "How can you ask why? I am a married woman, Mr. Quarternight. Dane Curtin is my husband."

"And you're so wildly in love with Curtin you're bravely willing to risk your life to find him?"

"Yes. Yes, I am." Elizabeth averted her eyes and stared down at the burgundy carpet.

"May I suggest, Mrs. Curtin, that your motives are not quite so noble. Isn't it a fact that you can't inherit your rich husband's money until he's dead? Until you can prove that he actually is dead?"

Her head snapped up. "Quarternight, the claim to the lost Grayson gold is in my name. It all belongs to me. I had no need to marry Dane Curtin for his wealth. I am risking my life for a man I love. *You* are doing it for money!"

"I said nothing about risking *my* life," he said evenly.

"The journey is dangerous." She reminded him of his own words, then added hatefully, "Perhaps you have nothing to live for."

Unruffled, West smiled and said, "Look at me, Mrs. Curtin." Exhaling loudly, Elizabeth looked into his eyes. His silver gaze holding hers, he said, "You and I understand each other. We're a lot alike."

"We are nothing alike!"

"For argument's sake, let's say you're right. Nevertheless, you came here tonight to strike a bargain with me."

"I didn't." She tossed her head proudly back and spoke the truth. "I came here to find out exactly what you intend to do with the information you have, Mr. Quarternight."

"Why, nothing," he said, and Elizabeth's heart speeded with relief. Then he added, "You want something from me. I want something from you. Am I right?" She said nothing. He went on, "You want me to keep quiet. That's easy enough." He fell silent, waiting for her to speak.

"And you? What is it you want, Mr. Quarternight?"

She noticed the ripple of muscles in his dark arms and chest when he again leaned up from the pillows. He said, "Make it worth my while."

Elizabeth found her resolve.

West smiled and patted the bed beside him.

Elizabeth smiled seductively back at him. She sucked in her breath so that her firm breasts would swell and press against the tight bodice of her peach silk gown. Putting out the pink tip of her tongue, she slowly wet her lips.

"And exactly what," she murmured in a honey-rich voice, "would you consider 'worth your while'?"

West swallowed hard. "You, baby. I want you. Spend the night with me."

Confident she was ready to capitulate, West began to lift one edge of the silky sheet. He was preparing to rise and take her in his arms when Elizabeth fell heavily down on him, almost knocking the breath from him.

She grabbed his bare shoulders and slammed him back up against the pillowed headboard. Her angry face inches from his own, she thrilled to the look of total surprise and disappointment in his widened gray eyes.

Coldly, she said, "Nobody blackmails me, Quarternight. Nobody! Nor am I a whore who offers her body in exchange for favors. The only thing I wanted from you that night we made love was just that, to make love! So listen to me, because I only mean to say this once. If you think you are going to hold something over my head, think again. As soon as we find Dane I will—"

"Tell him yourself?" West coolly interrupted, his composure returning.

"Yes! I'll tell him myself. Tell him everything."

"No you won't," said West accusingly. "If you meant to tell him, you already would have." His tanned fingers slowly rose to the sides of her throat and he gently urged her forward.

Elizabeth tore his hands away and leapt up.

Looking down at him, she hissed, "You, Mr. Quarternight, were and always will be a low-down, dirty yellow Yankee spy!"

Softly he replied, "And you, Mrs. Curtin, were and always will be the prettiest red-haired Rebel murderess who ever rolled in the old hay with a dirty yellow Yankee spy."

18

Having spent a sleepless night of worry, Elizabeth was pale and tired the next morning when she went downstairs to meet Edmund for breakfast. Walking through the double glass doors that led into the crowded La Fonda dining room from the hotel lobby, she paused and searched vainly through a sea of hard bitten, sun roughened male faces.

The dining hall was swarming with loud, hungry *vaqueros*, cowboys, ranchers, and merchants. Sprinkled in among the locals were a few hotel guests, easy to spot by the way they were dressed.

Squinting through a thick haze of blue cigar smoke, Elizabeth looked anxiously about for a pale golden head among all the dark ones, unaware of the glances of interest and inquiry she drew from the mainly male gathering.

Just then the morning sunlight, streaming in through a skylight, touched the shiny blond curls of a well-dressed man across the crowded restaurant. Seated near the front of the rectangular room, his back was to her, but there was no doubt in Elizabeth's mind that the fair-haired man was Edmund.

She started forward, cautiously working her way

through the maze of filled tables, the sounds of laughter and loud talk grating on her taut nerves, the aroma of freshly brewed coffee and hot baked biscuits doing little to whet her sluggish appetite.

Elizabeth was six feet away when she saw him.

West Quarternight, seated across the table from Edmund, pushed back his chair and rose to his feet. Elizabeth stopped stone still. But she knew he had seen her, knew it was too late to turn and run.

"Why, there she is now," said West, looking directly at her.

Elizabeth had only a split second to look daggers at West before Edmund was rising and turning. She smiled warmly at her brother-in-law.

"You look a bit tired, Mrs. Curtin," said West, stepping over to pull out a chair for her. "Didn't sleep well?" Looking anxiously at her, he leaned down close, his expression one of concern.

"My dear, West is right. You do look a bit pale," agreed Edmund, studying her fair face, detecting the dark smudges under her large blue eyes.

"I never felt better in my life," said Elizabeth evenly, moving toward the chair West held out. Noticing joyfully that the tall, dark man wore only soft Indian moccasins, she managed to bring the hard heel of her leather-shod foot down directly on his toes.

She did not look at him. Directing her full attention to Edmund, Elizabeth remained standing as long as possible, thoroughly enjoying the act of inflicting a small measure of pain on the tormenting teaser whose very presence was unsettling. She stood and turned her foot from side to side, grinding down her heel with the full weight of her body, longing to hear the impervious Quarternight yelp with pain.

"Sit down, Elizabeth," said Edmund. "Now that

you're here, we'll order some breakfast." He looked away and began hunting for a waitress.

Elizabeth immediately turned to look up at West Quarternight. Catching the distinct expression of discomfort on his tanned face, she experienced a quick surge of delight. She gave him a smug, triumphant smile. He merely grinned and shrugged muscular shoulders.

Then with his full, smooth lips, he silently mouthed the word, "Owwww."

Elizabeth left him with one last parting twist of her heel before moving around to take the seat he held for her. He politely pushed her close to the table and reclaimed his own chair on her left. Edmund had managed to attract the attention of a Mexican waitress, who hurried to the table, smiling and wishing them all a cheery *buenos días*.

It did not escape Elizabeth that the brown-skinned woman, pretty in a white ruffled Mexican blouse and colorful print skirt, came all the way around the table to stand directly beside West Quarternight's chair. Nor did Elizabeth miss the fact that the woman's dark, flashing eyes lighted with pleasure when West favored her with a lazy smile.

"Shall I order for us all?" West asked.

Edmund said gratefully, "Yes, why don't you. We'll trust you, won't we, Elizabeth?"

"Just coffee for me," she replied flatly.

West looked up at the hovering Mexican waitress and ordered breakfast in flawless, fluent Spanish while the woman nodded and giggled and acted as if she couldn't stand still. The woman's behavior—like Quarternight's—irritated Elizabeth. What could possibly be so amusing about a simple breakfast order?

Neither Elizabeth or Edmund spoke a word of Spanish, so they had no idea what West was saying to the laughing woman. But Elizabeth could tell that Edmund was impressed with West's easy command of Spanish. He regarded West with undisguised admiration, and obviously hoping he, too, might learn to speak the language, opened his red-leather menu to hunt items that sounded like the dishes West was spieling off so rapidly.

Elizabeth was not impressed.

And she was most definitely not amused when she sensed that West and the waitress were talking about something other than scrambled eggs. She knew she had guessed right when West eased a moccasined foot out from under the table and directed the Mexican woman's attention to it.

Of all the nerve! He was telling the Mexican woman about her giving him sore toes!

The waitress looked almost lovingly at his foot, shook her dark head in understanding sympathy, then glared hotly at Elizabeth. She muttered to herself as she hurried back to the kitchen with their breakfast orders.

West felt Elizabeth's snapping blue eyes on him.

All innocence, he asked quietly, "Something wrong?"

"Nothing *you* can fix!" She accentuated the word so wiltingly, Edmund looked up from his menu.

"A good breakfast will fix you up, Elizabeth," he said optimistically, puzzled by the friction between the pair. "Afterwards, West has promised to take us over and get us outfitted." He said it excitedly and his green eyes shone like those of a little boy about to get his first pony.

"That's very kind of Mr. Quarternight"—Elizabeth looked only at Edmund—"but since I have no idea what 'outfitting' means, I believe I'll pass."

West, slouching back in his chair, suddenly leaned up to the table. "You can't do that, miss."

"Ma'am," she quickly corrected him, turning to

meet his low-lidded gray eyes. "Ma'am. *Not* miss. I am a married woman, Mr. Quarternight."

"Sorry, ma'am," he said, not really sounding sorry. "You'll have to come with us, I'm afraid. 'Outfitting' means choosing all the equipment we'll need for the expedition."

At the mention of the expedition, Elizabeth brightened. She was anxious to get under way. Every hour they waited put her husband in further peril. She felt it was extremely urgent they get on the trail as quickly as possible.

"Then we'll be leaving right away?" she asked hopefully. "In the next day or two?"

"Soon as my partners come down out of the San Pedro Mountains," said West.

Edmund said, "So you've already communicated with them, West?"

West nodded.

"How?" asked Elizabeth. "The heliograph? You sent them a heliogram message this morning? Yesterday?"

"Nope." West again leaned back in his chair, the chambray of his gray shirt pulled across the flat muscles of his chest. "The mirror station up on No-name Mountain's been down for the past two weeks."

"The station's down?" Elizabeth felt her irritation rising again. "So you haven't been in touch with them! Well, that's just marvelous. Now we'll have to—"

"Simmer down, Mrs. Curtin," West broke in smoothly. "They've received the message to come down. They're on the way."

"Oh, really?" she said, more than a little skeptical. "You have some kind of magical powers, do you, Mr. Quarternight? You can merely wish someone here and they materialize?"

"No, ma'am," he said, and grinned. "You'll understand once you meet my partners."

Impatiently, Elizabeth said, "Are you capable of ever giving a straight answer, Quarternight?"

"Elizabeth," Edmund cautioned, surprised at her rudeness, concerned that she might antagonize their much-needed guide.

"It's all right, Edmund," West said. "It's a fair question. Let's see, today is Saturday the . . . the—"

"May fifteenth," said Elizabeth. "Saturday the fifteenth of May, 1869."

"Thanks, Mrs. Curtin."

"You're welcome, Mr. Quarternight."

"Okay. It's Saturday, May fifteenth," West repeated, unruffled. "Grady and Taos, my partners, will reach Santa Fe late this afternoon. If we're completely ready and outfitted—horses, pack mules, tools, everything—we can be on the trail no later than dawn Monday the seventeenth."

"So soon?" Elizabeth asked.

West grinned, then said, "Ah, just like a woman, Mrs. Curtin. Bellyaching when a man's too slow, then acting downright shocked when he makes a quick move." His voice got across the two-edged meaning of his remark and his silver eyes gleamed with devilment as he waited for her response.

Elizabeth's pale face flushed with anger. His casual statement clearly held a double meaning, but she couldn't properly respond without arousing Edmund's suspicions. She ground her teeth and quietly seethed to a count of five.

She smiled sweetly at West and replied, "Ah, just like a man, Mr. Quarternight. Always swaggering with supreme self-confidence, as long as he's never really put to the test."

Elizabeth was delighted to see the pleased expression quickly vanish from West's silver eyes. It was evident that she had hit a nerve, but in fact she was somewhat puzzled by her easy victory. While she did find him maddeningly self-assured, she would be the first to grudgingly admit that his confidence was not misplaced. She'd be willing to wager that the tall, dark man would not only meet but excel at any test.

"Oh, Good. Here's our breakfast." Edmund cut through the tension.

West's smile returned and Elizabeth's disappeared as the beaming Mexican waitress placed steaming platters of food before them.

Elizabeth heard West say, "Nothing like a hearty breakfast to start your day off right." Wrinkling her nose, she stared down at her plate as he pointed out what she was looking at. "These are very special enchiladas. Cornmeal pancakes stuffed with raw onions and melted cheese, smothered with hot chili sauce. And this is green peppers, filled with cheese and fried until they're golden brown. That's your scrambled eggs."

"That couldn't be scrambled eggs," Elizabeth said, shaking her head in disbelief.

"Yes, ma'am, that's fresh eggs soft scrambled with goat cheese and hot peppers and—"

"I'm not hungry," said Elizabeth, pushing the plate away.

"No?" said West. "Not even for a piece of spiced sausage sprinkled liberally with hot sauce?"

She made a face. "Edmund, I'd eat sparingly, were I you," she turned to her brother-in-law.

His mouth full of the hot, spicy food, his eyes watering, he could only nod. Elizabeth sat there sipping black coffee, her empty stomach churning, while the two men ate heartily, neither stopping until their plates were clean.

As they were leaving, the Mexican waitress made it a point to wander over to say good-bye. "You come back soon, no?" she said, looking only at West Quarternight.

"Sure we will," he told her, and the woman's dark eyes clung to him until they were well out of the dining hall.

Out in the La Fonda lobby, moving toward the plaza entrance, Edmund smilingly said, "West, I believe that pretty waitress has her eye on you."

Gently placing a brown hand to the small of Elizabeth's back as they stepped out onto the stone sidewalk, West replied, with mock resignation, "What can I do?"

Wrenching away from him, Elizabeth snapped, "You could stop leading her on!"

Smiling contentedly, West let the remark pass. In silence the trio strolled around the plaza, stopping when they reached a large, flat sand-colored adobe building on the square's west side.

Bold black letters on a long white sign mounted above the doors read Ruiz Brothers. West explained that in the Ruiz Brothers' store they would find all the supplies needed for the long, grueling journey ahead.

Inside the spacious, high-ceilinged store, the air smelled of plug tobacco and leather and fresh-ground coffee. Row upon row of tables and shelves along the walls were filled with a myriad of merchandise. Atop some of the large square tables were colorful bolts of fabric, ribbon-trimmed bonnets, and delicate lace mantillas. Men's trousers and bright-hued cowboy shirts and longjohns filled others.

From the ceiling hung hams and slabs of bacon and varicolored peppers. A glass-fronted display case was filled with nostrums: Oriental Wart Destroyer, Electric Rheumatism Syrup, Dr. Jacob's Female Tonic, and Sure-Help Toothache Drops. Atop the display case were big glass jars of peppermint sticks and jawbreakers and jet-black licorice twists.

One wall, containing no shelving, was covered with bridles and farm tools and brooms and baby cradles.

Everything from clothing to food to saddles to weapons to coffins could be found in Ruiz Brothers.

Two smiling slender mustachioed Mexican men hurried forth to greet them. *"Mi gringo amigo!"* said the taller of the men, vigorously shaking West's hand.

"¿Qué pasa, West?" said the other, his dark eyes and white teeth flashing.

Grinning, West greeted the pair in Spanish, then turned, laid a gentle hand on Elizabeth's arm, and said, inclining his head to the two smiling Mexicans, "Mrs. Curtin, Edmund, *los hermanos Ruiz."* To the brothers Ruiz, he said, "Rio, Roberto, may I present Senora Elizabeth Curtin and Senor Edmund Curtin."

"Señora, Señor," the Ruiz brothers said in unison, *"Buenos días. ¿Cómo están ustedes?"*

"Muy bien. Gracias," Elizabeth replied warmly, charmed by the two small, mannerly Mexican men.

All smiles, the brothers' dark eyes rested solely on her. Addressing West, they chattered excitedly in Spanish, and Elizabeth, able to catch a word here and there, heard *ojizarca* and *pelo rojo* and *hermosa* and *magnífica.* She was curious.

West answered the brothers in Spanish, shaking his head and smiling easily.

"What are they saying, Quarternight?" Elizabeth asked, smiling at the two Mexicans.

"The Ruiz brothers are amazed by your blue eyes and red hair. They say you are beautiful, a truly magnificent lady."

Elizabeth quickly thanked the Ruizes. Smiling, she said, *"Gracias, gracias."*

"Shall we get started?" Edmund asked eagerly, walking toward a square table loaded down with men's pants. Rio and Roberto Ruiz hurried after him, sizing him up, arguing over which cut of trousers would best fit him.

"And you"—Elizabeth turned slowly to West—

"when you answered the Ruiz brothers. What did you say?"

"Why, that I agree: *sí, con mucho gusto.*" His warm silver gaze slowly lowered from her face to where the soft light fell on the smooth slope of her exposed throat. "That I think you are a magnificent blue-eyed, red-haired beauty."

Feeling suddenly uncomfortably warm, Elizabeth wondered how West Quarternight managed to make the simplest of compliments sound decidedly familiar. Sexual even. She swallowed nervously.

"Gracias," she said, almost resentfully, turned, and walked away. She knew, without looking back, that those gleaming silver eyes followed, stripping the clothes from her body.

West and the Curtins spent more than two hours inside the Ruiz Brothers' general store. Leaning on one of the square merchandise tables, West smoked a cigar and watched, genuinely amused, as Edmund Curtin enthusiastically chose his personal gear for the upcoming journey.

Caught up in the excitement of being a rough, tough outdoorsman, Edmund chose several cotton shirts, some silk bandannas, a half-dozen pair of trousers of denim and twill and soft buckskin. A wide intaglioed leather belt with a silver buckle, a pair of matching leather cowboy cuffs. A leather vest. Some shotgun chaps. A fringed suede jacket. Two pair of handmade boots. And, finally, a wool-felt cowboy hat.

Elizabeth was far more conservative. She picked out only a pair of serviceable suede gloves, a brown flat-crowned hat with drawstring, and a couple of colorful silk bandannas.

"That all you're getting?" West walked over to her, toyed with the pair of rust suede gloves she had placed on the counter.

"It is. I already have everything I'll need."

"Really? You have tall leather boots and sturdy trousers and some long-tailed shirts? Wool socks and heavy cotton underwear?"

"Of course not! A lady, Mr. Quarternight, does not go about dressed like a man."

"The lady who goes where we're heading, Mrs. Curtin, is going to wish to hell she was dressed like a man."

19

"You won't tell, will you?"

"No, I won't tell."

"Thank you, Elizabeth," said Edmund gratefully. "I feel so foolish. I wouldn't want him to know that I—"

"He won't. Now just lie here quietly until you're feeling better."

"Yes, I'll do that," said the pale, suffering man.

It was not quite noon. After spending the better part of the morning purchasing supplies at Ruiz Brothers, Edmund had seemed more than anxious to return to the hotel. When West had suggested they all go out to Jorge Acosta's horse rancho, two miles east of Santa Fe, to pick out some saddle ponies and pack burros, Edmund had curiously begged off. Pointing out that he trusted West's judgment, he asked West to go on out alone, or to take Elizabeth, if she wished to go.

She did not care to go, she had quickly let it be known. She and Edmund had returned to their hotel while West promised to ride out to the Acosta rancho sometime after lunch.

Once back inside the comfort and privacy of the La

Fonda suite, Edmund had admitted the truth to his sister-in-law.

He was sick.

The hot, spicy breakfast had played havoc with his stomach and for the past hour he had been in agony. Tempted to say "I told you so," instead Elizabeth had sympathized. Urging him into his bedroom, she had ordered him to take off his coat and shoes and lie down. He hadn't argued.

While Edmund stretched out, she had poured cool, clean water into a porcelain pan, dipped a clean washcloth into the water, squeezed it out, folded it meticulously, and draped it across Edmund's perspiring forehead. She then went about pulling the heavy curtains and shutting out the harsh sunlight.

He murmured his thanks as she tiptoed out, closing the door behind her. Poor Edmund. He wouldn't feel like getting out of his room for the rest of the day.

Afraid she might bump into West if she went downstairs for lunch, Elizabeth had a light meal sent up. She couldn't interest Edmund in even trying some of the clear beef broth, so she ate alone. Afterwards, she took a long, cooling bath and stretched out on her bed. She read for a while, but found she was too restless, too full of energy, to get really interested in the book.

She dressed again, choosing a crisp cool blue-and-white gingham shirtwaist with a round collar and short puffy sleeves. She checked on Edmund and found him sleeping peacefully. She smiled and pulled his door shut.

Fidgety, she prowled the sitting room, crossed it, stepped out onto the hotel balcony, and stood looking out over the plaza. The city had suddenly become quiet and somnolent, the plaza nearly deserted. The shops surrounding the square were closing their doors.

Siesta time in Santa Fe.

A tranquil calm fell over the beautiful sky-high city. A hushed, peaceful silence descended over the verdant little valley and over its shuttered adobe residences. An atmosphere of total serenity settled over the calm, quiet valley.

Elizabeth pushed her long, unbound red hair back over her shoulders. While the warm alpine sun kissed her face, she looked down on the placid plaza. But she felt no peace. She was troubled. She was restless. She was confused.

She slowly lifted her eyes to gaze up at the towering mountains ringing the quiet valley.

Strong mountain winds swayed the scrubby juniper and tall green pines. Above the timberline, clouds veiled the highest summits and traces of snow still clung to the rugged cliffs and barren rock.

If the valley seemed serenely tame and safe, the majestic mountains with their soaring scarps and twisted peaks appeared wild and dangerous. The contrast was awesome. While charmed by the calm meadow village, Elizabeth felt a quickening of her pulse, a shortness of breath, as she gazed at those unreachable pinnacles framed against the clear blue sky.

As she stood there entranced, feeling helplessly drawn to the wild beauty of the forested slopes and barren sun-soaked plateaus and soaring peaks, the bothersome thought occurred to her.

Her husband, Dane Curtin, was like the pleasant peaceful valley. West Quarternight, like the beautiful, forbidding mountains.

Dane was blondly attractive, warmhearted, settled, trustworthy, respectful, and safe.

Quarternight was darkly handsome, callous, incorrigible, disreputable, disrespectful, and dangerous.

A chill shot up her spine.

Dear Lord, here she was, too close to admitting a terrible truth. Tearing her eyes from the mesmerizing mammoth monoliths, Elizabeth whirled about and rushed back indoors.

Once inside she reasoned that there was no real need for concern. Why not admit the truth and face the facts like the logical-thinking adult she prided herself on being? West Quarternight was a ruggedly handsome man with a sexual magnetism and self-assurance that women—all women, herself included—naturally feared, but were drawn to as well. His was the lethal brand of charm found in reckless, worthless scamps no woman could hope to hold. Which, of course, made every woman long to hold him.

Why did she suppose she should be immune? How could she be? Especially since she had certain guilty knowledge that the dark, dangerous Quarternight was all every woman dreamed he'd be and more. He was the hot, sexual animal they imagined. A skilled and exciting lover capable of stripping away any woman's inhibitions along with her clothes. If he were not the ultimate seducer, would she have allowed him to make love to her on a hay strewn floor while a guard slept just around the corner?

Certainly not.

West Quarternight, even with a bushy beard and a too-thin frame, had been powerfully persuasive.

Why should she expect herself to be so different from all the others? Hadn't she seen the beautiful Doña Hope slip away from the Governor's Spring Baile to spend one golden hour in Quarternight's arms? And the Mexican waitress at breakfast had made no secret of the fact she would be his for the taking.

All right, so she would admit it! She, too, Elizabeth Montbleau Curtin, was once unwillingly attracted by his strong allure; so sexual, so forceful, so powerfully male.

But that did not put her in the ranks with the blond doña or the Mexican waitress. She would be no man's fool, certainly not West Quarternight's.

Let women who court danger and hurt have the menacing mountains. As for herself, she'd had more than enough pain in her life. She would be perfectly content with the peaceful valley meadows for the rest of her days.

Elizabeth picked up her discarded book and sat down to read. Ten minutes later she again tossed it aside. Feeling she would scream if she stayed cooped up all afternoon, Elizabeth looked in on Edmund, found him still asleep, closed the door, and went to the pine writing desk on the east wall of the sitting room.

Not bothering to pull out the chair and sit down, she drew a sheet of beige parchment paper from the desk's middle drawer, took a pen from the inkwell, and hurriedly jotted a note informing her brother-in-law that she had gone shopping to pick up a few small items she needed for the trip.

It was not until she was downstairs, through the empty hotel lobby, and out on the quiet street that she remembered it was siesta time. All the shops were closed and would stay closed until four o'clock.

Elizabeth sighed.

She looked up one side of the deserted street, and down the other.

She supposed she should go back upstairs, but felt she couldn't bear it. She'd take a walk. Do some window shopping. See if she could spot a new hat for tomorrow morning's important church ceremonies, the laying of the cornerstone for Bishop Lamy's new St. Francis Cathedral.

Elizabeth sauntered around the plaza, stopping to

gaze into shop fronts, finding it strange to be the only person on the streets. It was eerily quiet. Even the cats and dogs were dozing in the warm sunshine. Smiling, Elizabeth started to step around a sleek black tomcat asleep on the flat stone *portal* of El Palacio Real.

She jumped, startled, when the pantherlike creature made low, growling sounds of menace deep in the back of his throat. Elizabeth stopped short. The shiny black cat slowly raised his regal head and opened his cold golden eyes. He lay there motionless, like the sphinx, staring at her. Not quite brave enough to stroke him, Elizabeth leaned down, put her hands on her knees, and said aloud, "If you think I'm afraid of you, you're wrong. I could have you purring in a matter of seconds." The golden eyes gleamed and a strange rattling sound came from down deep in the cat's black chest. Elizabeth straightened, shivered, and slowly backed away. Waiting until she was ten feet from the cat, she turned around and went on her way, smiling again.

She looked up, and her smile grew wider. At the far end of the palace, on the broad shaded *portal*, sat the old Navajo woman, Micoma. From the distance, Elizabeth couldn't tell if she was asleep, so she approached quietly, not wishing to disturb her if she was sleeping.

Elizabeth was still some distance away when the gray head turned in her direction, a toothless smile spread over the wrinkled brown face, and a bony, arthritic hand lifted.

"Micoma," Elizabeth said happily and hurried to her. Shaking the thin hand in both of her own, she said, "It seems we're the only ones awake. May I visit with you for a while?"

The watery black eyes shining, Micoma said, "I look for you sooner."

Like a little girl, Elizabeth dropped down on the porch. Drawing her legs up under her and spreading her skirts out, she said, "Sooner? Micoma, I didn't know I was coming here until—"

"But I know," Micoma interrupted. "I tell you to come. You not hear? You not come outdoors while others sleep?" Again the toothless smile.

"Why, I guess I did. I was in the hotel and I felt so restless, like I couldn't stay inside another minute." She smiled at Micoma. "Was that your doing?"

Micoma's black eyes disappeared into creases of weathered skin and she nodded, pleased with herself. "Micoma's doing," she bragged softly. Opening her eyes, she said, as she had the other time, "Never see such hair before. Hold out, so Micoma can get better look."

Glad to oblige, Elizabeth put the tips of her fingers through the ends of her long, unbound hair. She moved her hands out away from her head, allowing the fiery locks to spread like a huge silken fan.

While the ancient Indian woman stared in wonder at the "hair on fire," someone else was quietly admiring its blazing glory from afar.

A hat pulled low on his forehead, a cigar planted firmly between his teeth, West Quarternight was just across Lincoln Avenue, outside the now silent Red Dawg Saloon. Lolling lazily in a straight chair tipped back on two legs, his own long legs were stretched out before him, his moccasined feet resting atop the hitchrail.

His narrowed silver-gray eyes were on the blazing red hair.

Elizabeth might as well have waved a crimson red flag before a charging bull.

West had seen her the minute she stepped·out of the hotel. Had watched her idly stroll around the plaza, stopping to look in store windows. Had observed her shy flirtation with the dozing black cat. He had watched it all and remained totally still. When she quickly backed away from the cat, he was quietly amused, knowing she was a little bit afraid of the big black tom. He had watched as she headed down the long porch of the palace. Had caught her look of joy when she had seen Micoma. And he had smiled when —like an adorable child—she had sat down on the porch with Micoma.

All that, he had watched in unmoving silence. Keeping his distance. Purposely staying away from her. Allowing her the pleasure of the warm afternoon, the freedom of being out on her own and unbothered by him or anyone else.

But now she had gone too far.

That wild mane of bright cinnamon hair all spread out with the sunlight striking it was more than he could stand.

West urged the two front legs of his chair back down to the plank floor. He lifted his moccasined feet from the hitchrail, then lowered them to the sidewalk. He rose, took the cigar from his mouth, and flicked it out into the dusty street. He took off his hat, lifted his arm, and ran his long brown fingers through his hair, then put the pearl-gray hat back on, pulling the brim low.

He stepped down off the roofed walk, and as silently as an Indian, moved toward the seductive shimmer of that remarkable red hair blazing in the afternoon sunlight. Unhurried, West moved steadily closer, like a predator calmly stalking his unsuspecting prey.

Elizabeth was blissfully unaware of West's presence, but the old woman knew he was coming long before he got up from his chair.

And she knew more.

She knew that the tall, dark man calmly approaching didn't realize it, and would have laughed had she told him, but his role—the one he played so effortlessly, was so comfortable with—would one day change. The day would come when he would not be the predator, but the prey. No longer the hunter, but the hunted. And possibly, if he were not very careful, the victim instead of the victor.

But not now.

On this quiet warm afternoon the power was all his. He was coming for this red-haired woman. He would take her away. The woman would struggle against her fascination for him. She would fight him as no other woman ever had. But her attempts to resist him, her unwillingness to surrender, her strong indomitable spirit, would only further draw him to her.

So that finally her beautiful blazing hair, which was now pulling him to her, would one day ignite more than his body. His heart would burn as well.

Suddenly, Micoma frowned with worry and confusion.

Was this tall, dark man coming toward them one of her sons? This innocent-looking woman with hair of fire was married!

It was not good. These two had no future together. She couldn't allow this smiling red-haired woman to break her son's heart.

Abruptly Micoma leaned close to Elizabeth, clutched her arm in a death grip. She said firmly, "My son comes now to join us. You must ignore him! I will send him away."

"But why?" asked Elizabeth, releasing her hair, and turning her head to look around.

West Quarternight silently stood on the stone porch directly behind Elizabeth, between her and the sun. Removing his hat, he said, "Afternoon, Micoma, Mrs. Curtin."

Her flat black eyes flashing with alarm, Micoma said, "You go away! Do not take this woman with you!"

West stepped closer, but remained standing, his long brown fingers gripping the brim of his hat.

"What's wrong?" he asked softly, looking at Micoma. "What have I done?"

"Not done it yet," Micoma spit out. "And better not do!"

Elizabeth said nothing. She was baffled by the old Navajo's behavior. And she was uneasy with West Quarternight standing so close. His hard thigh was inches from her face and she couldn't help noticing the way his soft leather trousers clung to his slim hips and long legs.

She heard him saying calmly, "I'm going, Micoma. I'll see Mrs. Curtin back to her hotel." He put a firm hand under Elizabeth's arm and effortlessly drew her to her feet.

"No." Elizabeth protested weakly and looked down at Micoma for support.

She got none. The old woman who had so vehemently warned West away was now smiling and nodding, her reasons for wanting him to leave Elizabeth alone now forgotten.

Now she saw only her old friend, the brave mountain guide, West Quarternight, standing alongside her new friend, the beautiful Fire Hair, and she was pleased by the sight of them together.

West had no idea what the old woman was thinking, but he took full advantage of the change. His fingers imprisoning Elizabeth's upper arm, he smiled engagingly and said to the old Navajo, "Micoma, tell Fire Hair she must come along with me."

Micoma, disarmed by the smile, and supposing the pair belonged together, said to Elizabeth, "You go now with him."

"But, Micoma—"

"Mind old Micoma, Fire Hair."

"You heard her," said West triumphantly. "Say good-bye."

"Good-bye, Micoma. I'll see you again." Elizabeth said.

"Good afternoon, Micoma," West touched his hat brim with thumb and forefinger, gently turned Elizabeth about, and guided her down the stone porch.

"That was a high-handed trick, Mr. Quarternight, and it's just not going to work!"

His eyes on the cloud of shimmering red hair that had lured him across the square, he replied softly, "I believe, Mrs. Curtin, it already has. I have you, don't I?"

"You'll never have me, Quarternight!"

20
ᘒᘒᘒ

West didn't answer immediately. His fingers closing loosely but firmly around Elizabeth's upper arm, he silently ushered her back along the palace porch, the way she had come.

But at the end of the block, West drew her swiftly around the corner and headed in the opposite direction of the La Fonda. Frowning, Elizabeth stopped like a balky mule and tried to wrench herself away from him.

Almost roughly, West whirled her about into a shadowed doorway, pressed her up against the solid portal, and leaned close.

"Never, you said? I'll never have you?" West asked, his slate-gray eyes shining with a hot light, his brown hands spread on either side of the door, trapping her. "Perhaps you've forgotten Shreveport."

More angry than frightened, Elizabeth lifted both hands to push on his chest. Her blue eyes cold, she said truthfully, "I recall it every day, Quarternight. My shame is exceeded only by my fury."

"Ah, sweetheart, forget shame and fury." He lowered a hand, clasped a long lock of flaming red hair and lifted it to his face. Trailing the silky ends over his nose and mouth, he said softly, "Remember the passion and pleasure."

"Let go of my hair," Elizabeth ordered hotly. "And let go of me! What if someone should see us!"

"No one will. It's siesta time. Everyone's in bed." His gaze left her hair, went to her mouth. "And that's where we ought to be. Let's go to bed."

"You will *not* talk to me this way!"

Elizabeth gave West a forceful shove, but her hand slipped on the hard muscle of his chest and slid inside his half-open gray chambray shirt. Her sensitive fingertips encountered crisp, dark hair. Her gaze immediately dropped to that deep wedge of dark curling hair at the V of his open shirt. Flustered, she anxiously tried to withdraw her hand. But his came down atop it, pressing her palm to his heart.

"Leave it," West ordered. "Leave it and feel how fast my heart beats when I'm with you."

Her hand trapped beneath his, her palm flattened on his bare chest, Elizabeth felt the rapid, heavy cadence of his heartbeat thrumming against her spread fingers and couldn't help but be thrilled by the passion she aroused in him. Her knees weakened and for a long moment Elizabeth was smitten, frozen, suspended, in a hypnotic spell.

West sensed her resistance diminishing. He confidently moved closer, bent a knee forward, and nudged her legs apart. "Kiss me," he said, his dark head slowly bending. "Kiss me with your hand on my heart."

Half-tempted to do what he asked, curious to see if his heart would race from her kiss, Elizabeth slowly shook her head from side to side and murmured, "No . . . I . . . can't . . . I—"

"Sure you can, sweetheart," West murmured encouragingly, then foolishly pressed his luck by going on to say, "Then I'll kiss you with my hand on your heart."

"Never!" she hissed, jerked her hand out of his open shirt, and began struggling anew.

"Ah, no, don't—"

"You let go of me, West Quarternight!" Elizabeth shouted loudly, pushing on him with all her strength.

"Not yet. Not until you've kissed me."

"You're crazy if you think I'm going to kiss you. Now let me go, I mean it. Let me go . . . let me—"

From very near, a man growled loudly, startling them both.

And all at once a hand—the largest hand Elizabeth had ever seen—took hold of West's starched shirt collar. One minute West's tall, lean body was pressing her to the carved door, the next he was being yanked away as easily as if he were a helpless infant.

Elizabeth blinked in stunned horror.

Frozen in place, she saw West being hauled backward by a terrifying giant, a fierce, heavily muscled Indian who was so huge he towered over the tall, lean West. Heart hammering with fear, Elizabeth snapped out of her paralysis and instinctively became protective of West.

"No!" Elizabeth screamed, reacting. She lunged wildly at the huge Indian and pummeled the bullying giant with both fists, frantically shouting at him to let West alone. "Don't hurt him! He wasn't doing anything. He wasn't! Let him go at once!"

Surprised and relieved when the massive Indian suddenly released West, Elizabeth threw her arms around West's trim waist and buried her face in his brown throat.

"Are you all right, West? Did he hurt you?" she shuddered, near tears.

"I'm fine, sweetheart, fine," West assured her, embracing her.

Trembling against him, her eyes closed, Elizabeth heard laughter. Loud laughter. Masculine laughter. Coming from behind her.

West, his arms around her, his hand gently patting her back, was laughing too. Confused, Elizabeth opened her eyes, lifted her head, and gave West a questioning look. Gently he disengaged her arms from around him and slowly turned her about in front of him.

There stood the gigantic Indian before her, so tall the silver concho belt going around his big waist was almost at eye level. Fearfully, Elizabeth tipped her head way back and looked up at his face.

His features were blunt, harsh, as if carved out of hard, dark mahogany. His shoulders were massive and bulging muscles pulled the fabric of his bright turquoise Navajo blouse. A matching turquoise headband held the straight black hair off his face. Soft doeskin pants hugged his awesome thighs and muscled legs, and on his big feet were intricately beaded moccasins. A wide silver bracelet gleamed on his powerful right wrist, and rings of turquoise and silver flashed on his thick fingers.

With his unblinking black eyes and his immense size, Elizabeth found the Indian to be a figure so frightening she instinctively swayed back closer against West.

West lifted his hands and cupped her shoulders.

Elizabeth tore her gaze from the Indian and looked at the man beside him. Barely reaching to the Indian's shoulder stood a weathered-faced man in fringed buckskins. He had flowing white hair, a full white beard, and a drooping white mustache. Beneath the full mustache, pink lips were turned up into a broad smile. Bright blue eyes twinkled at her.

Close to her ear, West said, "Mrs. Curtin, I'd like you to meet my partners. The big guy is Taos." The giant Indian nodded, smiled down at Elizabeth, but said nothing. "And this white-haired rascal that was growling so loudly is Grady Downs."

Grady wiped his hand on his buckskin trousers, stepped eagerly forward, and thrust it out to Elizabeth. "Pleased to meet you, ma'am," he said, cut his eyes to West, then back to her. "Looks like we got here just in time." He grinned from ear to ear. The still-silent Indian was smiling too. So was West.

Elizabeth did not smile.

Incensed, she realized that neither of his partners had actually been appalled by West Quarternight's disgraceful caveman behavior. On the contrary, it seemed that they fully approved and were amused by his conduct. They had only been teasing West—not trying to save her! The entire incident had been nothing more than a good joke to the lot of them! And the laugh was on her! Well, she saw nothing funny about it!

"Mr. Downs, Taos," Elizabeth said coolly, quickly withdrawing her hand from Grady. "If you'll all excuse me, I must get back to the hotel."

"I'll see you safely back," said West.

"You're the only danger around!" she snapped acidly, whirled, and stalked angrily away while the three men, West, Grady, and Taos, smiled and watched her walk away.

His narrowed gray gaze on the flaming red hair bouncing on her shoulderblades, West said to Grady, "Why didn't my mama buy me one like that?"

Grady shook his white head, stroked his flowing white beard, and replied, "Sonny, 'cause that fiery redhead is likely more woman than you could ever handle." The feisty mountain man hooted with laughter and poked the giant Indian in the ribs. Taos nodded and laughed.

West laughed too.

"Hell, Grady, maybe you're right," admitted West. "Her temper sure matches her red hair."

Grady asked, "You say her name's Curtin? The same Mrs. Curtin—"

"She is," West slapped at his chest pocket, searching for a cigar, his eyes still clinging to Elizabeth's quickly retreating form. "She's the wife of the man we've been hired to find—our employer, no less."

Grady immediately frowned. "She ain't going down the trail with us, is she, Sonny? A woman on the search . . ." He started shaking his white head.

"Says she is."

"Thunderation!" Grady muttered. "Looky here, Sonny, all kiddin' aside, you gotta' leave her alone."

"Sure," said West, who turned, smiled, and gave Grady's hat brim a playful yank downward. "I will, *compadre.* I will."

Irritably shoving his dusty Stetson back up in place, Grady snorted, "It sure didn't look like you were leavin' her alone when me and Taos rode into town."

"As I recall, Grady," West said calmly, "you're the one who likes to say that things are not always what they appear."

"Weston Dale, you a-tellin' me you wasn't tryin' to steal a kiss from that red-haired woman?" Grady looked up at the big Indian. "Did you hear that, Taos? I never heard such a bald-faced lie in all my life, did you?"

The Indian nodded his head, agreeing.

"Jesus, Taos," West said, "don't get him started."

But it was too late.

Grady had already gotten started. He scolded and preached and shook his finger in West's face. Ignoring him, West drew a cigar from his breast pocket, lit it, and casually walked away.

". . . and never did cotton to no man messin' with another's wife. So if that's . . ." Grady paused, scratched his white head, and hollered, "Where you going, Sonny?"

Not bothering to stop, or even to turn around, West called over his shoulder, "Out to see Jorge Acosta about buying some horses and pack mules."

Grady looked up at Taos. He grabbed the big man's shirt sleeve and, dragging him, started after West. "Well, hell, Sonny, don't you want old Taos and me to help do the pickin'? I'm the one knows good horse-flesh when I see it!"

Finally West stopped walking. He took the cigar from his mouth, looked at the approaching pair. "Come along if you like, but not another word about Mrs. Curtin. You understand?"

Grady shot a glance at Taos. "You understand, Taos?" The Indian solemnly nodded his head. "We understand, Sonny," Grady said, turning back to West.

Over Grady's head, Taos grinned at West, lifted a big hand, pressed his fingers to his thumb, drew them wide apart, then repeated the gesture several times in imitation of Grady's constant tongue-wagging. West easily read the message as Taos rolled his black eyes skyward.

"Okay. Now that that's settled, let's go," said West.

"Sure thing, Sonny," Grady fell into step beside him. "What do you figure we'll need? Say, a dozen saddle ponies? Now, don't neither one of you two go lookin' at no white horses. Them white ones show up too good in the moonlight if there's any hostiles any-wheres about. I never did put much faith in chest-nuts, although . . . Did you have much trouble find-ing some Mexican hands to go with us on the expedition? They're all so doggone superstitious, them and the Indians . . . What's the Curtin fellow like that's come out here to hunt his brother? He like the rest of them Easterners, Sonny? Taking for granted all of us Westerners are uncouth illiterates?

Damnation, that makes me mad as a hornet, don't it you? Them silly-dressed tinhorns come out here acting superior like we was . . . You listenin' to me, Sonny? Taos, he listenin' to me?"

21

In all, they were thirteen.

The search party consisted of the three guides, the eight Mexican helpers, and Edmund and Elizabeth Curtin. Thirteen.

Nobody mentioned aloud that thirteen was an unlucky number, but the thought had occurred to several of them.

Not to Elizabeth, however. Not even momentarily did she consider its possible implication. When she came out of the La Fonda with Edmund at dawn Monday, the seventeenth of May, she felt optimistic and eager to begin what she hoped would prove to be a highly successful journey. A journey that would reconcile her with her missing husband.

The chill of the high desert night still clung to the thin morning air, but Elizabeth didn't mind. She knew it would soon be gone. Already the tallest peaks of the Jemez and the Sangre de Cristo ranges were tinged a pleasing pink from the rapidly rising sun. Within minutes the peaceful valley would start turning light.

Lined up in the dim, chill dawn at the edge of the hotel's roofed walk stood the Curtins' three hired

guides, West Quarternight, Grady Downs, and Taos.
Walking toward the trio, Elizabeth caught them exchanging quick, almost imperceptible looks. She saw
fleeting smiles cross their faces and knew immediately what was responsible for their amusement.

At her side, Edmund was decked out in all the western finery he had purchased at Ruiz Brothers. Compared with their scouts' comfortable buckskins, her
brother-in-law *was* a trifle overdressed. In his new
brown cowboy boots, stiff denim trousers, wide intaglioed belt with heavy silver buckle, red cotton shirt,
leather cowboy cuffs, white silk bandanna, fringed
suede jacket, and white, high-crowned felt hat, Edmund looked exactly like what he was: a cultured
Eastern gentleman eager to play the role of a tough
Westerner. Bless his heart, all he'd managed was to
look more like a greenhorn than ever.

Elizabeth was glad she had made no effort to appear more western. She felt completely comfortable
in the fashionable maroon gabardine traveling suit
she'd worn on the trip to Santa Fe. In a lace-trimmed,
high-throated blouse of pale pink, fitted, long-sleeved
suit jacket, wide-gored skirt, sensible kid slippers, and
the flat-crowned hat she had purchased at Ruiz Brothers, Elizabeth was confident she was dressed just
right.

Anxiously, she looked at Edmund, afraid her
brother-in-law might have caught the guides' knowing grins and glances.

But Edmund was smiling broadly, totally pleased
with himself, so proud of his new western wardrobe
he imagined the others were envious. Fond of her
good-hearted brother-in-law, Elizabeth was relieved.

Edmund stepped forward to shake West's hand and
speak to him. Having no desire to say so much as
"good morning" to West Quarternight, Elizabeth re-

mained where she was, quietly surveying the rest of the ready caravan.

West and Grady Downs stood beside a sturdy buckwagon, its bed covered with a tarp, pots and pans hanging over the side, and a water keg lashed to the tailgate. The giant Indian, Taos, listened to something Grady said, and nodded. Then Grady climbed up onto the wagon seat while Taos turned and walked toward his mount, a huge dun stallion tethered to the hitchpost.

Besides Taos's dun stallion, Elizabeth counted twenty horses, some saddled, some not, and a dozen pack burros loaded down with supplies.

Standing silently beside their saddled Navajo ponies, eight hired Mexican men waited for the command to get under way. Of the eight, a half dozen were poor peasants, dressed in cotton shirts and baggy pants, men chosen for their strong backs and willingness to work. The other two were small, trim leather-trousered vaqueros, hired to handle the horses on the trail.

Elizabeth's gaze slowly returned to Edmund and West. More specifically to West. He was lounging negligently against the wagon wheel, a knee bent, a boot heel hooked over a wooden spoke, smoking a cigar.

Her dislike of him was intense; still, she was glad that he and his partners were their escorts on this dangerous search.

West Quarternight, she mused as she watched him, was a hard, unfeeling man who had no respect for anyone, who seemed not to care about anything. But then, neither was he afraid of anyone or anything. Perhaps the fact that nothing mattered to him was responsible for his fearlessness. The idea had not occurred to her before, but it made a great deal of sense. She had always suspected that those men who were bravest in battle were ofttimes disillusioned, world-weary souls who purposely courted death because they cared so little for life.

"Ready, Elizabeth?" Edmund's voice broke into her thoughts.

"Yes. Yes, I'm ready." She hurried forward.

Edmund turned to face her, smiled, and lightly clasped her shoulders. He said, "It's not too late to back out. You can stay on safely right here at the La Fonda until we return."

Elizabeth was highly conscious of West, still lounging against the wagon wheel—not six feet away. She could feel, rather than see, the slight smirk on his handsome face. West knew, damn him, that she was leery of going and leery of staying. If she went, she'd be in constant danger of his getting her off alone. If she stayed behind, she was in danger of his telling the dirt on her. Either way, he had her, the dirty dark devil!

"Let's get going, Edmund," she said to her brother-in-law.

"All right, my dear. Good luck!" He squeezed her shoulders and rushed away. He walked hurriedly toward a saddled chestnut gelding, so excited he forgot to help her up into the wagon.

"Not to worry, Mrs. Curtin." West lazily pushed away from the wagon wheel and stepped forward. "I'll give you a hand up."

"I don't need your help," she said, brushing past him.

But she did.

Elizabeth had never in her life attempted climbing up onto a wagon. She had ridden in all manner of fancy carriages, she had ridden horseback, but never had she ridden in a strange-looking tarp-covered buckboard wagon such as this one. The padded seat where Grady Downs waited was so high up off the ground, she had no idea how to go about getting up onto it.

But she'd die before she'd admit it.

Her chin lifting, she flung her flat-crowned hat up onto the wagon, grabbed the whip stock with one hand, the seat with the other, and pulled herself upward, vainly attempting to find something to step onto so that she could hoist herself up into the wagon. But her slippered foot found only air and she hung there, helpless and frustrated.

From the corner of her eye, she caught West shaking his head at Grady, and she knew that the little white-haired man had aimed to reach out and pull her on up. West had stopped him with a look.

Damn him to hot, eternal hell!

Elizabeth put her feet back to the ground and released her hold on the wagon. She yanked the maroon jacket that had ridden up her midriff back down into place, pushed at a wayward lock of hair that had fallen into her eyes, and gave it another try. Struggling, striving futilely to climb up onto the wagon, she became miserably aware that the entire caravan had now mounted and was ready and waiting for her.

Those in the desert expedition were not the only ones witnessing her acute embarrassment. The sidewalks were quickly filling with the curious who had come into town at this early hour to watch the procession ride out of Santa Fe. From the restaurants ringing the plaza, vaqueros and cowboys, having rushed through their breakfasts, hurried outdoors to join in the fun.

Carriages with well-dressed gentlemen inside had parked just across San Francisco Street to get an unobstructed view. There were even several ladies who had turned out for the occasion at this ungodly hour. Elizabeth supposed that the tall, dark guide in buckskins was responsible for their presence.

Knowing every eye was on her, Elizabeth felt her face flush hotly. The heat intensified when she heard West calmly say, "You're the stubbornest woman I've ever met. Why don't you let me give you a lift?"

"I can take care of myself," she shrieked.

"You're doing a pretty lousy job of it."

Elizabeth's head whipped around. West stood with his arms crossed over his chest, smiling devilishly, just waiting for her to beg for assistance. Well, he would wait until Gabriel blew his horn!

Teeth grinding, fury rising, Elizabeth released her hold on the whip stock and wagon seat. She pushed West out of her way, turned around facing away from the wagon, put her hands behind her atop the wheel, and boosted herself up to sit on it. From there she was able to turn to her right and grab the wagon's splashboard with both hands, swing her feet up and around to the floorboard, and triumphantly climb up onto the seat beside Grady Downs.

"Good for you, missy!" said Grady approvingly.

Elizabeth's hot face blazed with fire when she heard applause and whistles coming from the men lining the plaza. Grinding her teeth so forcefully her jaws ached, she stared straight ahead, wishing she could duck out of sight under the canvas covering the buck wagon.

She flinched when West easily stepped up on the wheel hub and leaned across her. Longing to shout at him, knowing she couldn't, Elizabeth closed her eyes against the too-close sight of his chest and right arm. He leaned so near she felt his body heat, caught his scent, made all the more powerful because her eyes were shut. He smelled of shaving soap and tobacco and that unique, mysterious masculine scent that was his and his alone.

Her eyes flew open when she felt something being pulled tautly across her body. She looked down to see

West's dark hands tightly cinching wide leather straps across her, straps which were attached to the back of the seat on either side of her. The straps had a big buckle, which was now resting directly atop her naval.

Her face turned an even brighter shade of red as West calmly, deftly buckled the wide imprisoning belt. As if that were not enough, he then had the audacity to turn his hand over and hook his little finger up under the wide leather strap.

"What in heaven's name are you doing?" she said through clenched teeth, slapping at his intrusive hand, praying no one but Grady could see what was going on.

Not looking at her, West slid his three other fingers under, placed his thumb atop the wide strap, and then yanked firmly.

"There, that ought to hold you," he said, lifting his dark head, finding her red, angry face scant inches from his own. Proud of his handiwork, satisfied that the safety strap he had rigged up was tight enough, he told her, "Mrs. Curtin, I'm only seeing to it that you don't get thrown out of the wagon."

"That's all it was, missy," Grady quickly put it. "Sonny's just thinking of your safety."

Ignoring Grady, Elizabeth said to West, "Well, if you don't get down this minute, *you* are going to get thrown off the wagon!"

"You're very welcome," West said. "Think nothing of it." And he lithely dropped to the ground.

He didn't immediately move away. He leaned down, lifted the trailing maroon skirts of Elizabeth's traveling suit, and tucked them neatly in around her feet and beneath the seat.

With blazing blue eyes she glared at him and said beneath her breath, "Get away from here!"

"I'm only making sure," he said, a thumb and finger

toying with her hem, "that you don't get your skirt caught in the wagon wheel. That could be disastrous."

"It's going to be disastrous for you, Quarternight, if you don't get away from me this minute and stay away!"

"I'm going," said he, grinned, and slowly backed off.

Fuming, Elizabeth watched as West turned and unhurriedly walked toward a sleek red sorrel. Big and powerful-looking, the beautiful creature was a mare. The frisky mare tossed her head and danced in place, obviously eager to get out and race the wind.

West reached the magnificent animal, looped the long reins over its well-shaped head, and patted its sleek, shiny neck. When he was fully confident that the angry Mrs. Curtin was watching him, West looked straight at Elizabeth, again stroked the gleaming red mare's throat, and inclined his dark head meaningfully toward her.

Elizabeth made a sour face, having no idea what he was trying to tell her. Not that she cared.

With an easy grace, West swung up into the saddle, stuck his booted feet into the stirrups, and wheeled the shimmering red animal away from the hitchrail. Elizabeth tried to withdraw inside herself when she realized West was reining the mare toward the wagon.

What was the vain bastard up to now? Didn't he know the entire city of Santa Fe was watching?

West urged the big mount alongside the wagon where Elizabeth sat stiffly on the seat. When she turned to wither him with a look, West said, "Notice anything about my chosen mount?"

"Only that the unfortunate creature has a fool astride her."

Grady chuckled loudly, slapped his thigh, and said, "She got you good that time, Sonny."

West said to Elizabeth, "Her coat is the exact same color as your hair." His brown hand again tenderly stroked the mare's shiny red withers. "I think I'll call her Lizzie. You like that name?"

Her face as red as the shimmering coat West stroked, Elizabeth said, "I hope *Lizzie* throws you and you land on your head!"

"Why, missy, that's the hardest part of him," said Grady, joining in enjoying the fun.

Looking only at Elizabeth, West said softly, "She won't. I know just how to handle her."

Seething, Elizabeth held her tongue as West, showboating grandly, backed the shiny sorrel away, so obviously pleased with himself she longed to smack him a good one. When he was directly in front of the wagon, West reined the sorrel about in a semi-circle.

From the saddle horn he took his hat, put it on his head, and pulled the brim low. He then turned in the saddle and looked back at the long procession, at the men and the animals all itching to be off.

He turned back around, raised his long right arm, and brought it down just as he lightly touched his spurred heels to the shiny red sorrel's belly.

The expedition was officially under way!

Spectators waved and cheered loudly as the long procession moved slowly down San Francisco toward Calisteio, where it would turn south. West, atop the prancing red mare, led the parade. After him came the buck wagon with Grady driving, Elizabeth on the seat beside him.

Directly behind the wagon was an overdressed, very excited Edmund Curtin, flanked by the two Mexican vaqueros. Each vaquero led a string of well-bunched Navajo ponies. Next came the mounted peasants leading the pack mules loaded with supplies.

Bringing up the very rear was the big Navajo, Taos,

his flat, black eagle eyes trained and constantly at the ready to roam the changing countryside as he guarded their back trail.

Elizabeth, glad to be on the way at last, felt her anger quickly dissipating as she, too, got fully caught up in the excitement. The spoked wheels beneath her turned, the wagon lurched forward behind a team of strong-backed mules, and the white-bearded Grady Downs shouted loudly, "Yee-ha, we're off!"

"Yee-ha!" Elizabeth mimicked, and smiled warmly when Grady looked around at her, his blue eyes twinkling.

"Missy, we're gonna have us a good time!" he predicted happily, shouting to be heard.

"Yes, we are," she agreed, shouting back.

Feeling suddenly lighthearted, Elizabeth raised her hand to wave to the crowds lining the streets. The growing throng—mostly men—were fully appreciative. Seeing the beautiful red-haired lady from New York City smiling and waving brought louder shouts, long, low whistles, and doffing of hats.

Warmed by all the male attention, Elizabeth decided it only fair to turn and wave to the gentlemen lining the other side of the street. Her face aglow, her lips parted in a genuine smile, she turned on the seat.

But she never waved to the stomping, shouting men calling to her from the south side of San Francisco. The swarm of gentlemen well-wishers was forgotten as her narrowed eyes zeroed in on the dark-haired man astride a gleaming sorrel mare directly ahead of her.

West Quarternight held, of all things, a bouquet of spring flowers in his tanned right hand. It took only a second for Elizabeth to learn where he had gotten them. As he rode the prancing mare along the broad central plaza, he was steadily pelted with colorful blossoms coming from both sides of San Francisco Street.

The flowers were tossed by women.

Elizabeth was astounded. And revolted. Attractive, handsomely dressed ladies in gleaming parked carriages were throwing flowers at West Quarternight as though he were a conquering hero off to do battle! They were blowing kisses to him and calling his name.

She couldn't believe her eyes when a beautiful young woman bounded down out of a covered black victoria, lifted the skirts of her lush rose-hued dress, and dashed right out into the street, her hand outstretched, a lone pink rose clutched tightly in pale fingers.

The forward woman, whose long, loose hair was as black as West's, ran straight to him, held out the pink rose, then coyly withdrew it when he reached for it. Holding it teasingly behind her back, she smiled up at West and said something to him.

In a flash he leaned low, put a long arm around the woman's small waist, and swept her from the ground. Laughing happily, the woman clung to his neck while her feet dangled against the sorrel's side. Then, whispering something to West, the laughing dark-haired woman broke the long stem off the pink rose and tucked the vivid blossom behind his right ear. She then clasped his tanned jaws between her palms and turned her pretty, expectant face up to his.

West kissed her fully on the mouth.

The crowd hooted and hollered.

Grady Downs laughed and slapped his thigh.

Elizabeth forced a smile. But it didn't reach her blazing blue eyes.

22

❧ ❧ ❧

Once the gold-brown adobes of New Mexico's capital city receded in the background, Elizabeth's mood began to sweeten. The sun had climbed high, coloring the few puffy clouds hanging over the western hills a red, molten gold. The rest of the sky was a clear, cloudless blue.

It was a fine morning, despite Grady Downs's unending monologue. Within minutes of boarding the wagon with the twinkly-eyed white-haired mountain man, Elizabeth had learned only to half listen, to nod at the appropriate intervals, and to smile when he went into howls of laughter, signaling he had just told a tale he thought hilarious. Later, perhaps, she might pay more attention to the talkative Grady's stories, but for now she wanted to meditate quietly, to savor the freshness and beauty of the New Mexico morning.

The thin dry air was pleasantly cool and so clear that the distant peaks of the Sandias, far to the south, appeared to be within walking distance. Blankets of wildflowers covered the verdant valley, adding their vivid splashes of color to the usual greens, golds, and rusts. The dew-kissed blossoms swayed gently in a mild morning breeze and pleasantly perfumed the air with their subtle fragrance.

While the wagon followed the deeply rutted river road, Elizabeth examined the dramatic scenery surrounding her. She was suddenly struck by the idea that already she dreaded returning to New York. Shocked by the realization, she idly wondered if she might possibly persuade Dane to stay on here in this incredible land of towering mountains and extraordinary sunsets and peaceful solitude.

Elizabeth bit the inside of her cheek.

There was no chance of getting the sophisticated native New Yorker, Dane Curtin, to remain way out here in the Western wilderness. If he stayed, he would only be miserable. Dane loved the teeming city with all its bustle and excitement and varied culture. As grand as the Governor's Santa Fe Spring Baile had been, it would not have been an affair that met with Dane's approval.

The conversation at the baile had consisted of cattle prices, horse races, gold mines, and politics. Dane preferred discussing stock market rumors, art collections, the theater, trips to the Continent, and the latest gossip involving New York's rich social set.

No, Dane Curtin would never be happy living in the remote New Mexico Territory. Well, no matter. Likely as not, by the time this expedition ended, she, too, would be more than anxious to get back to New York City.

For now, she would simply relax and enjoy the journey. And to think that she had dreaded it! Had been afraid it would be hard and taxing. How wrong she had been. It was wonderful to ride along, cool and comfortable, admiring the ever-changing countryside, communing with nature at its finest.

Elizabeth drew a long, refreshing breath and felt the too-tight leather strap cut into her belly. Her eyes dropped to the wide, restraining belt and she exhaled irritably. Such idiocy, binding her to the seat as if she were a wiggling child in danger of falling from the wagon. Well, she would remedy that soon enough.

Pushing her flat-crowned hat back, Elizabeth stripped the tight kid gloves from her hands, stuffed them into a large triangular suit pocket over her right breast, and unbuckled the large buckle cutting into her flesh.

". . . and then by the time I found Taos, I was . . . was . . ." Grady's white head swung around. "Now, missy, I don't know as I'd unbuckle that, if I was you. Sonny won't like it."

"Then *Sonny* can lump it," Elizabeth replied calmly.

Grady laughed, but his white eyebrows knitted together. "I know you don't cotton much to Sonny and I can't say as I blame you, considerin' the way he was actin' Saturday when me and Taos rode into Santa Fe."

"Well, thank you, Grady. I had the distinct impression that both you and Taos were amused by his despicable behavior."

"Naw, naw. Nothin' like that. What tickled us was that you didn't want no part of him." Grady turned back to look straight ahead.

"Why should that tickle you?"

"No reason 'cept we ain't never seen nothin' like that happen before." Grady cut his blue eyes at her, then back to the road. "I don't know, there's somethin' about Sonny that makes him like catnip to all the ladies."

"Oh, really?" Elizabeth said, as though surprised.

Her gaze lifted to the raven-haired man several yards ahead riding astride a cantering sorrel mare.

He rode the way he moved. The way he did everything. With a quiet sureness and power, handling his mount with the effortless grace of the born horse-man.

Elizabeth's mouth tightened with displeasure and she wondered if there was anything West Quarternight did not do well. He was that rare man who was constantly relaxed and radiating a consistent confidence. He wore a casual and content smile that managed to be at once both warm and sardonic.

"What? I'm sorry." Elizabeth suddenly realized that Grady had asked something, and was waiting for her answer.

"I was jest sayin' that I think the reason all them women want him is 'cause they can't have him. What do you think?"

"Perhaps that has something to do with it."

"Yep, I seen lots of pretty gals set their caps for Sonny." Grady reached up, stroked his long white beard thoughtfully. "Beats any goddamned . . . ah . . . excuse me, missy . . . beats anything I ever saw." He shook his head. "All of 'em is wastin' their time if they think they can catch him. I know him too well. Now, back when I first met Sonny over in—"

"Grady," Elizabeth cut him, not wanting to hear anything more about West Quarternight, "what about you? How long have you been a guide? What did you do before?"

"Well, let me see, missy, I guess I been at this for the last three or four years. Got started by . . ."

And Grady gladly filled her in on his adventurous past. In his time he had been, he proudly told her, a West Point cadet cashiered for drinking in his room, an Indian fighter, a scout for Frémont, a gunman, a mustanger, a trapper, a cowhand, a prospector, a drummer, a mountain man, and finally, a guide.

Elizabeth listened as he told of his many escapades. But when an hour had passed and still he regaled her with tales of his glory days, she relapsed into nodding occasionally, smiling now and then, and not really paying attention.

By late morning the sun had burned the fresh coolness from the air. Cocking her flat-crowned hat to the left in a vain effort to shade her face from the bright glare, Elizabeth felt beads of perspiration pooling between her breasts, behind her knees, and above her upper lip.

With each mile they traveled, the temperature climbed and Elizabeth began to wish she had worn something lighter than the heat-attracting dark maroon gabardine suit. She crooked her forefinger, curled it under the tight, high band of her blouse collar, and pulled the fabric away from her dewy throat.

The higher the sun rose, the lower they dropped in elevation. And the hotter it got. Not only had she become uncomfortably warm, Elizabeth had also grown tired. Her back had begun to ache, her bottom felt battered from being bounced about all morning, and her legs were stiff.

She twisted and turned and tried to get comfortable. It was impossible. She looked up at the sun and wondered when they would stop for lunch. She broke into Grady's long-winded meanderings to ask and he told her that Sonny would pick a nice, cool spot when it got close to dinnertime.

Elizabeth looked up ahead at West. Slumped comfortably in the saddle, his feet out of the stirrups now and swinging with the sorrel's easy gait, he didn't appear to be the least bit tired. Or hot.

Frowning, placing a spread hand to the small of her aching back, Elizabeth turned in her seat and looked back to search for Edmund. She saw him bouncing along on the chestnut gelding, his new fringed suede jacket now shed and draped across the saddle. Large circles of perspiration stained his new red western shirt. His white felt hat was pulled low, but his fair face had now turned as red as his shirt. Wondering if hers had burned as well, she waved to him and smiled encouragingly, knowing he was likely even more miserable than she.

Minutes after she turned back around, West abruptly pulled up on the sorrel. He halted, looked about, and neck reined the mare off the narrow dusty road. Grady immediately pulled up on the team. Behind the wagon, men and horses of the long caravan came to a stop.

West cantered down a slight incline toward a copse of tall cottonwoods. While Elizabeth and the rest of the procession watched and waited, West and the sorrel disappeared into the trees. In minutes he rode back into sight and headed directly toward the wagon.

He was hatless now and the sun, straight overhead, made his jet-black hair glisten like the sorrel's shiny coat. The pale pink rose from the beauty back in Santa Fe was still tucked behind his right ear.

Dismounting when he was a short distance away, he dropped the long reins to the ground and signaled to the waiting riders to break ranks and take the horses down to the river for water. Grady pulled the wagon off to the side of the road, jumped down, and began unhitching the team.

Elizabeth took off her flat-crowned hat, dropped it to the seat, and lifted a hand to smooth back her damp, tousled red hair. West stepped up to the wagon, draped an arm along the splashboard in front of her, and said, "What about it? You ready to rest for a while?"

Elizabeth shrugged aching shoulders. "I'm not particularly tired, but if you want to stop here, you're the guide."

West shook his dark head. He could tell by looking at her that she was exhausted.

He said, "God, it must be hard, never saying what's really on your mind."

"I'm sure I don't know what you're talking about."

"Now, that's what I mean exactly."

Elizabeth's jaw hardened. Levelly, she said, "All right. How's this for saying what's on my mind? I don't much like you, Quarternight. In fact I *dislike* you intensely."

West cocked a dark eyebrow. "You sure it's not yourself you dislike?" She blinked at him. He dropped his arm from the wagon's splashboard, reached out, gripped her knees with both hands and turned her about on the seat to face him. "Maybe you're mad at yourself because you like me too much. Could that be it, Mrs. Curtin? One time you liked me a lot. Liked me so much you—"

"Hush!" She glanced around to be sure nobody had heard. "You ever so much as hint at that night again and I'll make you live to regret it."

"Ah, well, one more regret at my age won't make much difference," he drawled. Firmly clasping the backs of her knees with long fingers, his thumbs made lazy circles atop her legs through the maroon gabardine. "Let's make love now and regret it later."

"Get your hands off me, Quarternight."

"I will, but first let me see if . . . ah . . . there . . . I thought so." His thumbs were skimming along the top edges of Elizabeth's silk stockings. "This is where your stockings come to? It is, isn't it?"

"Unless you want them broken," Elizabeth warned, "you better get your thumbs off my knees!" Viciously she dug her long nails into the backs of his brown hands.

"Ouch! Jesus!" he swore, and quickly released her, but did not move away. Looking down at the tiny red half-moons decorating the backs of his hands, he said, "For a woman who's been around, you still have a lot to learn." His teasing gray gaze lifted to her snapping blue eyes. "It's my back you're supposed to claw, not my hands."

"That's it!" she hotly declared, pushing roughly on his chest. "Let me get down!"

West just laughed, reached out and spanned her narrow waist with his hands. "I'll help you out of the carriage."

"Thanks!" she snapped irritably, and avoiding his eyes, tentatively placed her hands on his muscular shoulders. Nervously she glanced about and saw that the others, including Edmund, had already gone down to the river. Her gaze returned to West and fell on the bright pink blossom tucked behind his right ear. The sight of it fueled her anger.

West lifted Elizabeth from the wagon deliberately slowly. His strong hands firmly gripping her waist, he plucked her from the seat, held her up before him, then turned slowly around with her in his arms.

He leaned back against the wagon and lifted Elizabeth higher. He tipped his head back and smiled up at her.

She didn't smile back. Her hands frantically clutching the buckskin shirt stretching across his wide shoulders, she kicked violently at his knees and hissed, "Put me down! I mean it, put . . . me . . . *down!*"

"Well, sure, you want down," he said, "I'll put you down."

Continuing to hold her high, West drew Elizabeth flush against his body. Held her there for a long moment with her pelvis pressing his chest. Then slowly, sensuously, he lowered her, feeling the soft, feminine curves of her slender body slide seductively against his hard-planed frame.

Elizabeth's long skirts did not slither down with her. The maroon gabardine bunched and clung to

West's buckskin shirt and pants. The lower he allowed her to drop, the higher her skirts rose.

West was aware of her anger and frustration, but far more aware of the soft female breasts an inch from his face, of the fiery red hair ablaze in the noon sunshine, of the pale, slender legs bared by the trapped skirts.

Inhaling deeply, West felt the soft kid gloves stuffed into her breast pocket tickle his jaw.

Grinning, he told her, "I'm afraid the finger of your left glove might poke my eye out. Think you could move them?"

"It would serve you right," Elizabeth said, but yanked the gloves from her pocket. And then wished she hadn't.

"That's better," he said and leaned closer to her breasts.

Elizabeth slapped him on the head with the gloves. "Get your face out of my . . . my . . . way!"

His dark face stayed where it was, his warm, smooth lips pressing the pink blouse to her flesh. He blew a long, hot breath through the thin cotton and felt, against his chest and belly, her involuntary shuddering response.

Satisfied he could arouse her when time and place presented itself, he let her go, allowing her to slide all the way to the ground. But he bent his dark head to catch a pleasing glimpse of her shapely stockinged legs before he released her.

As soon as she felt her toes touch the earth, Elizabeth straightened her skirts, whirled around, and stalked off.

West called after her, "Aren't you going to wait for me? Remember, I'm the guide here."

Not even slowing, she called over her shoulder, "Then guide yourself to the nearest lunatic asylum!"

West bent and picked up her dropped kid gloves.

He allowed Elizabeth to walk a little farther, then called, "Mrs. Curtin, you forgot something."

"You're lying, of course," she shouted back, but slowed.

"If Edmund sees me with your gloves in my pocket, he might wonder where I got them."

Elizabeth stopped walking. She looked down at her breast pocket. Slowly she turned and looked back.

West stood there leaning lazily against the wagon wheel, calmly dangling her gloves between thumb and forefinger.

"Would you kindly bring them to me?" she asked, knowing the answer before the words were out of her mouth.

"You want them. Come get them." He stuffed them into his breast pocket and crossed his arms over his chest.

As mad as a hornet, her hands balled into tight fists at her sides, Elizabeth stormed back across the meadow. When she reached him, she said nothing. She snatched her gloves from his shirt pocket, slapped him in the face with them, then spun around and marched off while his deep, infuriating laughter followed her.

But when she'd gone just a short distance, she stopped abruptly, turned, and again started back to him. Puzzled, wondering what she was up to, West came forward to meet her.

Elizabeth walked right up to him, reached out, and plucked the pink rose from behind his right ear. Making a face, she dropped it to the ground, forcefully crushed it under her heel, raised her eyes to his, and gave him a triumphant look.

And she said, "You silly son of a bitch!"

23

The sun vanished when Elizabeth reached the stand of tall green cottonwoods. The deep shade was an immediate cooling balm for her hot, prickled flesh. And her hot, prickled temper.

Out of sight of her tall, dark tormentor Elizabeth stopped, put her hand against a slender cottonwood trunk, and leaned against it for support while she gathered her scattered wits.

She unbuttoned her suit jacket and wrenched her arms free, tossing the jacket over her left shoulder. She pulled out the high, choking collar of her pink blouse, then spread a hand on her bosom. She shivered involuntarily as she recalled the feel of Quarternight's smooth warm lips boldly pressed to her breasts, breathing fire through the flimsy barrier of her blouse to the tingling flesh beneath.

Elizabeth sighed.

This journey was going to be a long and dangerous one in more ways than one. She would be in the close company of the cynical and unprincipled West Quarternight for weeks. She would have to be constantly on guard. She couldn't allow him to get her off alone. If he ever managed to catch her away from the others, he would try to compromise her once again. She could *not* let that happen.

Shaking her head, Elizabeth made her way down through the silvery willows and tall cottonwoods toward the sound of voices drifting up from the river. When she stepped out into a broad grassy clearing beside the rushing Rio Grande, she saw the men of the second Curtin expedition busily handling their individual tasks.

Edmund and the two vaqueros were far downriver, where they had led the string of ponies to water. The peasants, chattering in Spanish, were even further away, watering the burros.

Directly before her the big silent Indian, Taos, and the talkative white-haired Grady were laying out the noon meal on a large checkered cloth spread on the smooth, grassy banks beside the flowing river.

Soon everyone gathered to enjoy the delicious lunch prepared and packed by the La Fonda kitchen staff. Cold chicken, smoked ham, cheese, thick-sliced bread, fruit, and assorted nuts met with everyone's approval. Bottles of wine, stowed carefully in cracked ice, long since melted, were still pleasantly chilled.

Seated between Edmund and the silent Taos, Elizabeth ignored West, purposely keeping her eyes off him. When he had first strolled into the clearing she had stiffened, afraid he would head straight for her. But he hadn't. He had slowly circled the large checkered cloth, stood for a moment so that all she saw were his worn boots and the bottoms of his soft buckskin trousers. Then he dropped into a crouching position directly across from her. Their eyes had met and held for a second or two, and she looked away as he sat flat down on the grass and leaned on his stiffened right arm.

Now as she sat there in the shade at the edge of the checkered cloth, she ate with the same relish as the hungry men. The Mexican help shared the meal, so the conversation was light and lively with much good-natured laughter and Spanish words like *claro* and *bueno* and *Dios* sprinkled in.

When every last piece of chicken and slice of ham had been devoured, the Mexicans rose, thanked Señor Quarternight, and politely drifted away. The others stayed where they were, sated and resting. There was a lazy lull in the conversation.

Then Edmund, sipping the last of his wine, said to no one in particular, "A man could live a long time out here if he stayed on the river, couldn't he?"

West said flatly, "Ed, your brother couldn't stay on the Rio Grande and reach his destination."

"I know," Edmund admitted. "I know. Just what are his chances, West? Is there really any hope he's still alive?" Elizabeth finally looked at West, as eager as Edmund to be reassured of Dane's chances for survival.

Cupping his hands to light a cigar, West slowly puffed the smoke to life and took it from his lips. "At this time of year there's plenty of water in all the streams and creeks. There's always wild game in the mountains, even the deserts. Dane won't die of thirst or starvation if that's what's worrying you." His gray eyes met Edmund's. "His chances? As I've said before, I feel they're very good. What do think, Grady?" He turned his dark head to look at the drowsy white-haired scout sitting cross-legged beside him.

Grady immediately became alert. Stroking his flowing white beard, he said, "I believe they're alive, all right. So does Taos, don't you?" The big, stone-faced Indian calmly nodded. Grady continued, "If they are alive, why, we'll find 'em. The New Mexico Territory ain't a big enough place to hide in, once me and Weston and Taos start lookin'." His blue eyes shone and his pink lips stretched into a grin beneath his drooping white mustache. Quickly, he added, "Not that I aim to imply Dane Curtin's a-hidin'. That ain't what I meant."

"No, of course not," said Edmund. "But suppose they located the cache, but can't get it out of—"

"Now, you're jest a borrowin' trouble, Edmund," Grady told him. "Besides, I don't care what anybody says, I'm still not fully convinced there's a big cave down south with the Grayson gold hid in it. In my time I seen lots of them charts like your brother had. Some was good, some of em' just sets of directions, or waybills, others were maps. Seen some that was real old, others that had been artificially aged to dupe some tenderfoot. But I never did see one that showed any big caves or caverns."

Elizabeth had begun to doubt there was any gold hidden in a deep underground cavern, but she didn't care. If Grady was right, if Dane and the others were alive, nothing else mattered.

Engrossed in what Grady was telling them, Elizabeth paid little attention as West quietly rose to his feet and walked away. As Grady's raspy voice droned on and on, and he got off on a tale of flushing Apaches out of the hills back when he rode with Kit Carson, her mind began to wander. She turned her head and looked out at the river.

It was nice here. Very nice indeed.

The waters of the river tumbling and splashing over the smooth boulders had a rhythmic, musical sound. The tall cottonwoods murmured their soft accompaniment as a breeze out of the west stirred their shimmering leaves. It seemed almost as if she—as if they all—were only out for a Sunday picnic.

Lounging there in the shade by the river, Elizabeth easily lulled herself into supposing that the entire trip would be like this.

Travel during the morning when it was reasonably

cool, then stop in some shaded glade for a leisurely noon meal. Afterwards, rest and nap through the long, warm afternoon. Then get back on the trail for a couple of hours in the evening. When darkness came, stop again and make camp for the night.

Supposing that they would stay right here for the next three to four hours, Elizabeth lazily searched for a spot to take her much needed afternoon nap. Yawning, she casually looked around for West. He was directly behind her, not fifty feet away.

Like an animal sunning himself on a rock, he lay on his back atop a low, flat sandstone boulder. His bed of stone was not in the cool shade, but he appeared totally oblivious to the hot noonday sunshine beating down on his face and lean body.

His eyes were closed. His tanned fingers were laced atop his hard abdomen. His long legs were stretched out full length and crossed at the ankles. His breathing was slow and even, the rhythmic movement pulling the soft doeskin fabric of his shirt tight against the flat muscles of his chest.

In sleep he looked boyishly young and deceptively harmless. With those arresting silver eyes closed and all that raw power contained, he appeared innocent and benign.

Elizabeth knew better.

She turned away. She sat there not listening as Edmund and Grady continued to talk. Finally she was so sleepy she felt she couldn't hold her eyes open for another moment. Yet, even with West Quarternight sleeping, she was reluctant to wander too far from Edmund.

There was only one thing to do. Lie down right here where she was. Making sure her skirts were down over her legs, Elizabeth stretched out beside the checkered cloth, draped a bent arm over her closed eyes, and fell asleep.

Something tickled her nose.

She didn't waken, but rubbed at her itching nose with the back of her hand, licked her lips, and turned her head to the side. It happened again. A faint, almost imperceptible tickling of her nose. Again her hand rubbed back and forth and she sniffed, feeling as if she were going to sneeze.

Her heavy lashes finally fluttered open. The first thing she saw was a darkly tanned hand drawing a cottonwood catkin back and forth directly under her nose. Frowning, she knocked the hand away and saw the dark, smiling face of West Quarternight looming above. He was crouched on his heels beside her.

"Time to rise and shine, Mrs. Curtin," he said in that drawling resonant voice. "Got to get back on the trail."

"Go away!" she said groggily, squinting at him. "I just got to sleep."

Plucking a dead leaf from her tousled red hair, West rose to his feet. "We're pulling out. If you want to go with us, better get up." He turned and walked away.

"West is right, Elizabeth," Edmund said, gathering up their gear. "Perhaps you can rest in the wagon."

Reluctantly, Elizabeth sat up, yawned, and asked what time it was. When Edmund told her it was only one-thirty, she realized she'd slept about ten minutes. No wonder she still felt so sleepy! She was about to complain when from out of nowhere a huge hand appeared, startling her.

Elizabeth looked up to see Taos, his flat black eyes expressionless, reaching down to her. Elizabeth gratefully placed her hand in his and thanked him when he effortlessly drew her to her feet. But she protested strongly as she and Edmund walked together up the forested incline to the road.

She hoped West Quarternight didn't intend to push

them too far, too fast. She was anxious to find Dane, of course, but she wasn't sure she could travel all day every day. She was still exhausted from the long tiring morning. Wasn't he?

Yes, he was, Edmund admitted. He understood exactly how she felt. Still, West was their guide. He was the trail boss. They were paying him to lead them to Dane, so they were obliged to do it at his pace. Maybe West just wanted to make good time on this first day out when they were all fresh and eager. Once they had been on the trail for a day or two, he would surely slow down.

Hoping Edmund was right, Elizabeth suddenly noticed he was limping slightly. Stopping him, she put a hand on his arm and said worriedly, "Edmund, what is it? Are you hurt?"

Urging her on, he sheepishly said, "Blisters. These new boots have rubbed blisters on my feet. Both heels."

"Poor Edmund," she said. "Why didn't you take them off while we were stopped for lunch?"

"If I had, I couldn't have gotten them back on."

"You could have changed to shoes. Some of your comfortable English-made soft leather footwear."

They had reached the road. Edmund spoke softly so that no one could hear. "No, I couldn't. I foolishly left all my shoes in Santa Fe. I have another pair of new boots with me. Nothing else."

"I'm sorry," she said, and meant it.

"So am I," he admitted. Then, "Please, Elizabeth, I don't want to be a burden. Don't tell the others. Don't tell West."

"I won't," she promised, understanding completely.

At the buck wagon, Edmund lifted Elizabeth up onto the high seat, then went to his horse. He forced himself to walk as though nothing was wrong, manfully concealing his acute discomfort and his deep embarrassment.

If the morning had been long, the afternoon was interminable. Grady told Elizabeth that they would likely ride until they reached La Bajada, where they would stop for the night.

So, like a child, all afternoon Elizabeth kept asking how much farther it was to La Bajada. She envisioned it as a sleepy, pristine little community where they could all check into a quiet inn, have a hot bath, then enjoy a leisurely dinner before retiring to a clean, soft bed.

She could hardly wait. She was hot and tired and bored and thirsty and uncomfortable. When she complained of the heat, Grady smiled and told her they were still in the high desert.

"This here's the cool uplands, missy."

"Then Lord deliver me from the hot lowlands," she replied.

The white-haired old scout chuckled, then said, "Gawd Almighty. Jest wait till we reach the Malpais and the White Sands."

"I'm not even going to ask," she informed him.

Somehow the afternoon was finally gone.

The burning sun had dropped behind the purple mountain peaks and the air had started to cool. Elizabeth kept squinting into the gathering dusk, anxiously searching for the elusive twinkling lights of La Bajada.

She soon learned, to her despair, that there were no twinkling lights of La Bajada. No sleepy, pristine community. No inn. No nothing. La Bajada was only a name for a deserted spot by the Rio Grande where a stage way-station had once been. Not even that building remained.

Elizabeth loudly voiced her unhappiness to Grady,

told him she badly needed a bath and a hot meal and a clean bed!

"Well, now, this is the frontier, missy," said Grady flatly. "We're not out here for fun."

Out of the dusk, West reined his sorrel alongside the buck wagon, where the bitterly disappointed Elizabeth, arms crossed, sat looking around at all the nothingness.

"You seem less than thrilled to be stopping," West said, patting his winded sorrel's neck.

Elizabeth turned angry eyes on him. "If this is your idea of a joke, I'm not laughing. Since we've already been on the road for an eternity, I'd just as soon go on until we reach a town."

"Albuquerque is fifty miles away," West said, totally unsympathetic. "While I'm sure you could make it, Lizzie here might get a little tired."

Before Elizabeth could reply, he flashed his white, dazzling teeth, wheeled the mare about and rode away.

No sooner had he disappeared than Taos materialized out of the dusk. Silently, he held out his gargantuan arms to her. She nodded her ascent and the big Navajo plucked her from the high wagon seat.

Solicitously, he escorted her to the river, pushing trees limbs out of her way, alert and ready to catch her should she make a misstep in the dense underbrush. By her side, he saw her safely to the campsite and never so much as touched her arm. When they reached the river, Taos stayed with her until Edmund arrived, then disappeared back into the dusk.

Supper on the river was nothing like the lovely lunch had been. There was no more of the chicken and ham. No more fresh fruits and cheeses and nuts. No chilled wine.

Taos built a campfire while Grady got out an old tin coffee pot and filled it with water. West, straddling a

big rock, sliced a huge slab of bacon, the sharp knife
gleaming in the firelight. Edmund, boots now off,
squatted on stockinged feet pouring beans into a huge
skillet.

Elizabeth hated bacon. She hated beans. And
Grady's coffee was so strong she suspected he was
probably right when he bragged it would "put hair on
your chest."

When the unappetizing meal was over, full darkness had fallen and Elizabeth was forced to go to bed
without a bath. In the privacy of the tarped buck
wagon, she undressed and washed her face, throat,
and arms in a pail of water. She drew on her lacy
nightgown, stretched out on the blanketed wagon
floor, and reluctantly blew out the lamp.

As tired as she was, she lay there in the darkened
wagon, tense, listening, afraid. Bullfrogs kept up a
loud, steady chorus on the river. Crickets chirped. An
occasional male laugh carried on the still night air.

Lying in the close darkness, it occurred to her that
the others were camped at least fifty yards from the
wagon. A wild beast or dangerous outlaw or renegade
Indian could attack her while the men on the river
slept through the assault. She shuddered with fear,
then gritted her teeth in anger.

West Quarternight had simply shaken his dark head
and made no reply when she had announced she was
going to the wagon to spend the night. She would
have told Edmund, but he was already sound asleep.
Alone, she had picked her way through the darkness
back to the wagon while their lead guide remained
sprawled by the fire, calmly drinking coffee and
smoking a cigar.

Elizabeth continued to lie wide-eyed, listening to
the night sounds. Tired as she was, she could not relax. She would never be able to sleep. She was terrified.

Her heart in her throat, Elizabeth sat up, crawled on hands and knees to the end of the wagon, lifted the closed tarp, and fearfully peered out.

She saw the giant Taos standing there in the moonlight, a Remington rifle in one hand and a mug of coffee in the other. He leaned against an upthrust of rock not a stone's throw from the wagon. His big body was rigid, his head unmoving, the night breeze lifting strands of his shimmering black hair. But those alert black eyes were flashing and constantly sweeping the valley as he stood silent watch over her.

Elizabeth started to call to him, to ask him to stay there through the night. She didn't do it. There was no need. Instinctively she knew that the huge Navajo would watch over her until morning.

Yawning sleepily, the tension already leaving her body, she crawled back to her bed, stretched out, and sighed in the darkness. She was safe, totally safe. Lying on her back, she could feel her legs and arms growing limp, her eyelids getting heavy.

Sleep very close now, she recalled the way West Quarternight had looked sleeping in the sun like some big, lazy cat. The vision brought a smile to her lips. But the smile was quickly chased away by a frown of guilt, and she turned her thoughts to her husband.

Focusing on Dane, she wondered if he were lying in the darkness somewhere wondering about her. Was he alone and afraid down in some dark, cold cavern? Was he in misery, perhaps badly hurt? Was he helpless and lost, the sunny smile she remembered forever gone from his handsome face?

A tiny muscle twitching at the left corner of her full mouth, Elizabeth murmured softly, "My husband. My poor husband."

24

✿✿✿

"My master," the woman softly murmured, "my pale master."

His long black cape billowing out about him, the Master of the Depths stole silently across the chill stone floor toward his waiting female subject.

With his pearly translucent skin and enormous emerald eyes and long curling hair of spun gold, he was an ethereal, not-of-this-world being. A fair golden god to be worshiped and revered.

And feared.

Underneath the long ebony cape with its flanged shoulders and slits for arms, the golden-haired master's tall, lean body was as white as milk. He purposely kept it that way. Had his faithful minions spend long hours dutifully sponging his long, slim frame with various concoctions of lemon juice and cultured buttermilk and expensive bleaching creams favored by pampered belles of the Old South.

And he stayed out of the sun.

As graceful as a ballerina, as beautiful as Michelangelo's "David," as compelling as the world's most powerful rulers, the pale master stopped when he stood directly before his waiting vassal.

She was a Mexican woman—a girl really—of seventeen years. She lay upon a bed with her long, dark hair fanned out around her head. She was naked and her bare breasts, even as she lay flat, pointed proudly out from her chest, the large satiny nipples an appealing shade of wine. A fleshy girl, her belly was rounded and her thighs were plump and strong. Between them a forest of thick, dark hair was beaded with the perspiration of excitement.

And fear.

The bed on which the pretty young woman lay naked was not soft. It was not comfortable. It was not fashioned of downy feathers that gently cradled her luscious brown curves. The same height and shape of a regular bed, this one was unique. Unlike any bed in the world.

It was made of pure gold.

Blocks of smooth, hard gold had been meticulously stacked together. Dozens and dozens of heavy, precious gold ingots had been carried from other chambers to this, the pale master's enormous amphitheater with its high-domed ceiling and its natural half-oval-shaped stage.

A stage where the golden bed was positioned directly before footlights of burning pine torches. Beyond those smoking torches was a congregation of nothing but thick blackness—a vast chasm of darkness. A deep, bottomless pit that led straight to the stygian depths of hell.

The golden ruler of those depths moved gracefully toward the dark-haired naked woman whose brown satin body shimmered in the footlights. She lay prostrate and submissive upon the bed of glittering gold. A lovely offering placed on a golden altar to glorify her god. A human sacrifice to appease her jealous master. A gift of flesh and blood to satiate his satyr's hungers.

From the flaming torches located high up on the stone walls, flickering light cast shadows throughout the large eerie chamber. It was reflected in the golden blocks of the large bed and in the pale master's feral eyes.

When the tall, gold-haired master stood at the very foot of the golden bed, he lifted his artistic hands to the stand up collar of his black cape. With his eyes on the supine woman, he unclasped the lone hook, pulled the long cape apart, and let it slowly slither down his bare white body.

The supple cape whispered to the stone floor and pooled into a puddle of inky blackness around his bare feet. He stood in the torchlight, a golden, naked Adonis, allowing his lowly servant to adore his pale, godlike beauty. The grateful woman did just that.

Her dark eyes slowly moved from the glowing halo of golden curls adorning his handsome head, down to his wide white shoulders and to his broad chest where an appealing fanlike pattern of golden hair shimmered in the footlights. His leanly muscled arms and legs were long and beautifully shaped. His belly was flat and hard, and lower, from a glistening growth of golden curls rose his proud, precious instrument of sovereign power. That great throbbing staff of pain and pleasure. The glorious rod, magnificent provider of love and life.

And death.

The woman's sensuous mouth softened, the glistening tip of her tongue emerged and slid slowly across her full upper lip. She got up onto her knees and slowly, seductively edged toward her master, her full naked breasts swaying erotically with her every movement.

When the brown-skinned woman reached the edge of the golden bed, she sat back on her heels before her pale master. He lifted his bare white arms, placed his long, pale fingers on either side of her head. Holding her in the tight vise of his grip, his eyes gleamed demonically.

His low, modulated voice echoing off the walls of the cavernous amphitheater, he said, "I am the devil come to do the devil's work. You will obey me or I will loose from their world of darkness the winged demons and devils. I will call them forth from the dark shadows of their buried haunts, to slither like predatory beasts and stalk you, their helpless prey. Do you understand?"

"Yes, Pale Master." The woman was mesmerized by those glittering green eyes.

"And when they have finished with you," he went on in a low, murderous voice, "I will adjure the gods of the netherworld to damn your soul to roam in the scorching desert after death. Forever and ever."

"Yes, Master."

He smiled down at her. "You may kiss the staff of life."

"Oh, thank you, Pale Master," she said.

He released his deathlike grip on her head. She promptly bowed it and touched her worshiping lips and tongue to the smooth, hot tip of his pulsing masculinity.

For the next two hours the pale master and his dark subject, writhing about on that hard bed of gold, engaged in an erotic sexual performance for an audience of total blackness beyond the burning footlights. When the heated exhibition finally ended and the invisible curtain rang down, the dark-skinned subject, her voluptuous body shiny wet with the sweat of sex, lay limp and unmoving upon the bed of gold.

Her damp tangled hair fell away from her gleaming throat to reveal a set of blood marks midway down the left side of her neck. Without looking, the woman knew the marks were there. She was proud of them.

She would wear them like a badge of honor, would touch the tender flesh again and again when she was alone. And when she touched those marks that grew redder and deeper with each glorious encounter on the bed of gold, she would smile and recall the love and ecstasy that had come with them. She would run her fingers lovingly over the distinct pattern and flush with excitement remembering what had made them.

The master's teeth.

Swirling the long black cape back around his bare white body, the pale master strode from the theater, leaving the woman lying on the bed of gold, alone on the deserted stage.

Outside the spacious chamber, two lackeys waited.

Paco, a slim-hipped Mexican of medium height had small beady eyes, a big nose, and a pencil-thin mustache above a hard, slashing mouth. He stepped forward to strip the black cape from his leader's tall frame. The other man was Ortiz, a short, overweight Mexican with a badly crossed walleye, which he could not control. The bulging white cornea roamed at will and Ortiz had been whipped by his pale master more than once for daring to look upon the master's woman. His tearful explanations that he hadn't known he was looking fell on deaf ears.

Ortiz lifted a clean, dampened cloth and sponged away the woman's scent from his master's body. The master turned back to Paco, who held out a pair of trousers for the tall, pale man to step into. When the pants had been pulled up over his hips and the fly loosely laced, the blond master gave the two obedient thralls orders to rouse the spent Mexican woman, clean her up, and get her back to her own small, dark chamber.

After that, they were to get back to work hauling

the heavy ingots of shiny yellow gold up through the miles of darkened corridors and narrow tunnels and perilous stone catwalks.

While the two Mexican lackeys hurried forth to do his bidding, the pale master raked his long white fingers through his damp halo of golden curls, turned, and strode unhurriedly away.

Toward the deep shadows he moved with a quiet, deadly assurance. From the beckoning darkness came a low but persistent noise that started as a whisper. The whisper grew into a mighty roar as the pale master was swallowed up in the impenetrable blackness.

It had been three days, but it seemed more like three weeks.

At first Elizabeth had been genuinely bewitched by some of the most spectacular mountain and desert scenery in the west, country so remote it had changed little since Coronado had come in search of the Seven Cites of Cibola.

The bloodred arroyos slicing through the land, the green of the thick mesquites, and the distant blue mountains were a wondrous sight. The sunsets were unlike any she had ever witnessed, and just last evening she had stood on the edge of an escarpment, staring into the dying sun, mesmerized by the huge fiery ball on the western horizon and by the changing hues of the painted sky.

At first the sky was a bright, blood red, almost frightening in scope and color. Then swiftly the skyline lightened into a hot, vibrant pink. Next came a breathtaking shade of shy violet, the effect so sweetly beautiful, it caused an ache in Elizabeth's breast.

She stood unmoving, knowing the perfect peace shed by the violet sky would only last for a few precious minutes. She experienced those lovely, fleeting moments, drawing all the priceless pleasure she could squeeze from them.

And then, like all perfect things, the shy violet quickly darkened to a deep, foreboding purple. Elizabeth shivered involuntarily. She was suddenly struck with that feeling that someone was walking over her grave. She hugged herself and stayed where she was until the deep purple became a midnight blue and only a pale gloaming of light remained.

It was gone in an instant and pervasive darkness enclosed her. She sighed and hurried down the stone steps she had climbed to her high lookout.

Now, at midafternoon, as she bumped along atop the buck wagon, she found no magic in her surroundings, no thrill in studying the varied statues of sandstone dotting the Rio Grande valley.

But she could see what she hoped was the blue outline of Sandia Crest in the distance. If it was Sandia Crest, then they were nearing Albuquerque. As much as she hated even to speak to the man seated beside her, she was too curious to keep quiet.

Not looking at him, she said, "Correct me if I'm wrong. We are facing southwest, aren't we? I'm trying to locate Sandia Crest."

"Is that damned thing lost again?"

"You're not one bit funny, West Quarternight!" Elizabeth turned to face him. "I want to know if that is Sandia crest!"

"Why, I do believe it is."

"Will we get there by nightfall? Will we spend the night in Albuquerque?" Elizabeth held her breath.

"Nope."

She made no attempt to hide her disappointment. "You planned it this way, didn't you! You purposely let us take a longer lunch rest than usual so that we couldn't get to Albuquerque tonight."

His lanky body draped back in the seat, a long arm

behind her on the seat back, a booted foot lifted and riding the splashboard, West said conversationally, "Since you're absolutely unbeatable at figuring things out, maybe you'll tell me why I would do a thing like that."

"Because you really are a complete and total bastard," she was quick to answer.

He shot her an amused glance. "Practice makes perfect."

She huffed, crossed her arms over her chest, and refused to say anything more. There was no getting a straight answer from him. His biggest joy in life was to tease and torture her.

Her jaw hard, Elizabeth stared straight ahead, deciding that she didn't like any of their hired guides. When Grady Downs drove the buck wagon, he talked and talked until she sometimes felt her head was rattling. Big Taos was just the opposite, he never uttered a word, but it seemed like every time she turned around she was bumping into the big giant. It unnerved her.

But worst of all was the man seated beside her, whose full lips had gone slack in derision of her anger. She felt his gray eyes on her, glinting with contemptuous amusement. Never had she known a man with so much relentless audacity. She wondered if anything was sacred to him. He made fun of everything.

She hated it when he took a turn driving the wagon. He knew he had her then, that she couldn't get away. Knew he could say anything that was on his mind, and that's just what he did. He took perverse glee in bringing up things that had happened the night they had spent together in the Louisiana stockade.

He said things aloud that most people hardly dared to think. He brought up shared intimacies, and she was absolutely astounded. Both by the fact that he

could look right at her and say such forbidden things,
and by the fact that he had remembered them after
all this time. She had supposed that she was the only
one who remembered, the only one who had guiltily
relived those memories time and again in the darkness in her lonely bed.

Elizabeth came back to herself when West's booted
foot left the splashboard and he casually tossed the
reins across her lap. Automatically taking up the long
leather reins, she turned questioning eyes on him.

With an economy of motion, he reached a long arm
behind his head, wrapped tanned fingers around his
collar, and drew his shirt over his head. He wadded
up the pale blue cotton slipover shirt and tossed it
behind the seat. Looking straight at Elizabeth, he lazily scratched his hair-covered chest and said, "It's a
little hot out this afternoon. You don't mind, do you?"

"Would it matter if I did?"

Sun glinting on his sleek muscles, West reached
out, wrapped his fingers around her left elbow, lifted
her arm a little, and looked accusingly at the hint of
dampness circling her pale yellow long-sleeved
blouse.

"Looks like you're a little warm yourself."

Shaking his hand off, Elizabeth slapped at his chest
with the reins, and snapped, "It's a hundred degrees,
or hadn't you noticed!"

"I have," he said. "Too damned hot to wear clothes.
Why don't you slip out of your blouse."

"Not on your life."

"Don't tell me you don't trust me."

"I'm sure your feelings are hurt that I don't."

West deliberately leaned closer to Elizabeth. He
placed his hand over his heart. "Gets me right here."

"Oh, I'd like to get you right . . . right . . ." She
realized her eyes had fallen to the straining crotch of
his tight buckskins. Her head shot up, her fair face

flushed with color, and she twisted away from him, tossing the reins over his sprawled knee.

"You do, sweetheart," he told her. "You get me there most of all."

25

*** *** ***

The westering sun glared on the water where the Rio Grande took a slight bend eastward. Shading her eyes against the harsh reflection, Elizabeth looked out at the river and felt her exasperation grow. Behind her, the towering peak of Sandia Crest loomed close and majestic against the deep blue sky. A few low, scattered clouds cast long dark shadows on its sunny slopes.

It was a good two hours until sundown and Albuquerque was only seven miles to the south. As far as she was concerned, there was no good reason why they couldn't have ridden on in and spent the night in comfort. She had loudly voiced that opinion to West Quarternight when he had announced they were stopping and would camp here for the night.

"Stopping?" She had grabbed his bare forearm. "Why on earth would we stop? It's the middle of the afternoon, for heaven's sake. You told me yourself that when we reached Sandia Crest we'd be just seven miles out of Albuquerque. No one's tired. Not even the horses. Let's go on into town where we can check into a hotel and have some decent food. I badly need a bath—a real bath—and wouldn't it be nice to sleep in a soft bed with fresh sheets and . . . and . . . You're not listening to me!"

"What was that you said?" He finally turned to look at her, grinning like a wicked cherub.

"Oh, you!" She gave the hair on his arm a painful twist and wondered if anyone ever got through to the indifferent, pig-headed bastard. She doubted it.

Now, standing mute and angry on the riverbank, she paid little attention to all the activity going on around her as the men went about the ritual of setting up camp for the night. Her interest was piqued, however, when she heard West's voice behind her speaking softly to Grady.

Casually turning, she saw that he was no longer bare-chested. But it was not the wrinkled blue shirt he had put back on. He wore a fresh white pullover, the muscles of his chest outlined by the snugly fitting shirt. He stood absently slapping leather reins against his thigh and it dawned on Elizabeth that he was leading a saddled horse. Not his sorrel mare, Lizzie, but one of the Navajo ponies from the remuda they held in reserve as remounts.

Grady was pulling on his flowing white beard and nodding his white head while West did all the talking for a change. When Grady reached out, patted West's chest, then turned and walked away, Elizabeth's eyes narrowed. Sure enough, West looped the reins up over the paint's neck and that was when it struck her fully.

Quarternight was riding into Albuquerque!

"Just a minute!" she called, and marched over to where he stood framed between two thick willows. When she reached him, she stepped up close, her hands on her hips, and her chin jutting out. "Just where do you think you're going?"

"Wherever I want," was his calm reply.

"Oh, no, you're not!" She jabbed her forefinger into

his chest. "You park us way out here in the middle of the afternoon then selfishly ride into Albuquerque to enjoy yourself! You can't do that! I won't allow it. This time, Quarternight, you've gone too far!"

He shrugged. "There is no such place."

"I'm telling you—"

"You can tell me nothing, Mrs. Curtin," West smoothly cut in and smiled down at her. She stood with the sun at her back, her wild mane of hair aflame, her beautiful eyes snapping with heat. He felt a strong compulsion to reach out and seize her, pull her roughly into his arms, and kiss her until that fiery anger became fiery passion.

"Oh, yes I can," she said haughtily. "Perhaps you've forgotten that you are the employee and I am the employer. And I warn you that—"

"I think I should warn *you*, boss lady, that I always get my way."

"No, you don't. Nobody always gets what they want!"

"I do," he stated arrogantly, glanced about, then added in a low, calm voice, "And I want you, Mrs. Curtin."

A flare of fury came into her blue eyes. "You will *never* have me!" she hissed.

"Never?" His dark eyebrows lifted. "I've already had you once." His gray gaze lowered to her full, pouting mouth, then returned to her flashing eyes. "And remember, once the cork is drawn, it cannot be replaced."

"Get out of my sight this instant!"

"On my way, darlin', on my way."

Supper was early and unappetizing.

There was only one palatable thing about the meal of tough jerked beef, stale bread, and bitter black coffee. West Quarternight was not there to sit across from Elizabeth and pin her with those penetrating silver-gray eyes.

Chewing a bite of the crusty bread with little enthusiasm, Elizabeth looked up sharply when Grady, as if someone had asked, said that Sonny wouldn't be sharing supper with them. He had ridden over to a remote valley ranch five miles outside the small settlement of Bernalillo.

Swallowing with difficulty, Elizabeth, staring at Grady, quickly picked up her heavy mug and took a long drink of the inky black coffee to wash down the dry bread. She knew no one need ask *why* West had gone there. Grady would gladly supply the information.

He did.

"Yessem, Sonny makes it a point to drop in to see old Skeet Dozier and his three grown sons anytime we're down this a-way. I'd a-gone with him myself 'cept them boys of Skeet's yammer away about nothing till you can't hear yourself think. Old Skeet was in the war with Sonny, Sonny's commanding officer in the war's early days. Lost both his legs to a concealed Confederate cannon." Grady slurped his coffee. Then he laughed and slapped his thigh. "I know them boys of Skeet's, they'll hornswaggle Sonny into staying half the night. Them boys are worthless as they come, always a-drinkin' and cussin' and . . ."

Elizabeth no longer listened. She had heard all she needed to hear. The fierce anger she had felt earlier was quickly being replaced with anticipation. If Grady was right and West would be away until far into the night, it would be the perfect time for her to take that bath she'd been dreaming of since leaving Santa Fe. A real bath. Not the kind she'd had for the past three evenings. Not the hurried sponge baths from a pail of water under the wagon tarp as she knelt on the blankets and hurriedly washed her dirty flesh while she kept one ear open for the sound of Quarternight's voice.

Seated at supper in her hot, heavy skirts and high-collared, long-sleeved blouse, Elizabeth considered the prospect of stripping everything off and plunging into the cool, clean water of the river. It brought a smile to her lips and a quickening of her pulses.

She set her tin plate down on the checkered cloth and abruptly rose to her feet. "I'd like your attention, please," she said loudly, and several conversations trailed away and stopped. When all the men, including the eight Mexican helpers, had fallen completely silent and were looking at her, Elizabeth announced, "While you finish your supper, I am going to the wagon, get fresh clothes, then walk around that bend in the river. Once I am out of sight, I intend to take a nice, long bath. I expect each and every one of you to stay well away from that river bend. If you intend to bathe, make sure you go far to the south. Nobody, and I do mean nobody, is to take one step north of where you are now. Understood?"

The Mexicans smiled and eagerly nodded their heads. Grady stroked his white beard. Edmund wore a worried look. Taos's expression was, as usual, unreadable.

"Furthermore, I intend to stay in the river for a long time, so don't be getting worried and come down to see about me. I'll be perfectly safe and if I decide to stay for a couple of hours, that's just what I will do. Now, carry on with your meal." She took a step backward and Taos came abruptly to his feet.

"No," she warned, pointing a finger at him, "you are not to watch over me, even from a distance!" He looked almost hurt and she was immediately ashamed when she realized that the big, silent Indian had only drawn his heavy Colt .44 from the holster and was offering it to her, butt first. "Oh . . . I . . . well, yes, thank you, Taos. Thank you."

His black eyes said, "You're welcome, and be careful."

Carrying the heavy gun, Elizabeth went first to the wagon to get fresh clothes. She laid the Colt on the wagon bed, looked all around, jerked her skirts up high, and shimmied up onto the buck wagon. When she stuck her head inside the tarp, the first thing her eyes fell on were a neat stack of strange clothes lying atop her makeshift bed.

Kneeling there, she reached for the first article of clothing and held it up before her. A pullover shirt of pale yellow, it was far too small to belong to any of the men. She held it up to herself: a perfect fit. Next, a pair of velvet-soft rust suede trousers that laced on the left side instead of down the middle like those worn by the scouts. The pants looked as if they had been made for her. A pair of small, beaded moccasins and a silver concho belt completed the ensemble.

Elizabeth swallowed hard.

She was touched. She knew it was Taos who had left her the clothes. Just as the big Navajo had left a pair of moccasins beside the sleeping Edmund their first night on the trail. As if he had known Edmund's new boots had worn blisters on his heels, though Edmund had said nothing.

Now Taos was quietly helping her. She wondered where he had gotten pants and a shirt that fit her and why he had decided to give them to her now. Likely, he had sensed that this evening she would take a bath in the river.

Elizabeth smiled and pressed her cheek to the soft chamois cloth of the rust trousers. All men, she decided, should be as perceptive and as sensitive as the massive mute Indian. Her first impressions of Taos were quickly changing.

Gratefully tossing the new outfit over an arm, Elizabeth gathered up clean underwear, a big white towel, and a bar of perfumed soap. Ducking back out into the sunlight, she leapt down from the wagon, turned and picked up Taos's .44.

Down at the river she was well out of sight of the expedition. Still, just to be certain, she turned and determinedly headed north. Excited, she rushed along the grassy banks, walking fast, moving further and further upriver.

At last she found the ideal spot. A place so concealed with lush greenery and tall cottonwoods, she would feel totally at ease stripping. There was a small, flat patch of treeless grass sloping down to the water. Thick silvery willows enclosed the space, making it cozy and private.

The water, fed by melting mountain snows, was clean and so clear Elizabeth could see the rocky bottom. Best of all, as if Mother Nature knew she would be coming here, smooth flat boulders led in perfect stairsteps down from the smooth grassy banks into the water and on down well below the surface.

"There really is a God," Elizabeth said aloud, then dropped the new clothes to the grass, laid the heavy gun carefully down, and began disrobing as hurriedly as possible. When she had undressed down to her fancy satin underthings, she hesitated. She looked down the river, then up it. She turned about in a full, slow circle, her eyes sweeping the large Rio Grande valley that sloped gradually upward on both sides of the river. She saw nothing moving but a small herd of cattle far, far to the west.

She unhooked her satin chemise and let the dainty straps slide down her arms. When the wispy undergarment fell to the ground atop her discarded skirt, she wiggled out of her thigh-high underdrawers. When they reached the ground, she stepped out of them and impulsively picked them up by hooking a toe under the lacy leg and kicked them away.

Then, laughing like a child, her long red hair streaming down her bare back, she reached for the soap and the Colt .44 and excitedly headed for the water. When she stood on the stone stairsteps at river's edge, she tested the water with her right foot and was shocked by the coldness of the stream. It was icy.

Still giggling, Elizabeth stood on the stone steps while the fading sunlight kissed her bare white body, turning it a soft golden hue. Her deep red hair blazed around her head and between her sun-honeyed thighs.

She became indecisive, no longer certain she wanted to go into the water. Maybe she should sit down on a stone stairstep, lift handfuls of the chill water up and spritz herself. She took another cautious step downward, then another.

She laid the gun nearby, sat flat down on the smooth boulder, and dangled both feet in the water. She placed the bar of soap beside her. She leaned out, cupped her right hand to fill it with water, then splashed it on her bare left arm. She stiffened, drew in her breath, and pursed her lips.

But she went right back for more. She bent over from the waist, cupped both hands together in the water, brought them up to her naked chest and released the water. It sluiced down her bare breasts and she gave a loud breathy gasp as goosebumps popped out to cover her flesh.

While her bare breasts shimmered wetly and her nipples puckered from the shock of the cold water, Elizabeth laughed aloud, looking down from one breast to the other, and lifted a hand to rub at her gleaming midriff and belly. Quickly getting into the spirit of things, Elizabeth parted her long, white legs.

She sat with them spread wide, kicked her feet

playfully in the water, then leaned forward once
more with her hands cupped together.

Very slowly, very carefully, she straightened, taking
pains not to spill her precious cargo. When her filled
hands were no more than six inches from her open
thighs, Elizabeth thrust her pelvis forward, gritted
her even white teeth, and opened her hands.

"Ooooo! Soooo cold!" she gasped, feeling the icy
water trickle through the red curls and over the ultra-
sensitive flesh between. She tipped her head back.
Her long auburn hair spilled down her back and her
hands rode her wet thighs while her long legs remained parted, and she squirmed, murmuring, "Cold,
so cold."

"Hot, so goddamned hot," swore a tall, dark man
under his breath at the same time Elizabeth shivered
from the cold.

The dying sun to his back, he stood high on a jutting ledge above the west bank of the river, silhouetted against the orange sky. His heated silver eyes
were riveted to the beautiful red-haired woman below, unselfconsciously splashing water on the
sweetest part of her luscious naked body.

Sweat trickled down out of his thick black hair,
beaded on his long, dark eyelashes, and above the
hard line of his mouth. He lifted a forearm and wiped
his dark face.

"Hot," West muttered hoarsely, "Jesus, it's hot."

26

Elizabeth continued to splash water onto her bare body, playing happily as if she were a child, gradually getting used to the river's bracing coldness. Finally she was ready to take the plunge. Grabbing up the bar of perfumed soap, she rose to her feet and stood there in the dwindling summer sunshine, screwing up her courage.

She looked out at the river and debated exactly how she should go about it. She could slowly, carefully walk down the stone steps until she was submerged right up to her neck. Or she could just jump right into the river's depths and be done with it.

Considering both choices, she sprang up and down in place, laughing and trembling, a breeze off the river whipping her long red hair about her face and bare shoulders. Laying her soap aside, she took a deep, long breath.

She pinched her nose with thumb and forefinger, gave a loud whoop, and leapt into the water. In seconds she emerged, her head breaking the surface out in the middle of the river. Blinded by her long wet hair, she sputtered and gasped and gulped for air.

For a few minutes she was too chilled to do anything more than push the heavy wet hair out of her eyes and tread water against the gentle current. But in a remarkably short length of time, she thawed and began really to enjoy herself. She swam gracefully across the wide river from east to west.

The stream's western bank was in deep shadow, so she spent little time there. Pushing away with her feet, she swam back toward the sunny side, flopped over onto her back, and floated. Arms straight out to her sides, feet kicking rhythmically, she drifted dreamily along in the eddying river, her long hair spread out in perfect symmetry, lying on the water's surface like a gleaming scarlet fan.

Alone for the first time in days, Elizabeth felt her tired, tense muscles relax, her troubled thoughts recede to the far reaches of her brain. She had never fully realized just how precious privacy was, nor what a luxury it was to take a simple bath. Lying stretched out, buoyed by the lapping water, feeling its gentle slap against her flesh, she sighed contentedly, looked up at the lovely lavender sky, and pretended she was all alone in this magical world of wild, stark beauty.

She was the only human in this big, splendid outdoor wilderness, although of course she had the animals for her friends. As free and untamed as a mighty mountain lioness, she could move naked through the woods, unafraid, unashamed, followed by the now docile beasts of the forest to whom she was a ruling goddess.

Her vivid imagination taking her out of herself, Elizabeth continued to drift and dream until finally she realized she had better return to the real world, get her bath taken, and head back to camp. She sighed, turned over, and swam to the rock stair steps. She sat there on a flat, slippery stone with the water reaching to just below her waist.

Humming softly, she soaped her heavy wet hair and shampooed it, scratching at her scalp with sharp fingernails. When her hair was squeaky clean, she pushed it straight back to fall in a long wet rope down her back. Then she lathered her throat and arms and breasts and bent low to rinse away the suds. She bathed every inch of her body, lifting her long legs one at a time, pointing them skyward, soaping them leisurely.

When her body was as clean as her hair, she tossed the soap aside, leaned out into the water, rinsed herself thoroughly, then rose to her feet. Making a face, she realized she had left her towel—as well as all her clothes—back on the grassy banks out of reach. She shook herself like an animal, then bent, picked up the heavy Colt .44 with wet fingers, and started for her clothes.

She had gone only a couple of steps when she stopped short. Eyes wide and luminous, heart lurching in her naked chest, Elizabeth gasped in shocked surprise.

There in the very center of her own private willow-enclosed paradise lay West Quarternight sprawled out on his back. Hands folded under his head, one long leg was bent, his foot flat on the grass. The other leg was raised and crossed, the booted foot resting on his bent knee. Beneath his folded arms was her large white towel. And resting squarely atop his chest were *all* of her clothes, neatly folded and stacked, moving gently up and down with his slow, even breathing.

"Well, I've heard of taking nice, long baths, but I was beginning to think you were going to wash all your skin off," he said, letting her know he had been there all along.

"Oh, no!" Horrified, Elizabeth quickly turned away and splashed loudly back into the water, holding the heavy Colt aloft in her shaking hand.

West didn't bother to lift his dark head. Just lay there as calm as you please, yawning lazily, his raised, booted foot swinging slightly atop his knee.

Standing in water up to her shoulders, Elizabeth shouted venomously, "You get out of here right now, Quarternight!"

"Ready when you are, Mrs. Curtin," he replied, slowly turning his dark head. His silver eyes were heavy lidded, but his white teeth were flashing in a wide smile.

"I'm not about to get out of this stream until you go away!"

"I'll cover that bet," he said, continuing to smile broadly.

Furious, she warned, "So help me, if you don't get away from me this minute, I'll . . . I'll—"

"You'll what? Kill me?"

"Yes!" she said angrily, "I will! I'll kill you!"

"Well, I wouldn't be the first man you've killed, now, would I?"

Elizabeth was momentarily speechless. She had forgotten that this infuriating man believed her to be a cold-blooded killer. Well, good! This was the perfect time to take full advantage of his conviction.

She said, as calmly as possible, "That's right, Quarternight. One more killing won't make any difference to me." From the depths of the river where she stood shivering, Elizabeth pointed the weapon at him and tried to sound cold and dangerous when she warned, "A dead man holding all my clothes. I'd be no-billed by any judge in the country. You have exactly sixty seconds to leave."

Idly fingering the lacy strap of her satin chemise, West looked at her, cocked one eye shut, and said, "You're not that good a shot, sweetheart. You might manage to plug me from there, but I'd live." His full attention returned to the wispy underwear lying on his chest. He drew Elizabeth's underpants up to his face and inhaled deeply. "Better come closer if you mean to do the job right."

Elizabeth closed her eyes in deep frustration. How could she scare a man who apparently didn't care if he lived or died! Her eyes came open. Or was he bluffing? If she got out of the water and leveled the Colt directly at his chest, would *that* get his attention?

She called, "You're right, Quarternight. I sure wouldn't want to miss." Turning, she started toward the stone stair steps. Her teeth chattering from the cold and from nervousness, she coolly warned, "I'm giving you one last chance. Leave now and I won't hurt you."

She couldn't believe her eyes. The dauntless man continued coolly to lie there on his back, grinning. Well, the steel barrel of the Colt .44 stuck in his ribs would wipe that cocky smile off his face!

Emerging fully from the water, desperately wishing there was something—anything—she could throw over herself to hide her nakedness, Elizabeth determinedly started toward West.

Watching her every movement, he finally set her clothes aside and rolled agilely to his feet. He stood waiting for her, booted feet planted firmly apart, the white towel clutched in his right hand.

He was still smiling.

Her modesty partially preserved by the rapidly falling dusk, Elizabeth stopped several yards from West, raised the gun in both hands, and gave him his last warning.

"Drop the towel, turn and walk away, Quarternight."

"Lower the gun, come and get it, Mrs. Curtin."

It wasn't the answer she had expected. Uncertain what to do, Elizabeth stood there trembling, the heavy gun wavering in her shaking, outstretched arms, the breeze off the river chilling her bare wet body.

Her finger toyed with the trigger and she threatened, "I mean it, Quarternight! I'll shoot you!"

"No," he said insolently, "you won't shoot me, sweetheart."

"I will, I swear it!"

"You do and every man in camp will be over here before you can get your underwear on."

Elizabeth knew he was right. In her mind's eye she saw the entire expedition swarming around the corner. She sighed and began to lower the gun.

West said, "Yes. Just lay the gun down on the grass and you can have your towel."

"You promise?"

"Would I lie?"

Elizabeth whirled about so that she no longer faced him. She crouched down, reluctantly laid the heavy gun on the ground, and rose to her feet again.

Over her shoulder she called, "Okay. I've put the gun down. Now toss the towel to me."

"Come here and get it."

White with anger, Elizabeth felt as if she might explode. How could this reckless bastard manage always to get the upper hand? What other man on earth would consider behaving as he did? Edmund Curtin was paying Quarternight a small fortune to escort this expedition, yet he was willing to gamble it away. To lose it all. And that's exactly what would happen if Edmund were to find out about this little encounter.

Well, unlike Quarternight, she *wasn't* willing to gamble away her future. She had to get that towel, get dressed, and back to camp before Edmund or Taos got worried and came looking for her. If they did, she would be hard pressed to explain why she was calmly standing naked with West Quarternight, instead of screaming at the top of her lungs.

"All right," she said, "I'll come for the towel."

"It's waiting for you," said West. "And so am I."

Refusing to face him, Elizabeth started cautiously backing toward West. Immediately, the muscles tensed in his arms and back. Continuing to smile, he blinked and watched the pale, naked woman slowly edging her way toward him, her wet heavy hair pressed to her slender back and dripping rivulets of water down over her bare shapely buttocks.

His eyes roving restlessly over her slender form as she awkwardly backed toward him, he grinned and said, "You're getting a little off course, Mrs. Curtin. Swing back a little more to your right."

Elizabeth caught her lip between her teeth, hesitating. But she did as he told her. Feeling like the world's biggest fool, she moved steadily closer to a man she hated beyond all reason.

Her hand out behind her, she said, "You've had your fun. Give me the towel."

"I'm holding it out to you. All you have to do is turn around and take it."

Livid, Elizabeth made a couple of frantic swipes behind her with her right hand and heard him chuckle. "My arm's not *that* long. You're still a good twenty feet from me."

Elizabeth continued to back slowly toward him, despising him for his ridiculous jesting guidance. "Warmer, you're getting warmer," he said, the sound of laughter in his voice, Then abruptly, "No, now you're getting colder. Move more to the left. To your left. Not that far, ease back a little to your right. That's it. Aaah, yes. Warmer. You're definitely getting warmer. W-a-r-m-e-r."

The nearer his voice, the angrier Elizabeth became, and the more she made frantic, reckless swipes behind her with her hands. At last her outstretched fingers connected with the heavy towel and a little gasp of triumph fell from her open lips.

But before she could yank it from him, West snatched it away, draped it around her bare shoulders, and spun her to face him.

Looking down into her angry face, he said, "Hot. Now you're hot."

"I've never been colder in my life!" she spat, squirming to free herself.

Against his leanly muscled arms, her struggles were in vain. West smiled in quiet amusement, drew her closer, and kissed her. Her mouth stayed tight and cool beneath his searching lips. When at last the unwanted kiss ended, she lifted blazing eyes to his.

He grinned and teased, "Ah, don't worry. There's more where that came from."

"You fool!" she hissed. "You conceited fool. Can't you tell that I can't stand you in my sight!"

His strong arms still encircling her, he said, "Look, if you've got something on your mind, just say it."

"I hate you!"

"Feel better now?"

"Yes, I do."

An expression of mock confusion on his tanned face, he said, "Let me get this straight. You hate me. You can't stand me in your sight."

"Good for you," she said. "You've finally caught on."

"Well, does this mean that you don't want to make love to me?"

"You're not funny, damn you," Elizabeth said, struggling anew. She was surprised when his arms fell away from her.

Quickly stepping back, she drew the white towel tightly around herself, looking warily at him. She wondered what he was up to now. And immediately found out.

Bending, he swiftly gathered up all her clothes and

coolly informed her that if she wanted to get dressed and back to camp before the others grew worried, she would wisely allow him to assist her.

She learned further that his idea of assisting was to loll there on the ground, smoking a cigar, and watching as if he were a ticket-buying patron at the theater.

Awkwardly, Elizabeth struggled to get dressed without fully exposing herself to his penetrating silver eyes. It was not an easy feat. She was turned away from him, but he held her clothes and handed them to her, one article at a time.

If Elizabeth was in a great hurry, West was not. Enjoying himself immensely, he observed her every move, managing to catch captivating glimpses of bare ivory flesh despite all her best efforts to hide herself from him.

"You know," he mused aloud, "I never noticed that tiny little mole on the inside of your—"

"Why must you always do this to me?" She whirled to face him. "Why don't you leave me alone?"

Her hands were at the laces going up the side of the rust suede trousers. West had not yet given her the shirt. She wore only the flimsy chemise and the unlaced leather pants. The satin chemise clung to her damp skin, outlining her nipples as if she wore nothing at all.

West instantly came to his feet before her. His swiftly heating silver gaze holding hers, he tossed the withheld shirt over his shoulder, reached out, and wrapped her long wet hair around his right hand. Urging her head back, he slowly bent to her.

His mouth hovering a scant inch from her parted lips, he said, "I'm not sure I *can* leave you alone." His eyes dropped to her mouth and his hand tightened its grip on her hair. "Are you? Can you leave me alone, Mrs. Curtin?"

"Don't be absurd," she said, with far more conviction than she actually felt. "You know I can."

"No, I don't."

"You most certainly do, or at least you should. I realize it's almost impossible for you to believe, but not every woman in this world wants you."

"You're kidding."

She rolled her eyes, at the same time pushing on his chest. "Quarternight, you're confusing me with a frightened young girl in a darkened Louisiana death cell. No firing squad awaits us. I'm in no need of a man's strong arms to shelter me. I'm a married woman with a handsome, loving husband who gives me all the love I need."

As if she hadn't spoken, West said, "Kiss me first, then answer."

"Let go of my hair!" she said irritably, squirming. "Answer what?"

"The question. Can you leave me alone?" He placed a kiss on her parted, startled lips.

After a timeless, dizzy interval, her soft mouth, even as she made murmuring sounds of protest, began to answer the pressure of his. West drew her closer, released her wet, heavy hair, and deepened the kiss. His hands spanned her ribcage, but he held her gently, lightly, allowing her the opportunity to slip from his tender embrace.

If she wanted to.

She did want to. Or at least she wanted to want to, but his marvelous lips were so skilled at kissing, and his tongue sliding inside her mouth brought a hot excitement that was devastating. She was responding in spite of herself. Of their own volition, her weak arms stole up around West's neck, her fingers grabbed anxiously at the thick black hair that curled over the top of his white shirt collar.

As abruptly as it had begun, the scorching kiss

ended. West lifted his mouth from hers and set her from him. While she stared questioningly at him, he handed her her shirt. Then he reached up behind his head, grabbed his collar, and pulled his own shirt up and off.

"What do you think you're doing?" she asked.

"I can't make love to you with my clothes on," he said matter-of-factly, and his hands went to the fly of his trousers.

Holding her shirt up in front of her, Elizabeth said, "You are *not* going to make love to me!"

"Sure I am. You gave me the answer I was looking for when you kissed me."

Shaking her head in denial, Elizabeth said, "No, I never . . . I didn't mean . . . you . . . you kissed me, and I—"

"And you kissed me back." He took a step closer and she trembled. His devilish smile returning, he slipped a long tanned finger beneath a lacy strap of her chemise that had fallen down her arm. He said, "Don't look so worried. I was teasing about making love to you here." He urged the fallen strap back up onto her shoulder. "We don't have time tonight and I don't want to hurry. But I'm going to see you again."

"Not if I'm lucky and die tonight in my sleep," she quickly replied.

Anxiously, Elizabeth pulled on the slipover shirt and allowed West to lace up her pants and fasten the silver concho belt around her waist. When he crouched down before her, lifted a bare foot to his thigh and slipped a soft beaded moccasin on, she heard him say, "Remember this, sweetheart, it will happen and soon. We will make love again. I want it. You want it."

He lowered her foot back to the grass and Elizabeth gasped when he impulsively clasped her hips tightly in his hands, pulled her forcefully to him, and pressed his tanned jaw to her belly.

She stopped breathing completely when he turned his face inward and lowered it until his mouth was directly between her legs.

Through the soft chamois of her britches, his breath was a hot flame on her flesh when he promised, his deep voice muffled against her, "And with you begging me to stop, I'm going to kiss you right here." Gently, West kissed her there and added, "Until you beg me never to stop."

27

🙌

The Second Curtin Expedition continued moving steadily on down the old Rio. Through the sprawling city of Albuquerque—located on a high desert plain at the base of the Sandia mountains—they went, then alongside the Bosque Redono, the big reservation in the shadow of the Manzano Mountains into which thousands of unhappy Navajos had once been herded.

Next came Los Chavez. Then Belen. Las Nutrias. Socorro.

Riding the river all the way, they dropped steadily lower into the cacti-dotted desertlands of New Mexico. The changing scenery continued to be stunning. Flat-topped mesas rose majestically from the barren terrain and cracked arroyos cut through stark, jagged hillsides. Lancelike yuccas spiked the broad desert floor, dwarfed by the rugged sandstone boulders rising to meet the clear azure sky.

The river changed along with the topography. At first it had been a surging, fast-flowing stream cutting through deep gorges. Now it was a slow, meandering river winding its lazy way south through treacherous sandbars and quicksand, its banks still canopied with tall, green cottonwoods and silvery willows.

Far more comfortable since exchanging her hot traveling suits and petticoats for the suede pants, cotton shirt, and soft moccasins Taos had provided, Elizabeth was in a genial mood when the contingent stopped for the night at a wide, lush bend in the river fifteen miles below Socorro.

Her lighthearted feelings were due entirely to the fact that she had not been alone with West Quarternight since that horrid evening four days ago when he had sneaked up on her while she bathed. Taos or Grady had driven the wagon since then, and she much preferred Grady's rambling monologues and Taos's solemn silence to West's flirtatious needling.

She had been in West's company only briefly at mealtime. On those occasions she had avoided him totally when possible and had fixed him with a frosty stare when it was not. Still, she longed to get even with him and had spent a lot of her idle time silently plotting revenge.

Just when she least expected it, the golden opportunity fell right into her lap.

It was after supper at the river encampment south of Socorro. Everyone was lazing about, full, half sleepy. Elizabeth, sipping the last of Grady's strong black coffee from a tin mug, looked languidly about and realized, suddenly, that West was nowhere around. She said nothing and continued to sip the coffee and look out at the placid river.

But when she heard Grady telling Edmund over their endless game of checkers that West had gone downriver for a bath, her fingers tightened on her mug and it was all she could do to keep from smiling foolishly. Instead, she stayed just as she was for a few minutes more.

Then, setting the tin mug aside, she rose to her feet,

stretched her arms high over her head, and yawned. She sauntered over to Edmund, touched his shoulder, and casually announced to both men that she was going to lie down in the wagon for a short rest. When she came back, she would take on the checker game's winner.

"Be careful," said Grady and Edmund in unison.

She looked up and her eyes met the alert black ones of Taos, standing at the water's edge. He nodded his head. She turned and strolled away in no discernible hurry, thumbs hooked into the waistband of her britches.

But as soon as she was out of sight, Elizabeth let out a loud exhalation of breath and began to smile. She quickly changed directions, heading toward the river south of the camp. Pushing low limbs out of her path and shielding her face from the slap of willow branches, Elizabeth could hardly contain her excitement.

Mr. Weston Dale Quarternight was about to get a dose of his own devilish medicine. She was turning the tables. Now he was going to find out that it was no fun being the one caught without clothes. Let him squirm in embarrassment and shame. See how he liked it!

It didn't take her long to find him. She just followed the sound of that unmistakable baritone voice. He was singing loudly:

> "Yo ho ho, you and me,
>   Little brown jug do I love thee,
>   Yo ho ho, you and me . . ."

Elizabeth's heart began to drum with excitement when she caught sight of the dark head, the bare brown shoulders. West was out in the middle of the river, blissfully unaware he was not alone. Best of all, his clothes—including his underwear—lay on the grassy banks.

Clamping a hand over her mouth to keep from laughing aloud, Elizabeth knew victory was within reach. Even should he catch sight of her, she was closer to his discarded clothing than he was. Elizabeth stayed where she was for a moment longer, screwing up her courage.

Then carefully, quietly, she sneaked out into the clearing, keeping a watchful eye on the unsuspecting man caught up in the pleasure of his evening bath. West continued to sing as Elizabeth moved silently forward toward his clothes. When she reached them, she swiftly scooped them up from the ground and immediately felt light-headed and dizzy with power.

She wouldn't alert him to her presence. She would do to him what he had done to her. Let him continue to make a fool of himself while she calmly spied on him. Wait patiently until he finally looked up, saw her, and tried to cover his shame!

Grinning from ear to ear, Elizabeth clutched West's clothes to her chest and eased down onto the grassy banks to wait. Eyes sparkling with mischief, she found it was very satisfying to be the one with the upper hand. For a change, she was in charge. She was playing a cruel joke on him and enjoying every delicious moment of it!

Her laughing eyes trained on West, she kept them there, afraid to look away even for a second. She certainly didn't want to miss the expression on his dark face when at last he looked up and was surprised to find he was not alone.

West continued to sing and to soap his dark chest in obvious ignorance of her presence. When he ducked under the water's surface to rinse himself, Elizabeth's eyes remained on the spot where his dark head had disappeared.

But West didn't come up.

Elizabeth watched and waited and felt her bright smile becoming a little forced. Lifting a hand to shade them, she squinted her eyes, growing mildly uneasy. Why was he staying under so long? Had something happened to him? Had he perhaps hit his head on the rocky bottom and was lying unconscious under the water?

Her smile was now completely gone. The wispy hair at the nape of her neck lifted and her heart was no longer speeding from excitement but from apprehension and fear. Her legs weak, Elizabeth slowly rose to her feet.

She almost jumped out of her skin when with a loud splash West lunged up out of the water directly before her. Easily levering himself up onto the bank in one fluid movement, he stood there, brown and shimmering in the last rays of the sun.

As naked as the day he was born.

Thunderstruck, Elizabeth could only stare, her lips parted in surprise and awe. With the unconscious grace that was so much a part of him, he came directly toward her while the water sluiced down his lean brown body. Muscles bunched and stretched, the sleek dark skin rippling smoothly, his stomach falling away in a succession of hard ridges, all gleaming. His arms and legs were long and powerful beneath the sleek wet skin. His blue-black hair was plastered to his head and diamonds of water beaded the thick curling hair on his chest and at his groin.

His gray eyes glinted silver in the dying sunlight and his teeth—those perfect straight white teeth—shone in a disarmingly devilish smile. Overwhelmed by his startling dark good looks, Elizabeth hugged his clothes to her chest and shook her head as if to clear it.

That habitual teasing nature of his more strongly in

evidence than ever, he stepped right up to her and placed the tip of his wet forefinger against the pulse in her throat. He felt its furious drumming.

Smiling broadly, he took his clothes away from her, dropped them to the ground, and lowered his hand to the silver concho belt circling Elizabeth's small waist. None too gently he pulled her by the belt up against his tall, wet frame, letting her feel the hard, naked contours.

"Hell, I surrender," he teased. "If you want me this badly, you can have me."

He bent his head to kiss her, but she turned her face away. Against his wet, muscular shoulder she warned, "Let go of me, Quarternight, or I'll scream!"

His lips in her flaming red hair, he said, "Do and you'll have one devil of a time explaining why you sneaked down here to join me."

Her head snapped up. She glared at him. "I didn't come down here to join you. I came to—"

"To get a glimpse of me naked? Here, I'll stand back a little so you can get a good look." He loosened his hold on her.

"No!" She clasped his slick biceps and pulled him back to her. "I do *not* want to look at you."

"No?"

"No."

West covered one of her clasping hands with his own and drew it between them. "Then you may touch me. Don't feel ashamed. Is that what you're after?"

"I am after nothing," Elizabeth said, irritably scraping her long, punishing nails down his wet chest until he flinched. "It was foolish of me to come here. I'm sorry that I did."

"Don't be. I'm always delighted to have your company."

"Yes, well, your delight is about to come to an end.

Drop your hands from me, but don't move back. Stay right where you are while I turn around."

"As you wish, Mrs. Curtin." West allowed his hands to fall to his sides.

"Thank you. I appreciate that," she said, looking into his silver eyes.

She swiftly did an about-face, her turn executed so close to him, she avoided again seeing his nakedness. She drew in a long breath and was about to step away from him. But that breath came out in a loud rush when his long, wet arms came around her and West slammed her back against his hard body.

"So you don't want to see me?" he said, his arms tightening dangerously. "You don't want to touch me?" The words came out in a low, steady voice made more frightening by its lack of expression.

"That's what I said."

"Are you telling the truth?" he asked, in a tone that said he knew damn well she wasn't.

"Yes," she managed, wanting it to be the truth, hoping that it was.

"Ah, that's too bad," he said. "With me it's just the opposite. When I came down to the river where you were bathing, it was just to see you. And I didn't see nearly enough to suit me." His hand abruptly lifted from her waist, his long brown fingers wrapped themselves gently around her throat and pressed her head back against his wet chest. He leaned down and said just above her ear, "And I want to touch you, even though you swear you don't want to touch me."

"Yes, well, touching me wouldn't do you a bit of good," she said coldly, hoping he didn't mean to touch her now, knowing full well that he did.

"We'll see," he said, and his fingertips began gently to stroke her throat. To her disgust Elizabeth felt her face grow flush and warm. She hoped he hadn't caught the quickening tempo of her breathing and knew he had when those stroking fingers slid down inside the opening of her pullover shirt.

While his thumb rested on her collarbone, his fingers fanned tantalizingly over her flesh and settled into the nervous warmth of her underarm. It was then that his other hand began to move. Deserting the silver concho belt around her waist, it moved down to spread over her flat belly, the tips of his fingers gently applying pressure.

At once her clothes felt tight and confining and she became very aware of his body, naked and hot, pressed against hers. Her lips parted, her neck arched, and she leaned back against him, his bare hard frame supporting hers.

His hand returned to the silver concho belt at her waist, and Elizabeth felt relief. Her head came up off his chest, her eyes lowered to the tanned fingers toying with one of the circular silver disks. She started to say something, to make some cutting comment. But before she could speak those tanned wet fingers again deserted the belt.

West bent his head so that his dark, glistening cheek was pressed to hers. They both silently watched as the tips of his fingers found and settled on the seam that went down the center of Elizabeth's rust suede pants.

Elizabeth's breath caught in her throat when those fingertips slowly, enticingly moved downward, tracing the fabric's seam, igniting the flesh beneath. Mesmerized by the sensual sight of those lean brown fingers gliding down the middle of her quivering belly, Elizabeth swallowed hard when at last those moving magical fingers reached the spot where the seam of the trousers met the seam of her pliant woman's body.

West turned his face in and kissed her flushed cheek as his fingers gently caressed her. Allowing his middle finger to dominate, to slip between her legs and apply just the right amount of pressure, he kissed the corner of her open mouth.

A sweet warm suffusion began deep inside Elizabeth, thrilling her, frightening her. Arms hanging limply at her sides, she stood there waiting for him to stop, hoping that he would, and soon.

She was just beginning to hope that he wouldn't when his hands abruptly fell away from her, his droll sense of humor returning. "Well, what do you know, you were right. Touching you didn't do me a bit of good. Get on back to camp. Heck, I know when I'm beat."

28

❧❧❧

Dane Curtin stared at his empty glass. He smiled, poured himself another, and sipped, allowing the smooth rich brandy to spill over his tongue and glide down his throat. When the warmth reached his chest, he sighed and stretched contentedly.

Dane licked his wide lips and gazed about his dazzling palace. The underground palace was filled with deep, clear pools and rock-embellished grottos and rare crystal formations—vast chambers with soaring domed ceilings and dense forests of pure white stalactites, stalagmites, and great hanging curtains of vari-colored stone.

And gold.

A treasure of glittering, spendable gold!

Thick dusky lashes fluttering low over his gleaming emerald eyes, Dane smiled with deep satisfaction. Here in his cool, shadowy kingdom eight hundred feet below the parched deserts above, he ruled supreme. To those whom he governed he was more than a mere monarch. He was god and master.

Dane laughed suddenly, the sound of his laughter echoing off the shadowed rocky walls of his private chambers. Twisting a glistening golden curl around his long, pale forefinger, he continued to laugh almost giddily.

Stretched out on his fur-covered couch, his long diaphanous robes hiding nothing of his slender, glorious physique, even Dane Curtin felt he truly was a god. A beautiful god. His hair, grown quite long from his weeks below ground, was a mass of gleaming golden curls and his flesh was as pale as ice. No wonder he was worshiped.

Dane poured himself another brandy and drank thirstily. He had found that if he kept himself a little tipsy at all times, it was much easier to stay way down in this dank, eerie, underworld without fear of losing his mind. Soon enough his self-imposed exile would be over. Rich and victorious, he would emerge into the sunshine, return to New York, collect his beautiful flame-haired bride, strip her naked, and make love to her on a bed strewn with gold.

Licking the brandy from his lips, Dane continued to toy with his golden curls and to daydream about his reconciliation with the lovely, innocent Elizabeth. But soon he tired of the game and wished, as he had on more than one occasion, that killing his business associate, Tom Lancaster, hadn't been necessary. He missed Tom. Missed him terribly. Tom had been enjoyable company and an intelligent, witty, likable comrade.

Dane sighed a little sadly as his thoughts went back to that unforgettable evening when he and Tom had found the gold. It was the week after they first discovered the caverns. They were exploring one of the many chambers and it came to be the hour when the bats awoke and flew en masse from the cave. One, a small gray-brown furry little creature that had apparently lost his way, darted into the chamber. The Mexican minions, slim Paco and the fat, walleyed Ortiz and their compadres quaked in fear at seeing the "winged creature." When it swooped down and bit Dane on the cheek, drawing blood, they gasped and were frozen with terror.

Tired and angered by the bat bite and the foolishness of the superstitious Mexicans, Dane decided it was time to quit for the day. But Tom, a few steps ahead of Dane, suddenly let out a low whistle of disbelief. His irritation forgotten, Dane hurried forth and his eyes widened as they beheld an unbelievable sight.

There in a vast, dome-ceilinged natural amphitheater he stood up to his neck in gold! Transfixed, he held his pine torch high and stared. At the amphitheater's center, gold ingots, stacked like cordwood, were surrounded by thirteen guarding skeletons chained to colorful stalagmites.

Gold!

Yards and yards of gold. Stacks and stacks. Tons and tons.

The lost Grayson gold.

Lifting his torch high, Dane couldn't believe his ears when Tom Lancaster said they should leave the gold as they had found it. Leave the bodies and cave and never return. The legend of the lost Grayson gold was true. The skeletons proved it. They would die if they attempted to take the gold from the caverns. They'd wind up skeletons themselves.

The frightened Mexicans were crossing themselves and shaking their heads in agreement with Tom. Deliriously happy but ever-resourceful, Dane Curtain, ignoring his partner, turned to face the big-eyed Mexicans.

Holding the pine torch close, he touched the pinpoint of blood left by the bat's bite. In a voice soft yet deadly cold, he said, "Only I am unafraid of the 'winged creatures of the night.' I am one of their number. I am their leader. Their master. And yours. Do you understand?"

Trembling, the peasants could only nod, too frightened to speak.

"My creatures and I feed on blood." Dane licked his full, sensual lips until they glistened in the torch light. "Human blood. I am all-powerful. Unless you obey me, I will unleash from their hiding place millions and millions of vampire bats. The very air will be black with their number."

Their terror was absolute. From that night the peasants did anything he asked of them. What he asked was that they transport the heavy gold bars topside to be stashed in a well-concealed hiding place until every last ingot was above earth.

He sent Paco and Ortiz into villages to bring back liquor and food and women. They obeyed without question and were far too intimidated to consider telling anyone of the pale master who ruled an underground golden kingdom of winged night creatures.

In time, Tom Lancaster came around to Dane's way of thinking. There was no curse on the gold; such an idea was ridiculous. Why leave the gold untouched? It was theirs for the taking.

Theirs? Dane didn't like the sound of that. Patiently he pointed out to Tom that the claim was registered in *his* wife's name. The gold belonged entirely to Mrs. Elizabeth Montbleau Curtin. And to her loving husband and heir, Dane Curtin.

Dane had thought that was the end of it. But one night Dane had spent the evening entertaining a young woman in his private chambers, a pretty Mexican senorita his minions had brought to him from Malaga. When he tired of her, Dane got up, strapped a leather-sheathed dagger around his trim waist, swirled his long black loden cape around his naked body, and moved quietly through the shadowed passageways toward the amphitheater. There in the torchlight he caught the unsuspecting Tom staring at the gold.

"What are you doing here?" Dane's voice startled Tom.

Tom turned, smiled, and said, "Nothing really. Couldn't sleep is all."

"You're stealing from me!"

"Stealing?" Tom lifted his empty hands. "I've never stolen a penny in my life."

"Liar! You're carrying away my gold while I sleep."

"You're crazy, Curtin. Nuts! You've been down here too long. Look at yourself. Roaming around here in that black cape like some kind of—"

"Be quiet!" Dane snarled, reaching inside his cape and drawing a jewel-handled dagger. "I am the Pale Master, damn you! I rule this underground kingdom and all that is in it! I will not have you stealing my gold!"

"You *are* insane," Tom said calmly. "I'm getting the hell out of here and . . ."

Dane rushed forward and plunged the razor-sharp dagger into Tom's stomach. A look of disbelief and horror in his eyes, Tom's lips moved, but no sound came. Only a slight trickle of blood appeared at the left corner of his mouth. His hands clasped around the dagger's hilt, Tom crumpled to his knees and died.

"I didn't want to do that," Dane defended himself to the dead man. "You gave me no choice."

Dane pulled the dagger free of Tom's body, wiped the blood off on his shirtfront, and resheathed the weapon. He stood looking down at the body for a long moment before going down on his knees beside it, his black cape billowing out around him.

Dane's hand went to Tom's chin. He turned Tom's head to one side and let his long, pale fingers flutter over the length of Tom's exposed neck, from earlobe to collarbone. He smiled demonically, leaned down to the dead man, put his lips to Tom's throat, opened his mouth wide and sank his sharp, white teeth into the warm flesh.

Moments later Dane crossed the vast amphitheater, stepped out into the shadowy corridor, clapped his hands loudly three times, and waited impatiently as Paco and the walleyed Ortiz scurried forward. Dane motioned them to follow him.

He led them directly to Tom's body. They saw the teeth marks on Tom's throat and shuddered.

Dane ordered them to toss the body over the apron of the amphitheater stage into the chasm of blackness. Stricken with terror, the pair quickly obeyed.

With Paco trembling uncontrollably and Ortiz biting on a knuckle, his bulging white walleye roaming wildly, they stood respectfully behind the pale master while the body of Tom Lancaster fell through the thick blackness.

They never heard it hit bottom.

29

She had learned her lesson.

Elizabeth was firmly resolved to stay away from West Quarternight. He was a cynical, amoral man to whom the concept of decency and honor meant nothing. He never regretted the sins of his yesterdays, nor intended to live better tomorrows. This life apparently meant nothing to him and he was surely headed for hell and damnation in the next.

Well, he wasn't going to take her along with him. She did care. She cared a great deal, about both this life and the one to follow. Morality and self-esteem were vital to her well-being in this life and the state of her immortal soul was important in the next, and she was in danger of losing both with Quarternight around. Any time she was with him, she felt an intense sexual excitement she could not deny. Her fear was as strong as her excitement.

The solution to her predicament, however, was actually quite simple.

Stay out of his way. Never again foolishly suppose that she could successfully play a joke on him. She could never get even. Never embarrass him the way he had embarrassed her. Never tempt him and tease

him and bring him to his knees. It was virtually impossible to get the best of a man who cared about
nothing and no one.

Those were the thoughts in Elizabeth's mind the
next afternoon as she bumped along on the wagon
seat beside Grady. She was vaguely aware that Grady
was talking again—or still. She wasn't sure which.
But, for the past hour, she had heard nothing of what
he said.

Feeling half mean about her inattention, Elizabeth
turned to look at the white-bearded scout. As Grady
talked, he smiled—as usual. His blue eyes were twinkling, his face was ruddy with good health, and his
lion's mane of absolutely white hair appeared as he
took off his sweat-stained Stetson and wiped his face
on his forearm.

". . . and then after that, I was a lawmen for better
than a year." Grady, putting his hat back on, felt Elizabeth's eyes and turned.

Elizabeth smiled at him. "You were a policeman?"

"Policeman, hell!" he said, frowning at her as
though she were dim-witted. "This ain't New York
City, missy, and I wasn't running around with no
night stick! I was a New Mexico Ranger. I still got
some souvenirs from them days." He started smiling
again. "Yep, I got, among other things, a couple of
double-barreled shotguns, six Bowie knives, three
Mexican daggers, and a couple of nail-studded clubs
—all taken single-handedly from felons and outlaws."

Grady told her of knifings, murders, domestic violence, Indian raids, and bank and stagecoach holdups.

Aghast, Elizabeth said, "Grady, you're lucky to be
alive!"

The white-haired mountain man was totally sincere
when he replied, "Aw, I don't believe I've ever been in
anything that was serious, missy."

The earnest statement struck Elizabeth as hilarious. Murders and holdups and Indians raids not serious? Then what on earth would he find dangerous? She began to laugh and couldn't stop. She was laughing when West, riding just ahead, turned his sorrel mare Lizzie and came trotting back toward the wagon.

While Elizabeth wiped tears of laughter from her eyes, West pulled up on the mare, reined her about in a semicircle, and rode alongside the wagon. He gave Grady a questioning look. Grady shrugged.

"Had too much sun, Mrs. Curtin?" West asked her.

Elizabeth tossed her red hair with girlish abandon. "No, Quarternight, I have *not* had too much sun, thank you very much. The only thing I've had too much of is you."

"Now, that could be," West mused aloud. "Or perhaps not nearly enough."

"Sonny, you shouldn't say things like that," Grady scolded.

"Oh, let him run his head," Elizabeth said. "He's enjoying it."

"Not really, Mrs. Curtin. I'm a man of few words," West teased, his lips stretching into a wide grin. "A man of action."

"Is that so?" she replied. "Then let's hope you locate some action somewhere soon." Her blue eyes lifted to meet his gaze. "Looks like you won't be finding any along this trail."

"Oh, I don't know about that," West calmly replied. "I rode back here to let you know you'll be enjoying a real bathtub, a superb meal, and a soft, clean bed tonight."

Elizabeth's eyes immediately widened. "You mean it? We'll stay the night in an inn?"

"Better than that. We'll spend the night in a private mansion," West said. "I've an old and dear friend who has a large rancho up ahead about eight miles. We should arrive there well before sundown. How does that sound?"

"Are you certain your friend won't mind putting us up?"

West's gray eyes gleamed devilishly. "My friend will be delighted—very hospitable."

With that, he neck-reined the sorrel away, and Elizabeth immediately began looking forward to the evening. Grady immediately started talking again. He began telling her about Rancho Caballo and the huge hacienda and the royal welcome they would all receive.

But Elizabeth wasn't listening. She was too preoccupied with looking forward to a hot bath in a real tub and a good night's sleep in a soft bed. She could hardly wait.

The sun was sliding toward the distant western mountains when the contingent approached the ranch of West's old and dear friend. Elizabeth had just caught her first glimpse of a large sand-colored adobe hacienda in the distance when Edmund excitedly brought his chestnut gelding up alongside the buck wagon.

Elizabeth looked up at her brother-in-law, smiled, and said, "Did West tell you, Edmund?"

"Yes, he did," Edmund replied. "Looks like we'll be spending the night in comfort."

"Yes! Isn't that wonderful?"

"It is, my dear," Edmund agreed. "And won't it be pleasant seeing Doña Hope again?"

The smile immediately left Elizabeth's face. Her high brow knitted. "Doña Hope? Where will we be seeing Doña Hope again?"

Edmund smiled. "Didn't West tell you? We're spending the night at the Rancho Caballo, the doña's rancho." Edmund looked toward the looming sand-colored hacienda. "Who would have supposed that West was a good friend of the lovely Doña Hope?"

"Who indeed?" Elizabeth said, exasperated.

The location of her elegant home was as beautiful as the woman who lived there. Built on the left bank of the Rio Grande, at a point where the long river was at its widest and joined on the west by the Alamosa River, Rancho Caballo sat in a wide lush valley framed by the rising peaks of the Fra Cristobal and Sierra Caballo mountain ranges.

Elizabeth began to get some sense of the doña's true wealth long before she stood before the heavy hand-carved oak door that graced the entrance to the huge sand-colored hacienda.

As the buck wagon started up a long graveled drive that led to the handsome two-story structure, the sky turned scarlet and the stucco walls of the sprawling desert palace took on the appearance of pink frosting.

Beyond the main house were many adobe outbuildings of the same hue: barns and stables and whitewashed corrals. Far to the back, directly between two mountain crests, was a quarter-mile racetrack for exercising Baca thoroughbred horses.

For once Elizabeth listened with undivided interest as Grady pointed out the supply store, the bakery, the laundry, even the infirmary, all right there at the ranch. There was much activity going on. The shouted commands of lean, leather-trousered vaqueros mingled with the chatter and laughter of happy Mexican women in colorful dresses and lots of turquoise and silver jewelry. All were going about their evening chores. All were employed at and living on Rancho Caballo.

The thought occurred to Elizabeth that Rancho Caballo was like a well-run, self-contained little city. Grudgingly, she decided that there must be a great deal more to the Baca woman than her rare blond beauty. To run such an empire would surely take a healthy portion of brains and ability.

The buck wagon rolled to a stop before the impressive mansion fashioned of eighteen-inch double-adobe walls. Elizabeth, removing her flat-crowned hat and attempting to smooth back her tangled hair, wondered what the doña's reaction would be on seeing her. The last time they had met Doña Hope was slipping out of West Quarternight's hotel room after . . . after . . .

Elizabeth soon stood in the cool wide corridor of the two-story hacienda. A Mexican servant had let them in and had gone upstairs to fetch her mistress. Now the five of them—Taos, Grady, Edmund, West, and she—stood waiting, all silent save Grady.

Very shortly Doña Hope appeared at the top of the wide oak staircase. She was radiant in a white lacy Mexican blouse and full white matching skirts. A wide sash of pale blue accentuated her tiny waist. The white blouse was gathered around the low neckline and short puffed sleeves, and one side had fallen down over a bare ivory shoulder. Her white-blond hair was a shimmering mass of soft loose curls framing her lovely face. One stray, gleaming strand lay atop her full bosom.

"Darling!" the doña exclaimed loudly, looking only at West, and came flying down the stairs.

Smiling at her, West took a couple of steps toward the base of the stairs and held his arms open wide. On reaching him, Doña Hope threw her arms around his neck, drew his dark head down, and kissed him fully on the lips.

While the men all laughed and Grady clapped his hands, Elizabeth averted her eyes, choosing to admire the fine woodwork and moldings that bordered the mansion's doors and windows. But from the corner of her eye she witnessed the kiss and thought the pair terribly rude and disgusting.

Finally the doña released West, turned, and warmly hugged Grady, then Taos. She then turned her full attention to Elizabeth and Edmund.

Doña Hope's smile remained warm and totally confident when she said over her shoulder to West, "Why, darling, I've met the Curtins." To them she trilled, "So wonderful to see you both again. Welcome to my home." Her eyes met Elizabeth's levelly and Elizabeth detected not one trace of uneasiness, at least not on Doña Hope's part. She herself felt awkward and unreasonably irritated. "You do recall, don't you, Mrs. Curtin," the doña went on sweetly, "we met at the Governor's Spring Baile?"

"How could we forget such a gracious, lovely lady, Doña Hope," said Edmund gallantly, beaming at the beautiful blonde.

"Of course, I remember," said Elizabeth, and couldn't resist adding softly, "everything."

"Good, good," said the doña, unperturbed. She turned immediately back to West and hugged one of his long arms to her breast. "If you'll excuse me, I'll go tell the cooks we're having company for dinner. I'll have them fix something special!" She looked up at West and asked, "Darling, will you pour drinks for the gentlemen and the lady or shall I ring for Hernando?"

"Will do," said West.

Elizabeth quietly gritted her teeth when Doña Hope pressed her face to West's muscular arm, bit his biceps playfully, and growled low in her throat like a disturbed feline before hurrying away.

West directed them all into a spacious rectangular sitting room where the high ceiling was beamed and a Spanish fireplace dominated the entire end wall. Massive sofas of rich yellow velvet were complimented with several man-sized easy chairs covered in supple brown suede. A plush Aubusson carpet, patterned in shades of yellows, rusts, and browns, topped the smooth oak floor and handmade shutters of oak adorned each tall window.

It was more than evident that West Quarternight was completely at home in the doña's rambling hacienda. He had found no need to ask where he was to take the guests. Once in the well-appointed room, he walked directly to a long oak cabinet upon which were dozens of handsome cut-crystal decanters. An oak cupboard was above the cabinet. West opened it and Elizabeth saw row upon row of sparkling glasses of all shapes and sizes.

West took down six tiny shot glasses. He unstoppered a squat, square bottle containing a dark amber liquid and poured. From behind another cupboard door he took a small round silver tray, set the shot glasses on it, and moved forward to pass out the drinks.

Doña Hope came rushing into the room and Elizabeth automatically stiffened when the blond woman headed straight for West. The doña laid a possessive hand to the small of his back and said, "Darling, Elizabeth and I have time for only one whiskey." She smiled at the men and then at Elizabeth. "Then we will leave you gentlemen to do as you please while we make ourselves lovely for dinner."

Everyone was still standing. They remained respectfully standing as the beautiful blond woman in the lacy white blouse and skirts hovered over West as he bore the silver tray with three small glasses remaining atop it. He had come to Elizabeth first, but she had refused. Now the doña insisted that Elizabeth join them all in a drink. Again Elizabeth shook her head.

"Oh, come on, Mrs. Curtin," Doña Hope said, "have one little jigger of whisky. It will do you good."

"I'd really rather not." Elizabeth declined as graciously as possible.

"Why, Elizabeth . . . may I call you Elizabeth . . . this is a celebration," said the doña. "And I'm serving no ordinary whiskey. It's the finest Kentucky bourbon ever distilled. I only offer it to my most special guests."

Elizabeth didn't feel like arguing. She took the glass. Doña Hope smiled approvingly and took her own glass from the tray. West picked up the last one and set the silver tray aside.

Everyone now had a glass of the aged bourbon. Doña Hope wrapped her hand around West's left arm, looked up at him with adoration shining in her wide blue eyes, and said, "Now I'd like to propose a toast."

"Yes, yes," everyone murmured, watching her.

Her eyes finally leaving West, the doña held up her shot glass and addressed the small gathering. "To you all. To my old friends, Grady and Taos." She favored each with a smile. "And to my new friends, Elizabeth and Edmund Curtin. Welcome to Rancho Caballo." She paused, laughed, and warned, "No, wait, Grady, not yet. I have one more little toast to make before we drink."

"Well, hurry it up, will you, Doña," Grady said, "I'm powerful thirsty."

Doña Hope ran her caressing fingers up and down West's arm. "To the Territory's best scout."

She held her glass out to West. Smiling, he touched it with his own.

Everyone murmured, "Here, here," and drank.

Including Elizabeth.

Lifting the heavy glass to her lips, Elizabeth closed her eyes and drank the fiery whiskey down in one long powerful swallow. Although it tasted awful and her eyes watered and her throat and chest burned and her arms felt strangely heavy, she was grateful that the doña had bullied her into accepting the bourbon.

A good stiff drink was an absolute necessity if she was to make it through this disagreeable evening without screaming!

30

"Oh, no, really, I couldn't."

"But of course you can."

"I could just as easily ask Taos to bring one of my traveling suits up from the wagon," Elizabeth said.

"A traveling suit for this very special dinner?" Doña Hope's perfectly arched eyebrows lifted. "Come now, do you wear a traveling suit when your husband takes you out to dinner in New York? Hardly."

The two women were upstairs in Doña Hope's dressing room. Elizabeth had never seen a dressing room one quarter as large. Located off the doña's spacious white bath, the dressing room had no windows, but there were skylights overhead for daytime illumination and gaslights shimmering in white porcelain wall sconces for the nights.

The room was entirely of fragrant cedar, and an abundance of riding habits and afternoon dresses and expensive evening gowns—arranged by color—lined three of the cedar walls. The remaining wall was home to dozens of pairs of expensive boots and shoes sitting in neat columns on cedar shelves. There were also gloves and hats and scarves and parasols. Tall rows of cedar drawers held satin chemises and lacy underpants and filmy nightgowns and sheer silk stockings.

Carpeted in fine plush wool that had been dyed as white as the doña's hair, the cedar-lined dressing room had at its center not one, but four free-standing full-length mirrors and a pair of matching white silk chaise lounges. Between the couches was a low oval table of white marble atop which sat a silver pitcher filled with ice water, a carafe of red wine, and a half-dozen crystal glasses.

"Here, what about this one?" Doña Hope took from the rack a dazzling black brocade trimmed with white chiffon and spangles. She eagerly held it up to Elizabeth, cocked her head to one side, and pondered. "No. It just isn't right for you." She tossed it across one of the white silk chaises.

Looking about at the tens of thousands of dollars worth of luxurious clothing, Elizabeth, thinking aloud, said, "My goodness, Doña, you certainly have everything a woman could ever want."

"No, my dear. Not quite everything," the doña said, but didn't elaborate. "Ah! I have it. Look at this one, Elizabeth."

The blonde held up a totally exquisite gown of shimmering turquoise silk. Of the very latest style, the gown's bodice was cut into a deep V, which was partially filled with net ruching of the same turquoise hue. Tightly fitted around the waist, it was fashioned in the pointed peplum style. Tiny cap sleeves were nothing but net and covered only the tops of the wearer's shoulders. The skirts were long and full, edged with a deep ruffle and drawn back.

"I can't pretend that it isn't gorgeous," said Elizabeth truthfully.

"With your red hair it will be perfect! How fortunate that we're so near the same size."

"Fortunate for me." Elizabeth replied.

Doña Hope tossed the turquoise silk on the white chaise, took Elizabeth's arm, and led her from the dressing room, saying, "I'll put you in my favorite guest room and have one of the servants bring the turquoise dress and all the accessories you'll need. Feel free to keep Juanita with you for as long as you like. She's an excellent back scrubber and she will help you get dressed and fix your hair."

The guest quarters to which Elizabeth was shown, a bright airy beige bedroom opening onto a wide upstairs front balcony, was at the opposite end of the hacienda from Doña Hope's large suite. Doña left Elizabeth there, reminding her to ring for anything she needed and telling her they would all meet downstairs for dinner at precisely nine o'clock.

Elizabeth was glad to be alone. Feeling the effects of the strong bourbon, she sighed, crossed to the bed, and fell lazily over onto her back, stretching her arms up over her head. The bed was very soft, very comfortable. How enjoyable it would be just to take a nice long bath, crawl in between the cool silky sheets, and stay there until it was time to leave in the morning.

A wry smile touched her lips. She might as well stay upstairs. With the rich, beautiful Doña Hope around, who would notice that Elizabeth Curtin was missing?

It was still twenty minutes of nine, but Elizabeth was restless. She'd been dressed for the past fifteen minutes and was tired of waiting. So why do it? She would go downstairs, perhaps take a short stroll out on the grounds until the others came down for dinner.

She took one last look at herself and frowned. She had refused the offer of Doña's maid in helping with her hair. Now she wished she hadn't been so stubborn. She'd washed her long auburn hair, and while it shone with highlights, she hadn't been able to do much with it. Finally giving up, she had pinned it atop her head, but already wispy strands were slipping down around her cheeks and along the nape of her neck.

The doña's turquoise gown fit as though it had been made for her, but the bodice was cut so severely low, Elizabeth felt naked. The net ruching was all that covered the tops of her full, pushed-up breasts, and she would have to remember not to bend over.

Elizabeth stepped out into the silent corridor, went to the wide oaken staircase at the center of the big hacienda, and swept noiselessly down the stairs. She peeked into the sitting room where they had all shared drinks earlier. It was empty. Glad that it was, Elizabeth went inside, immediately crossed to a pair of heavy double doors thrown open to the night, and stepped outside.

She crossed the portaled flagstone porch and paused at the edge of the flower-filled courtyard. Water splashed lyrically from a three-tiered fountain and soft guitar music floated over the high adobe walls enclosing the private courtyard. Diamond-bright stars filled a black velvet sky. A gentle breeze from out of the west stirred the wispy curls framing her face. It was a cool, beautiful night and Elizabeth stood inhaling deeply of the fragrant blossoms and clean desert air.

She jumped when a match flared out in the shadowy courtyard. Her startled gaze went to the tiny orange flame. Lighting a thin brown cigar, West Quarternight sat alone on an iron-lace settee, half hidden by a smothering bougainvillea. Silently, Elizabeth counted to ten before moving forward. Then, as calmly as possible she lifted her turquoise silk skirts and approached him.

His long legs stretched out and crossed before him, West wore superbly tailored evening clothes of midnight black, a fact that annoyed Elizabeth. She felt sure the rugged scout had not packed such a suit for the journey. Apparently he kept a wardrobe at the doña's hacienda.

Moving toward him, she noticed that the well-fitted jacket was unbuttoned and parted. The ruffled white shirt was half open down his dark chest, a black silk neck piece was untied and hanging loose around his stiff white collar. One long arm was resting on the settee's high back, two inches of white shirt cuff thrusting from the jacket sleeve. Long, tanned fingers curled around the white iron lace.

When she neared him, West took the thin brown cigar from his lips and smiled engagingly.

"You look as though you're waiting for someone," said Elizabeth, attempting to sound casual.

"For the next beautiful woman that happens by," was West's low, teasing response. He patted the seat beside him.

Elizabeth shook her head. "Only, you assumed the next beautiful woman would be Doña Hope," she said, and couldn't stop herself from adding, "I'm fully aware, Quarternight, that you and the blond widow are more than just friends."

Unperturbed, West shrugged wide shoulders. "You listened to idle gossip in Santa Fe, Mrs. Curtin. Few things flourish as well as rumor." He put the brown cigar in his mouth and drew on it, its red ember glowing hotly, lighting his dark handsome features.

"I heard no rumors," Elizabeth said. "I *saw* the doña leaving your hotel room the night of the Governor's Spring Baile. And I know what she was doing there," she continued smugly.

West took the cigar from his lips, studied it thoughtfully for a few seconds, then lifted his eyes to meet hers. "Do you, now?" His voice remained low, calm. "Well, spare me your self-righteousness, Mrs. Curtin.

You and I have also been more than friends, as I fondly recall."

Elizabeth let that pass, but snapped, "Why must you constantly be such a womanizer?"

"I've got that special calling, I guess," he drawled lazily. "Like some people hear the calling to be a preacher." He laughed.

Elizabeth did not. "I think you should marry Doña Hope," she said acidly, reaching up and plucking a fuchsia blossom from the bougainvillea.

"What? And make every other woman in the Territory unhappy?" West flashed his white dazzling teeth. He came to his feet, dropped the cigar, and crushed it under his heel. "Let's get back to you. I find you breathtaking tonight, Mrs. Curtin. And believe me, I've got a keen eye for beauty."

"Yes, well, I've got a keen nose for trouble, Quarternight, so I think I'll go back inside." She handed him the fuchsia blossom. "For your lapel."

West took it. Holding her gaze, he rolled the flower's fragile stem between thumb and forefinger, then held it back out to her. "Won't you do the honors? You're so good at it."

"No," she said, hastily adding the first thing that came into her mind, "you're too tall."

West swiftly reached out, caught her wrist, drew her forward, and sat back down on the settee. "Now I'm not." His silver eyes glittered in the dusky desert twilight. He again held out the blossom. "Please." He paused, then added, "Elizabeth."

It was the first time he had ever called her by her given name. The way he said it—as though he liked the taste of it on his tongue—made Elizabeth suddenly weak-kneed and faint. Or was it simply this afternoon's whiskey? Tentatively, she reached out and took the fuchsia blossom from him. Nervously, she came nearer, moved to the left of his bent knees, and slowly leaned down to him.

Inexplicably shaky, she fumbled with his black satin lapel and made several futile attempts before she was successful in placing the blossom's stem through the small buttonhole. Her eyes on her task, she had completely forgotten about the borrowed turquoise gown's low-cut bodice. She was doing exactly what she had cautioned herself against. Bending over. Allowing her bare bosom to come dangerously close to spilling from the dress. And giving West Quarternight an eyeful.

"Elizabeth"—again he called her by her name— "may I say you have the most beautiful breasts I've ever—"

"Oh, God!" She gasped, straightened immediately, and quickly pressed both hands modestly over her bosom.

For a split second West's silver eyes went flat and still above his prominent cheekbones. Then he laughed and again came to his feet. His voice cool, faintly mocking, he said, "A woman more concerned with virtue than vanity. What a waste."

"Why must you never miss a chance to torment me! Haven't you any heart at all?"

"Yes," he replied levelly, "and I intend to keep it right where it is."

"Well, while you're at it you can also keep your—"

"West, are you out here?" Doña Hope's voice came from the flagstone porch. "Darling, where are you?"

"Be right there," West called evenly and didn't move —just kept standing there, looking at Elizabeth with those compelling silver eyes. He must have sensed her helpless attraction to his remarkable sexual power, because he said in a low, determined tone, "I do want you, Mrs. Curtin. You know that don't you?"

"Yes," she said, unable to tear her gaze from his, "I'm afraid I do."

"Don't be afraid," he said softly, hooking his little finger under a wispy red curl at her cheek. "I'm not."

Breathless, attracted, Elizabeth feebly shook her head and brushed his hand away. "Quarternight, you're just no good."

"The good die young," he responded immediately, and the smile left his handsome face, his features became sharpened, hardened. For the first time ever, Elizabeth got a tiny glimpse of a very different West Quarternight. Flatly, almost wearily, he continued, "The rest of us came back from the war and no one wanted us. All the good boys were killed in the war, or should have been." His lashes lowered over strangely wistful gray eyes. "The good died young."

"West, I never meant—"

"We'd better go in." His smile was already back in place. He took her arm. "You wouldn't want your hostess getting jealous."

Elizabeth had supposed that Doña Hope would serve the traditional southwestern fare that everyone in this part of the world so favored; beans, beef, rice, cornmeal tortillas, and black coffee. She might have known better. Doña Hope was no ordinary hostess, no ordinary woman.

Absolutely dazzling in a long white gown of shimmering satin, her white-blond hair elaborately dressed atop her head, diamonds flashing on her pale throat and at her earlobes, the doña ushered them all into a salon she called the small dining room. It was small when compared to the huge one at the front of the mansion, where a long mahogany table could comfortably seat fifty.

In the small dining room a silk-covered table was set for six with crystal goblets and heavy English ster-

ling and fine bone china. Tall white candles in silver
candelabra bathed the room in soft, romantic light,
and a bouquet of purple mariposa and pink roses perfumed the air. As for the food—well, it was no typical
meal.

A large silver tray held raw oysters on a bed of
chipped ice. In a deep silver bowl was black Russian
caviar. There was stuffed quail. Lobster tails. Smoked
salmon. Leg of lamb. A half-dozen vegetables. In addition, there was also tender Baca-raised beef and
plenty of spicy Mexican dishes because the thoughtful
doña knew that Taos and Grady wouldn't touch the
other fare.

The seating arrangements placed Doña Hope at the
head of the table with West opposite, facing her. Elizabeth and Edmund were across from Grady and
Taos, Elizabeth nearest to West, Edmund beside the
doña. Uncomfortably conscious of West's nearness,
Elizabeth was unusually quiet during the long meal.

The others talked plenty, including Edmund, who
was obviously charmed by their lovely hostess. It was
apparent that Doña Hope was used to entertaining
and was practiced at putting everyone at their ease—
especially men.

After Doña Hope had expressed her concern for
Dane Curtin's fate, she steered the conversation back
toward more lighthearted subjects. At her encourage-
ment, Grady told one of his wild Frémont tales and
Doña Hope threw back her blond head and laughed
uproariously. Elizabeth decided she had never known
a woman more confident and charming, in addition
to being a rare beauty. No wonder she was one of
West Quarternight's favorite lovers.

Inwardly sighing, Elizabeth lifted her stemmed
glass, took a sip of champagne, and stole a glance at
West. He was smiling and he was looking at the doña
as she talked. His long, tanned fingers were wrapped

around a crystal water tumbler. Slowly he lifted the glass to his lips and took a drink.

Elizabeth noted, and not for the first time, that his hands, like everything else about him, were attractive. Never hurried, never awkward, those lean brown fingers could reach up, snag a cigar from his pocket, flash out a match, snap it into flame, and light up . . . all in one neat, controlled motion.

Just as easily, just as smoothly, they could help a woman out of her clothes.

West set his glass back on the silk-covered table and Elizabeth watched as that intriguing hand moved gracefully to pick up his heavy sterling fork. In her mind's eye Elizabeth saw those lean fingers pulling the white satin gown away from Doña Hope's flawless flesh. Elizabeth's throat grew dry and her stomach tightened painfully. Seconds later, when Doña Hope told an amusing story with more than subtle sexual undertones, the bold blond woman looked longingly down the table at West as if she could hardly wait to get him alone.

The wine and sparkling champagne freely flowed and by the time dessert arrived, everyone was in high spirits, with the exception of Elizabeth. Taking only a couple of bites of the sweet concoction of whipped cream and Marsala wine, Elizabeth wondered miserably if the meal would ever end.

Finally, it did.

Doña Hope rose and led them into a small cozy parlor at the back of the hacienda with interior walls unlike any Elizabeth had ever seen. Watered silk of deep burgundy met intricately carved leather at a height of three feet. The effect was stunning. Deep wine leather couches faced each other before a brightly burning fire of fragrant piñon wood. A heavy square piano sat in the corner, facing the room.

Brandy was splashed into snifters and cigars were lighted by the men. From her place on one of the long leather sofas, Elizabeth consciously tried to keep her eyes off West. But Doña Hope made that near to impossible. The beautiful woman in the slinky white satin gown insisted that West play the piano.

Shrugging out of his black evening jacket, West obligingly carried his brandy to the piano, took a long drink, and set the glass down. Tugging gently at the creases in his snug black trousers, he took a seat on the bench and kneaded his hands together. He played masterfully, but Elizabeth was not surprised. After all, his were the hands of an artist.

She *was* surprised by the tune he chose. Somehow the sweet sadness of "My Old Kentucky Home" didn't seem to fit the cynical, unfeeling West Quarternight.

"Guess Sonny still ain't completely forgot his old home place," Grady said in a loud stage whisper. He shook his white head.

West Quarternight from Kentucky? She hadn't known that. Come to think of it, she knew next to nothing about the enigmatic man. He certainly never spoke of his home, his family, his past.

When West began to sing in that deep, smooth baritone voice, Elizabeth couldn't help but stare. Doña Hope stared as well. Standing with her back to the fireplace, the doña looked at him with unveiled adoration. Soon she drained her brandy glass, crossed the parlor, and stepped around behind West.

Smiling, she placed her well-manicured hands atop his wide shoulders and sang the sentimental song with him. When the number was completed, West stayed at the piano, but played no more. Waving away the applause and calls for an encore, he reached for his brandy glass and said, with a laugh, that he had completed his limited repertoire. Edmund suggested his sister-in-law play, but Elizabeth quickly declined.

She didn't feel like playing. She didn't even feel like being in the room. As conversation swirled around her, she could think of nothing but West and the doña. Doña Hope and West Quarternight. The beautiful blond widow and the dark, handsome scout. The bold, sensual woman who had come out of the La Fonda hotel room where she had left the dark, sated man naked on the bed.

Doña Hope continued to stand behind West. As she talked, she lifted her hands from West's wide shoulders and affectionately ran her fingers through his thick blue-black hair. Pressing his dark head back against her soft bosom, she lovingly fingered the thick glossy locks and stroked his tanned face.

Elizabeth felt uncomfortably warm.

She told herself she was seated too near the piñon fire, but knew that wasn't the cause. She found it extremely unsettling to see Doña Hope with her hands roaming possessively over West Quarternight.

While the others laughed and talked and paid no mind to the tender scene, Elizabeth gritted her teeth, looked away, and wished she could flee from the room. Shortly, Taos and Grady bade their good nights, Grady admitting they were anxious to get down to the bunkhouse for some serious stud poker with the Rancho Caballo vaqueros.

The two men were hardly out the door before Edmund yawned, apologized for his rudeness—blamed the desert air—and said it was time he went up to bed. Elizabeth quickly followed suit.

Climbing the wide oaken staircase with her brother-in-law, Elizabeth was silent as Edmund spoke of how much he had enjoyed the evening. Forcing a smile, she nodded. When they reached the second-floor landing, Elizabeth cast one last curious look back downstairs.

In the wide corridor below, Doña Hope turned to West, slipped a pale hand inside his half open white shirt, raked her nails through the dense dark chest hair, smiled suggestively, and said, "Bedtime at last, my love."

31

❧❧❧

Bare-chested, a snifter of brandy in his dark right hand, West sat sprawled comfortably on a white silk-covered chair in Doña Hope's capacious white bedroom suite. A knee hooked over the chair's arm, foot dangling, he wore only his tight black trousers and patent-leather shoes.

Directly before him, twenty feet from his chair, a sweetly scented piñon fire burned in the white marble fireplace. Behind him, across the room, the white silk sheets on the doña's huge bed had been turned down for the night. On either side of the bed, candles in sparkling crystal holders burned atop white marble night tables. The firelight and the candlelight were the large white room's only illumination.

A set of white double doors to the front balcony were thrown open to the cool evening. A pleasant breeze ruffled the room's silky white curtains and somewhere a vaquero still strummed a guitar, the haunting Latin music adding to the romance of the desert night.

Staring into the fire's leaping orange flames, West waited for a woman to come to him. A blond, sensual woman who enjoyed and expected physical pleasure.

An erotic woman willing to do anything he desired. A wanton woman eager to perform the most unorthodox of sexual acts so long as it gave them both ecstasy.

His kind of woman.

And yet, his thoughts were on another woman.

A beautiful flame-haired woman in a shimmering turquoise gown who also enjoyed physical pleasure, but insisted on denying it was so. An erotic woman by nature, whose ladylike pretense had everyone fooled. Except him. A wanton woman who was willing to perform the most unorthodox of sexual acts—but only when there was a payoff that had nothing to do with ecstasy.

West ground his even white teeth and his silver-gray eyes narrowed. The lovely redhead had given herself to him that night in the stockade in exchange for her life. Now she had married wealthy easterner Dane Curtin in exchange for luxury and social position. Flesh bartered for gain.

West knew her kind. He could have her body this very night in exchange for his silence. The deceitful Elizabeth Curtin would take him into her bed faster than Doña Hope, if she believed for one minute it was that or be exposed for what she really was—a deceptively sweet-looking imposter capable of coldly committing murder and adultery.

Lost in thought, West never noticed when Doña Hope came floating in from her dressing room. Determined she would get and hold his undivided attention, the doña silently circled his white chair, and came to stand between him and the fireplace.

West look up at her and smiled.

In a nightgown of pale ivory satin, her long white-blond hair brushed out and falling around her shoulders, she was nothing short of gorgeous. The gown hugged her slim body so tightly her large nipples

showed clearly. Curved in at her small waist, the soft
satin hung on the bias to outline her hips and thighs,
and fall to her slender ankles. Holding his gaze, Doña
Hope moved her white slippered feet apart and licked
her lips.

With the firelight behind her, every provocative
curve of her lush body was outlined. Slowly she
turned about to show him the rest of his carefully
wrapped package. In back, the white satin gown was
slashed to her waist and hugged her rounded buttocks snugly. Her bare slender back was pale as porcelain, her long platinum hair the texture of fine silk.

The doña turned back to face West and said in a
low, husky voice, "Would you like to have a peek at
the legs you'll soon have wrapped around your back?"

West grinned. "I'd like a nice, long look, please." He
took a big swallow of brandy.

Doña Hope smiled and placed her fingertips on her
flared hips. She gathered two handfuls of the slippery
satin fabric and very slowly, very seductively drew
the long white gown up, up until it was bunched between her firm naked thighs. Her long, slender legs
were completely exposed.

She stood there, bathed in the firelight, allowing the
seated man to take a long, leisurely look at her many
charms. The gown hiked high, Doña Hope shook her
long platinum mane about her face, moved her feet
apart, and posed provocatively. Aware that the firelight playing on her near-naked body enhanced her
pale blond beauty, she again pirouetted slowly, allowing him the pleasure of languidly admiring her.

She knew him so well. West was a man who could
become highly aroused by the sight of a beautiful naked woman. She wanted her lover to be highly
aroused on this May evening. She wanted him hot
and hard and insatiable. She wanted him so aroused
he was scary. She wanted to spend the long warm

night on the edge, engaging in scary sex with this
scary man. She wanted her lover to become so blood-
poundingly excited it would take an entire night of
uninhibited lovemaking to satisfy him.

She was just the woman who could do both! Arouse
him so thoroughly he would lustily, savagely take her
again and again. And then, satisfy him so completely
he wouldn't want another woman for weeks!

Not even a blue-eyed, flame-haired, apricot-
skinned, gentle-spoken beauty who didn't fool her for
a second! The very married Mrs. Dane Curtin was
helplessly attracted to the handsome West Quarternight. And West was dangerously attracted to the
regal redhead, whether he realized it or not.

So if a tiny spark existed between West and Elizabeth Curtin, it was strictly up to her, Doña Hope, to
extinguish it before it had a chance to burst into
flame. She would fight fire with fire. She would make
her handsome lover burn for her. Then she would
envelop him in a blaze of love so hot and consuming,
there would be nothing left for any other woman.

Confident, Doña Hope came to West.

She cupped his brown jaws in her small white
hands and tipped his face up. She leaned down to him
and inhaled deeply, offering him a tempting view of
her full, ivory breasts pressing against the thin satin,
her nipples already tightened in arousal.

"I'm going to kiss you all over your hard, brown
body," she promised tantalizingly, lowering her wet
red lips to his and kissing his mouth.

West's left hand covered a breast, his right slid
around her waist and, with open palm against the
curve of her back, pulled her down to him. When the
long kiss ended, the doña was draped atop his bent
knee, leaning back in his arms.

Breathless, she murmured, "My darling, I'm going
to give you exquisite pleasure tonight. All night long."

His trousered leg still hooked over the chair's arm, West squeezed her narrow waist, settled her so that her hip and thigh were pressed against his groin, and said, "You never fail to give me exquisite pleasure, Doña." His fingertips traced a jutting nipple through the clinging white satin.

Sliding her thigh provocatively back and forth over his lower belly and crotch, she said, "And I'll never fail. Anything you want me to do to you, I will." Her fingers raked through the dark hair on his naked chest. "Anything you want to do to me—anything— I'll let you."

"You're a lot of woman," West replied, knowing she meant every word she said.

"All you'll ever need," she assured him.

"Shall we go to bed?"

"No," she whispered. "Let's make love right here. In the chair before the fire."

"Anyplace you want it," was his agreeable reply.

"Kiss me, West. Kiss me."

West kissed her. It was a long, hot kiss and Doña Hope, already on fire for the hard-muscled man upon whose knee she sat, ground her open mouth to his, sucked at his tongue, and allowed her erect nipples to graze his bare chest.

At last she tore her flaming mouth from his, gasped for air, and experienced a fleeting second of uneasiness. While she was already trembling and her flesh was flushed and heated, her thigh, pressed flush between his legs, told her that West was not yet ready for lovemaking.

She would make him ready.

Doña drew West's mouth back to hers and kissed him wildly, playfully nipping and biting him, sensuously licking at his wide, smooth lips, and plunging her tongue deeply into his mouth. Over and over she kissed him and as they kissed, she changed their positions.

Snatching her gown up with one hand, she wiggled about to straddle his body. Climbing atop him, she pressed her knees tightly to his trim waist and rhythmically ground her pelvis to his. She took her lips from his mouth, pushed his dark head against the chair's back, and set about brushing wet, open-mouthed kisses to his bare chest. She flicked the tip of her tongue over his flat brown nipples and circled them. She licked the heavy line of black hair leading down into his trousers.

Finally she lifted her head, looked into his eyes, and felt her apprehension escalate. Those beautiful, expressive eyes were not the hot molten silver she longed to see, but a calm, almost penitent gray. Heart pounding, she jerked her gown's narrow satin straps down over her shoulders, and wiggled free of the flimsy bodice, allowing her full, throbbing breasts to spill onto his chest.

"Doña, sweetheart, I . . ." West began, but she wouldn't allow him to finish.

Grabbing the thick, dark hair at the sides of his head, Doña Hope again covered his mouth with her flaming lips. Desperately she kissed him, and when she took her mouth from his, she arched toward him and brushed a hard nipple back and forth across his gleaming lips.

"Doña, listen to me, sweetheart—"

"No!" She wouldn't allow him to say what she couldn't bear to hear. She clutched the dark hair of his head and pressed his face to her naked breasts. "Darling, darling," she breathed, kissing the top of his head, praying his wide, wonderful mouth would search out and warmly enclose an aching nipple.

It didn't.

Still the doña clung to his hair, willing him to want

her as much as she wanted him. Her knees hugged him tightly. Between her clasping thighs the sensitive feminine flesh was swollen with her need and a hot wetness was flowing from her. A deep, painful longing was causing her belly to contract sharply.

But Doña Hope knew her lover wasn't experiencing the same urgency, the hot desire that seized her. She pushed West's face away from her breasts, slid off his lap, and knelt between his spread legs. Sadly she looked at his groin and laid caressing fingers on the flaccid flesh. West's hand immediately covered hers.

Sheepishly, he apologized, "I'm sorry, Doña. I guess I'm tired from the—"

"Tired?" she interrupted, hurt and angry. Snatching her hand away, she rose to her feet, and said, "You have come to me after seventy-two hours without sleep and grown hard with my first kiss!"

"Maybe I have"—he reached for her hand, pulled her back to him—"but sometimes—"

"Maybe? You don't remember?" Her brown eyes flashed with pain and fury and she again pulled away from him. "You think I don't know what's wrong with you tonight?"

"Hell, honey, nothing's wrong with me," he said, shrugging. "I had too much to drink and I'm tired. I'm not an eighteen-year-old boy, for Christ sake."

"That's not it!" she snarled, angrier than he had ever seen her. Tears gathering in her eyes, Doña Hope pulled the lowered satin gown up over her naked breasts and said, "You're in the wrong damned bedroom!"

West grinned, attempting to jolly her. "I thought you wanted me here."

"Oh, I did! You know I did, but somebody else wants you in her room as well, eh, West?"

The smile left West's dark face. "You're talking foolishness and you know it."

"Do I know it? Do you?" She stood holding up her gown with one hand while pointing with the other. "Maybe you ought to go right down the hall to the redhead's room, see if she can make you get it—"

"Hush! Hush, now," he warned, coming to his feet. He stepped up to her, clasped her bare shoulders in his hands, and said, "You know more about a man's body than any woman I've ever known, so surely you understand that the only thing wrong with me is exhaustion and too much brandy."

"Liar," she accused, flinching away from him. "Liar. You want another woman. A married woman!"

"I'm going to forget you said that, Doña," West told her in a flat, low voice. "Let's put a stop to this nonsense and get in bed. I told you I'm tired." He turned and started for the bed. Over his shoulder, he said, "Maybe we'll make love in the morning."

Doña Hope flew at him, grabbed his arm, and spun him to face her. "If you only intend to sleep in bed, then go to your guest room. I am not sleepy!"

West said placatingly, "Well, now, darlin', I never said I wouldn't take care of you, did I? There are all sorts of ways to—"

"Never!" She would not be appeased. "You think I'll lie in your arms and allow you to touch me while you think of another woman?"

"Jesus, what is it with you? I haven't said two words to Elizabeth Curtin since we've been here."

Tears spilling down her flushed cheeks, Doña Hope shook her head and said, "Leave me now. Leave me. Get some sleep. Maybe you are only tired," she said hopefully. "When you awaken, if it's in the middle of the night or tomorrow morning, and you want me— only me—I'll be here. Waiting." She started pushing him toward the door. "Otherwise I'll see you at breakfast with the others."

They were at the door. Doña Hope opened it, West stepped out into the corridor, turned back and touched her tear-stained cheek. " 'Night, sweetheart."

The doña didn't answer. She closed the door in his face. Sighing, West shrugged bare shoulders and walked away. Several doors down he stepped into his darkened guest room. He didn't bother to light any lamps. Bone tired, he crossed directly to the bed and threw back the covers. He kicked off his shoes, pulled off his black stockings, and hunched out of his tight black trousers.

Naked, he climbed into bed, stretched out on his back, yawned, and waited for sleep to come. An hour later, he still waited. Irritable, edgy, he got up. A black silk robe lay at the foot of the bed. West put on the robe, tied the sash loosely at his waist, and picked up a cigar and match from the night table.

He went out onto the shadowy balcony, and walked over to lean against the black wrought-iron railing. He automatically cast a glance down the long balcony toward the doña's bedroom. No lights shone from her open double doors. Apparently, she was asleep.

West inhaled deeply, put the cigar in his mouth, and was about to light it when in the opposite direction a pair of double doors suddenly opened. Suffused light spilled out of the room onto the balcony.

Curious, his dark brows knitted together, West lowered the match without striking it, his gaze narrowed. The unlighted cigar between his lips, he stared, wondering who could still be up at this late hour.

His heart kicked against his ribs when a tall, slender woman with flaming red hair stepped out into the square of pale light. Perfectly framed, she was barefoot and wore only a nightgown. An incredibly alluring nightgown. The bodice was entirely of delicate aqua-colored lace, the skirt of pale aqua satin.

West's sharp teeth cut into his unlighted cigar when
Elizabeth moved forward, clutched the railing, and
inhaled deeply. Her full, high breasts strained against
the alluring aqua lace. A night wind blew from out of
the south, pressing the soft aqua satin against her
shapely thighs and long slender legs and tossing locks
of her wild red hair about her ivory shoulders.

Afraid to move, afraid to breathe, West stood there
concealed in deep shadow, an unashamed voyeur, eagerly watching the unsuspecting Elizabeth put on a
sensual performance for his eyes only.

Slowly, his dark hand moved up to pluck the cigar
from lips that could no longer stay closed around it.
Lowering the cigar, his strong fingers reflexively
crushed it as he stared unblinking at the beautiful
red-haired woman.

She stood there in the night, in the wind, a fiery,
near-naked temptress so alluring that the sight of her
sent an involuntary shudder of pleasure through
his body. He trembled. His belly tightened. Blood
pounded in his temples. And in his groin.

His hot silver eyes never leaving the night vision
before him, West felt the slithery black satin of his
robe rising with his untimely arousal. He stood
cloaked in the darkness, his powerful erection throbbing with a need more fierce than any he had ever
known.

It frightened him, he wanted her so badly. Frightened him because it was *her*—Elizabeth—not just a
beautiful woman he wanted. He wanted *her*. Only
her, and he was terrified. And because he was terrified, he grew angry. Angry with himself for being so
weak. Angry with her for making him weak.

Slowly Elizabeth turned about, threw her head
back, leaned against the railing, and unwittingly
showed her angry, suffering voyeur pale pink satiny

nipples peeking through aqua lace and shadowy red curls outlined against clinging aqua satin.

Hot silver eyes blazed, then turned icy cold.

Under his breath West uttered the oath, "Goddamn you, Mrs. Curtin."

32

❦❦❦

He couldn't have stayed away had the penalty of going to her been certain death. He was more than a little afraid of her. He was unreasonably angry with her. But the white-hot passion she aroused in him was far greater than fear or anger.

The beautiful red-haired siren stood there in the night wind guilelessly exhibiting her charms, and West couldn't resist. Helpless, he started toward her, his heart beating so forcefully he could hear it drumming in his ears.

Barefooted, he moved as swiftly and quietly as a sleek panther. But he had taken only a few steps before she sensed his approach. One hand reaching out to the balcony's solid railing, Elizabeth slowly turned.

She saw him coming. A tall, dark-robed figure moving toward her from out of the darkness, but she didn't scream or dash inside to safety. She was afraid, yet she didn't move. Just stood there clutching the cool railing, awaiting her inevitable fate. She knew, well before he reached the pale square of light, who was coming to her.

For her.

And she knew what was going to happen.

West stepped out of the shadow into the light and he had the look of a villain about him. His blue-black hair was disheveled and falling over his forehead, a shadow of whiskers was already beginning to darken his lower face, and his eyes were a frightening, fascinating mixture of deadly gray coldness and vibrant silver heat.

He stood there a long second, watching her carefully for some slight gesture or movement. He caught the quickening tempo of her breathing, saw the faint pulse at the base of her throat and he knew he could have her. Knew he *would* have her.

Elizabeth couldn't slow the quickening of her pulse. She couldn't back away from this tall, dark man who loomed dangerously close before her, emanating a fierce animal strength. He was, she breathlessly realized, already erect in anticipation, the hard male flesh rising and surging beneath the black silk of his robe.

Neither spoke a word.

They were totally silent. The silence between them grew heavier and was charged with a taut electric excitement that each felt and knew—had always known—was shared by the other.

West moved closer. Trembling, Elizabeth released her hold on the balcony's railing and stepped forward to meet him. His body already hardened with desire, West's hungry gaze swiftly skimmed over her. His molten silver eyes touched the pale pink satin nipples pressing aqua lace, swept over the flat belly and the tiny indentation of her naval, and settled with rising excitement on the shadowy triangle between her legs.

Elizabeth anxiously lifted her hands and placed them on his chest. West drew her to him. Their gazes locked. Elizabeth's heart pumped wildly in her throat. West's pounded painfully against his ribs. His dark face lowered. Her fair face tipped up. Mouths, tongues, met in a blazing kiss of surrendering consent.

After that, it was like a wild fire spreading unchecked over parched dry land. With one swift kiss they both burst into devastating flame. There was no turning back, no having second thoughts. It was too late. The fire, once ignited, was so hot, so destructive, it could only be extinguished by raging completely out of control and then quickly burning itself out.

That's exactly what happened.

Roughly, West clasped Elizabeth's fragile wrist, propelled her back inside her bedroom, lifted the globe from the single burning lamp atop a drum table. He extinguished the tiny flame with thumb and forefinger and the large beige room was at once cast into shadowy moonlight.

West made no move to shut the open balcony doors. He made no move to carry Elizabeth to the silk-sheeted bed. There was no time for that. He was so hot. He was covered with a sheen of perspiration and every nerve and muscle in his body was tense.

Elizabeth was just as excited, just as eager. Her face was flushed, there was gooseflesh on her arms and beads of moisture between her breasts.

West's hands clasped her shoulders, his passion-hardened mouth came back to hers. He kissed her as his tanned fingers deftly swept the aqua-lace bodice away from her aching breasts. He pushed the wispy gown down past her waist where it snagged on her rounded hips.

Unwilling to break the kiss, the electrified pair began shedding their unwanted garments. West's hands spanned her delicate ribcage and he pressed her body close. Her pebble-hard nipples were buried in the crisp hair of his chest. His thrusting erection pulsed against her belly.

While West eagerly urged the slippery satin gown

down over Elizabeth's hips, she found his robe's tied sash, yanked on it, and began frantically pushing the black silk robe apart.

In their urgency, they became like animals. Between quick, hot kisses they madly struggled to strip each other naked. Patience and good manners were totally abandoned as they went at one another, each fighting to bare the other's flesh first. Wanting her so badly he was physically hurting, a savagely determined West pulled on, shoved down, and yanked at the aqua satin gown keeping Elizabeth's bare, pale loveliness from him. At the same time a rash, willful Elizabeth clawed at, jerked on, and peeled away the black satin robe concealing West's magnificent bare brown body from her.

In seconds his black robe and her aqua gown lay discarded on the carpeted floor and they were naked together. Still they made no move toward the waiting bed. They stayed where they were, in front of the open balcony doors, kissing aggressively, as if they would devour each other, their bare sensitive bodies pressed hotly together. Finally, West tore his flaming mouth from hers. He pushed her tousled red hair back, leaned down, and buried his lips in the curve of her neck and shoulder.

His hands roaming possessively over her, his mouth never leaving her tingling flesh, he kissed her throat, her pale shoulders, her hard pink nipples, slipping to one knee before her. Elizabeth's nervous fingers went into his dark hair at the sides of his head. She pressed his hot face to her, luxuriating in the wild joy of his wet, warm mouth sucking so violently on her aching, swollen breasts.

She pushed her breast more fully against that marvelous hot mouth, longing to have him draw as much of the pale rounded flesh as possible inside. She was sure he sensed it when his hand slid up, cupped and lifted her breast, and his mouth opened wider. In frenzied delight she watched as more and more of her full white breast disappeared into his flexing brown jaws.

In seconds she was so weak with pleasure her legs wouldn't support her. She urged his dazzling mouth away and slid to her knees facing him. Again they kissed and as they anxiously embraced, they sank together to the plush beige carpet.

Elizabeth felt his hard nakedness against her, felt the animal heat of him pressing her down. His hands moved enticingly over her body, one going to the downy auburn triangle. Her hands were just as bold. Her shaky fingers found and wrapped themselves around his awesome erection.

The explosively hot pair spent only a few seconds in play, he caressing her, urging her legs further and further apart, she simply clinging, holding him tightly as though afraid he might take that throbbing power away from her.

In the next second, he did exactly that.

But then he gave it back.

Driven beyond endurance by the touch of her naked body, West quickly positioned himself between Elizabeth's widely parted legs, gripped himself, and thrust into her, the hot wetness supplied by her receptive body making it incredibly easy for him to slide deeply into her.

Their gazes locked. Her fingers curled around his hard biceps. She pulled him down to her, tilted her pelvis more fully to his, and enveloped him in warmth and sweetness. They made wordless sounds and clung to each other.

Violently, they mated on the plush beige carpet. West drove forcefully into her with the quickness and urgency of a young boy. Elizabeth was just as delirious. She drew her knees up, wrapped her long, slender legs tightly around his back to press him closer, loving the exquisite pain-pleasure of his driving so fast and forcefully into her.

In seconds it was over.

Together they exploded into riotous climax. So turbulent, so stirring was their shared orgasm, the sounds of their mutual joy might have awakened the entire household had they not muted the noise by kissing. When the deep fulfillment began, West saw Elizabeth's beautiful blue eyes widening in shock and hurriedly kissed her. Into his mouth she cried out in her ecstasy while he groaned with his own shuddering rapture.

When it was over they broke apart and lay on their backs, panting for breath. The thundering of their heartbeats began to slow, the involuntary jerking of their limbs ceased. For a few seconds more they stayed as they were.

Then, reality intruded harshly. Logical thought returned. Disbelief struck.

Two naked people who had just been the most intimate of lovers felt suddenly ill at ease. Ashamed. Disgusted. Sorry for what they had done.

West coughed needlessly, rolled to a sitting position, picked up Elizabeth's aqua gown and draped it between her pale legs. Her knees closed around it and she folded her arms over her bare breasts.

Turning away, West picked up his black satin robe. Seated on the beige carpet, he shoved long arms into the sleeves, pulled the robe around himself and tied the sash at his waist.

He warily glanced at her. She, too, had sat up. Turned away from him, she was pulling the aqua gown down over her head. West rose quietly to his feet. Elizabeth settled the gown down over her hips and cautiously stood up.

She turned to face him. For a long moment they

stared at each other, but neither spoke. West started toward the double doors. Elizabeth stayed where she was as he walked away. He reached the open portal and didn't pause to turn and look at her. He walked out into the night and disappeared back into the darkness from which he had come exactly fifteen minutes earlier.

In that fifteen minutes they had made fast, wild love, and had not spoken one word to each other.

For a long while after West left her, Elizabeth continued to stand in the shadowy room, unmoving, unfeeling, telling herself it couldn't be true. This hadn't really happened. It had all been a dream, a wicked nightmare. She hadn't actually writhed naked on the floor of Doña Hope's desert home with West Quarternight.

All at once Elizabeth was in motion. She flew across the room, pulled the tall doors shut, and locked them. Then stood there trembling uncontrollably, knowing it was a foolish wasted gesture.

It was too late. Too late to lock him out of her room. Too late to lock him out of her body. It was not, she told herself, too late to lock him out of her heart.

33

Again dressed in her suede rust trousers, pullover shirt, and soft beaded moccasins, Elizabeth nervously walked into the small dining room at Doña Hope's Rancho Caballo.

"Well, there she is now!" boomed Grady Downs, and Elizabeth felt herself being scrutinized by the beaming Grady, a silent Taos, the patient Edmund, and an inquisitive Doña Hope. "You enjoyed the nice soft bed so much you didn't want to get out of it this morning, eh, missy?" Grady asked, his pink lips stretching into a wide smile between his white mustache and flowing beard.

A blue linen napkin tucked into the opening of his buckskin shirt, Grady hurried to pull out a chair for Elizabeth as Taos and Edmund respectfully rose to their feet.

From the head of the table, Doña Hope, looking glamorous and self-assured even at this early hour, said pointedly, "We were beginning to wonder about you and West."

Elizabeth felt her face burn. Scooting up close to the table, she glanced at Doña Hope, smiled, and said, "Grady's right, Doña. The bed in your guest room was so comfortable, I was reluctant to get up." She reached for a freshly poured cup of strong black coffee, hoping no one noticed the slight trembling of her hand.

"I'm glad you found your accommodations to be adequate," said Doña Hope, her heavily lashed brown eyes remaining on Elizabeth. "Do you suppose West was as content with his?"

Not sure if the keenly astute Doña Hope somehow knew the awful truth or if the blond widow was merely making conversation, Elizabeth took a long spine-stiffening drink of coffee, carefully set the cup back in its saucer, and replied, "Well, now, Doña Hope, I suppose you would know a great deal more about that than I." Sweetly she smiled, and added, "The rancho's accommodations, I mean."

Doña Hope, just like Elizabeth, was determined she would keep up a false front. Telling herself that everyone—including Elizabeth Curtin—believed that West had spent the night in *her* big white bedroom, she gave Elizabeth a knowing smile, shook her blond head, and said, as if slightly embarrassed, "I told West we were fooling no one." She laughed girlishly, and added, "He worries about my reputation more than I." Her glance swept around the table. "I assured him that you are all adult and not the least bit shocked by the close relationship that has existed between the two of us"—she paused, her gaze purposely returning to Elizabeth—"for more than three years."

Grady nodded enthusiastically, Taos smiled, and Edmund courteously said, "My dear Doña, let me assure you that we're all fully approving of your friendship with West." Smiling directly at the stunning blond woman, he said, "Aren't we, Elizabeth?" No answer. Edmund turned to his silent sister-in-law. "Elizabeth?"

"Of course. Why wouldn't we be?" Elizabeth said,

choking on the words, forcing herself to smile while every nerve in her body screamed with despair and pain and guilt.

Relieved when Grady quickly jumped in to reclaim the conversation, guiding it away from her—and from West—Elizabeth picked up her china plate, rose, and moved to the sideboard, pretending interest in breakfast.

Atop the long gleaming buffet were silver dome-covered dishes. Lifting the lids, Elizabeth saw crisply fried bacon, thick sliced ham, fluffy scrambled eggs, tender browned potatoes, feather-light hotcakes, and an array of biscuits and muffins and breads. There was plenty of sweet creamery butter, small silver pots of jams and jellies and maple syrup, and silver platters of fresh fruits.

None of it tempted Elizabeth. She was not hungry. Maybe she would never be hungry again. Dispiritedly, she laid a blueberry muffin on her plate, speared a slice of honeydew melon, and returned to the table. Conversation swirled around her, but she heard little of it.

Any minute now West would come down for breakfast. How would he behave? Would he be as self-conscious and heartsick as she? Would he appear as awkward and embarrassed as any other man in similar circumstances? Would his habitually cocksure manner desert him this morning? Would he fumble for words, avoid looking her in the eye, and be so hesitant and nervous that the others would be sure to notice . . . and know?

She soon found out.

The door from the kitchen abruptly opened and through it stepped West Quarternight. Irascible, impatient, irreverent. Touching her, then Doña Hope, with his narrow-eyed gray gaze, nodding almost imperceptibly, then swiftly dismissing them both, he strode through the dining room calling for Grady, Taos, and Edmund with all the assurance of a lifetime of leadership.

Unquestioning, the men rose and followed West from the room, through the big hacienda, and out the front door. Elizabeth and Doña Hope exchanged puzzled glances. The doña rose, crossed to a tall window, and pulled back the heavy wine curtains. Elizabeth stayed at the table.

Out on the graveled driveway a pair of brown-twill-uniformed New Mexico rangers dismounted amidst a growing gathering of excited Baca vaqueros. West made his way through the crowd as the taller of the two rangers removed his trooper hat and stepped forward.

The slim, hawk-nosed ranger shook West's outstretched hand and said, "Quarternight, glad you're at Rancho Caballo. We rode out to warn Doña Hope that another body has turned up."

Drawing a cigar from his breast pocket, West said evenly, "Go on, sir."

"A young Mexican woman was discovered on the plaza in La Luz before dawn this morning. The body was nude, very pale, and had deep teeth marks on the left side of her throat."

"Madre de Dios!" exclaimed several vaqueros, and anxiously crossed themselves.

"Well, I'll be go to hell!" rasped Grady Downs, stroking his white beard and looking up at Taos.

"God in heaven!" said Edmund Curtin.

"What about the young woman?" said West calmly. "Any family? If so, do they know where she had gone? When? With whom?"

The veteran ranger told all he knew. The young woman had gone with her beau to a Mesilla cantina one night more than three weeks ago. While there they met a couple of Mexican charros. One was a slim, cold-eyed man with a pencil-thin mustache, the other was fat with a bad walleye.

Drinks flowed freely and soon the slim, mustachioed man asked the young woman to dance. When the pair went out into the night together, her jealous sweetheart followed, but there was no sign of the couple. Nor of the fat walleyed man.

"Apparently the young woman was kidnapped, taken somewhere and held captive," the ranger concluded.

Outraged, the growing gathering of Caballo ranchhands erupted into loud mutterings and Spanish curses. West held up his hand for silence.

"We appreciate your coming," West said to the rangers. "I'll caution Doña Hope not to ride alone."

The tall ranger nodded, put his trooper hat back on, and said, "I'd do more than that, Quarternight." He glanced at Edmund. "I'd persuade the young lady with your search expedition to remain at Rancho Caballo until you get back."

West made no reply to that suggestion. "Thanks again. Won't you come in and have some breakfast with us?"

Declining, the rangers mounted, rode away, and the gathering quickly dispersed. Returning to their interrupted meal, Grady, Taos, and Edmund reclaimed their places at the table. Waiting until they were seated, West pulled out a chair, twirled it about and straddled it, resting his crossed arms on the back of it.

Mincing no words, he said, "A young woman's pale, naked body was found on the La Luz plaza early this morning." He nodded his thanks to a Mexican servant when she set a cup of steaming hot coffee before him. He looked straight down the table at Doña Hope. "I wouldn't go riding alone for a while."

Her answer was a question. "How long will you be gone?"

West unhurriedly reached out, picked up his coffee cup, and said, "I don't know. Maybe a week, maybe a month. I've never taken a woman into the desert before." He took a drink of coffee.

"Elizabeth," said Doña Hope, "you're more than welcome to remain here at Rancho Caballo until—"

"Stay here, Mrs. Curtin," West cut in, his tone one of quiet force. "Stay." He glanced at Elizabeth and his look was unbearably cold and detached.

The dull ache in her breast quickly became a sharp, stabbing pain. The others backed up West.

But Elizabeth heard herself say, "I am going all the way, Quarternight, and that's final."

West shrugged indifferently. The meal continued. Silent, Elizabeth sat uncomfortably close to West, more miserable than she had ever been in her life.

Her misery was magnified by the fact that he was not miserable. Not awkward. Not embarrassed. His wry, cynical, offhand charm was as much in evidence as ever. Obviously, he was neither sorry nor upset by what had happened last night. It had meant nothing to him. Nothing. He had probably gone straight from her to Doña Hope's bed. Or he had come to her from the doña's bed!

That thought sickened her. She felt as if she was going to be violently ill. Dear God, he was without scruples and she was as bad as he. No, she was worse! She was a married woman who had allowed a man, still warm from another woman's bed, to . . . to . . .

Elizabeth felt those penetrating gray eyes on her. She slowly turned her head.

"Did you say something to me?" she asked as calmly as possible.

"I said you'd better finish your meal. It's time we hit

the trail." He slid up out of his chair, turned it back around, and added, "You do realize that we won't be taking the wagon. You'll have to ride a horse across the—"

"I can stay in the saddle as long as you," she interrupted.

He said no more to her. While the others pushed back their chairs to get up, West walked the length of the table to his hostess. Her eyes clinging to him as he came, Doña Hope rose to meet him.

Still angry and hurt, the blond widow sighed, laid a hand on his chest and toyed with the loose lacings of his snug buckskin shirt.

West smiled at her, his hand came up to cup her chin, and he said softly, "Forgive me?"

"Always," she admitted helplessly, her parted lips eagerly lifting for a kiss that never came.

West brushed his lips against her cheek, thanked her for everything, said good-bye, turned, and walked out of the room.

"By doggie, we're on the way!" exclaimed Grady, hurrying after West.

Out on the graveled drive, the expedition was swiftly forming up. Vaqueros shouted and horses whinnied and pack burros kicked and snorted.

Two women, one blond, one with hair of flame, turned to face each other in the rising sun.

"Thank you so much, Doña, for your warm hospitality," said Elizabeth Curtin.

Doña Hope smiled weakly. "You could stay and enjoy it longer. The *Jornada del Muerto* really is no place for a woman."

Elizabeth's smile was as weak as the blonde's. "Now you're sounding like Mr. Quarternight."

"I think you should be flattered by West's concern." Doña Hope defended him. She paused and added, "And perhaps you are."

Elizabeth made a face. "Doña Hope, I want no part of West Quarternight. You can have him on a silver platter!"

"No, I can't," said the blond woman. She smiled and added, "but then, Mrs. Dane Curtin, neither can you."

34

🙟🙟🙟

The sprawling Rancho Caballo was still within sight when the mounted contingent began its gradual climb out of the Rio Grande valley into the foothills of the Sierra Caballos. Mounted astride a responsive iron-gray stallion, Elizabeth looked at the forested slopes and sandstone spires rising on the near horizon. They didn't appear to be particularly foreboding. Not nearly as foreboding as the tanned, handsome face of the expedition's lead scout.

West hadn't spoken a word since leaving Doña Hope's ranch. In his customary place at the head of the prossession, he rode the sorrel mare several yards forward of the contingent, which in itself was not unusual. What was unusual was that he never turned to glance over his shoulder, never wheeled the sorrel about to observe the long train's progress, never gave any indication that he was alert and or even alive.

Nor did he ride in the typical comfortably slouched position she had become so used to seeing. Instead, his back was held militarily straight, the fabric of his soft buckskin shirt pulling tightly over rigidly erect shoulders. The level attitude of his dark head never altered. He might have been a statue, carved from stone.

Even without the opportunity to see his face, Elizabeth could easily have guessed that it was set in hard ungiving lines, the smoky eyes cold, the sensuously sculpted mouth grim. The abundant Quarternight charm was markedly missing. It had been left behind at Rancho Caballo. Elizabeth had never seen West this way and she felt a numbing chill just looking at his tense back.

Forcing her gaze and her thoughts away from him, Elizabeth turned to glance at Grady, riding along beside her. He was going on—as usual—about something. She had no idea what; she hadn't been listening. She interrupted him, which was about the only way to get a word in edgewise.

"Grady, I know you've told me before, but could you refresh my memory about the route we'll be taking?"

Grady yanked off his battered Stetson, slapped it against his thigh, and fixed her with snapping blue eyes. "Thunderation, missy, what's wrong with you young folks?"

"Wrong?" Elizabeth repeated nervously, terrified the white-haired mountain man suspected something. "Why, nothing's wrong."

"Well, then, how come you can't remember a thing I tell you?" He jammed his hat back on his head. "You're just like Sonny. Can't remember your own name. I tell him he's got his brains in his butt—beggin' your pardon—but I don't know what in the Sam Hill is the matter with you! If I've told you once, I've told you a dozen times exactly the route we're a-takin'."

"I'm sorry, Grady. You're right, of course, I should have listened more closely. Never mind, I'll—"

"Well, now hold your horses, missy. I don't mind

going over it *one* more time." His snapping blue eyes began to twinkle. Onto him, Elizabeth smiled, knowing he couldn't wait to tell her again.

"I'll listen closely this time, Grady," she said, and meant it.

"Well, you better, 'cause this is the last time I'm a-tellin' you." He lifted a hand, pointed a forefinger toward the horizon. "We'll be well up into the Sierra Caballos by sunset. Then down their gentle rise right into the hostile lands the Spanish conquistadors called *Jornada del Muerto,* Journey of the Dead. Ain't nothin' out there 'cept bone-dry deserts, snakes, scorpions, stinging ants, and savage Indians.

"We'll ride across them burning deserts and canyons, then up into the towering San Andres Range with peaks soaring nigh on to nine thousand feet.

"No sooner do we get down the other side of the San Andres than we're slap dab in the middle of El Malpais, the Badlands. We'll have to ride through that big ol' hell of black basalt and lava pits and on down the Tularosa Valley into the White Sands." He looked at Elizabeth to be sure she was properly attentive. "Missy, I'm talking about a huge lake of sand as white as the virgin snow, as far as the eye can see. You ain't never seen nothin' like it in your life!

"Out of the White Sands and into the Tularosa Basin till we hit the Sacramentos. Them mountains are some big ones. Hell, Alamo Peak is right at ten thousand foot, give or take a hundred feet."

"That tall?" said Elizabeth, letting him know she was listening closely and was appropriately impressed.

"That's what I said. Might be some snow still up on the summits, I wouldn't doubt it. So we'll likely skirt the Sacramentos, be in the foothills for a while, and then wind our way right on over into the Guadalupes. Then down into the cussed hot deserts again and keep on a-dropping southeast till we get to where we're a-goin'.

"There ain't gonna be nothin' easy about this part of the trip. We got endless deserts and mountains ahead to wind through and unending passes and mesas to cross. Ain't no place for a lady, which is why Weston tried to get you to stay at Rancho Caballo. Why didn't you do it, missy?"

Elizabeth shook her head, didn't answer. She drew a deep breath and said, "I take it West and Doña are . . . are—"

"Have been for years," Grady assured her, nodding. "Ever since she was in Santa Fe one spring morning and Sonny seen her sittin' in her fine carriage right out there in front of the La Fonda Hotel. Prettiest thing you ever did see. That white-blond hair a-gleamin' in the sunlight and a bright pink dress that looked like somebody had poured her right into it." He chuckled and stroked his beard.

"Go on," Elizabeth softly prompted. "They were introduced that day?"

"Introduced?" He hooted. "Sure, they was introduced, but it was Sonny who done the introducin'. You see, we was comin' out the hotel dining room that mornin', me an' Sonny an' Taos and we seen her sittin' there. Well, wouldn't you know it, without so much as a 'by your leave' Sonny went right over to her, opened the door of her carriage, stepped up into it, and dropped down into the seat beside her, big as you please. And there he didn't have no idea who she was." Remembering, Grady laughed, his whole body shaking.

"Then what, Grady?" Elizabeth was mildly annoyed. She wanted him to complete the story.

"Well, sir, Sonny picked up one of her small, gloved hands, looked into her eyes, and said, 'Where would you like to take me?' Can you imagine that? Just jumps right up in there and asks where *she* would like to take *him*!" Again Grady roared with laughter, wiping the tears from his eyes.

Forcing herself to laugh along with him, Elizabeth waited for him to calm down a little, then continuing to smile easily, she said, "Such appalling impudence! What was the poor startled woman's answer?"

"This you gotta hear," said Grady merrily. "Even if it ain't real proper for me to be a-tellin' it or you to be a-hearin' it. Now, what do you suppose Doña Hope said?"

All too certain she knew, Elizabeth replied, "I have no idea."

"You ain't gonna believe it. That sweet smellin', blond-haired, filthy rich widow woman looked right at Sonny and said, 'Cowboy, I'd take you home with me, but the ranch is too far away. Let's go upstairs to my La Fonda suite.'"

And Grady laughed again, then added, "They been mighty close ever since."

"I see. Are they . . . in love?"

"Love, naw, nothin' like that. Leastways, Sonny's not in love." The wide smile abruptly left Grady's weathered face. He turned almost somber. "West is not a man for no woman to be lovin'." He looked off in the distance as if he were seeing things that she did not. "His way of life is pretty much what the Mexicans call the *no le hace.*"

"Which means?"

"It doesn't matter after all."

Across the woolly patches of buffalo grass the expedition rode. Through rabbit brush and yucca spears, they crossed the high grasslands of southern New Mexico. By suppertime, they were well up onto the cedar-dotted slopes of the cool Sierra Caballos.

They stopped in a rolling mountain meadow covered with thousands of purple mariposa lilies. Golden butterflies darted dizzily from blossom to blossom. A bluebird with sunlight glinting on its outstretched indigo wings flew gracefully to the meadow's edge, where a tiny stream trickled with cold, clear water.

The bluebird made a perfect landing atop a jutting boulder in midstream, tiptoed down the slippery rock, wet his beak several times, then was again airborne, soaring to the top of a fragrant cedar bordering the stream's far side.

Seated in the lengthening shade on a smooth overturned boulder, Elizabeth looked around. She was in a peaceful, beautiful glade and under different circumstances she would have been thoroughly enchanted. But not today. Not after last night.

Warily she kept an eye on West as he and the rest of the men set up camp. It struck her that his physical movements were those of a caged but dangerous animal. And nobody knew better than she just how dangerous he was. Looking at him now, noticing the way the muscles pulled in his long legs as he crouched down to unpack a food hamper, she felt her throat grow dry. She vividly recalled the sight of those powerful muscles bunching under sweat-slick brown flesh as he crouched naked before her in the shadowy moonlight.

Inwardly shuddering, Elizabeth told herself that what had happened last night must never happen again.

Most likely West supposed that she was now his for the taking, anytime, anyplace. Well, he was mistaken. For reasons she herself couldn't understand, she had totally lost her head last night. And she felt miserable about it today. Her guilt and remorse were devastating. She'd give anything if she could turn back the clock twenty-four hours.

If only she could go back to yesterday afternoon,

before they had reached Rancho Caballo. Or, if she could go back to twilight last evening, before she stepped out into a flower-scented courtyard where a dark man in evening clothes waited in the dusk.

Dear God, if she could just go back to midnight when she looked up to see a dark, dangerous man coming for her from out of the night. Even then she could have stopped him. She could have hurried back inside and locked the doors against him.

No. That wouldn't have been necessary. Much as she hated to admit it, Elizabeth knew that West would not have forced her. If she hadn't wanted him, he would have let her go. He was not like Colonel Frederick C. Dobbs, the rapacious officer back in Louisiana whom she had . . .

Elizabeth's troubled thoughts were interrupted when Taos handed her a filled plate. She smiled her thanks, took it, but was no hungrier now than she had been at breakfast or noon. Holding the plate on her knees, she forced herself to swallow a few bites. Moments later she sighed, set the plate aside, swiveled slowly about, and saw West. He stood directly across the narrow stream leaning against a rock upthrust, arms folded, face turned away, an untouched plate of food on a sandstone ledge at his elbow.

He turned, caught her staring, and Elizabeth half expected him to toss her one of those teasing, predatory Quarternight grins and perhaps a conspiratorial wink.

He didn't.

His steady gray gaze exerted an almost physical pull, but his was not a look of teasing warmth. A shadow of rapidly growing whiskers already darkening his face, he stared at her coldly, impersonally. Unintentionally, he projected a chilling air of dark, raw sexuality.

Elizabeth quickly turned away, confused by the

startling change in him. The entire trip he had seized every opportunity to torment her, to pester her, to get her off alone. Now he looked at her as if he had never seen her before. Suddenly cold in spite the day's warmth, she was more afraid of him than ever.

And more attracted.

Elizabeth was not the only one to notice that something was bothering the lead guide. West Quarternight had not been himself all day and nobody knew the reason.

"What's botherin' you, boy?" Grady walked over to where West sat alone and apart after supper that evening.

West shrugged. "Who said anything's bothering me?"

"Hellfire, what do you take me for? A double-damned fool?" Grady hotly responded. "Sonny, I been a-knowin' you now for nigh on to four years. I been with you night and day for months at a time. I seen you blind drunk. I seen you hopping mad. I seen you having a rip-roaring good time. I seen you when you was lazy, seen you when you pushed yourself too hard. Seen you go for weeks without a woman. Seen you hole up with a woman and refuse to get out of her bed. Seen you behave like a wise man, seen you act a derned fool. Seen you sick, seen you well. Seen you fight and win. Seen you fight and get knocked flat on your ass." Grady paused, waiting.

Never looking up, West said in level tones, "Guess that about sums me up."

"Not quite," said Grady. "I ain't never seen you actin' like you have today. What's stickin' in your craw, Sonny? You and the doña have a fuss?"

"No."

"Well, then what? You ain't said two words all day and your face looks like a big ole' black thundercloud. If I've done somethin' to chap you, spit it out, son."

West finally lifted his eyes to Grady. "Partner, you haven't done anything. Nobody has. I'll see if I can't be a little better company tomorrow."

"Tomorrow, hell," bellowed Grady. "The sun ain't even completely down on this day yet! How about takin' some of them sweet pills right now and comin' on over to join the rest of us for a little jawin' around the campfire."

West smiled. "You go on. Truth is, I'm a little tired this evening. Think I'll just catch up on my shut-eye."

Grady's frown slowly changed to a grin. "I get it, now. You ain't mad. You're just all tuckered out from Doña Hope. That there's it, ain't it? You and the doña romped around her bedroom all night and she drained the life right out of you, huh, Sonny?" Grady slapped his knee and guffawed loudly. "Hell, why didn't you say so. Can't find no fault with a man what spends his night makin' a pretty young woman happy. No, sirree. Nothin' wrong with that. You go on and turn in, I'll tell the others you're just a little tired is all."

West said nothing.

But his smile swiftly disappeared when Grady stepped aside and West caught sight of a long-legged vision in tight rust pants. His gray eyes narrowed and his full mouth tightened as he watched the willowy young woman move about with an easy, upright posture and graceful fluid motion.

His narrowed gaze lingered on the seductive swell of her lush, ripe breasts beneath her blue pullover shirt, then slid slowly down to the appealing arch of her hip, the rounded firmness of her bottom so well defined in the tight rust trousers.

Elizabeth slowly circled the campfire. She stopped, stood for a long moment bending her head back to look up at the darkening sky. She lifted her arms, unpinned her hair, and it fell around her shoulders and down her back almost to her waist.

Vivid, shimmering, that flaming red hair blazed in the campfire's glow.

And set West's aching heart afire.

35

❧❧❧

"Captain Brooks! Captain Brooks, where are you? Oh, my God, Brooks! No, No!"

"Wake up, West. Wake up. You're havin' one of them nightmares again."

"What? What is it?" West bolted up from his bedroll, a hand clawing madly at the choking laces of his buckskin shirt. His breath was loud and labored, his dark face wet with sweat.

"You were dreamin', son," Grady said, crouching down beside West, his long white hair gleaming in the starlight. "You was puttin' up an awful racket."

West swallowed hard, raked a tanned hand through his damp hair, and shook his head. A deep shudder passed through his long, lean body. "Sorry, Grady. Didn't mean to wake you."

Grady gently patted West's shoulder. "No harm done. The others never heard you. They're all sleepin' like babies."

Grady was right. West's recurring nightmare had not awakened the others. But someone else had heard West's strangled cries of terror.

Across the remote desert camp, Elizabeth had been lying on her back under the stars. Wide awake. She had been awake since bedtime, hours earlier. Troubled and confused, she had been unable to fall asleep despite her total exhaustion.

When the deep nighttime silence was suddenly shattered with West's panicked shouts, her heart leapt into her throat. She pushed herself up on her elbows, stared openmouthed across the moon-splashed camp, and saw West thrashing wildly about in his bedroll.

Her immediate instinct was to go to him. Anxiously, she pushed down her blankets, her heart hammering against her ribs. By the time she was on her feet, she saw the white-haired Grady move to West, crouch down beside him, and shake him awake. A hand on her pounding heart, she sank weakly back down to her blankets, her eyes wide as she watched and listened.

She heard the two men clearly; their voices, though soft and low, carried on the still, thin air. She heard every word that was said. When Grady made a move to return to his own bedroll a few feet from West's, Elizabeth quickly lay back down, not wanting either man to know she was awake. She heard the pair say goodnight, watched Grady crawl back under his blanket, pull his long white beard on the outside of the covers, and carefully spread it out. He sighed and folded an arm under his head.

Elizabeth knew that he had immediately fallen back to sleep by the sound of his soft snores. West did not lie back down. He waited until he, too, heard Grady's snores. Then he rose to his feet, reached up behind his head, yanked off his buckskin shirt, and moved silently toward the low-burning campfire.

In the dying firelight his bare brown torso glistened as if oiled and Elizabeth realized he was drenched with the sweat of fear from his dark, troubled nightmares. Staring at him, she bit her lip and wondered what those tortured dreams had been. What frighten-

ing monsters had his slumbering mind unearthed?
What demons had been unleashed to stalk him? What
did it take to scare a hard, virile man she thought of
as being totally impervious and fearless?

Shivering, she watched him. Unaware he was being
observed, West dropped to the ground and sat cross-
legged directly before the fire, staring into the flames.
His gray eyes widened, caught the firelight, and
glowed. Elizabeth saw the fear that remained in their
silver depths. She noted the uncontrollable trembling
of his powerful brown shoulders, the jerking of his
flat belly.

West Quarternight was afraid. Afraid to go back to
sleep!

Inexplicably touched to the depths of her soul, Elizabeth felt tears spring to her eyes. She clasped a hand
over her mouth as her slender body trembled in em-
pathy with his lean frame.

He looked for all the world like a vulnerable,
frightened little boy. Elizabeth felt the strong mother-
ing instinct, so much a part of every woman God ever
created, surface fully as she lay there watching him.

It was all she could do to keep from tossing back
the covers and going to him. She had an almost overwhelming desire to get up, go over, and drop to her
knees beside him. To reach out, wrap her comforting
arms around his trembling shoulders, and press his
dark head to her breast. To hold him close and comfort him until his fears were all gone and forgotten.

It was out of the question, of course. So she did
nothing, continuing to lie unmoving, quietly watching, hoping he wouldn't catch his death of cold sitting
bare-chested in the chill desert night.

At last, he rose to his feet but did not immediately
leave. He thrust his hands, palms flat, down inside the
waistband of his tight buckskin trousers. His eyes

slowly lifting, he turned his dark head slightly and looked straight at her.

The distance between them was too great for him to see that her eyes were open, so she stared unblinking at the tall, dark man looking at her from across the campfire. She caught the definite tensing of his muscles. Saw his hands come out of his waistband and ball into fists at his sides. Saw the tendons in his neck and long arms stand out in bold relief. Saw the handsome face change from appealing boyish vulnerability to intimidating masculine hardness.

The transformation was swift and awesome. Gone was the petrified child awaking from a horrible nightmare. In his place stood a powerful man, rigid with the tautness of passion leashed. The change in him brought about a similar one in her.

Gone instantly was the need to comfort him as a mother, replaced with a craving to thrill him as a lover. Both emotions were equally strong. Only moments before she had been tempted to throw back the covers, go to him, and offer solace and understanding. No longer.

Now she yearned to throw back the covers, go to him, sensuously stroke those tensed brown shoulders and kiss that hard, cruel mouth until his unyielding stance crumbled. She longed to embrace him in the firelight, to brush tender kisses across his gleaming chest and down his flat abdomen. To press her open lips to his heart until it speeded out of control, and he trembled as violently with hot desire as he had with cold fear.

For what seemed an eternity, West continued to stand there staring, his naked chest shimmering in the firelight, his feet apart, his fists tight at his sides. Through it all Elizabeth silently waited, scarcely able to breathe, half expecting him to come for her as he had at Rancho Caballo. Praying she could turn him down, doubting that she would.

At last West moved and Elizabeth tensed.

And then sighed with relief and disappointment when he turned away, walked back to his bedroll, and stretched out on his back. She was thoroughly baffled by his behavior and had been since they had left Rancho Caballo five days ago.

Not once in all that time had he attempted to get her off alone. In fact, he ignored her, hardly spoke to her. She had quickly decided it was because he no longer wanted her. She supposed that her easy surrender at Rancho Caballo had forever ended the chase. There, in the darkened bedroom, she had given him what he had been after, so now he was no longer interested. She had been a challenge to his male ego. Then she had fallen right into his arms and ended the quest. It was as simple as that.

But he wanted her badly tonight; he wanted her right now. She was sure of it. Why was he holding back? The others were sleeping soundly. The two of them could easily have slipped away from camp and made love with no one the wiser. Why had he stayed away?

She didn't understand him. Just when she was sure she had him figured out, he again surprised her. Elizabeth was still pondering West's strange actions when at last she fell into fitful sleep.

Too soon, morning came in the wretched Land of the Dead.

Bright stars dulled and disappeared. Elizabeth moaned in disbelief when Edmund awakened her, saying it was time to get up: five-thirty already.

Shivering, she lay there for a minute. A glaze of hoar frost covered her blankets, and she was stiff and chilled to the bone. Shortly before six o'clock the sun rose.

Three hours later the temperature had risen to one hundred degrees. Like every other member of the expedition, Elizabeth wore a heavy, long-sleeved shirt, batwing chaps over her rust trousers, tall leather boots, and suede gloves. The drawstring of her flat-crowned hat was pulled tight under her throat, and around her neck was a silk bandanna, its flowing ends threaded through the silver and turquoise ring Micoma had given her.

The sun quickly climbed high into a cloudless sky each day, and the heat grew almost unbearable. It baked her brains and left her limp from midmorning to dusk. Her head ached relentlessly. Her lips were badly chapped and her fevered flesh itched so badly, she longed to tear off all the heavy smothering clothes and claw at her perspiring, prickling flesh.

But she didn't.

To have done so would be almost suicidal in a hostile wilderness of cactus, quicksand, cutbacks, deeply etched canyons, jutting rock columns, cracked arroyos, sand-blown dunes, dry lake beds, and brutal mesquite. Without the added protection of the heavy clothing her slender body would have been torn to pieces by the vicious thorns that scratched the horses' legs and fetlocks.

If she were to survive the pitiless heat and the blowing sands, the prickly pears and brittlebush and wavy thistles, the spiders and centipedes and scorpions, it was imperative that she stay covered from head to toe no matter how uncomfortable she became.

And so, miserable but uncomplaining, a well-protected Elizabeth rode the iron-gray stallion through the stark, awesome Land of the Dead, firmly resolved that the caravan would not be slowed nor hampered by having a woman along. In a harsh, mean region where physical prowess and deadly skill were needed merely to survive, Elizabeth pulled her own weight.

At least, most of the time.

She'd had more than one narrow escape in the five long days since leaving Rancho Caballo, but then so had Edmund and a couple of the Mexican peasants, and even one of the rugged vaqueros.

Elizabeth made a face. It seemed to her it was grossly unfair that when one of the men got a nasty cut or bruise or fell from his mount or came down with a touch of desert fever, nothing much was made of it.

But let her run into a bit of difficulty and West flared with anger and acted as though she were a terrible burden to him and the entire expedition. Which was doubly unfair since he was never the one who rushed to her aid. It was always Big Taos. The silent Navajo was unfailingly there when she needed him.

Like the incident a couple of mornings ago when her winded iron gray had struggled up a steep cutback through a thicket of mesquite. The stallion had made a misstep and tumbled into a four-foot-deep hole. She had leapt off and the gray had swiftly clambered out, leaving her frightened but unhurt.

Almost before she even realized what had happened, Taos was beside her, his gargantuan arms were gently lifting her up out of the crater. Eyes still wide with fear and surprise, she had looked up to see a mounted, scowling West Quarternight come to a plunging halt a few feet away.

He swung down out of the saddle, swiftly advanced on her, grabbed her upper arms so forcefully his fingers bit into the flesh, and said coldly, "You hurt?" Trembling, on the verge of nervous tears, she hadn't answered soon enough to suit him and he had become unreasonably angry. The muscles along his tanned jaw rigid, he said, "When people don't answer me, I get furious. Have you ever seen me furious?"

"Yes. I mean no—"

"No double-talk, Mrs. Curtin. I asked if you're hurt?"

"No. No, I am not hurt," she said, "and you can believe this or not, I am trying very hard not to annoy you."

"I know," he said, releasing her, "and that annoys me."

Later that same day they had pitched camp against the western bastion of the San Andres Range beside the bubbling Turquesa spring. Sweltering and uncomfortable, she had anxiously stripped off her hat, gloves, and batwing chaps, then rolled her shirt sleeves up past her elbows and jerked the long tails up out of her pants.

She turned to see West watching her, his gray eyes narrowed with disapproval. Not caring a fig what he or anyone thought, she yanked the shirttails up and tied them into a knot around her bare midriff, then sank to the ground and stretched her weary body out on the pebble strewn sand.

She closed her eyes, enjoying tremendously the deep shade cast by a rising spire of sandstone. She was about to doze when she felt a slight tickling on the exposed flesh of her midriff. Her eyelashes fluttered open just in time to see a small brown scorpion, its pincers thrust forward and open, its stinger-tipped tail arching forward over its body.

The scorpion was ready to inject venom with a lightning-swift forward snap of its stinger into her pale white flesh. Swifter still was the huge bronzed hand of Taos as he swooped down and plucked the scorpion from her trembling stomach, pinched it to death between his powerful thumb and forefinger, and flung it far away.

Before she could thank the protective Navajo, West stepped forward, grabbed her by an arm, and hauled her to her feet. His mean-looking face, inches from her own, was made meaner still by its dark growth of beard. His lips thinned, his voice icy cold, he said, "Do you know what happens when the *Centruroides sculptureatus*—the scorpion that was crawling on your belly—bites you, Mrs. Curtin?

"No, I guess—" Elizabeth began, only to be cut off by West.

"You thought it would cause a little swelling and inflammation, like a wasp sting, right?"

"Well, yes. I . . . I guess if the scorpion had bitten me, I would have been very uncomfortable for a while." She clawed at the imprisoning fingers circling her upper arm.

"Uncomfortable for a while?" A muscle danced inside his tanned jaw. "The *Centruroides sculptureatus* is the most deadly scorpion in the Southwest. When it bites, the venom quickly diffuses into the body tissues. It acts violently on the nerves. You go into convulsions. You can't breathe and your heart goes wild, then stops. It's an ugly, painful way to die, Mrs. Curtin."

Shaken, Elizabeth stammered, "If . . . if Taos . . . hadn't been close by . . ." She trembled, adding, "I'm so grateful."

"I'd be grateful if you'd keep your clothes on, Mrs. Curtin," West said coldly, finally releasing her. "You can't go around half naked out here without getting yourself into trouble. See if you can't remember that." He turned on his heel and stalked away.

Now, remembering that unpleasant episode, Elizabeth gritted her teeth and lifted bloodshot, scratchy eyes to the dark man who was becoming more disagreeable with every passing day.

Riding alone at the head of the contingent, West neck-reined his sorrel mare along the crusty edge of an escarpment and was momentarily silhouetted against a white-hot sun. Her stinging eyes clinging to him as he crossed the rocky ramparts above, Elizabeth frowned.

After lecturing her on the dangers of going about half naked, he was bare-chested in the fierce midday heat. He had removed his buckskin shirt and wrapped it around his head like a desert sheik. As dark as any Arab, his bare torso gleamed with sweat and a glaze of fine sand. His rapidly growing beard was scraggly, but as black as night. He looked mean and menacing. Had he been a stranger she happened upon, she would have been afraid of him.

Elizabeth made a sour face.

Back in Santa Fe and all the way down the Rio Grande to Rancho Caballo, West Quarternight had been an impeccable man. Meticulous about wearing clean shirts and pressed buckskins, he had bathed a couple of times a day and also shaved twice each day. His blue black hair had always been shiny clean, well trimmed, and neatly brushed.

Not anymore.

While he did still bathe at least once a day, he was no longer well groomed. His black hair was shaggy and badly in need of a comb and a cut. A fierce growth of heavy black whiskers covered his lower face. Sweat ran in rivulets down his deeply clefted brown back. His soft buckskins were wrinkled, covered with sand, and torn by thorns. He lifted a long arm to rub at his neck, and black perspiration-soaked hair flashed under his arm.

He was, Elizabeth told herself, revolting. Without scruples or pride. He was everything she found offensive and contemptible in a man.

Dane Curtin was his opposite. Handsome, blond,

and always immaculate, Dane was sensitive and caring. His morals were high, his deep respect for women unerring.

She wasn't worthy of such a man.

36

❧❧❧

"They were not worthy of me!" cried the pale, distraught madman perched atop his hard bed of gold. "I must have a beautiful young angel deserving of my attentions!"

The stocky, walleyed servant, down on his knees before the chalky-faced satyr, bobbed his dark head in agreement. "Sí, sí," said Ortiz. "A beautiful senorita."

"Yes, beautiful," murmured the pale man seated atop the shiny gold bars. "Beautiful and sweet and innocent, like my wife. A fair, refined, red-haired woman like my lovely Elizabeth."

A smile spreading over his face, the pale man lapsed into a kind of dreamy trance. Languidly raising a white hand to lift the hot, dampened curls from his nape, Dane Curtin was blissfully unaware he was no longer the man Elizabeth Montbleau had agreed to marry.

In his mind's eye he was a fit, lean, blondly beautiful man of untold riches to whom any woman would willingly subjugate herself. His mouth slightly open, a finger idly twisting a damp curl, he clearly envisioned the sweet moment when at last the two of

them, he and his trusting Elizabeth, would come together in all their splendid naked beauty.

As he daydreamed, he began to drool. A thin string
of saliva dribbled from the left corner of his open
lips. His bloodshot green eyes rolled heavenward. His
head lolled to one side.

It had been less than six months since he'd left New
York, three since finding the gold, but Dane had
changed drastically. He would not have recognized
himself had he looked into a mirror. His hair, down
to his shoulders, no longer shone with golden glory.
It was a tangled, dirty mass of limp ringlets, dulled to
a drab brassy yellow-brown. His once handsome face
was puffy with the first signs of dissipation, his jaws,
chin, and throat covered with a growth of untrimmed
brownish whiskers.

His superb physique—the hard, slender body—was
gone. His pale arms and legs had lost their muscle
tone and the pallid skin was beginning to sag. Along
with his gluttonous indulgence in rich, fattening
foods had come a paunch that protruded beneath his
transparent robes where once the board-flat belly had
brought sighs of approval from entranced lovers.

Worse, he was no longer immaculate. Dane had
grown extremely slovenly in his personal hygiene.
The flimsy, see-through robe he wore was soiled and
spotted with spilled liquor, stale sweat, and grime.
Beneath the thin, stained covering, his pasty flesh was
unclean and smelly. Half drunk at all times, halluci-
nating with ever greater frequency, he had no idea it
had been days since he had last washed his ripe flesh.

His ragged fingernails had grown excessively long
and dirt had collected beneath them. Dane never noticed. With those sullied clawlike nails, he scratched
obscenely at his itching crotch and underarms, oblivious to the fact he had become a revolting, filthy ani-

mal. An unwashed, unhealthy, scabrous creature, unclean in body and mind.

In his state of deepening insanity, Dane vacillated between the exquisite satisfaction of knowing he possessed untold riches in gold and the insatiable hunger for a beautiful woman whom he could physically possess upon his golden bed.

It was the hunger that ruled him now.

Coming out of his stupor, Dane reached out for the black leather riding crop that he kept always within reach. He picked it up from the bed of gold and looked at the trembling man kneeling before him.

Flicking the vicious whip underneath his arm, Dane slid off the hard gold bed, rose fully, and smiled with pleasure on seeing a look of fear quickly spread over Ortiz's brown upturned face.

Dane stood with his dirty bare feet wide apart, the thin, soiled robe indecently exposing the pale, naked body beneath. He tossed his head back, supposing he was still the beautiful golden-haired god worshiped by all his brown-skinned servants in this underground kingdom he ruled. He didn't remember that, one by one, his subjects had fled. Didn't realize that the terrified Ortiz was the only vassal left in his kingdom of evil. He looked down on the kneeling thrall and issued orders.

"Ortiz, turn and face the other direction, but remain on your knees." The walleyed Ortiz swiftly obeyed. Never rising, he turned all the way about, so that he was facing away from his demented master. Terrified, he waited for further instruction from the madman standing behind him. "Take off your shirt," said Dane. Ortiz stripped off his white shirt. "Now the sash at your waist. Remove it." With trembling fingers, the walleyed Ortiz untied the knot resting atop his fat middle and pulled the wide crimson sash away from his stocky body. "Now lower your trousers to your knees."

"Please, Pale Master, I—"

"You heard me," said Dane as he took the riding crop from under his arm and began flicking it in the air.

The frightened Ortiz began to cry as he obediently lowered his white peasant's trousers past his fleshy hips and down over his trembling brown bottom. Bawling like a baby, he reluctantly released the pants. They whispered down around his knees.

Ortiz's stubby fingers had hardly let go of the white linen fabric before he felt the first stinging blow of the whip on his bare buttocks. He fell over onto his hands and knees as the sounds of his screams bounced off the walls of the huge natural amphitheater and echoed throughout the dark reaches of the vast underground caverns.

It was over quickly. Dane tired, dropped the whip, and fell back, pleased and exhausted, atop his bed of gold. Breathing heavily and sweating profusely, he issued his final order. "Now get up, get dressed, get out of here. And bring me a beautiful young woman." Dane sighed deeply, yanked the tail of his long, dirty robe up to wipe his perspiring face, and added, "A refined woman with fair skin and red hair. Go, now!"

In the western foothills of the Oscura Mountains, the afternoon shimmered in palpable waves of heat. West dismounted by drawing his right leg up over the saddle horn and sliding to the ground. Leaving his sorrel mare with reins trailing, he climbed a turret of red sandstone and stood looking out at the lines of mountain ranges through the layers of heat.

Elizabeth also looked through those distorting heat waves, but not at the distant mountains. Astride her iron gray she silently watched the tall, dark man who looked as if he belonged here in these low-lying broken mountains called the Oscuras. Grady had told her that *oscuro* meant "dark" in Spanish. Both man and mountains were *oscuro* and forbidding.

Her tired, stinging eyes clung to the *oscuro* man standing somber and alone atop the jutting turret. She couldn't help but wonder, as she often did of late, what West was thinking. What was really on his mind? What thoughts filled his head at this moment? And on those occasions when he was silent and uncommunicative for long stretches at a time?

From the beginning there had been an aura of mystery about West Quarternight, and his tight-lipped refusal to discuss his past was maddening. Now, since his devilish teasing and easygoing manner had entirely vanished, he was even more mysterious.

He continued to be a highly competent scout, knowledgeable and brave, but he was growing increasingly distant. To her. To the rest of the crew. He had little to say to anyone, answering questions with a distinct economy of words.

At times he was almost sullen. His dark moodiness was apparently so uncharacteristic that his two partners—men who had been with him for the past four years—seemed genuinely baffled. Further, she had noticed a brooding expression in the depths of West's beautiful silver eyes on occasions when he thought no one was looking at him.

Puzzling over the enigmatic man, Elizabeth had begun to suspect that the impassive Quarternight was nursing some secret sorrow, some hidden wound. She recalled snatches of conversations she'd had with him. Remembered things he had said before their bantering relationship had so abruptly ended. Like the evening in the courtyard at Rancho Caballo when he'd said all the good boys had been killed in the war and that others had come home and nobody wanted them. She remembered, too, when she had asked if he had no heart at all, he had said he did and intended to keep it right where it was.

Before that night, when they were still riding the Rio Grande, she had said to him once, "Perhaps, Quarternight, your toughness and self-interest mask some shattered ideals." A strange expression had flickered into his teasing gray eyes and she had anxiously pressed on, asking, "Was your trust in someone misplaced?"

"I have little faith in most men," he had swiftly replied, "and none at all in women."

At the time, she had paid little attention to the rather telling remark, but now as she thought back on it, she wondered if he had meant it. Or was she reading more into the offhand remark than it warranted?

Squinting now at the tall, long-legged man with his hands on his slim hips, booted feet apart, Elizabeth frowned, then mentally shook herself, feeling guilty and confused. What did she care what West Quarternight was thinking? What was it Grady had told her? *No le hace.*

It doesn't matter after all.

By midafternoon the caravan was down out of the Oscuras and into the most awesomely ugly terrain imaginable. Blackened, lava-scorched earth stretched in all directions, the flatness of the desert floor scored and scarred with black basalt twists and peaks, thick, ropy cords and tall, jutting ridges of black volcanic stone.

Elizabeth thought that the stunningly grotesque region appeared as if the flat black earth had at one time been a vast kettle of black liquid cooking atop a huge stove. The thick, boiling concoction had bubbled hotly, leaving large, deep craters scattered over its black surface. At the same time it had spewed up great plumes of ebony fire, leaving trails of cliffs and ledges from the eruptions.

She wasn't that far off the mark.

While she and Edmund stood staring at the burned, twisted lands in astonishment, Grady told them they were standing in the Valley of Fires. The blackened, twisted lava formations were formed from volcanic eruptions that had happened thousands of years before. He said the huge piles of black lava covered more than a hundred square miles.

Lifting a hand to shade her eyes, Elizabeth looked out at the vast blackened Valley of Fires in mute amazement. Pointing and gesturing, Grady moved forward. Taos and Edmund followed. Elizabeth didn't move. She stayed where she was, rooted to the spot.

So engrossed was she by the stark, foreboding scenery, she didn't notice the dark, foreboding man who silently stepped up beside her. Then she felt his presence. Close. At once, she could hardly breathe. It was his fault. He was making her miserable. He was making everyone miserable.

Suddenly Elizabeth was overwhelmingly angry with him. He had chased her mercilessly until he caught her and made swift, profane love to her. Now he treated her with cold contempt. As if what had happened between them had been all her fault. As if she were the one without morals!

Elizabeth dropped her hand away from her eyes, quickly turned, and snapped, "What is it? What do you want?"

His narrowed gaze never leaving the distant horizon, West calmly replied, "Not a thing. Nothing at all. And you?"

"Me? I don't . . . I have everything . . . I . . . oh, damnation, is your only goal in life to cause trouble, Quarternight?"

At last he turned his head and his low-lidded eyes finally met hers. They were expressionless. He said, "Lady, I have but one goal. To escort you and Edmund to wherever the hell your loving husband is holed up, collect my money, and go."

Stung by his harshness, Elizabeth said, "Quarternight, you truly are a cold bastard!"

"Sin duda," he replied levelly. "Without doubt."

Tension between the two became almost palpable as the expedition continued to wind its sure way toward the southeastern corner of the wild New Mexico Territory.

Determined to forget West Quarternight existed, Elizabeth went out of her way to ignore him and to appear gay and carefree. When the contingent reached the spectacular White Sands that Grady had been telling them about, Elizabeth paid no attention to West's stern warning that everyone was to stay mounted, that they would waste no time on foolishness.

Had he not issued such a high-handed command, Elizabeth might have contented herself with staying in the saddle. As it was, she immediately felt obliged to take off her flat-crowned hat, hook it on the saddle horn, and climb down off the iron-gray stallion. Turning around and around, she soon fell to her knees and scooped up double handfuls of the white, sugary sand.

Laughing like a child, she played in the glistening sand, completely captivated by the vast shimmering wavelike dunes, as fresh and unspoiled as a wilderness snowfall. A vast ocean of sparkling gypsum crystals, as bright and as beautiful as fine diamonds. An unbelievably extraordinary place of almost blinding brightness.

Totally absorbed with the pristine beauty surrounding her, Elizabeth romped about on the dazzling white sands, oblivious to the men's shouts of appreciative laughter at her childlike antics. Oblivious as well to the narrowed silver-gray eyes that followed her every move.

While the others in the caravan dismounted to stretch, West stayed in the saddle. With a knee hooked around the horn and a thin brown cigar clenched between his teeth, he stared unsmiling at the laughing, frolicking woman. When he saw her spin dizzily about, then fall giggling down onto the sand, a vein begin to pulse on his high forehead.

Elizabeth lay on her back, spreading her outstretched arms and legs enthusiastically, shouting to Edmund that she was making a sand angel, just the way she used to make angels in the snow. Her long, red hair had come unbound and was fanned out atop the white sands. Millions of tiny glistening crystals clung to her tight pants and her long-sleeved shirt. The sound of her girlish laughter echoed across the billowing dunes.

Growing angrier by the second, West felt every muscle in his body tighten. His sharp teeth clenched so tightly, his cigar was almost cut in two. He lowered his leg back over the horse, thrust his booted feet into the stirrups, wheeled the sorrel mare about, and shouted over his shoulder, "That's enough, Mrs. Curtin. We're moving out!"

West was equally disgruntled the next day when they reached the beginning foothills of the Sacramentos and Elizabeth insisted on leisurely stopping to study the fascinating petroglyphs decorating the huge rocks.

"What's botherin' you, Sonny?" Grady asked the scowling West. "It ain't gonna make no difference if we spend a few minutes here. I been a-tellin' the Curtins I'd show 'em the picture carvin's."

"Make it snappy," West bit out irritably. He swung down out of the saddle and sat on an overturned boulder while Grady herded the others up into the rocks. Glorying in his roll of knowledgeable guide, Grady told how the Anasazi—ancient ones—had carved the pictures on the rocks hundreds of years ago. Enchanted, Elizabeth went from rock to rock, touching, studying, asking questions. It was more than two hours before they returned to where West waited below. One glance at his granite face, and no one needed to wonder if he was angry.

The next day, when the caravan came upon one of the many closed turquoise mines that dotted the rugged slopes of the Sacramentos, Elizabeth wanted to go inside and explore. West put his foot down.

"No, Mrs. Curtin," he said calmly. "Out of the question. I won't allow it."

Aware of the building tension between the pair, the others held their collective breaths and turned to look at Elizabeth, wondering what she would do, hoping she would quietly acquiesce.

She didn't.

Sick and tired of putting up with the dark disgruntled man who was forever spoiling everything for everybody, Elizabeth again challenged him.

She loosened the drawstrings of her flat-crowned hat, took it off, and hung it on the saddle horn. Looking straight at the scowling, mounted West, she tossed the reins to the ground, threw her leg over the saddle just the way she'd seen him do, and slid from the iron gray's back.

Three sets of eyeballs clicked in unison as Edmund, Grady, and Taos all looked anxiously from Elizabeth to West.

West sighed.

Just as Elizabeth had done, he slowly removed his sweat-stained Stetson and hooked it on the horn. He released the sorrel mare's reins, threw his long leg over, and dropped agilely to the ground.

Like a couple of gunfighters in a high-noon show-down on the dusty street of a frontier town, the pair started toward each other. The rest of the caravan, still mounted, watched in nervous silence.

Her chin lifted defiantly, shoulders thrown back, Elizabeth walked steadily forward to meet the dark, angry man purposely bearing down on her. The fateful march lasted but a few seconds; it seemed much longer. At last they stood toe to toe, facing each other, so close Elizabeth noticed a tiny muscle twitching at the corner of his stern mouth, and West saw the rapid throbbing of the pulse in her creamy throat.

Elizabeth swallowed hard.

Never had she seen a man look meaner than West Quarternight looked at that moment. She sensed him drawing in, coiling like a great spring. The muscles along his dark jaw became tense and ridgid. His gray eyes were murderous.

Still, she was not to be bullied. She had opened her mouth to inform him she would "do any damned thing" she pleased, when he thoroughly shocked her by saying, barely above a whisper, "Don't do it. Please don't go in that old mine. It isn't safe."

For a fraction of a second his mean gray eyes lost their hardness, and she could have sworn she caught a fleeting glimpse of naked fear in their silver-gray depths. Flustered, she frowned at him, hesitated, but felt compelled to go on with the speech she had planned to make.

Hands on her hips, face tilted up to his, she said, "Quarternight, you can't tell me what you will and will not allow me to do." She watched his expressive gray eyes immediately flare with rage and was strangely relieved. She was back on safe ground now. Knew right where she stood. "I am going into that mine to have a look around. And you cannot stop me!"

She thought for a minute he was going to strike her. She knew he wanted to. Instead he turned and walked away and Elizabeth caught his almost imperceptible nod to Taos.

Minutes later when Elizabeth stepped into the shadowed mouth of the long-abandoned mine, she glanced over her shoulder to see West leaning negligently back against a shoulder-high boulder, arms crossed over his chest. There was about him that usual air of quiet defiance which she found both irritating and attractive. Apparently his concern for her safety had been short-lived. She tossed her head and hurried into the abandoned turquoise mine, Taos, Grady, and Edmund close behind.

When the last glimpse of her flaming red hair was swallowed up in the mine's yawning darkness, West's long arms came uncrossed. He pushed away from his rocky resting place, his body taut, his heart hammering in his chest.

He could feel the perspiration beading in his hairline and along his upper lip. He tried to take slow, calming breaths. It did no good. He felt weak, as if his legs would not support him. A bitter taste of fear filled his mouth, and he trembled violently.

In the blinding sunlight of the New Mexican wilderness, West's recurring nightmare caught up with him again, this time while he was wide awake.

He was again a sickly, starving twenty-four-year-old Yankee prisoner locked up in that hellhole the South called Andersonville. With him was the best friend he had ever had in his life. Captain Darin Brooks and he had been together since the first days of the war, when they had both been strong and eager.

Now they were thin and disillusioned but determined they'd escape. They had to escape. They were going to die if they didn't get out. It had taken weeks to dig the long tunnel under the prison floor. At last the night came when they were ready. All they had to do was crawl the length of the dark narrow tunnel in the middle of the night and freedom would be theirs.

They had almost made it. Liberty was within reach, when the tunnel began to collapse on top of them. Great clods of dirt fell into their eyes, their mouths, shutting off their breath. Suffocating them. Burying them alive.

Now West weakly crouched down on his heels in the glaring New Mexico sunshine. He leaned over and put his head between his legs, gasping for breath. He put his face in his hands, trembling and sweating. He felt sick. Sick that he had survived that night and Brooks had died. It was Brooks who'd had everything to live for. Brooks who had a wife and two baby boys waiting for him back in Ohio. Brooks who was too good to die young.

West stayed crouched there shaking in the heat, his fearful gray eyes riveted on the mine's mouth. When at last he caught sight of flaming red hair flashing like a beacon in the night, he shot to his feet and a grin of relief spread over his dark face.

Quickly, West checked himself, wiped the smile off, leaned back against his rock upthrust, crossed his arms over his chest, and pretended nonchalance. He was confident that none of them suspected he was a man so afraid of mines and tunnels and caves and caverns, the prospect of going into one literally paralyzed him with terror.

What, he wondered miserably, what would he do if they actually located the vast underground caverns of the Legend?

37

❧❧❧

"By doggies, we been on the trail ten days now since leaving Rancho Caballo and ain't run into no trouble yet," said Grady. He rode along beside West under a white New Mexico sun.

West, his alert gray eyes sweeping the serrated mountain peaks rising just off to the left, said, "Don't go tempting fate."

To which Grady quickly replied, "Well, what do you know? He can talk. I was beginnin' to think you'd gone as mute as Taos."

West managed a slight grin, but it was quickly gone. His face, covered with a ten-day growth of black woolly beard, again took on that shuttered, glowering expression Grady had come to dread.

Grady couldn't help himself. He had to ask. "Why are you so all-fired mad at Elizabeth Curtin?"

"Who said I was?"

"It's plain as the nose on your old sour puss. What in tarnation's wrong? I'm a-gettin' tired of askin'."

"Then quit asking," said West. He glanced at Grady, and added, "Nothing is wrong. *Nada.*"

But it wasn't true. He was angry with Elizabeth. Everything she did rankled him, made him mad as hell. He longed for the moment when he safely deposited her at her husband's feet and was done with her once and for all. She was what the Mexicans would call *la bruja*—the witch. Elizabeth Curtin was a tempting, flame-haired witch who was driving him nuts. Damn the beautiful bruja!

West pulled his thoughts back to the trail ahead. The caravan had managed to skirt the western edges of the towering Sacramentos, but there was no way around the Guadalupes, looming now against the clear blue sky. Already they were leaving the flat sagebrush and saltbush country behind, gradually climbing up into the foothills toward a series of rough ridges and unspoiled canyons.

"That's it, ain't it, Sonny?" said Grady abruptly, pointing to a big rocky talus rising just ahead. "That the entrance to the pass?"

"Yep," said West, "right on the other side of that rippled slope we'll turn up into the pass. Barring any unforeseen trouble, we should be through the mountains and on the other side by four or five this afternoon."

"I 'spect so," said Grady. "You 'member, Sonny, that time we was a-ridin' through the pass and them two 'Paches was hid up there on some high rocks and they jumped us when we . . ."

Nodding, West remembered. He was not worried about Apaches today, but he was edgy. He felt as if somebody was walking over his grave. Couldn't shake the nagging premonition that something was going to happen.

He said nothing about it to Grady. But he did resolve to be extra alert and cautious as he led the contingent through the crisscrossing maze of peaks, spires, and craters in the inner reaches of the towering Guadalupes.

Immediately he blamed his mild case of jitters on

Elizabeth Curtin. If she hadn't insisted on coming along on a perilous journey meant only for men, he wouldn't be feeling apprehensive. He could damned sure take care of himself. So could the others. Even Edmund Curtin had toughened considerably since leaving Santa Fe.

West glanced back over his shoulder. Edmund, who rode several yards back alongside one of the vaqueros, was no longer the fancy-garbed tinhorn who had ridden out of Santa Fe that May dawn. Gone was the fringed suede jacket, the leather cowboy cuffs, the stiff denim trousers, the bright red shirt, the bolo tie, and even the wide intaglioed belt with the big silver buckle.

Edmund now wore a sun-faded pullover collarless shirt and a pair of soft buckskins beneath his protective batwing chaps. His felt hat was creased and sweat-stained. His brown leather boots were scarred and the worn heels sported a pair of big roweled Mexican spurs. Slouched in the saddle, hat brim pulled low, Edmund Curtin looked completely at home astride the Navajo pony. The urbane Easterner had adapted. He no longer needed anyone watching after him. Edmund Curtin, West suspected, wouldn't be afraid to go down into a deep, dark cavern.

"Where the hell you goin'?" Grady's raspy voice cut into West's troubled musings.

Stopping abruptly, West realized he had ridden past the distinctive sandstone landmark denoting the opening of the mountain pass. Grady pulled up and jerked the bit against his mount's mouth. His horse danced in place and shook its head.

West shrugged, turned his sorrel about, and came riding back. Without a word, he reined the mare right past the frowning, swearing Grady and up into the narrow rocky entrance of the pass.

Shaking his white head and muttering, Grady trot-

ted after West and the rest of the caravan followed.
Soon every last person and animal had been swallowed up in the soaring mountains. The scouts knew
the winding pass well. They expected the crossing to
be easy and uneventful. The trail was no more treacherous than some they had already traveled.

The cooling shade cast by the steep-sided canyons
and the strong winds that whistled through the deeply
cut valleys offered welcome relief from the broiling
heat of the sun. Hats came off heads and eyes no
longer squinted in the blinding brightness. Sighs of
relief went up, Elizabeth's being the loudest. She took
off her flat-crowned hat and let her long red hair tumble down around her shoulders.

It was shortly after one o'clock in the afternoon
and all was exactly as it should be as the caravan
made its way across a grassy mountain meadow between towering rocky ramparts. On and on and up
and up they rode, across rocky draws and over dry
washes and alongside deep gulches.

Skirting the jutting faces of soaring sandstone
walls, they sidetracked deep arroyos and vast yawning chasms. They splashed through shallow, sandy-
bottomed springs that were perfect for filling near-
empty canteens with cold, clear water. They rode
across sheets of flat, smooth rock, their horses'
hooves striking the stone with pinging sounds in the
quiet of the afternoon.

Further into the mountains they traveled, threading
their way through brush-choked ravines, climbing up
flat-topped mesas and past spiraling buttes. They circled great piles of rocks scattered on the valley floors.
From tiny pebbles to gigantic boulders weighing ten,
twenty tons, the fallen rock had come from high
above. The sun-heated stone had cooled during the
chill nights, broken off from ridges hundreds of feet

above, and rained down into the canyon floor, taking great chunks of the sandstone wall with it.

When West neck-reined his sorrel mare into the mouth of Cajita Canyon, he pulled up to look around. Hand resting on the saddle horn, he leaned his head back and looked up at the sky. He nudged the mare with his knees and the sorrel dutifully turned in a slow, complete circle while West studied the heavens.

Not a sign of cloud anywhere. The sky was a dome of uninterrupted blue.

Satisfied, West rode on into Cajita Canyon. Cajita was three and half miles long, but only a half mile wide. Its steep sides rose to five hundred feet, almost straight up. Ragged ridges, deep crevices, and cupped-out craters scarred the soaring sandstone walls.

More than a mile into the canyon a lone thunderhead moved abruptly into sight over the jagged ridges high above. The air suddenly became ominous, heavy. West's sorrel mare pricked up her ears, snorting nervously. A squirrel skittered into the sagebrush. A hawk took quick flight, veering away toward the canyon's mouth.

A storm was brewing.

It was too late for the caravan to turn back. West rode back and issued the order for all riders to dismount and loosen the cinches of their saddles. Pulling up, Edmund swung down and obeyed without question.

Elizabeth frowned, stayed mounted, and said, "Why would I want to loosen the cinch? I want my saddle to be—"

"Get off that horse and do as I said," West snarled, and wheeled away as Grady came riding up.

"You always loosen the cinches before you swim em'," Grady said to Elizabeth, unnotching the cinch buckle under her iron gray's belly.

"Swim the horses?" Elizabeth said, and looked up at

the sky. "It's not even raining. And if starts, surely it can't rain enough to fill an entire canyon."

"There, all finished," said Grady. "Now, get your slicker out from behind the cantle and put it on. You're gonna need it, missy!"

As the scouts helped untie the bunched ponies and pack burros, they reminded everyone to take care of themselves first, the stock and supplies second. Knowing what could happen in a summer storm in these mountains, West and Taos exchanged worried glances, then West headed back to the head of the caravan and Taos moved to the rear.

The single thunderhead billowed swiftly into a huge black cloud that sailed in front of the sun. The canyon was immediately cast in strange eerie blue light. A great flash of lightning streaked across the darkened sky. A deafening rumble of thunder followed.

The cloudburst began.

Elizabeth, squinting through the fast-falling rain, caught sight of West. A dark hand lifted to the brim of his cocked Stetson as rain dripped from the side of his hat onto his shoulder. Suddenly, she could no longer see him through the downfall and within seconds she was gasping for breath in an unbelievable torrent of pounding rain unlike anything she had ever seen. The wind-driven rain felt like needles stinging her face. It plastered her long hair to her head and hammered against her yellow slicker.

Clinging to the reins of her nervous stallion, she blinked and squinted, automatically searching for the big bronzed Navajo who would take care of her, just as always. Turning in the saddle, she spotted Taos through the blinding rain. But he was far back, pulling on the bridles of badly spooked ponies.

She shouted to him just as a huge wall of water materialized from out of nowhere and came roaring down the canyon. Eyes enormous with fright and disbelief, Elizabeth turned back around and braced herself. She managed to stay in the saddle when the water reached her, but not for long. The current was incredibly swift. Her feet came out of the stirrups. Frantically she clung to the reins with one hand, the saddle horn with the other, as the stallion lunged sideways then began swimming through the raging water.

Suddenly, all around her was utter chaos. Big-eyed horses whinnied and neighed, plunging wildly about in the rising tide. Pack mules struggled under their loads, went under the eddying surface, came up and bobbed along, swept by the tide. Cargo broke loose and swirled away down the canyon. Guns, food, and medical supplies were lost in the flood.

One of the Mexican helpers, arms and legs flailing, was swept away with the current, the sounds of his choking screams echoing off the canyon walls. The pounding rain continued to fall in great sheets, the canyon rapidly filling with frothy, surging water. The swift current became deadly. Debris rushed dangerously down the swollen stream. A tree limb struck Elizabeth in the back. She was unhurt, but the blow knocked her off her horse.

She clung to the long reins and was dragged along beside the struggling, swimming stallion. Like a child counting on a dependable parent, she foolishly looked about for Taos and felt her pounding heart sink with despair. He was still far back in the canyon, swimming his mount toward Edmund. Grady had leapt from his horse and was scrambling up a rocky trail on the canyon's far side.

Elizabeth felt the wet leather reins being wrenched from her fingers as the struggling, blowing stallion made a kicking lunge forward. Desperate, she attempted to swim against the rushing tide and felt herself being dragged under. Her head bobbed up, she spit out water, and grabbed for her horse's tail. Floundering and thrashing, she was dragged downstream with the boiling current. My God, she was going to drown! And it was West Quarternight's fault. He had led them into this canyon, this death trap that was to be her watery grave!

At that instant somebody took hold of Elizabeth's slicker collar and jerked her sinking head up out of the water. She was flopped over onto her back and dragged through the dirty, rushing water toward the rocky canyon wall. She felt herself bumping against a hard side, felt legs kicking against hers, but didn't attempt to see who had saved her. Eyes closed against the pelting deluge, she felt herself being tugged through the rapidly rising water and was tremendously thankful.

They reached the canyon wall and West scrambled up out of the stream, pulling Elizabeth up with him. His lungs aching, his legs throbbing and weak, he hauled Elizabeth out of the water. With one hand tightly clinging to her collar, the other clutching a rain-slick ledge jutting out from the canyon wall, he pulled her against his chest and braced a bent knee between her legs to support her weight.

"You okay?" he shouted above the rumbling thunder and crashing water.

"You!" she shouted back, seeing at last who had her. She began to struggle within his encircling arm. "Let me go!"

"Don't be a fool," he warned, tightening his hold. "Either we get to higher ground quickly or we drown." He drew her around in front of him and shouted, "Start climbing!"

"No! Not with you!"

"Yes, damnit, with me. Get going!"

"No! I won't!"

West's strong arm tightened reflexively around her. He squeezed so hard she couldn't breathe, and she knew if his hand had been free, he would have hit her. He slammed her against the jagged canyon wall with his body and his wet, bearded face was inches from hers.

"Start climbing, goddamn it! Climb, and don't you look back and don't talk back, either!" He found better footing, released his hold on the rock, spun her roughly about, and shoved her up the face of the wet canyon wall. He slammed his long, lean body against hers with such angry force she nearly lost her breath. He lifted her up, then gave her another hard shove.

Frightened, crying now, Elizabeth clutched at handholds above, desperate to get away from him. She slipped, staggered, and fell back. He was atop her in the blinking of an eye and he literally hurled her up the trail, throwing a hard forearm up underneath her buttocks, lifting, pushing.

"Move it, damn you! I'm not about to die because of you. And you're not going to die either, and let me take the blame for it!" Nodding, Elizabeth tried valiantly, but couldn't climb fast enough to suit him. He shouted after her, "Get moving, you little bitch. You've been nothing but trouble to me from the start. Get your ass up that wall or I'll spank it until you can't sit down!"

Pushed by his harsh words, Elizabeth found strength and agility she didn't know she had. Crying loudly, her tears mixing with the rain peppering her upturned face, she scrambled up the pock-marked canyon wall, finding jutting ridges to grab, slippery ledges to tread on. More than once she made a misstep or lost her hold and came sliding back down. West was there to shove her roughly back up.

Blinded by tears and sick with fear and anger, Elizabeth crawled up the rugged perpendicular face of wet, slippery granite. She climbed the canyon wall while ominous gusts of wind howled around her head and driving rain beat on her back and a black-bearded, black-hearted man threatened her.

West climbed, too, with single-minded purpose: to get another man's spoiled, flame-haired wife safely up into the shelter of a cupped-out crater a hundred feet above the canyon floor. Keeping a watchful eye on Elizabeth, he moved around her, scaled the last ten feet to the crater, and tumbled into the dry, small-mouthed cavelike crevice.

Immediately he was up and turning about. Quickly he sat flat down on the stone floor at the very center of the cave's opening, positioning himself a few feet back from the lip. Spreading his long legs wide apart, he braced his booted feet on either side of the crater's mouth, then leaned out and reached for Elizabeth.

Catching both her wrists, he hauled her up the canyon's craggy face and into the cupped-out crater. Leaning farther and farther back as he pulled her inside, West finally collapsed onto the dry stone floor.

They were safe inside; he flat on his back, his chest heaving, his breath labored, she lying atop him, shivering and weeping.

38

West immediately rolled over, asked if she was all right, and not waiting for an answer, leapt to his feet. He left her lying on the stone floor, weeping and gasping for breath. He rushed back to the crater's mouth, poked his dark head out, and squinted through the driving, pounding rain.

Across the canyon he caught sight of the others and waved a long arm to signal. Over his shoulder he called to Elizabeth, "They're safe. Edmund's with Taos under a high overhang back in the direction of the canyon's mouth." He quickly pulled his head back inside. "Grady and the others are holed up in a big, protected crevice several yards up canyon." West lifted his hands, swept the thick, wet hair back off his face, shrugged out of his rain slicker, dropped it, and turned around.

"Looks like we made . . ." His sentence was never finished. Elizabeth, on her feet now, her eyes wild, stepped aggressively up to him and slapped his dark, wet face with such ferocity, his ears rang and his head turned to the side. "Jesus," he muttered in stunned disbelief, "what was that for?"

"You think me a bitch! I'll show you just how a

bitch acts. You'll see what a bitch I really am!" She
slapped him again, this blow harder than the first.
Her hand tingling, she gritted her teeth and slapped
him yet again.

"You've shown me," he said calmly. "Now let it go."

"No, I won't let it go, you bastard," she raged, the
hot tears surging down her cheeks. "If all I am to you
is trouble, why didn't you let me drown?"

"Christ, I didn't—"

She slapped him again. "I wish you had let me
drown! Wish you hadn't bothered saving me! I'd
rather be dead than trapped here with you."

Another open-handed slap connected squarely with
West's bearded right jaw. His silver eyes narrowed
with rage, and his hands balled into tight fists at his
sides. A vein bulged on his wet forehead. His tall, lean
body was tightly coiled, rigid with leashed ire.

Elizabeth was far too upset to notice or to care. All
the anger, all the tension, all the guilt that had been
building since that first evening she had gone to his
La Fonda Hotel room poured from her now. In a fit
of fury and passion she took out all her frustration on
him

"Bastard, you bastard," she screamed loudly, slapping him repeatedly, some of her wildly thrown
blows connecting, others going awry and glancing off
his muscular shoulders, his chest, his arms. "I hate
you, I hate you," she shouted, coughing and gasping,
her nose running, her tears blinding her, long wet
locks of her hair whipping into her face. "You call me
a bitch, you bastard! You no-good son of a bitch! You
corrupt, debased, vile, heartless user of women!"

Elizabeth continued to call West every bad name
she could think of, shouting to be heard above the
violent storm raging six feet from where they stood.
Completely out of control, she sobbed and hit at him
until she could no longer lift her trembling arms. Out

of breath, exhausted, her eyes swollen and red, she valiantly tried to continue the assault.

Totally spent, she sagged against him, still trying to hit at him. Her knees buckled and she knew she was going down, could no longer stand. Fighting against it, she clutched at West's chamois shirt, but her hands were wet and she couldn't get a grip on the soft fabric. Her fingernails scraping down the shirt and the corded ribs beneath, she sagged helplessly to her knees before him. Jerking with sobs, trembling with fatigue and emotion, she sank back on her heels, and her head dropped to her chest.

Above her, West stood as he had throughout her tirade, rigid as a statue. He had made no move to subdue her; had not so much as lifted a hand to deflect the stinging blows to his face.

But he *was* angry.

As angry as he had ever been in his life. Never had he been this angry without hurting somebody. His short fingernails cutting into the palms of his hands, he was tempted to hit her, which was what she deserved. But he had never hit a woman in his life. He couldn't hit this one.

His heart hammering against his ribs, his teeth so tightly clenched his jaws were aching, West stood there trying to maintain his fragile self-control. Cool intellect at war with hot emotion, he struggled to keep his head.

But, God, she made him mad!

His gray eyes twin points of silver fire, West reached out and grabbed a handful of thick, wet hair atop Elizabeth's bowed head. At once her hands flew up to wrap themselves around his wrist and her red-rimmed blue eyes lifted and clashed with his.

"Stop it!" she screamed as he roughly pulled her to her feet by her hair. "You're hurting me!"

"Good," he said, continuing to clutch her hair

tightly even when she stood facing him. "Good," he said again, and gave her hair a painful yank, forcing her head back, her body against his.

"Let go of my hair!" she snarled, clawing at his wrist with long, punishing nails.

"Goddamn you," he said through clenched teeth, and Elizabeth could feel through their clothing the granite hardness of his tensed, powerful body. "I don't know what to do with you," he admitted angrily. For a long moment they stood glaring at each other, the tension building. Then West's angry silver eyes shifted to her wet, trembling lips. A muscle flexed in his bearded jaw. "I don't know," he said, "whether to kill you or kiss you."

With the last ounce of defiance left in her, Elizabeth pushed on his hard, ungiving chest with shaking hands and told him hatefully, "I'd much prefer you kill me!"

It was the wrong thing to say.

The stinging remark had hardly passed her lips before his mouth was on hers, cruel and hard and invasive. His long fingers, tangled in her hair, cupped the back of her head and held it firmly so she couldn't turn away. She was trapped against him, one arm caught between them, the other delivering tired, weak punches to his back.

In that long, punishing kiss was all his hunger, all his frustration, all his guilt. He had caught her with her mouth open and he took full advantage. No tender exploration this, no gentle seeking of permission, no slow, sweet buildup to passion. His kiss was at once ravenous and ruthless. Brutally he explored the soft, warm recesses of her mouth, his tongue thrusting deeply, meeting and melding with hers.

Elizabeth struggled as he kissed her hotly, demandingly. Her head held immobile in the vise of his hand, she beat on his back, pushed on his chest, and made moaning sounds of protest. West paid no attention. He continued to kiss her with such unleashed ferocity and animal passion, Elizabeth was shocked and frightened. And was quickly becoming aroused.

Never had he kissed her like this.

West's searing mouth stayed fused with hers in a savage, prolonged kiss that Elizabeth knew she should find repugnant. She should have been thoroughly insulted and outraged by his fierce caveman brutality. And yet, as his flaming lips moved on hers and his silky tongue thrust deeply, she felt her anger and disgust giving way to rising passion.

She suspected that West knew what was happening to her when all at once he abruptly lifted his burning lips from hers and looked into her eyes. He said nothing. The only sound was that of the wild, raging storm blowing rain into the open mouth of the shallow cave at West's back.

Their gazes were locked. Their bodies were pressed close. Their hearts were galloping. Her rain-wet face was turned up to his. His dark face was bent to hers. Elizabeth saw all the hunger and desire inside him showing clearly out of his hot silver eyes. She knew how much he wanted her. She wanted him just as badly.

The silence between them was charged with as much electricity as the violent heat lightning of the sudden summer storm. And it was just as dangerous.

The strained silence continued as both became achingly aware of each other and of the fact that they were alone together in this dim, sheltered mountain cave. Might be here for hours. The others were far across the canyon with a rising sea of water in between.

"We're alone," West murmured, his heavy-lidded gaze settling on her kiss-swollen lips, his hand cupping her wet face. "All alone."

"Yes," she managed, noticing the tiny droplets of water clinging to his long, dusky eyelashes. "The others are—"

"On the far side of the canyon." His dreamy silver gaze again lifted to her red-rimmed blue eyes. "Cut off by the flash flood. They can't see us, can't hear us, can't get to us." His hand moved between them. He began flipping open the clasps going down the center of Elizabeth's yellow rain slicker.

"West, we can't . . . we can't do this," Elizabeth whispered with little conviction.

"We can't keep from it, no more than we can keep from breathing." He pushed the wet slicker over her shoulders and off. It fell in a wet yellow heap to the stone floor.

Mesmerized by his sultry silver eyes, tingling with excitement and indecision, she said, "We must try to . . . to . . . stop before it's too late."

"It's already too late. It was too late back in Shreveport." He gently brushed wet strands of auburn hair back off her face, bent, and kissed her. Gently, he sucked her full bottom lip into his mouth. "Too late, sweetheart." His sharp teeth nipped at the fleshy inside of her lip. "I'm going to make love to you here in this canyon crater"—he brushed a kiss to the left corner of her mouth—"and you're going to make love to me as well."

Elizabeth's eyelashes fluttered restlessly and her breathing became shallow as his lips, warm and persuasive, moved over her tear-streaked cheek to the sensitive spot just below her ear. Nibbling on the tender flesh at the side of her throat, West said, "Ah, yes. Until the storm passes and the floodtides subside, we are going to make love. If it's a half hour"—his lips slid lower on her throat—"or all night long, this time is ours alone."

"This is so wrong . . ." she murmured, loving the

touch of his lips on her tingling skin, the feel of his hard thighs pressing against hers.

"Yes, it is," he agreed as he deftly drew the tails of her shirt up out of her rust suede trousers. His lips left her throat, and he pulled her shirt up over her head. His eyes immediately dropping to the hard points of her nipples rising against her damp chemise, he said in a low, husky voice, "This is the only way. The only thing for us to do is to give in fully."

"No . . . that won't work," she said, attempting to keep her wits, to think of a good solid argument against what was about to happen. "We've given in before and—"

"This is different," he said, deftly relieving her of the damp satin chemise, his silver-gray eyes caressing the bare ivory breasts he'd uncovered.

"It's not," she said, and watched as he pulled his chamois shirt up over his head and discarded it. "It's the same."

"No, sweetheart." His hands came up, cupped the sides of her throat, and he drew her against him. Elizabeth shivered involuntarily when her naked breasts touched his chest. The crisp black hair felt mildly abrasive and ticklish to her hardened nipples.

West wrapped his arms around her, pressed her close, and said, "Let me explain, so you'll understand why it's different."

Weakened by the feel, the heat, the scent of his body, Elizabeth clasped her hands around his trim, hard waist and laid her head on his shoulder. Her face turned inward, she stared entranced at his slick brown throat while he spoke in a low, calm voice, the sound vibrating from his chest. She could feel it against her breasts.

"When I was a boy," he said, stroking her back, "I loved hot peach cobbler. It was my all-time favorite. Nothing else could compare." Elizabeth smiled and snuggled closer. He continued, "I loved peach cobbler so much, my mouth would start to water anytime I saw it, smelled it, or even thought about it."

"Mmmmm, it is good," murmured Elizabeth.

"I never could have as much as I wanted. I always had to make do with one small serving and all that did was leave me starving for more. Ravenously hungry for more delicious hot peach cobbler."

Elizabeth stirred, started to speak, but he stopped her. "Let me finish. One morning when I was walking into Hopkinsville, I passed the preacher's house and there on the window sill sat a hot peach cobbler. I stole that peach cobbler from the window, sat down under a shade tree, and ate the whole thing."

"West Quarternight!" Her head came up off his shoulder, and she looked into his eyes to see if he was teasing.

"I ate every last bite of that peach cobbler and I haven't wanted any since."

"You should have been severely punished," she said, lifting a hand to stroke his woolly black beard.

"I was. First by the preacher. He blistered my butt with a willow tree switch, then told my daddy. Daddy whipped me with his belt. Hurt like hell. I had to stand for a week. But that's not the reason I never wanted any more peach cobbler."

"I . . . I'm not sure I understand."

West's hand covered hers as he drew it to his lips, kissed the palm, and said, "I knew when I stole the pie I'd get a licking for it, but I didn't care. I wanted that pie so badly, I didn't care what happened when I got caught. The reason I've never wanted any more peach cobbler is I ate so much that morning I got sick. *Finally* I'd had my fill of hot peach cobbler. I never wanted any more."

Again he kissed her hand, then drew it down between them to the rigid erection straining the fabric of his tight, rain-dampened buckskins. "Every time I see you, smell you, touch you, I want you so badly this is what happens to me. I've had a couple of tastes of you, but not nearly enough to satisfy my hunger."

Her hand shyly toying with the hardness throbbing against his damp trousers, Elizabeth said, "So I'm to be your stolen peach cobbler?"

Trembling from her touch, West nodded. "I don't care what happens if we're caught. I don't give a damn what punishment waits for me. All I care about is having my fill of you just once. If this storm lasts long enough for us to make love again and again, if you'll let me love you in every way and any way I want, then I'll finally be satisfied and never want you again." He paused, and added, "And you'll never want me again."

Elizabeth realized that his twisted logic should seem farfetched and out of the question, but at this time and place, it didn't. She understood fully. Knew exactly what he meant, how he felt, because she felt as he did. She felt that if she could completely get her fill of him just one time, then maybe her heart would no longer pound whenever he came into view. Maybe she would be able to look at his sensual lips without wishing she could kiss them.

Maybe if here in this dim, cozy hideout high up in the Guadalupe mountains with a summer thunderstorm raging, she made love to this dark, bearded man over and over again, she could purge herself of him once and for all and be free. Maybe if, as he suggested, she allowed him to love her in any way and every way he wanted, she would be so repulsed and sickened by his lovemaking she would never want him to touch her again for as long as she lived.

Her hand left his erection, moved up to the tied laces going down the fly of his buckskin pants. She pulled on one end of the leather string and the laces came untied. She crooked a forefinger underneath and began loosening the laces. West caught his breath when her other hand came up to help. His lungs starving for air, he watched transfixed as the beautiful red-haired bare-breasted woman unlaced his pants, pulled them apart, then hooked that same forefinger into the low-riding waistband of his underwear.

Elizabeth watched, too, as slowly, with that one finger, she pulled the white linen down, down his wet brown belly until the huge tip of his surging masculinity popped out.

The air exploded from West's tight chest when Elizabeth, awed by the size and heat of him, pressed all five fingers to the smooth head of his pulsing flesh, lifted her eyes to his, and said boldly, "I'm famished, Quarternight. Promise you'll fill me so full I'll never want peach cobbler," her fingers gently caressed him, "or this again."

Hoarsely, he said, "I promise."

39

West drew her hand away, placed it on his pounding heart, bent and kissed her with such sweet tenderness it was almost impossible for Elizabeth to believe he was the same man who had just kissed her so violently. The feel of his warm, soft lips caressing hers with such unexpected sensitivity was utterly devastating.

Sighing, Elizabeth lazily slid her arms up around his neck and thrilled to the feel of muscles rippling across his smooth broad shoulders, the pleasant tickling of his woolly beard against her face. His hands were as gentle as his lips as they lightly spanned her naked waist and drew her close.

Their lips melding in a soft, liquid movement, the pair stood there kissing for a long lovely time while the summer storm worsened. Gale-force winds howled down through the canyon and bright bolts of lightning crashed on the steep rocky walls above. Answering thunder boomed with deafening loudness and the wind-driven rain continued to pour from the cloud-blackened heavens.

The embracing pair didn't care.

The heavy deluge provided a concealing curtain

across the mouth of their cupped-out crater, ensuring total privacy. The noisy din of the turbulent thunderstorm could drown out even the loudest cries of ecstasy this afternoon of uninhibited loving might produce.

Grateful for the continuing violence of the sudden rainstorm, West stood with his back to the roar and the rage, holding Elizabeth close yet gently in his arms, purposely kissing her as if she were a young, treasured sweetheart whom he had just begun to court.

He had her here, was going to have her here, all to himself, for the duration of the storm. His intent was to squeeze a complete relationship into the course of the afternoon. To start at the very beginning and see it patiently to its end while time and opportunity were his. To tenderly woo and win the beautiful flame-haired woman as if she were totally innocent.

As if she were totally his.

In this high hidden place with her on this night-black afternoon, he would take the time to make all the careful steps. He would lead her from this first tender kiss all the way to the final ultimate ecstasy. He would live a lifetime in a few golden hours. He would kiss and hold and arouse her so completely, Elizabeth Curtin would be totally his for as long as this stolen interlude lasted.

As West continued to kiss her with such heart-stopping tenderness, Elizabeth tried hard to keep in mind some intentions of her own. She, too, was resolved to take full advantage of this turbulent afternoon. And of this turbulent man.

She was ready, even eager for him to take her right now, this minute. Wished that he would. If he was brutal and violent in his lovemaking, so be it. If he did wicked, shocking things to her, fine. If he forced her to do base things to him, all the better.

And the sooner the better, because when the furious storm passed and they left this mountain grotto, she meant to leave her unhealthy attraction to this man here as well. She aimed to end this unforgivable madness once and for all. She was going to have her fill of the darkly handsome West Quarternight.

She would touch him, kiss him, make love to him until his touch turned her stomach, his kiss made her gag, and his body made her flesh crawl.

That was Elizabeth's firm intention, but already she was forgetting her well-laid plan. The way West was kissing her, the way he was holding her, made her feel warm and safe and wonderful. His hands—those gorgeous lean brown hands—were caressing her bare back with such gentleness and care she felt she might swoon. It was as if he found her fragile, breakable, so precious he was taking the utmost care not to hurt her. His warm, smooth lips moving on hers were just as considerate, just as caring.

Swaying helplessly to him, feeling as though she could never get enough of this maddeningly paradoxical man, Elizabeth lifted her hands up into the wet, raven hair at the back of his head. Combing through the damp, silky locks, she eagerly pressed her naked breasts against his bare chest and trembled when she felt the hot hardness of his half-exposed erection stabbing against her stomach.

The kiss West meant to keep feather-light immediately deepened when Elizabeth rose on tiptoes and provocatively pressed herself closer. He couldn't help himself. The taut, tempting crests of her breasts grazed his chest and through her wet trousers her flat belly rubbed against his aching tumescence. His hands slipped from her bare, slender back to her narrow waist, then moved quickly along the flare of her hips and down over her rounded buttocks. Spreading

his long fingers, he clutched the twin cheeks of her
firm rounded bottom and drew her more fully to him.

His careful plan to slowly take the step-by-step path
from sweet romance to blazing passion was immediately forgotten. The caress that had begun so gently,
so sweetly, ended in an explosive kiss of unrestrained
hunger.

His lips had hardly left hers before he began undressing her. Elizabeth didn't mind; she was glad. She
helped with the stubborn wet laces at the side of her
suede pants and wriggled her hips as West knelt before her and peeled the soaking trousers down her
body.

"God, honey, you'll freeze," he said, when she stood
naked before him, wet from head to toe from her
dunking in the raging stream. "Stay right here," he
commanded, urging her up against the crater's low-
ceilinged back wall. Nodding, Elizabeth hugged herself while West retrieved his discarded chamois shirt,
hurried back, and used the shirt for a towel.

The stone ceiling was too low for West to stand
erect, so he crouched on his heels before her and began blotting the wetness from her slender ivory body.

Elizabeth wasn't chilly for long.

While she wound her wet hair into a long rope and
squeezed the excess moisture from it, West dried her
breasts, her belly, her long legs. As he was in all
things, West Quarternight was adept at this task, and
Elizabeth wondered idly if he were enjoying the exercise as much as she. Those marvelous hands of his
kept pressing, rubbing, swiping the soft chamois shirt
to her flesh in an excitingly erotic way.

"Turn around," he said finally and Elizabeth slowly
pivoted to show him her back. She sighed heavily and
pressed her hands to the stone wall while he dried her
shoulders, her back, her buttocks. He went down
each leg, toweling away any lingering traces of water

while she closed her eyes and relaxed. Or tried to. When he had finished with her left heel, he said, "That about does it."

Elizabeth started to turn, but his hands at her waist stopped her. She gasped in startled surprise when she felt his bearded face tickle her buttocks. Then shivered involuntarily when she felt his smooth warm lips settle briefly on the twin dimples at the base of her spine.

"West . . ." she murmured, thrilled, embarrassed.

"Turn around, sweetheart," he said softly. "Let's see if you're completely dry."

Blushing, Elizabeth turned to face him. His silver eyes swept slowly, searchingly up her body.

"I believe you've done a thorough job," she said, her own eyes helplessly drawn to the opened fly of his buckskins. What she had boldly exposed was covered once more, but it surged against the restraining white underwear, as awesome and exciting as ever.

"I missed a spot," announced West, as if glad.

"You did?" Her throat was dry.

She followed his eyes to her left breast where a lone bead of water clung to her tight nipple. West didn't lift the chamois shirt to wipe the tiny diamond drop away and when Elizabeth started to brush it off, he gripped her wrist and stopped her. He dropped his damp shirt, rose to his knees, and drew her to him. He looked directly into her eyes as his mouth opened and moved unerringly toward her left breast. His long sooty lashes lowered as he put out his tongue and delicately licked away the errant drop of water.

Elizabeth shivered, then sighed with pleasure when his mouth stayed to suck on her sensitive nipple. It was glorious, wonderful, nothing could be better. She brought her hand up to nestle in his damp raven hair. She smiled dreamily, pressed her breast closer to his bearded face, and murmured, "Yes, oh yes" when his sharp teeth teasingly bit at the distended nipple, and his tongue flicked tormentingly over it.

When West moved to her right breast Elizabeth thanked him and then shuddered deeply when his expression of "You're welcome" was to playfully nibble on the diamond-hard tip and then suck on it so forcefully she felt the fierce pulling all the way down to her lower belly and between her legs.

When at last his warm, wet mouth allowed the shiny nipple to pop free and his bearded face moved down over her ribs, Elizabeth regretted its departure. But not for long.

West's dark face never lifted from her flesh. His lips tracked her fragile ribs, kissed a line across her waist, then went to her flat stomach and began slowly moving downward. On fire, urgently excited, wanting him to wait no longer to take her completely, Elizabeth clasped a handful of his hair and murmured, "Please, West. Make love to me."

His lips brushing kisses to her quivering belly, he said, "I am, sweetheart. I am."

"Yes, yes and it's . . . it's wonderful, but I want . . . I need . . ."

West languidly lifted his head and gave her a lazy smile. "I know, sweetheart. I know exactly what you need. What you want."

Her breath coming in short little pants, every muscle screaming out for the fulfillment his hard body could bring her, she whispered anxiously, "Then give it to me. Take off your trousers and—"

"Ah, baby, baby. I can give you what you want without taking off my pants."

"No . . . you can't," she said frantically, and began slowly slipping downward, reaching greedily for the restrained male flesh he withheld. Her fingertips fluttering nervously in a half attempt to draw him free of his clothing, she said, "I want this. You'll have to give me this."

West pushed her back up. "I don't have to give you that now, sweetheart," he said. "First I can give you my mouth."

"Your mouth?" she said, bewildered, still an innocent to all the ways there were of loving. "But how can . . . I mean . . . you can't . . ."

West placed a lean brown hand atop the triangle of flaming red curls between her pale apricot thighs. He said, "Move your legs apart, sweetheart."

Pressing her palms back against the cool stone wall of the crater, Elizabeth moved her bare feet a few inches apart. West gently raked through the tight auburn coils and then slipped his fingers between her parted legs. His lean middle finger touched her in that most sensitive of all spots and again he said, "I'll give you my mouth, baby." His finger lightly caressed her. "I'll kiss you right here for as long as it takes to give you ecstasy."

Half horrified, half curious, Elizabeth squirmed excitedly, but shook her head. "No. You wouldn't . . . you can't do that."

"I would. I can," he said, moved his hands to her thighs, and added, "I will." And proceeded to show her.

"West . . ." she gasped as his hands clutched her hips and his bearded face came back to her naked stomach.

He was kissing her again. Over and over. His kisses went down her stomach, probing her navel, working their way along the insides of her thighs. Wet, hot, licking kisses. Then back up her thighs and slowly, as if in a dream, his bearded face moved directly to that flaming triangle and his hands commandingly gripped her buttocks.

Straining with anticipation, Elizabeth watched

with unashamed gratitude as that dark, bearded face sank lower. His bushy beard tickled and his breath was fiery hot and his lips, as they placed a gentle kiss on the swollen, throbbing flesh begging for his kiss, literally took her breath away.

Her breath exploded from her tight lungs when his mouth opened possessively on her and his tongue began to stroke, to caress, to circle. Sharp jolts of incredible joy shot through Elizabeth's entire body, and that tiny source of her pleasure which he so artfully tongued was on fire.

West felt the immediate response of her shuddering body, the shocks surging through that hard little bud that shared with him all her darkest secrets, conveyed all her private fantasies, assured him that for now, for as long as his lips were fused to that glorious tiny nubbin of female flesh, she was his and his alone.

Elizabeth was both frightened and elated by the heights of ecstasy she was attaining. At a fever pitch, she wriggled and gasped and clawed at the rock wall behind her. She closed her eyes, she opened them. She gritted her teeth, she bit her lip. She knitted her brow. She smiled foolishly.

She stood naked against that rocky wall of their canyon crater while outside the wild thunderstorm raged and gathered ferocity. Great bolts of lightning flashed to light the shallow shelter with blinding brightness. Thunder rocked the valley, its booming sound reverberating off the canyon walls. Great torrents of water fell, splashing onto the stone apron of their cozy hideout.

It was as violent a storm as Elizabeth had lived through. But its threatening fury was nothing compared to the wild love-storm enveloping her. Her pleasure-widened eyes lowered to the man responsible for the savage turbulence claiming her.

She saw what seemed to her at that particular moment in time the most pleasingly erotic sight she had ever looked on. West's dark, handsome face was sweetly buried in her, his thick beard a startling blue-black against the fiery auburn curls in which it was immersed. His eyes were closed, long black lashes feathered on his tanned cheeks. His strong hands were clasping her to him, as if he would feast on her forever.

Elizabeth watched for only a moment, then quickly closed her eyes. But it was too late. Her release was coming in a tidal wave that couldn't be held back. Her head tossing to the side, her weak knees helplessly bending, she totally gave herself up to the frenzied ecstasy she couldn't control.

"Please, don't stop, don't stop," she begged her kneeling lover. "Oh, darling, darling . . . don't ever stop!"

And he didn't.

West licked and lashed and loved her until Elizabeth screamed out, shuddering violently, clutching madly at the hair of his head, bucking her pelvis against his pleasuring mouth until the joy became so great, she couldn't bear it for one second more.

Frantically she gripped his hair, tore his mouth from her, and sagged gratefully down into his waiting arms, her slender body jerking, tears of sheer ecstasy spilling from her eyes.

40

West sat on his heels, knees spread, enfolding Elizabeth in his arms as she cried and trembled and clung to him. Soothingly he stroked her back and kissed her hair and softly murmured, "Sweet, so sweet. Sweet baby. There, there, it's okay, darlin'."

When her bare, slender body quit jerking with tiny aftershocks, and her sobs of hysterical joy turned to soft sighs of serenity, West eased her head up from his chest and back into the crook of his arm. He brushed her damp, tangled hair off her face and smiled down at her.

"You all right, sweetheart?" he asked, the timbre of his low, smooth voice further calming her.

"Mmmmmm," was all she could manage, but the expression in her shining blue eyes spoke volumes.

He leaned down, kissed her, and Elizabeth tasted herself on his lips. But instead of finding it repugnant, it seemed somehow incredibly intimate and pleasing.

When his lips left hers, West drew her back up into a sitting position between his knees. While Elizabeth clasped his ribs, he deftly spread his damp chamois shirt out on the stone floor. He kissed her again and gently urged her over, following her down.

Totally relaxed, Elizabeth lay on her back, stretching and purring like a lazy cat. West lay on his side facing her, his weight supported on an elbow. For a while he caressed only her tousled red hair, her flushed face. Then his gentle hand moved down her limp body as his lips brushed kisses to her closed eyes, her hot cheeks, her delicate chin.

It wasn't long before Elizabeth was surging up to meet his gliding hand and her parted lips were lifting eagerly for his kiss. West continued to kiss her and to stroke her silky flesh until he knew he had her sensually awakened again.

Abruptly he pulled away, rolled to his feet, and stooping, crossed to the crater's adjacent wall, where the ceiling was higher. There he rose to his full imposing height, turned to face Elizabeth, and began swiftly undressing.

Curling up onto her side, Elizabeth openly stared while he shed his wet boots, then hunched out of his buckskin trousers and underwear. Naked, West closed his eyes, took the discarded pants and blotted at the residue of moisture beading his shaggy raven hair and beard. Watching, Elizabeth decided he was surely the most physically magnificent man the Almighty had ever created. Splendidly perfect from any and every angle. The blood warm and syrupy in her veins, she rolled up from her stone bed.

After only a careless attempt at drying his hair and beard, West opened his eyes and tossed the pants aside, ready to rush back to Elizabeth. But he immediately hesitated, his silver-gray eyes widening.

Elizabeth, on all fours, was slowly, seductively crawling toward him, her blue eyes hot, her red lips parted, her pale breasts swaying. Speechless, unable to move, West stood there gaping. She was, he decided, the most exquisite woman that God had ever created. Breathtakingly gorgeous from the top of her fiery head to the tip of her cute little toes.

Elizabeth crawled directly to him, purred teasingly, and sat back on her heels before him. West braced himself to keep his knees from buckling. Almost shyly he put out a hand and touched her cheek. Then, frantic with desire, he clutched her upper arms and drew her swiftly to her feet and into his close embrace. Anxiously he kissed her, his hands sweeping possessively over her silky skin, his heart thundering in his bare chest.

After only one hot, lingering kiss, he tried to urge her back to the spread chamois shirt. Shaking her head, Elizabeth refused. Instead she pressed him against the wall and wrapped her arms tightly around his neck.

Wanting her so badly he was almost ill with desire, West kissed her ear, slid his hand around and down between the firm cheeks of her buttocks and slipped his fingers between her legs. He found, to his relief, she was wet and ready.

Huskily, he said against her ear, "Oh, baby, please, please let me. Give it to me. Make love to me, sweetheart."

"I am making love to you," Elizabeth whispered, undulating against him, kissing his shoulder, biting him playfully.

"I know, I know, and it's great, but . . . I need this." His fingertip touched her. "I want it."

Elizabeth tipped her head back. "I know exactly what you need. What you want."

The blood pounding through his veins, every nerve and muscle crying out for the satisfaction her soft pliant body could bring him, West said raggedly, "Then, give it to me, baby. Let me put it—"

"I can give you what you want without—"

"No, no you can't," he interrupted hoarsely, the tip of his finger slipping up inside her. "I want this, baby. Give me this."

Elizabeth wriggled free of his gently probing finger. "I don't have to give you that now," she said sweetly, "first I can give you my mouth."

"Ah . . . no . . . no . . . baby," West shook his dark head. "You can't do—"

"Move your feet apart," she commanded and slowly sank to her knees before him.

Refusing to obey, West reached down and took her arm, meaning to pull her up. But Elizabeth deliberately laid her cheek directly against his throbbing erection and said, "I'll give you my mouth. I'll kiss you here for as long as it takes."

"Oh, God, Elizabeth," his trembling fingers left her arm, settled gently atop her head. "Don't, sweetheart . . . you can't . . . Jesus, honey . . ."

His words trailed away and he sagged back against the rock wall as her pert nose nestled in the crisp black hair of his groin and she murmured, "I would. I can. I will."

Her hands gripped West's hard thighs and her face came up to his stomach.

And then she was kissing him, over and over, and her soft, sweet lips on his burning flesh felt so good he was helpless to stop her. Her feathery kisses moved over his tight abdomen, probing his navel, then moved downward, working their way along the inside of his thigh.

His breath labored, his perspiring palms flattened against the wall, West anxiously moved his feet apart when she kissed her way along the insides of his taut thighs. Warm, sweet, plucking kisses. Then back up his thighs and languidly, as if in a fantasy, her lovely face moved directly to his straining erection and her soft hands assertively clasped him.

Tense with expectation, West watched with frank appreciation as that beautiful face bent to him. Her soft lips pressed a kiss to the tip of his pulsing flesh and he groaned. When she opened her mouth and cautiously touched her tongue to him, West's hands went to her head, tangled in her hair.

Elizabeth felt the immediate response of his tall, trembling body, the power jolting through that shaft of hard male flesh that shared with her his secret desires, transmitted his confidential dreams, guaranteed her that for now, for as long as her lips enclosed him, he was hers and hers alone.

West allowed himself only a brief sweet moment of the delicious torment. His feet apart, he stood against the rock wall as if in a beautiful dream. He vaguely was aware of the howling winds whistling through the canyon, of the deep rumbles of thunder. Of the close bolts of lightning illuminating the rocky crater with blinding brightness.

His molten eyes lowering to the pretty woman kneeling between his legs, he was rewarded with the most carnally pleasing sight he had ever seen. Elizabeth's beautiful face was pressed to him. Her large blue eyes were shut, the spiky lashes resting on her fragile white cheekbones. Her soft pink lips enclosed him warmly. His hands, entwined in her hair, drew long strands forward to brush his lower belly. The sight of those fiery tresses mingling with the black hair of his groin was electrifying.

West closed his eyes, reluctantly jerked her loving mouth away, and bit the inside of his jaw to inflict distracting pain, knowing he was dangerously close to exploding release. Forcefully, he drew Elizabeth up into his arms, kissed her hotly, and maneuvered her back to his spread shirt.

The smell of the fresh rain was heavy in the air when they sank anxiously to the stone floor. Throbbing in full erection, West eagerly rolled Elizabeth onto her back and moved between her legs. Before he came into her, a radiant bolt of lightning illuminated his dark-bearded face, looming just above hers.

"Wait," Elizabeth said, her hands pressing on his bare brown shoulders. "There's something I have to tell you." Thunder boomed loudly and she had to shout to be heard above it. "I didn't murder that Southern officer back in Shreveport, West."

"Baby, I don't care," he said hoarsely and thrust forcefully into her.

She felt him fill and stretch her and his handsome face came closer, his molten silver eyes looking into hers. Forgetting everything but him, Elizabeth looped her arms around his neck, longing for this perfect melding of flesh in flesh to go on forever. But both were far too hot for it to last. In a matter of seconds both were in the deep throes of ecstasy, the sounds of their mutual joy carried away on the winds of the raging rainstorm.

But it was not the end.

Both knew that there was only one way to put out the fire consuming them. Even as Elizabeth moaned in orgasmic delight and West spasmed with rapture and the scent of sex mingled with that of the rain, they knew they had not had enough. Not nearly enough. Trapped in a passion beyond their control, they had firmly decided to do something about it. Neither had the slightest intention of stopping until they had enough—no, too much—of each other.

So the uninhibited pair spent the stormy afternoon making love. Equally amazed at how soon they could again become aroused by a few well-placed caresses, a few hot kisses, each proved the ideal match for the other. They made love in any and every way imaginable, shocking and thrilling each other so much neither noticed when the turbulent summer storm ended.

They had no idea what time it was. Had no conception of how long they had been there. They were so enraptured, so single-mindedly focused on the pleasure their bare willing bodies could give and take, they never even noticed when the hot sun came out to flood their high canyon retreat with bright, intrusive daylight.

Hours might have passed. Or perhaps it had only been minutes when Grady called loudly to them. At that moment West was stretched out on his back with Elizabeth astride, grinding her pelvis to his, both very near a climax.

"Sonny, you and missy okay? Storm's been passed for half an hour. What you a-waitin' on? Want Taos to climb up there and help ya'll get down?"

Elizabeth's eyes widened with horror and indecision. Her head told her to leap up at once and get dressed, her body told her she couldn't leave West before . . . before—

"No, Grady," West shouted calmly, his hands gripping Elizabeth's waist, holding her where she was. "We're on our way. Be down in ten minutes." And West's lean hips kept lifting and thrusting, as he whispered softly, "It's okay. Just relax. Plenty of time, sweetheart."

He continued to make love to her, giving her all he had, guiding her hips with his hands, looking into her eyes. From the canyon below came the sounds of the men stirring about, their voices loud and clear as they shouted to each other, rounding up the loose horses, taking inventory of what had been lost in the flood.

Ignoring the activity below, West whispered encouragingly, "Ah, baby, baby, that's it. Yes, oh yes. That's good. So . . . good. Let it all out, sweetheart."

"West . . . West . . ." she breathed, and he swiftly

wrapped a hand around her nape, drew her face down to his, and covered her mouth with his lips. He kissed her until their final shared ecstasy ended.

Once it was over, they broke apart. Frantically they dressed, their limbs still weak from pleasure, their hearts pounding. Within minutes they had dressed and scaled down the canyon walls.

Edmund anxiously stepped forward, glanced at West, put an arm around Elizabeth's slender shoulders, and asked, "Are you all right, my dear? Did West take good care of you? Are your unhurt?"

"I'm fine," she said, avoiding his questioning eyes, "just fine."

41

Twilight on the trail.

Through and out of the Guadalupes, the contingent descended the final low cliffs of the eastern foothills. The sun had set behind the mountains. Open desert again stretched before them. It was eight-thirty in the evening and darkness was falling fast.

Stopping, they made camp on a long, timber-fringed spit of land overlooking the desert floor. A clear, narrow brook spilled down from the higher elevations, broadened and splashed over variously sized boulders, trickling between grassy banks in a shallow stream.

The afternoon's flash flood had left the Mexican crew quiet and upset. But Grady pointed out that despite the loss of time, horses, and equipment to the raging flood, the important thing was that not a single human life had been lost. Even the terrified peasant whom they'd all seen being washed away, had been found later, clinging to a clump of spindly sagebrush two miles down canyon, battered but alive.

All the horses had undoubtedly made it, although the vaqueros were able to round up only half the remuda. The loss of pack burros and equipment was a heavy one, the unfortunate animals having been too weighted down to swim out of the canyon. Supplies had broken loose from packs and washed away, the biggest loss being that of the weapons. Of the many pistols and rifles brought along from Santa Fe, the only ones left were the Colt. 44 Grady wore strapped around his hips and the Winchester rifle Taos had snatched from his saddle scabbard.

Discussions of the day's storm and the losses went on over a late supper. Listening quietly, Elizabeth inwardly cringed when she heard Grady say—again— that the cloudburst had started shortly after one o'clock in the afternoon and had lasted until exactly five-thirty-five. Which meant that she had spent four and a half hours making love to West Quarternight.

And it had not been enough.

Risking a glance across the campfire at West, Elizabeth caught him staring at her. She calmly looked away, held her head high, but the little muscles in her throat trembled. She looked at Edmund and was uneasy to find that he, too, was staring at her, a puzzling expression on his face.

She gave him a small smile, which he returned, but she couldn't shake the feeling that something was on his mind. When, moments later, Edmund pleaded tiredness and said he was going to bed, she knew something was bothering him. Always before he had stayed up to the very last man, drinking his coffee, enjoying the camaraderie and the checker games with Grady.

Five minutes after Edmund had gone, West quietly rose and walked away. Grady called after him, "Now where you goin', Sonny? I thought we'd all—"

"For a walk," said West, and never slowed his pace.

Soon the Mexican helpers scattered and only Elizabeth, Grady, and Taos were left at the campfire. Chuckling, Grady produced the checkerboard, overjoyed that it had survived the flood. Elizabeth inwardly sighed. He would insist she play him, and a game of checkers was simply more than she could bear tonight.

Board and checkers in hand, Grady started toward her, grinning broadly. But Taos stepped forward, put a hand on Grady's shoulder, and stopped him. Grady looked up at the big Navajo, frowned, and said, "What do you mean she don't wanna play checkers? How do you know?" Taos gave his head a decisive shake, tapped his own massive chest with a forefinger, and Grady smiled again. "You'll play me? Hellfire, you ain't played me in ages. You wanna make a little bet on the outcome? Got any money on you?"

Chuckling happily again, Grady hunkered down close to the campfire to set up the board. Elizabeth exchanged glances with Taos, silently thanking him for intervening. Looking back into the brightly burning fire, she wondered if the mute Navajo, who seemed to see and know everything, knew about West and her.

Lost immediately in troubled thought, Elizabeth was hardly aware of Grady and Taos's presence. After today with West, she was more confused than ever. There was, however, one thing of which she was absolutely certain. She couldn't stay married to Dane Curtin. She could not be his wife. She would tell Edmund of her decision tomorrow and Dane as soon as they found him.

"Owww!" Grady's loud yelp interrupted Elizabeth's thoughts. "Damnation!" he swore.

"What is it?" she moved to him, her brows knit.

"A gol-darned splinter," he told her, making a face, squeezing on his forefinger. "Came off this ol' beat-up checkerboard."

Taos, ever resourceful, had already gone for a needle and a salvaged bottle of whiskey. When he returned, Elizabeth volunteered to remove the pesky splinter. Nodding, the Navajo uncorked the whiskey, poured a trickle over Grady's finger, turned him over to Elizabeth, and sat down beside her. Using the campfire's glow for light, Elizabeth bent to her work.

"Hope the sight of blood don't make you sick, missy," said Grady.

Eyes trained on her task, Elizabeth idly replied, "Don't worry, I saw plenty of blood in a field hospital in Shreveport."

"Shreveport, Louisiana?" Grady said. "Why, Sonny was in Shreveport during the last days of the war."

Elizabeth's head snapped up. Grady was grinning from ear to ear and looking like the cat who swallowed the canary. Her aching heart plummeted. West had told them about her. Had told them everything, the bastard!

"He told you about me," she said, "didn't he! Didn't he! Damn him, he told you about the night in the stockade and everything else!"

"Huh?" Grady said, still grinning, but puzzled.

Sure both men knew everything, Elizabeth said, "You knew West first met me years ago in the Shreveport stockade! Admit it." She released Grady's finger, handing him the needle. "He told you everything. He told you I'm a murderess, but he doesn't know the whole story. I'm no murderess. I'm not, I'm not!"

The splinter forgotten, Grady stuck the needle in his collar, grabbed Elizabeth's elbow, and made her look at him. He was no longer smiling. "Listen to me, missy. If West knew you back in Shreveport, he never mentioned it to us, did he, Taos?" The Navajo forcefully shook his head. Grady continued. "And he danged sure never has said nothin' about you being no murderer."

"He didn't?" Elizabeth was skeptical, yet hopeful. "He didn't say that . . . he never told . . ." Her words trailed away and she regretted she had jumped to conclusions.

She could feel Grady's blue, questioning eyes on her face. And the unreadable black ones of Taos. When she heard Grady say, "Now, missy, I'd be the first one to admit that Sonny can be the bastard of all times when he wants to be. He's willful and stubborn and it seems like there ain't nothin' means much to him. Lately, he's been downright mean and inconsiderate. But he ain't a man to go carryin' tales. West is one close-mouthed feller, if ever there was one."

"He is?" Elizabeth turned and lifted her eyes to his. "He never—"

"Swear to God," said Grady. "He don't talk much about hisself nor nobody else. Why, I'll bet you don't know hardly a thing about him, do you? He ain't told you nothin' about hisself, now, has he?"

"No. No, he hasn't," said Elizabeth. "Tell me about him, Grady. Please. Tell me about West Quarternight."

"I'll tell you all I know, which ain't that much." Grady smiled suddenly and added, "And it would be even less if I hadn't a caught him dead drunk a couple a times and took to questionin' him."

Grady stroked his flowing white beard and began. "Weston Dale was born and raised back in Hopkinsville, Kentucky. He was the first of . . ."

Grady told her that West had been brought up in bone-crushing poverty on a sharecropper's farm outside Hopkinsville by a shiftless father who rarely worked and a loving mother who was always tired and frail. From the time he was four years old, West was working in the fields from sun to sun. The oldest of six children, West took care of the family after his father ran off and left them.

When war broke out, West joined the Union Army and sent every penny he earned to his mother. Still, it was not enough. In the cold winter of sixty-three, the entire Quarternight family, without means to keep warm, came down with influenza and died. That same year, the young woman West had loved since boyhood married a wealthy landowner from Louisville without so much as writing to let West know.

Grady watched Elizabeth as he talked. He saw the many changing emotions march across her expressive features. Soon she was asking questions, and he supplied answers. Recalling the night in camp when she'd seen West awaken from a bad dream calling to a Captain Brooks, she said softly, "Grady, who is Captain Brooks?"

Grady didn't ask where she had heard the name. "Brooks was West's closest friend back in the army. They was like brothers, them two." He shook his white head and added, "West saw every one of his best buddies die in the war. Sometimes I think he wonders why they died and he lived." He again shook his head, contemplating. "I don't know how Brooks died, but I do know that Sonny still has nightmares about it and I can't help but wonder if he don't blame hisself for Brooks's death. I've asked over and over, but he won't talk about it." Grady fell silent again, then finally added, "Guess lots a folks got somethin' that bothers 'em." He yawned and stroked his beard. "Sometimes the only cure is to face up to it."

"Yes," murmured Elizabeth thoughtfully, "I think you're probably right."

Before Elizabeth knew it, she was telling Grady and Taos about herself. How she'd been a pampered, happy girl in Natchez, Mississippi. How she had lost all her family except her father in the war. She told them of being accused of murder. Said she was innocent, that a drunken officer, Colonel Frederick C. Dobbs, had assaulted her outside a field hospital in Shreveport, Louisiana.

Tears sprang to Elizabeth's eyes and she made no attempt to wipe them away. Her slender shoulders shook as she told how the colonel had dragged her into the forest and tried to rape her. She had picked up a rock and hit him on the head, but she'd never meant to kill him. The army tribunal had seen it differently. She had been accused of murder and sentenced to die. They threw her into a stockade cell with West Quarternight. Ultimately, West had saved her life.

Elizabeth paused and stared silently into the fire with tear-blurred vision, then continued. She went on to tell about teaching in New York and looking after her ailing father until he died. She said she had married Dane Curtin by proxy because she was tired of being lonely, tired of being poor, and she had nowhere else to turn.

"But it was a mistake," she admitted sadly. "I did Dane a terrible injustice. I don't love him; I never did."

The silent Taos, who had listened as attentively as Grady, reached out and laid a gentle hand on her shoulder. She slowly turned to look at him and was surprised and touched to see big tears swimming in his flat black eyes.

"Oh, Taos," she said, pressing her cheek to his hand, "what would I do without you and Grady?" He squeezed her shoulder, smiled understandingly, blinked back his tears, and she could see in his eyes that he knew—had known all along—what had happened between West and her.

Looking straight into those intelligent black eyes, Elizabeth said, "Taos, you see everything. Please, tell me. How does West really feel about me?" Taos smiled, laid his big spread hand directly over his heart, and patted up and down in a rapid fluttering motion. Elizabeth's own heart lurched with hope.

Behind her, she heard Grady say, "Sonny went for a walk, but I bet Taos could find him for you." Elizabeth turned back to Grady. He stroked his white beard and added, "You might wanna tell him what you've been a-tellin' us."

"Yes," Elizabeth said, knowing suddenly it was the thing to do. She *had* to talk to West, to tell him the truth. To tell him everything. Even if it made no difference to him. Even if he remained cold and uncaring, she had to tell him. "I must talk to him."

"Now, miss, you have to approach West without fear," was Grady's advice. "You have to be strong and totally honest with him. If you hesitate, well, you're lost. Now go on, Taos will help you find him."

West sat atop a jagged table of sandstone overlooking the starlit desert far below. Long legs dangling over the lip of the ledge, he was grim-faced and melancholy. To his left was an almost perpendicular dropoff of the boulder-strewn bluff. To the right was the path through thick cedars back to the camp. Below was the broad expanse of desertlands they would traverse come morning. Above was a sky filled with millions of bright, glittering stars.

But West saw none of it.

It made no difference where he looked, left, right, below, or above, he saw only Elizabeth Curtin. Her beautiful face was there before him, even when he closed his eyes. Try as he might, he couldn't get her off his mind, out of his heart.

He felt like a foolish lovesick schoolboy, only he was a far bigger fool than any young boy. He was mooning over another man's wife, a woman who was not only an adulteress, but a murderess as well. West ground his teeth.

The afternoon's loving hadn't cured him as he had hoped. West trembled as a longing that was deeply physical swept through him. He *still* wanted her. Wanted her now more than ever. Was sick with wanting her.

Lost in troubled thought, West didn't notice Elizabeth when she stepped out from the dense growth of trees into the starlight.

Elizabeth paused, looked at the solitary figure poised on the edge of the rimrock cliff, and felt a wave of dizziness sweep over her. Before her was a very different West than the one she'd come to know. Gone was the cocksure, impatient, impervious Quarternight. Missing also was the fun-loving, tormenting, teasing Quarternight. Nowhere in sight was the sexy, hot-blooded, immoral Quarternight.

The man sitting on the rocky ledge with his shoulders slumped minutely and his head bent slightly, appeared to be vulnerable, lonely, and unhappy. Elizabeth bit her lip. She could stand to be unhappy herself, but she couldn't bear to see him unhappy.

She hurried up the path toward him. West heard the pebbles crunch beneath her feet, turned his dark head, and saw her, but said nothing. Her heartbeat drumming in her ears, Elizabeth climbed up to him, sank to her knees beside him, and said nervously, "I've come to see you, West."

"Well, now you have," was his reply, but his voice was low, soft, and in his silver eyes was a sad, brooding expression. A forelock tumbled across his brow and for a brief moment he looked like a little boy. An unhappy little boy.

Elizabeth sat down beside him. "We have to talk."

His head swung back around. He looked out at the shimmering desert. "Do we really have anything to say to each other?"

"Look at me, West," she commanded, placing a gentle hand on his arm. He turned to face her. "You may have nothing to say to me, but I have plenty to say to you. Will you listen?"

He shrugged dismissively. "All the conversation in the world won't change a thing."

"Maybe not. But at least I can go to my grave one day knowing I tried." She took a deep breath and thrust out her closed fist before him. Opening it, she lifted her hand up to his face and said, "Do you know what this is?"

West's eyes fell on the shiny little object resting in her palm. "Looks like a button. A brass button."

"Not just any brass button, West. It's the brass button I pulled from your uniform jacket in my excitement that night in the Shreveport stockade. I kept it all these years and there hasn't been one bedtime in my life that I haven't looked at this brass button and remembered that night with you."

"Oh, Jesus," West said, shaking his head, his eyes closing in agony, "I wish I'd never seen you, kissed you, held you in my arms."

Elizabeth couldn't have heard him utter any sweeter words. He had given himself away. He did care. He couldn't forget her, any more than she could forget him.

"Don't be sorry," she said. "Please, West, open your eyes and look at me."

He sighed wearily, lifted his eyes to hers, and said, "What do you want me to say? That it was all my fault. All right, I will. It was my fault and I—"

"No, it wasn't. I'm as much to blame as you, if not more. What I've done was very wrong, unforgivable. But I'm not quite as bad as you think me. If you'll give me the chance, I'll explain what I mean."

Before he could reply, she told him all about herself, leaving out nothing. It was the strangest of sensations. Suddenly she wanted them to know each other well. To understand their shared secrets. She started to move closer, warming to her story.

West listened in silence as she spoke. Elizabeth nervously fingered the ring old Micoma had given her; it rested in the hollow of her throat, a silk bandanna threaded through the shiny silver and deep turquoise band.

She told West she had accidentally killed Colonel Frederick C. Dobbs when he attempted to rape her. She swore to him that she had been a virgin that night in the Shreveport stockade. That she had married Dane Curtin by proxy, that the marriage had not been consummated. On hearing that, he looked as if he were about to speak. She quickly pressed a finger to his lips. "Please, West," she pleaded, "you have to believe me. Please listen."

He kissed her finger, but his eyes remained brooding.

She hurried on, "The marriage will *never* be consummated; I am going to have it annulled."

He looked at her for a long moment. "You'll be making a big mistake if you do that."

"No, I won't. The mistake was marrying him when I couldn't even bear to throw away a silly little brass button." Her hand reached out to his dark, bearded face. The touch of love. Cherishing him. Sending a bolt of pain through his chest.

He took her hand and enclosed it in both of his. "Elizabeth, I'm all the things you've accused me of being." He smiled fleetingly. "Worthless, heartless, selfish, no good—"

"I know about you, West. Grady told me."

He stiffened. "What did Grady tell you?"

"About your boyhood when you were poor. About you losing your family. Of losing the girl you loved to a rich man. And of losing all your friends in the war."

To her surprise, West began to talk about the past.

He told more than Grady had known. He told her more than he'd ever told anyone else. He talked at length about his family, about the pretty young girl who had promised to love him forever and then had married a rich landowner's son while he was away at war. Told her about the horrors he saw in war, the friends he had loved and lost.

"Sometimes I think," he said wistfully, "all that was good and soft in me died in the war."

"No, West, that isn't true. I've seen you with old Micoma. No man could be more kind and gentle than you are to her. There's still plenty of good in you."

"I'm not so sure." He shrugged. "After the war, there was nothing left but guilt that I had lived through it and they had died. They were the ones with families who needed them. They were the ones who should have come back, not me. What did I have to come for?" He shook his dark head. "I'm hard and cynical, I know it. I guess . . . I guess I'm—"

"Afraid to care?" she finished for him. "Don't be, darling. Don't turn your back on the world because of your losses. And don't feel guilty because you lived when the others didn't. It wasn't your fault."

"Wasn't it?" he said. West told her about the night he and Captain Brooks had attempted to escape from Andersonville Prison. How the tunnel they'd dug collapsed, trapping them. How he tried and tried to get to Brooks, but by the time he found him, it was too late. Brooks had suffocated.

"He was a husband, Elizabeth, and the father of two little boys who needed him. God, it should have been me, not him." His face was a study in pain as tears filled his silver eyes.

"Oh, my darling," she said, and threw her arms around him. "Stop blaming yourself. You did all you could to save him; let it go now. Put it behind you and forget." She pressed her cheek to his bearded face for a moment, then pulled back to look at him. "No life is any more precious than any other. Besides, just because you were not a husband and father then, doesn't mean you'll never be."

"Elizabeth," he brokenly whispered her name.

"The important thing is you did come home from the war and now we're here together. I love you, West Quarternight," she said. "I love you."

At last he smiled. "Don't tell me, sweetheart, show me."

She did. She kissed him with all the love in her heart and for West the sweetness of her kiss was enhanced by the knowledge that he alone knew what a fiery lover she was. No other man had had her, no other ever would. She belonged to him.

When their lips separated, West said, "You actually kept my uniform button all that time?"

"It was all I had," said she with emotion, trembling against him. Tears of happiness filled her eyes.

"Relax, my sweet love," West said soothingly, as he would quiet a fretful child in the night. "Everything is going to be all right."

"I must tell Edmund first thing tomorrow," Elizabeth said, loving the feel of his strong arms wrapped around her.

"I'll handle it," said West. "I'll talk to Ed."

"No, I really think I should be the one."

"We'll tell him together," said West. He looked into her eyes and said, "Elizabeth, there's something I must confess to you."

"Tell me anything, anything at all."

"I know a great deal about making love, but very little about love itself. Will you teach me, honey?"

"I don't know. It may take fifty or sixty years for you to learn," she said, smiling. Then her smile vanished and she said, "You can start by telling me you love me."

"I love you, Elizabeth." A muscle flexed in his jaw. "*So* much."

42

The happy pair remained on that starlit ledge long after midnight had come and gone. There was so much to say to each other. So many plans to be made. So many dreams to be shared. Curious about anything and everything that concerned the other, they asked and answered numerous questions. Neither held back; neither attempted to hide anything.

Well, almost nothing.

West did keep one small secret from Elizabeth. He didn't admit to having an almost paralyzing fear of going down inside dark caves and caverns. Praying he wouldn't fail when he was put to the test, he pushed the worrisome doubts to the back of his mind and listened as Elizabeth enchanted him with stories of her childhood.

He watched her closely as she spoke, charmed with the way her lovely eyes sparkled and her delicate hands gestured, and by her sudden eruptions of soft feminine laughter. She looked so young and pretty in the starlight, it was as if she were a child even now, as if she were still an adorable little girl.

He could envision her flying down the steps of the big river-bluff mansion in Natchez, her blazing curls framing the small, perfect features of her child's face. So carefree, so safe and protected, so much the apple of her distinguished father's eye.

While Elizabeth talked, it occurred to West that she had been little more than a child when the unprincipled Southern officer had tried to rape her. Barely nineteen years old and as innocent as a baby. A trusting little girl, alone and helpless, trying desperately to fight off the rapacious Colonel Dobbs. The bastard got exactly what he deserved!

West's moral indignation swiftly turned to guilt. Jesus, he himself was as bad as Dobbs. He had cunningly seduced her the minute she was thrown in the stockade with him. Hadn't bothered taking the time to find out anything about her. When he made love to her that very first time, he had disregarded the nagging suspicion that she might well be a virgin. Vividly he recalled the feel and fit of her that night. How could he have been so damned blind and callous?

His heart hurting for the unspoiled girl he had carelessly violated, West reached out, gently taking Elizabeth's chin in his hand. Interrupting, he said, "Sweetheart, I'm so sorry for all I've done to you. I'll make it up to you, I swear it."

Elizabeth's bubbling laughter subsided and she looked at him with total trust and love. Softly, she said, "I know you will, West." Then, before his very eyes, her sweet child's face changed into that of a beautiful, seductive woman. She laid a hand on his heart. She licked her lips, ran the tip of her tongue under her teeth, and said, "Know what I want right now more than anything in the world?"

"Tell me, baby."

"More peach cobbler."

West threw back his head and laughed. He drew her into his arms, kissed her, and said, "Sweetheart, have you any idea how much I love you?"

"Show me."

It was past three in the morning when the tired, in-love pair walked back into camp. Holding hands and yawning, they stepped into the clearing and saw Edmund alone before the dying campfire, staring fixedly into the glowing embers. West and Elizabeth looked at each other. West squeezed her hand reassuringly and they went to join Edmund.

Edmund didn't seem surprised to see them together in the middle of the night. Nor was he astonished when they told him they were in love and Elizabeth intended to have her marriage to Dane annulled. Silently he listened as they spoke, West doing most of the talking, taking all of the blame.

At last it was all out in the open and Elizabeth said, "Edmund, I hope one day you can forgive me for the dishonesty—"

"My dear," Edmund interrupted, "I haven't been totally honest, either. You see, what our Santa Fe agent, Martin Exley, and I failed to mention is that he and Dane are almost positive they've located the Grayson gold." Edmund rubbed his tired eyes and sighed. "The truth is, I selfishly helped persuade you to marry Dane because I saw it as my only way out."

Edmund went on to tell them that the stock market crash had totally ruined him; the Curtin fortune had been wiped out. He had sold his wife's jewels to afford the trip to New Mexico and the search for Dane and the gold. He admitted he was so afraid of losing Louisa, that he saw the Grayson gold as his only hope.

"Elizabeth, I must ask forgiveness of you. Of both of you." He looked at West. "I've seen the attraction growing between the two of you and I've struggled with my conscience, knowing I should tell you the truth." He paused, drew a slow breath, and added, "Elizabeth, you're far too good a woman to be Dane's wife. Even had you loved him, Dane wouldn't have made you happy. I'm afraid Dane has never loved anyone but himself." Edmund miserably shook his blond head. "But then I'm as bad as my brother. My greed for gold has made me party to this unforgivable deception."

Elizabeth reached out and laid a hand on Edmund's arm. "Edmund, it wasn't your greed for gold, it was your love for Louisa. I can understand loving someone so much you'd do anything to keep from losing them."

Edmund's troubled green eyes met hers. "You are a kind, intelligent, and understanding young woman, Elizabeth."

"No, Edmund, just a woman in love." She smiled at West. West affectionately squeezed her waist as she said to Edmund, "If there is gold, if we find it, then certainly half of it belongs to you."

"No, no, I won't hear of it," protested Edmund. "West, I can't allow—"

"You heard the lady," said West, smiling. "Ed, you financed this whole expedition, of course you should share in any found treasure."

At sunrise it was discovered that four of the Mexican peasants had fled during the night. West was not surprised. The expedition was heading steadily deeper into the heartland of Navajo mysticism and the Latins were as superstitious as the Indians. The nervous men had seen the flash flood as a warning to stay away.

West studied the brown faces of the men who remained. Fear shone out of their dark eyes and he doubted they could be counted on to go all the way. He looked from man to man as he eased the bridle onto his sorrel mare's head and fastened the throat lash in preparation to ride.

He was lifting the saddle up onto the mare's back when Elizabeth saw him for the first time that morning. His back to her, she watched the lifting and lowering of his shoulderblades beneath his shirt, the play of muscles in his back and long legs.

A mug of hot steaming coffee cupped in her hands, she felt a tingle of pleasure shoot through her limbs, recalling last night's loving atop a stone ledge in the starlight. She felt again those powerful muscles rigid and straining against her hands and the skill of his exploring mouth.

Abruptly West's arms fell to his sides. He remained totally still for a moment, then he turned around. Elizabeth's lips fell open. Gone was the black, bushy beard. His handsome, sun-bronzed face was smoothly shaven and his thick raven hair was neatly brushed. That old reckless grin came back to his face and it was all she could do to keep from running and throwing herself into his arms.

Thinking he must have read her mind, Elizabeth caught her breath as he strode purposely toward her. When he reached her, West wrapped long fingers around the nape of her neck, glanced hurriedly about, leaned down and kissed her fully on the mouth.

"Mornin', sweetheart," he said. "Still love me in the cold light of day?" His silver eyes danced with happiness. Suddenly shy and in awe of him, Elizabeth could only nod wordlessly. West hugged her to him and said against her ear, "I know. I feel the same way about you."

By midmorning the contingent was down out of the Guadalupes and riding across the flat, burning desertlands of eastern New Mexico. To the northeast was the *Llano Estacado,* the Staked Plain. Due west, in the distance, the Ocotillo Hills rose against the azure sky.

And southeast, the direction in which they were headed, was the Texas border. Hopefully, just north of that border were the vast underground caverns of the Legend.

A constant Sonoran wind blew, kicking up dust devils and swirling brittle tumbleweeds across the flat basin. The sand, the heat, the wind bothered some of the riders.

Not West Quarternight.

Not when he could turn and see Elizabeth riding beside him, facing the wind, her hair blowing around her beautiful face like a scarlet storm.

Elizabeth felt his eyes on her, laughed, and shouted, "I'll race you!" She dug her booted heels into the iron gray's belly and he shot away.

Grinning, West eased his grip on the reins and the sorrel mare's stride lengthened into a gallop. Gray eyes squinting against the stinging wind, West good-naturedly pursued his playful lover. And wondered why, after Elizabeth had gone less than half a mile, she abruptly pulled up, bringing her stallion to a dirt-flinging halt.

"Give up already?" he shouted as he cantered up to her.

"West, look!" Frowning, Elizabeth pointed toward a figure lying beside a tumble of rocks.

"Wait here," said West. He swung down out of the saddle and went to investigate.

Moments later the others caught up and Edmund, Grady, and Taos quickly dismounted and hurried to where West knelt in the sand, his long arm supporting a half-dead Mexican. He was tipping his canteen of water to the man's parched, cracked lips.

Cautiously, Elizabeth climbed down from the saddle and ventured closer. She got a glimpse of the man cradled in West's arms and she shuddered. The stocky man's clothing was in tatters. Vicious-looking whelps scored his exposed brown back and dried blood was caked on his white linen shirt and trousers.

Gasping and coughing, the badly injured man clutched at West's shirtfront and talked, telling him what had happened. Elizabeth, several yards away, caught only a few phrases.

"El máximo jefe . . . Diablo alado . . . mucho oro . . ."

The poor man anxiously went on and on and Elizabeth noticed, when she got a better look at his dirty, sunburned face, that he had a bad walleye.

West spoke to the man in Spanish, calming him, and assuring him they would get him to a doctor. But the man weakly shook his head, knowing he was dying, determined to tell all he knew before it was too late.

West stayed with the dying man until he drew his last breath, then carefully laid him on the sand and rose to his feet. Everyone waited for West to speak.

He took a deep breath. "His name was Ortiz. He says he's been held prisoner in an underground cavern by the maximum *jefe* or boss . . . a winged devil with long golden hair." West's gaze met Edmund's, he caught the quick flash of horror that came into Edmund's eyes. "He said there are tons of gold bars down deep in the earth and that the pale master had been making his servants haul the heavy gold up out of the cavern." West fell silent.

"Anything more?" It was Edmund, his face mirroring his suspicions. "Does the ruler still live? Is he . . ."

West minced no words. "The master is alive; yesterday he beat Ortiz, then sent him out to bring a beautiful young woman back to the caverns for his pleasure."

"Dear God!" said Edmund, stricken. "Do you suppose . . . could it possibly be—"

"Ed, I'm only repeating what the dying Ortiz said. This desert can do strange things to a man dying of thirst." He added reassuringly, "The poor fellow was probably out of his head. Babbling about winged devils and maximum rulers . . . he made little sense."

But even as West spoke, he knew better. Before he died, the walleyed Ortiz had said that the pale master had killed two young Mexican women after using them for his own sexual gratification. The body of the last young woman had been left on the plaza at La Luz about two weeks ago. Now the evil master wanted another woman to share his bed of gold, but he had warned Ortiz not to bring back another brown-skinned woman. He wanted a woman whose skin was as pale as his own.

And her hair *must* be flaming red.

West inwardly shuddered as his eyes fell on Elizabeth's flaming tresses, gleaming in the desert sunlight. The thought of what would happen if the depraved maniac got his hands on her made the blood in his veins congeal.

He would have to keep very close watch on her, not allow her to be alone for even a second. The danger was real, and it was close.

A long, frustrating search for the elusive caverns would not be necessary. The dying Ortiz had revealed their exact location marked by telltale landmarks, less than twenty miles away.

By sundown they'd be there.

43

Darkness was beginning to claim the sky.

The hot winds had died. A gentle breeze blew from out of the west. The air had begun to cool. A sleek, sleepy-eyed bobcat stood poised on the low ridge line of a rocky hill, the sun's dying rays tinting his downy fur a soft apricot hue.

West recognized the promontory where the yawning bobcat stood as the first of the landmarks Ortiz had described. Its shape distinctive, the sandstone hillock looked like the huge, solemn face of an old Indian warrior.

West's gray eyes left the landmark and turned to scan the southern horizon. In the distance he saw a tiny speck of black soaring against the lavender heavens. Within seconds a cloud of free-tailed bats filled the night sky. Millions of the furry little creatures flew from the opening of an unseen cave to spend the hours of darkness in a foray for insects.

"West, what is it?" asked Elizabeth anxiously, her eyes lifting to the dense black cloud rising steadily higher.

"Just little bats, sweetheart," West said, smiling at her. "Means we're very near the caverns."

Speechless, she nodded, and reined her iron gray a little closer to West. "There are so many of them," she said, feeling the hair at the nape of her neck lifting.

"Millions," he confirmed, and quickly added, "but harmless. They sleep in the cave all day, then fly out at sundown to search for food."

She turned in the saddle to look back at the others. "West, did you realize that all the Mexicans have left us? I see only Grady, Taos, and Edmund."

"I know," West said calmly, nodding. "Throughout the afternoon they've been falling back, one by one, and riding away. I'm not surprised."

"But won't we need them now more than ever?"

He grinned. "Hope not." Turning to her, he said, "When we found Ortiz this morning, I knew we'd lose the rest of the crew. Honey, Mexicans and Indians are incredibly superstitious, so when they heard Ortiz's wild tales about 'winged devils,' there was no chance of keeping them."

"You don't believe Ortiz's ravings, do you?"

West shrugged wide shoulders. "Sweetheart, the only winged devils we're apt to see are those ugly little bats."

Lowering her voice, Elizabeth said, "Are you thinking what I'm thinking? That perhaps Dane found the gold and he's down there holding prisoners and—"

"If Dane's down there, he's alone. Ortiz swore all the others fled in the past few days."

Elizabeth shook her head thoughtfully. "But what about Dane's partner, Tom Lancaster? Did Ortiz mention him? Surely Tom stayed."

Reluctant to tell her, West glanced at her, then admitted, "Ortiz said Lancaster is dead."

"Dear God!" Elizabeth murmured, afraid even to ask how he died.

* * *

With the last traces of dying light, the riders came upon the gaping mouth of a dark, open cave and knew they had found the caverns of the legend. Dismounting, they stood on the rim, peering into the yawning blackness, wondering what fate waited deep down inside the uncharted abyss.

Even the talkative Grady was uncharacteristically quiet as they set up camp near the cave's wide mouth. Looking down into that inky darkness was an unsettling experience and the faint, strangled cries of the cave swallows fluttering from perch to perch on the cliffs above made them all a little edgy.

Bedtime came and a jittery Elizabeth decided she wasn't about to place her bedroll discreetly away from the men. She slept right beside West, lying so close she was able to hold tightly to his hand until she fell asleep. Directly across the fire from them, Grady and Edmund stretched out, Grady still wearing his holstered Colt.

Taos didn't lie down. The big Navajo agreed to stand watch through the night, then go to sleep at dawn. The Winchester rifle resting between his knees, he sat propped up against a dead tree trunk, his unblinking black eyes focused on the cave's dark mouth.

When the stars faded and dawn was not far off, Grady awakened. Opening his eyes he was surprised to see Edmund stretching and rising to his feet. Grady threw back his blanket, rose, and nodding to Edmund, walked over to tell Taos he could go get some sleep. The big Navajo nodded, handed Grady the rifle, stretched out right where he was, closed his eyes, and fell immediately into a deep slumber.

Whispering quietly so he wouldn't disturb the others, Edmund said to Grady over their morning coffee, "Grady, it may be hours before West wakes up. I don't want to wait. I'm going down and have a look around."

Grady frowned and shook his head violently. "No, you can't do that, Ed! No tellin' what you might find. It ain't safe to be goin' in no cave alone."

"I'm not frightened," said Edmund. Then he added, "My brother's down there, Grady. I have to find him, to see for myself . . ." His words trailed away and the expression on his face was one of deep worry.

"I understand," whispered Grady, "really I do. Want me to wake West and—"

"No, I won't hear of it. West and Elizabeth got only a couple of hours sleep last night. West is tired; he needs to rest."

Grady screwed up his face, stroked his long white beard, and finally said, "Tell you what, why don't we let 'em sleep and you an' me go on down in the cave together. Hellfire, we could get down inside, have a look around, and be back topside in time for breakfast with Sonny and Elizabeth. What do you say?"

Relieved, Edmund said, "Let's grab some rope and a safety lantern and be on our way."

The sun was high in the sky before West finally began to stir. He lay stretched out flat on his back, his head turned to one side. Struggling to open his eyes, West finally raised his thick lashes.

Filling the entire scope of his sleepy vision was an angelic face with one tangle of flaming red hair sheafed across sleeping eyes, shining strands falling around an ivory throat.

Still more asleep than awake, West rolled over, brushed her hair back, and covered her soft mouth in a warm kiss. His drowsy gray eyes closing again, he sighed as her lips opened beneath his. She moaned and tilted her head slightly, sliding the tip of her tongue between his teeth and into his mouth.

Eyes still tightly closed, Elizabeth sleepily snuggled to him, kissing him dreamily, while in her mind's eye she could see his dark, handsome face, the blue-black hair, the straight nose, the sensual lips that were moving so warmly on hers.

She inhaled the unique fragrance of him and lay there willing and ready to play, supposing that, since all was totally silent around them, it was very early and the others were still sleeping. Kissing him fully on the mouth, Elizabeth licked at West's lips and sighed when his hand rubbed across the front of her shirt.

Mouth sweetly fused with his, her lashes lifted to see that his silver eyes were wide open, looking at her. It was so wildly exciting, her heart began to pound. For a few seconds more he continued to look at her as he kissed her. Then his lips lifted an inch from her own, his hand covered her soft right breast, and he whispered, "I want you. Let's slip away before the others stir." A muscle twitched in his jaw. "Will you?"

"Of course," she murmured, and he smiled, lowered his head, and kissed her throat.

Lips moving against her warm flesh, he lovingly warned her, "Sweetheart, when I get you alone, I'm going to—"

"Help! West, Taos, help!" Grady's raspy shout shattered their warm cocoon of romance. "Help us! Oh, God, help!"

West was on his feet immediately, as was Taos. Both men ran directly toward the sound of Grady's voice, which was coming from the cave's large entrance.

Elizabeth, on her feet, hands pressed to her cheeks, saw Grady's white head and Edmund's blond one bob into sight just as West and Taos reached the cave's entrance. Limping badly, Grady supported Edmund, an arm around his waist, struggling under the heavy burden.

Elizabeth screamed when she saw the blood saturating Edmund's shirt, and she felt her legs buckle beneath her. But she quickly got control of herself and grabbed a canteen of water and a towel, ready to help. She saw the strong Taos lift Edmund up into his arms as if he were no heavier than a child. Taos carried him to a spread bedroll and gently laid him down while West supported the hobbling Grady.

Bleeding badly but fully conscious, Edmund unashamedly wept as he told them that his only brother had become a deranged and highly dangerous madman.

"Don't talk, Ed," said West. "Save your strength."

Grady, grimacing from the pain of a broken leg, explained what had happened when he and Edmund had awakened before dawn and decided to go down in the caverns.

Once inside, they got so caught up with the wondrous sights and exploring the many underground rooms and corridors, they became temporarily separated.

"I was lookin' at a still pool that mirrored them limestone icicles hangin' from the ceilin' when I heard Ed's scream. I went a-runnin' and I seen Ed strugglin' with a . . . a—"

"My brother is like nothing human," said Edmund miserably, as Taos worked to stanch the flow of blood from the knife wound just below his ribs. "His hair and his fingernails have grown long. He's as pale as snow and as filthy as a beggar."

Edmund swallowed hard and tears spilled down his cheeks. Elizabeth, kneeling beside him, pressed a wet cloth to his perspiring forehead, her heart aching for him.

"Even when I saw what he has become," said Edmund, "I didn't believe that Dane would actually harm me. Not his own brother. I begged him to come with me, to leave the caverns, to let me help him." Edmund's red-rimmed eyes closed, then opened again.

"He accused me of being greedy, of wanting to steal his gold. Nothing I said convinced him that he was wrong. I told him I love him and I'd get help for him, but he . . . he . . . his eyes grew wild and he drew a dagger from under the long cape he wore and he . . . he . . . stabbed me. He would have killed me if Grady hadn't heard me scream and come running."

Nodding, Grady said, "I started shoutin' as I ran and I guess that scared Dane off. By the time I got there, he was runnin' away and I didn't see nothin' of him but his back; just that long dirty hair, black cape billowin' out behind him, and the dagger dripping blood. And there Ed was on his knees clutching his belly, blood a-pourin' between his fingers.

"I helped him up and I was in such a hurry to get him topside, I took a misstep, fell, and busted my danged leg."

Working with quiet efficiency, Taos cleaned the deep knife wound and bandaged Edmund's ribs with strips from one of Elizabeth's white petticoats while West made a splint for Grady's broken leg.

As West worked, he said, "Taos, the closest hospital is in Malaga. You'll leave right away, we'll rig up a travois for Ed. I think Grady will be able to ride; I'll put him in the saddle. Take Elizabeth with you and—"

"No," Elizabeth quickly interrupted, "I'm not going."

"Yes, you are." West never looked up, just kept securing Grady's broken leg to the splint. Addressing Edmund, he said softly, "Now, Ed, don't be worrying about Dane. I'll go down and bring him out of the cave." Finally he glanced at Elizabeth. "I don't want you around when I bring Dane up."

"If you're staying, I am staying," Elizabeth said, looking him squarely in the eye. Softly, she added, "Whether you want me to or not."

Elizabeth stayed.

She and West watched the trio ride away. Edmund, unconscious now, was cradled in the quickly constructed travois behind Taos's horse. Grady rode with his splinted leg dangling beside the empty stirrup.

"Don't worry," said West, as they rode out of sight. "Taos will get them to Malaga and the hospital."

"How could Dane attempt to murder his own brother?"

West's comforting arm went around her slender shoulders. "He didn't, darling. The monster Ed described is no longer Dane Curtin."

She looked up at him. "Quarternight, you're an imposter; you're actually a perceptive and sensitive man."

He grinned. "I have my moments."

44

Gently cupping the back of Elizabeth's head, West said, "Promise you'll do exactly as I tell you." She didn't answer. "Elizabeth?"

"I can't," she said, "I won't. Not if you're going to say I can't go down in the—"

Her sentence was never finished. West grabbed her upper arms and spun her to face him, his face turning hard as stone. "Don't," he said, "make the mistake of thinking you can run over me, just because I love you."

"West, I certainly don't—"

"Yes, you do, but you're wrong, Elizabeth. Dead wrong." He continued to hold her in a viselike grip, his silver eyes dark with emotion. "I should have sent you with Taos; I went against my better judgment."

Looking up at him, she said, "Darling, I wanted to stay here with you."

"You can't have everything you want, Elizabeth. I let you stay, but I shouldn't have." His grip remained tight, the strong fingers cutting into her flesh. "I will not allow you to go down into that cavern." Abruptly, his snapping slate-gray eyes softened and he pulled her into his close embrace, pressing her head to his chest. Against her hair he said, "Oh, sweetheart, sweetheart, I can't risk something happening to you." He hugged her tightly. "I'm so afraid I'll lose you, like—"

"You won't, my love," Elizabeth said, thrilling to the forceful beating of his heart beneath her cheek. "I'll stay right here above ground and wait for you."

Sighing with relief, West instructed, "Here, keep Grady's Colt .44 with you. Remain at the entrance of the cave with the gun always in your hand. Under no circumstances are you to go farther into the caverns. Fire at anyone except me who tries to get near you. Will you do that?"

"I will," she said, "but I wish you'd take the gun."

She was still wishing he'd take their only weapon when West kissed her quickly and walked away, winding his way down the narrow zigzag path descending into the cool throat of the caverns. Elizabeth looked up over her shoulder at the sun's location. It was directly overhead.

Straight up noon.

Pride made West assume a demeanor of self-confidence as he strode purposefully down the slanting path. The woman he loved was watching, so he went out of his way to appear totally calm and unafraid. As he moved beyond the sun's reach and into the shadowy emptiness, he wondered if all men were like him. Did they put on a brave show of courage at times when they felt weak and helpless?

Safety lantern in one hand, rope slung over his shoulder, he continued to drop farther down the narrow path into the eerie darkness until the cave's wide, sunny entrance—and Elizabeth—was no longer in sight. Even then he continued on his way, determined he'd not think about his unreasonable fear of tunnels and caves.

But as West dropped lower into the depths of the dark, silent world, the old debilitating anxiety rose up to overwhelm him. His knees and hands began to tremble. The awesome silence and solid blackness were too much. He stopped, sagged against a rocky wall, and fought for breath, his chest constricting painfully. He felt sick and panicky, unable to think or to act. His heartbeat doubled and thumped so forcefully against his chest wall, he was afraid it would explode.

His head started spinning. He became dizzy and feared he might black out. Anxiously he sucked for breath, imagining that there was no air way down here in this dark netherworld, just as there had been none in that small, dark tunnel beneath Andersonville Prison.

He felt the caverns were closing behind him, that the entrance above was disappearing, caving in on itself, burying him under tons and tons of rock. His heart racing, sweat pouring off his face, he lifted the lantern in his shaking hand and waved it about, attempting to ward off the close, smothering darkness.

Knowing he had to get a grip on himself, he gasped for air, tore at the choking laces of his shirt, and said aloud, "You can do it." He kept repeating the litany in his brain, *you can do it, you can do it.* Soon it seemed as if the entire underground cavern was shouting, "You can do it, you can do it," the sound echoing through every connected room and mazelike passageway and narrow corridor and tiny crawl space.

Thousands of stalactites and stalagmites took up the chorus, mocking him, ridiculing him, knowing what a pitiful coward he actually was. Knowing he couldn't make himself go one more step into the confusing labyrinth of passages leading farther down into this ominous underworld kingdom of darkness and death.

Trembling, West forced himself to move one weak foot forward, then the other. Like an infant just learning to walk, he toddled shakily forward, arms held out to balance himself, eyes round as saucers. It was hard, but it became a little easier as he made himself doggedly go on.

He moved down a dark, wide passageway, looking cautiously about. He shuddered involuntarily when the swinging lantern, casting yellow light on limestone ledges and shallow crevices on both sides of the narrow path, illuminated coiled diamondback rattlers and black widow spiders taking refuge from the desert heat.

On he went, realizing finally that he could breathe, that he was breathing. There *was* air down here. He wasn't going to suffocate. He wasn't going to die. Gratefully, he pulled long, revitalizing breaths deep into his chest and felt his heart begin to slow its rapid beating. He felt a little strength returning to his weak, watery legs.

Confidence swiftly growing, in no time West began to feel fine. At long last he had come face to face with his worst fear and had triumphed over it! Heartened by the knowledge, he grinned and headed down the path armed with his old self-assurance.

And walked straight into a spider web that covered and clung damply to his face, bringing a loud shout of terror from him. But it was quickly followed by a nervous laugh of embarrassment.

Then he heard the faint flutter of wings. Thousands of tiny wings.

Elizabeth looked again at the sky.

The white hot sun had moved from directly overhead halfway to the western horizon. It had surely been three or four hours since West had disappeared into the cavern's mouth. He should have been back by now. She was tense from waiting, sick with worry.

Sighing, she peered once more into the yawning blackness below. She saw nothing. But finally, after another half hour had passed, she heard what she had been listening for all afternoon. The sound of West's feet striking the stone path. A smile of relief quickly coming to her face, Elizabeth laid the gun aside and happily shot to her feet.

When the top of his head appeared, Elizabeth eagerly ran to meet him, shouting, "Darling, darling, I was so worried. I thought you . . . I . . . I . . ." She stopped short and stared in horror as a long-haired, wild-eyed man wearing a flowing black cape and carrying an ebony leather riding crop approached her.

He reached her before she had time to think, before she could run back for the gun. In seconds he stood directly before her. Pale fingers with long dirty nails tightly enclosed her right wrist and Elizabeth was forcefully yanked up against the vile creature who smiled down at her, teeth bared, wolflike.

He brought the leather whip up under her chin and said, "Just where did Ortiz find you, pet?" His gleaming green eyes settled on her red hair. "I must reward him. I'm very pleased with his selection. You're far prettier than the others."

"My God," Elizabeth murmured, recognizing the familiar voice. "Dane? Is it you?"

He blinked at her in confusion. His eyes narrowed, and he studied her face. "My lovely, how dare you mention the name of the Pale Master? Have I had you before?"

"It can't be true," breathed Elizabeth in disbelief. "Dane, what has happened to you? Dane . . . my God, Dane Curtin!"

"Elizabeth? Is that you, my love?" His fevered green eyes took on an expression of added excitement.

"Why, it is! You've come to me at last. How I've waited for this. I've so much to show you. Come."

"No!" she screamed, her brain starting to function. She tried to break from his tight grasp. "Let me go!" she shouted.

"Let you go?" He was insulted. "You're my wife, Elizabeth. This, finally, is our honeymoon."

"No, no, please," she begged, her senses assailed with the sour smell of him, her heart frozen with fear. "You can't do this, you . . ."

Frowning, Dane wrapped a hand over her mouth, quieting her, forcing her back against him. He reached inside his black cape and tugged loose the wide gold sash from around his waist, withdrew it, and swiftly gagged Elizabeth. When she could make only soft pleading sounds in the back of her throat, he pulled her silver concho belt free of her suede trousers and used it to truss her hands behind her.

"Now," he said, pleased with his ingenuity, "you're a little nervous, Elizabeth, but you'll be fine once I get you down to our magnificent quarters, where we'll consummate our wedding vows."

Balking, refusing to take a step, Elizabeth shook her head violently, her eyes as wild as his.

"Elizabeth, I'm hurt and surprised by this strange reluctance on your part to begin the wonderful honeymoon I have planned for us." Casually, with the leather riding crop, he swept back one side of his black cape to reveal a sheathed dagger. Elizabeth caught sight of more than the dagger. Beneath the black cape, he wore only a soiled transparent robe over his pale, naked body. Wickedly he grinned and allowed the cape to fall back into place.

And then he swiftly dragged her into the caverns. The sun disappeared behind them, but he did not stop or even slow his pace. He continued to drag the struggling woman down, down into the depths. Elizabeth could see nothing. She was drowned in a pit of total darkness and she felt as if any second they would make a fatal misstep and plunge to their deaths.

On he took her, his pace steady and confident. It was as if he could see in the dark. As if the thick blackness could be penetrated by those wild green eyes. Elizabeth had no idea how far down into the earth they went, but when finally they stopped, her legs were tired and aching, her heart was hammering with fear and exhaustion, and her face was beaded with perspiration.

In the inky darkness, from just above her ear, he announced, as if she had asked, "We are now nine hundred feet below the surface of the earth. To get here, we walked approximately two and one half miles." He added, "All that way in darkness and not once did I stumble. You see, my beautiful red-haired wife, I *am* the Pale Master. The ruler of the depths. I can see in total darkness, just like my vampire followers."

Elizabeth winced when suddenly a torch flared to life. With its circle of illumination lighting the pale, smiling face of the demented man, he said, "There's something I want to show you, my dear."

He ushered her into a large, dark chamber. He raised his smoking torch high and said, "Look at my subjects, Elizabeth."

Elizabeth's eyes automatically lifted, and a fierce tremor of revulsion raced through her at the sight. Thousands and thousands of gray-brown vampire bats hung upside down, almost within reach. A gruesome tapestry of bats literally covered the ceiling as far as the eye could see.

"Impressive, isn't it?" Dane said. "Did you know that during winter's long sleep, the bats become stiff and cold, and they almost stop breathing?" He lowered the torch, looked at her, and said, "I'm trying to perfect that for myself." He sighed wistfully. "I suppose I'll have to wait until winter. Why, Elizabeth, you're shivering. Perhaps it was too soon to show you my winged subjects."

She tried to speak, to scream; it came out nothing more than sobs muffled by the gold sash gagging her.

He said, "What's that? You think me mad or sick? My dear, you're greatest fault is that you reason only in black and white; good and bad." He shook his blond head accusingly. "You've never dealt with a gray or devious world. The world where I now exclusively exist."

Elizabeth looked up at the towering figure in the dark loden cape and knew there would be no reasoning with him.

"Come," he said, escorting her back out into the passageway. "I sense your aversion to the bats. Later this evening I'll show you around my vast domain; you'll find that much of it is quite beautiful."

He took her further down the corridor and into a huge room where smoking wall torches cast so much light Elizabeth was momentarily blinded, her pupils still dilated from the darkness. When she could see, she gaped up at the high-domed ceiling and then at the huge stack of shiny gold ingots stacked at the very center of the vast natural amphitheater. Pleased by her awe, he led her forward—past the bed of gold—and several yards beyond. He directed her attention to the smoking floor torches bordering the edge of where the stone floor fell away into darkness.

He instructed her to look out into the blackness. Then he told her he liked to think of this natural amphitheater as his own majestic auditorium. They were standing at the edge of the stage on which they would shortly perform. Their audience? "Why, imagine thousands of admirers out there in the darkness, applauding us, mesmerized by our exhibition of talent and beauty."

He pointed a long-nailed finger downward and then warned her to be very careful after the performance when they came down to the front of the stage to take their bows before the torch footlights.

"To the best of my knowledge," he said, "the black, yawning pit below has no bottom."

Elizabeth trembled and instinctively moved back. He smiled, took her arm, and led her back around to the other side of the solid gold bed. He turned her to face the bed.

From just behind, Dane said, "Darling, I would like to share my gold with you, but I can't. There just isn't enough."

He removed the gagging sash from her mouth. Before she could make a sound, he added, "I will, however, immensely enjoy your company until I—"

"I'm not alone, Dane," she warned him, torn between the hope that West would find them and the fear that Dane would kill West if he did. "My companion will miss me and come looking. He'll find us."

Leisurely removing the concho belt binding her wrists, Dane said, "No one has ever come close to this well-hidden chamber."

"Edmund," she reminded him. "Edmund did."

"Edmund was nowhere near this amphitheater." He chuckled, then added, "But I didn't appreciate his nosing around in my personal kingdom. I suspect he was looking for my gold, trying to steal it from me."

"You're mistaken, Dane. We've come here to help you, not to harm you or steal from you," she said desperately. "I don't want any of the gold. You can keep it all. Just let me go."

He turned her to face him. "I want," he said, his green eyes glowing demonically, "to make love to you here, where I can watch my gold as I take you." His

eyes turned brighter and he bared his teeth like an
animal. "I've found the sight of all this hard, gleaming
gold to be the ultimate aphrodisiac."

"My God, you're hopelessly insane!" she murmured, backing away from him.

The leering smile still on his face, he advanced on
her. "Take off your clothes, Elizabeth. Now." He
seized her shoulders. "Unless you want to end up like
brother Edmund, you'll obey me."

Trapped, terrified, Elizabeth stood directly before
the bed of gold and began undressing. She pulled her
shirt up over her head and off. "Please . . ." she
begged.

"Continue," said Dane, and removed his long black
cape, allowing it to fall to the floor at his feet. "Take
off your boots and trousers." Watching her with palm-
rubbing eagerness, he said, almost idly, "Do you realize, Elizabeth, I've never even seen your bare legs."

When she stood before him wearing only her thin
satin chemise and thigh-high underpants, Dane licked
his lips, twirled a long, dirty blond curl in nervous
fingers, and said, "You have no idea how many times
I've dreamed of this moment. Just the two of us alone
down here in my secret kingdom of pleasure. Just
you and me far, far down in the bowels of the earth
where no matter what I may do to you, your screams
cannot be heard. I can have you as my love slave for
all eternity . . . or at least until I tire of you." He
shivered with anticipation. "Now, start backing away,
move toward the bed of gold."

Elizabeth shook her head, but when he took a step
toward her, she began backing away from him. He
slowly advanced on her, his filmy gown revealing his
bare, unwashed body. The dagger was still strapped
to his waist.

"When you reach the bed," he commanded, "take
off your underthings, climb up onto the gold, and

crawl to the bed's center. Then turn to face me, take the pins from your hair and let it fall down your back. Kneel there on my golden bed so I can admire your naked beauty at the same time I admire my shiny gold."

Gooseflesh covering her bare arms and legs, tears of fear and despair stinging her frightened eyes, Elizabeth said, "I won't do it! You can't make me, you depraved monster!"

Her fear tickled Dane's mad whimsy. He threw back his head and laughed, the sound echoing off the stone walls. "I'm no monster, my pet. We are mammals. Vampires. The highest class of vertebrates. Surely we are the richest." He laughed, and added, "We are in the same form as human beings, even though some people think us monsters."

"You are obviously deranged," she sobbed.

"Were you aware that the old testament called bats 'unclean birds'? Did you know that my winged creatures and I are so powerful, people have become rabid just sharing the same air we breathe." He continued to move slowly closer. "I've always known that I am compelled and driven by the force of some dark star, just as I know full well that though you are afraid, you are helplessly attracted to my erotic power." He smiled and calmly said, "Take everything off."

Sick with fear, Elizabeth shouted, "No! No, damn you, no!"

The wicked smile never leaving his face, Dane drew the sharp dagger from its sheath and held it up so that it gleamed in the torchlight. He came at her, and Elizabeth let out a blood-curdling scream.

That loud piercing scream carried through the large amphitheater and out into the corridor beyond. In a small chamber not far away, West heard the scream, just faintly, and followed its sound, the safety lantern swinging in his hand. Running faster than he knew he could run, he bolted into the giant amphitheater just as Dane slipped the dagger beneath the delicate strap of Elizabeth's chemise and cut it in two.

Waiting until the madman had moved the knife away from Elizabeth's shoulder, West shouted loudly, "Curtin!"

Dane whirled around in surprise, the dagger in his hand. West had nothing but the miner's safety lantern. "Come on," West goaded, gesturing, moving further inside the chamber. Quickly advancing, he widely skirted around the gold where they stood, determined to draw Dane away from Elizabeth. "Come and get me."

"Who are you?" Dane demanded, turning, his eyes following West as he slowly circled. "You have no right to be here. No right at all. If you wish to watch the performance, then kindly go join the rest of the audience, just beyond the floodlights."

"West," Elizabeth screamed, "there's a sheer drop off on the far side of those torches lining the floor!"

"I'm not one of the audience," goaded West. "I'm part of this performance."

"You are not!" thundered Dane. "Get off my stage!"

"Come throw me off," said West, clutching the lantern tightly in his right hand. He watched Dane size him up, knew he was checking to see if he was armed.

"I'll kill you," said Dane, and moved toward West, dagger poised. There was only one chance, but West took it. He threw the heavy lantern at Dane's right hand so swiftly Dane had no time to react. Dane screamed and the dagger went flying. It skittered across the stone floor and Dane lunged after it. West reached him just as Dane's fingers touched the knife's handle. West forcefully kicked the dagger and it sailed across the stone floor past the torches and over the edge into blackness.

Dane straightened and threw a punch at West. He missed. West's fist lashed out and slammed squarely into Dane's left jaw, turning his head to one side. West followed up with a fierce blow to his ear.

Enraged, Dane growled like an animal and punched West in the stomach. West gasped and Dane tagged him with a punishing right hook to the chin, driving West's sharp teeth together, catching the fleshy inside of his bottom lip between. Flecks of blood flew.

While Elizabeth watched in helpless horror the vicious fight went on and on. Blow after pounding blow struck flesh, until both men were staggering and punch-drunk. All the skin had come off their knuckles and blood covered their battered faces and their clothes.

Worse, as they fought on, they moved closer and closer to the smoking floor torches that bordered the deep black bottomless pit, until West's booted feet were not more than a foot from the sheer drop-off.

Dane was aware of his advantage. Victory within reach, he used every ounce of his strength to throw a punch at West, putting the full force of his body behind it. At just the last second, West managed to duck out of the way and Dane Curtin went flying over the ledge. Elizabeth threw herself into West's tired arms while the sound of Dane's screams echoed throughout the underground palace.

They never heard him hit bottom.

45

❦❦❦

The old Navajo woman, her hands adorned with silver and turquoise rings, sat on the broad, flat porch of Santa Fe's El Palacio Real. Her ancient face was as burnished brown and as deeply carved as the rugged Sangre de Cristo Mountains. She leaned back against the wall of the one-story adobe building, her watery black eyes twinkling, the wrinkled, tissue-thin lids open wide. Her old bones were warmed by the June morning's brilliant sunlight, and her old heart was warmed by an inner peace.

The contented Indian woman did not stop passersby to ask if they had seen her sons. She knew where they were. They were safe from harm and in a better place.

Or were they?

If so, who was that raven-haired young man waiting nervously inside a many-roomed low adobe building far, far away?

With her eyes open wide, Micoma could not see much. But when they were closed, she could see everything. So she leaned her head back, shut her eyes, and fell into a deep trance.

And then she could see all the way to Malaga, New Mexico.

So much in love they couldn't bear to wait, West Quarternight and Elizabeth Curtin decided to marry in the Malaga *clínica* where Edmund and Grady were recuperating.

At straight up noon on that beautiful June day, West, the typical nervous bridegroom, stood beside the robed padre between Edmund and Grady's hospital beds in the immaculate sunlit ward.

Edmund was still weak from loss of blood, but grateful to be alive. Grady was feeling so fine he was sitting up in bed, his long white beard and hair neatly brushed for his role in the wedding. He was West's best man.

Out in the spotless white corridor, Elizabeth, carrying a small bouquet of pink primroses, clung tightly to Taos's big arm as he escorted her into the room and down the very short aisle to where West and the old padre waited.

West watched her come toward him, overwhelmed by her startling beauty. When she teasingly winked at him, he felt his trembly knees buckle.

The ceremony began.

The padre asked, "Who giveth this woman away?"

Beaming like a proud father, Taos took Elizabeth's small hand and placed it atop West's. Smiling, Elizabeth waited for the giant Navajo to nod his head decisively. Instead, she heard him speak for the first time ever.

The towering Taos looked at her and said in a surprisingly soft, pleasing voice, "I do."

Afterword

↭↭↭

The Albuquerque Tribune
Monday, October 30, 1989

Victorio Gold Hunt Revived
Skeen provision would
open up missile range

By Peter Copeland
Scripps Howard News Service

WASHINGTON—Deep under the White Sands
Missile Range, in a cavern big enough to hold a
freight train, is a cache of gold bars stacked in
rows like firewood.

That's the story, anyway, and it's so persistent
that Congress is about to require the Army to
open up the missile range in southern New Mexico for a treasure hunt.

But put down your shovels. The search will be

limited to a partnership set up by the heirs of the man who claims to have found the gold fifty years ago at Victorio Peak.

The West is filled with stories about lost mines and hidden gold, but this story is different because everybody knows exactly where the gold is supposed to be. The only trouble is, it's buried under 400 feet of earth at a place where the Army is shooting rockets and blowing up airplanes.

New Mexico Republican Rep. Joe Skeen managed to put a provision into the House Defense Authorization Act that would require the Army to allow a search for the gold. The legislation has been in conference committee since July.

The searchers will have to pay all the expenses, and the fate of any recovered treasure will be decided by the courts.

"The mystery should be solved once and for all," said Sherry Kiesling, an aide to Skeen.

The Army has agreed to go along. "We want it laid to rest once and for all," said Deborah Bingham, a spokeswoman for White Sands.

The story begins in 1937 when, according to New Mexico folklore, Milton "Doc" Noss dodged into a cavern to escape the rain while hunting deer on the side of Victorio Peak near Las Cruces.

The peak is set in a deep, bowl-shaped valley. Noss said he walked into a huge cavern and found "gold bars stacked like cordwood" and twenty-seven skeletons chained to heavy wooden posts.

Noss said he went back to the peak with dynamite to make the hole bigger but ended up caving in the shaft and burying the gold. Noss spent days digging in the hot sun and convinced a Texan, Charles Ryan, to invest in the hunt.

But Ryan was frustrated by the lack of progress. He fought with Noss and gunned him down in 1949.

Noss's ex-wife, Ova Noss, then filed a claim for the gold. After World War II, the peak became part of the 3,200-square mile White Sands Missile Range, but Ova Noss convinced the Army to open up the range for unsuccessful searches in 1963 and 1977.

Ova Noss has since died, but lobbying for a new hunt was taken up by her grandson and a professional treasure hunter, Expeditions Unlimited of Pompano, Fla., which also led the 1977 hunt.

Jerry Lee, a vice president of the company, said his ground-penetrating radar found a cavern at the base of the peak in 1977. "Is there anything in the cavern?" Lee asked. "Who knows."

The company wants fifteen days to do engineering studies on the site, forty-five days to excavate and forty days to bring out the gold. The company's budget is $1 million, Lee said, which would include money to cover the Army's expenses.

Expeditions Unlimited would receive a "small percentage" of the booty, Lee said, but he won't say how small.

Lee says he could get started before the end of the year, but the Army says it can't act until Congress approves the legislation and an environmental-impact study is done.

If any gold is found, there's going to be a fight over who owns it. Any number of people claim it, including the Apache Nation (the peak is named after Chief Victorio), other relatives of Noss, and a group of Air Force veterans who say they saw the gold in 1958.

Just where the gold came from is also a mystery.

Howard Bryan, a retired reporter for *The Tribune* who covered the 1977 search, says his favorite theory is that the cavern was an Apache cache.

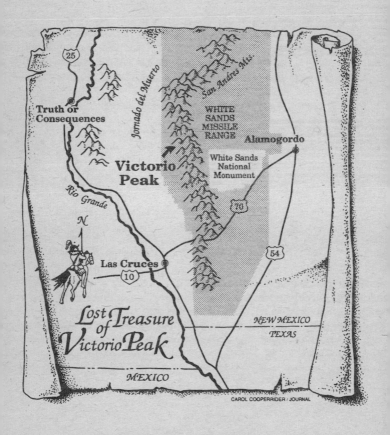

Lost Treasure of Victorio Peak

CAROL COOPERRIDER / JOURNAL

NAN RYAN

"Nan Ryan is one of Passion's leading ladies." —ROMANTIC TIMES